Street Smart

BOOKS BY TEYLA BRANTON

Unbounded Series
The Change
The Cure
The Escape
The Reckoning
The Takeover

Unbounded Novellas
Ava's Revenge
Mortal Brother
Lethal Engagement
Set Ablaze

Colony Six Series
Insight (prequel)
Sketches
Visions
Travels

Imprints Series
First Touch (prequel)
Touch of Rain
On The Hunt
Upstaged
Under Fire
Blinded
Street Smart
Hidden Intent

Other
Times Nine

UNDER THE NAME RACHEL BRANTON

Lily's House Series
House Without Lies
Tell Me No Lies
Hearts Never Lie
Your Eyes Don't Lie
Broken Lies
No Secrets or Lies
Cowboys Can't Lie

Noble Hearts
Royal Quest
Royal Dance

Finding Home Series
Take Me Home
All That I Love
Then I Found You

Other
How Far

Picture Books
I Don't Want To Eat Bugs
I Don't Want to Have Hot Toes

Street Smart

TEYLA BRANTON

WHITE
STAR
PRESS

This is a work of fiction, and the views expressed herein are the sole responsibility of the author. Likewise, certain characters, places, and incidents are the product of the author's imagination, and any resemblance to actual persons, living or dead, or actual events or locales, is entirely coincidental.

Street Smart (Imprints Book 6)

Published by White Star Press
P.O. Box 353
American Fork, Utah 84003

Printed in the United States of America
ISBN: 978-1-948982-14-6
Year of first printing: 2019

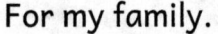

For my family.

Chapter 1

With gloved fingers, I put the final Little People wooden character in the merry-go-round next to the schoolhouse and stood back to admire my handiwork before closing the case. I bought the black tea gloves off eBay by the dozens these days, a buck a pair. Their function was twofold—they kept body oils off my antiques, and they protected me from reliving the often-incapacitating emotions imprinted on their surfaces.

After temporarily losing my psychometry ability in early May, a little over a month ago, I was careful to avoid as many casual imprints as I could. I still checked everything I put in my store to make sure any imprints they contained were positive, or at least neutral, but after that I limited contact, even with the good ones that usually made me feel revitalized. I was still healing from my mental blindness, and according to Dr. Easton Godfrey, a self-proclaimed expert in psychometry, reading any imprint was effort and could delay my progress.

Not that I'd been called on to read much of anything this past month since taking down the mobster Frank O'Donald. Truthfully, those events still had me looking over my shoulder, even though he was dead and all of his top people were in jail. I wasn't too upset that most people coming into my antiques shop carrying objects for me to read only wanted to know if their husbands were cheating or if their bosses were thinking of giving them a promotion.

Friday afternoons at Autumn's Antiques were always slow, and today only two customers, a blond-haired woman and a young boy, were browsing the shelves that held the music boxes. As I moved away from the Fisher-Price case, the woman left her son and approached me.

"May I help you?" I asked.

"Yes." She leaned toward me confidentially, lowering her voice. "I'm here with my little boy. He insisted on coming. It's my birthday soon, and I think he wants to buy me something special. I've tried to show him a few things, but . . ." She glanced at the child, who had moved from the music boxes and now had his nose pressed up against a case containing antique metal cars. "He doesn't want me around while he chooses, but if you could please steer him to something that isn't expensive? He's been working so hard the past year doing odd jobs for my father-in-law. We're living with my in-laws, you see, while my husband and I finish school." A frown marred her perfect heart-shaped face, and the bleakness of her tone made me wonder if there was trouble at home. "Anyway, he's a generous kid, but I'd like him to save for something he wants, not spend it all on me."

"I'm glad to help," I said. "Is there a certain limit you had in mind?"

Red stained the woman's pale cheeks. "I don't really know how much he has, but maybe around ten or twenty dollars?" She gave a self-deprecating chuckle. "Not much in here for that, I know. But there's a little pewter jewelry box that I like. My wedding ring would fit in it nicely."

I knew the piece immediately. It had belonged to an old woman before her death, given to her by a long-dead beau. The tender imprinted memories from both of them, though fading, had made me tear up the first time I'd held it.

"I'll do my best," I said. "Are you going to wait outside or in another part of the store?"

She smiled. "I think I'll go next door to that herb shop. Since they have the adjoining door, I can peek in on him, and they have some black licorice Kylan really loves." For the first time, her gaze went to my bare feet and then away again as quickly. If she thought it strange that a full-grown woman chose to go around barefoot, she was polite enough not to comment.

"I love that licorice too," I said, giving her a smile. "Go ahead. I'll help Kylan."

"Thank you. I'm sure that right now he's nowhere near what he intends to buy." She glanced around at the boy, who was staring hard at her. "See? He's waiting for me to leave."

"Then you'd better go," I said with a laugh.

After another glance at my feet, she disappeared through the double doors connecting my store with the Herb Shoppe that had once belonged to my father, Winter Rain, but now belonged to my best friend, Jake Ryan. Or my formerly-best-friend-turned-boyfriend-then-turned-friend-again Jake. We were finding our way back to friendship since my engagement to a local homicide detective and Jake's subsequent meeting of his current girlfriend, but it was sometimes awkward. I missed the old days of being regular best friends.

Since my store was dead, our shared full-time employee, Thera Brinker, was selling herbs in Jake's shop, and our part-time helper, Jazzy Storm, aka Jessica Sandstrom, who I'd recently put over my online sales, was off today. That left just Kylan and me.

The minute his mother vanished, the boy rushed over. He was a pretty child, with his mother's blond hair and an appealing round face. His expression was somber, though, and he didn't smile as he approached. He wore a T-shirt, faded jeans, and worn tennis shoes. A black backpack with frayed trim hung over one shoulder.

"I need your help," he said, his gaze flicking past me to the Little People display with unveiled disinterest. Not even the nineteen seventy-four castle with the turquoise flag caught his attention, and it was everyone's favorite.

"Would you like to see something?" I asked the boy, reaching in my dress pocket for the keys. "You were looking at the cars, right?" Recently, I'd taken to locking small items in cases, an action my adoptive parents, diehard flower children, would have decried.

"I don't want to buy anything right now," he said, which surprised me.

"Oh, okay. How can I help you then?"

He glanced toward the doors leading into the Herb Shoppe and then around my store. When he was sure no one was watching, the boy shrugged off his backpack, unzipped it, and pulled out a decidedly wrinkled white sheet of paper.

"It's about this," he said, shoving it at me. "I need your help."

I knew the article the moment I saw it—the one that talked about me solving a murder at a local theatrical company. While I'd been careful to keep my connection to the recent mobster incident from the paper, this was out on the Internet for anyone to see. But Kylan couldn't be more than nine or ten. What was he doing reading online newspapers? Kids were supposed to be addicted to games these days, not keeping up on current events.

"You need me to read something for you?" I guessed.

He nodded solemnly. "Is it free like it says?"

I removed my gloves, tucking them into my pocket. "Yes." I usually encouraged people to buy something they loved from my store after using my special services, but he didn't need to know that. "Come on over to the counter."

He followed me to the back of my store, where I slipped behind the counter and sat on my tall stool. Sitting when reading imprints was always the best idea, just in case, though what he'd brought couldn't be all that serious.

"How come your eyes are different colors?" he asked, studying me. He pointed to my left eye. That's one's blue, but the other is, uh . . ."

"Hazel. I was born that way. It's called heterochromia." In my case, it was hereditary, a condition I shared with my biological father and my twin sister.

"Oh." Setting his backpack on the floor, Kylan bent over, nearly disappearing from my sight. Seconds later, he brought out an old chest about eight inches long, holding it carefully with both hands. He hefted it onto the counter. "This is my treasure chest. I put all my money in here. I was saving for something special—for my mom's birthday." His gaze again strayed briefly toward the Herb Shoppe before coming back to me.

"That's great," I said. The cherry-stained wood chest wasn't anything special, antique-wise, but I could see why the boy liked it. The rounded top and the black hasp reminded me of pirates and hidden treasure. There was a place for a padlock, though he didn't seem to have one.

"No, it's *not* great." He frowned, and moisture glinted in his eyes. Brown eyes, I noted. Deep brown, though I was sure his mother's eyes were blue. He opened the chest and turned it around so I could see into it. "Because it's gone. All of it except some coins."

Inside the chest were a few folded pieces of paper, a dirty string, a crystal-shaped object that had likely been a pull to a set of blinds, a small ball, and a handful of change. Not one bill of any denomination in sight.

"I had seventy-six dollars," Kylan said, blinking back tears. "I've been mowing my grandpa's lawn and cleaning out my neighbor's birdcage for a year and a half to get that money. Whoever took it also took my silver dollars." He paused and added hurriedly, "They weren't *real* silver, but sometimes my neighbor pays me that way. I like the big coins. They're cool. So can you tell me who took my money? I gotta get it back, and I can't tell my mom because she already has too much stress."

I wanted to assure him that I could find his culprit, but if whoever had taken his money hadn't left an imprint on the chest, I wouldn't be able to help him at all.

"I'll certainly try," I said.

Not even that brought a hint of a smile to the child's cherubic face. Instead, he nodded solemnly. "Thank you."

"A few questions first," I said. Getting background would help me understand any imprints I'd read. "Where do you normally keep the chest?"

"Under my bed. But everyone knows I have it."

"Everyone?"

He bent back over until I could only see the top of his head. The next minute, he showed me a tiny notebook and a pencil covered with little cars. He stretched his arms out over the counter and opened the notebook to a page, tapping it with his pencil. "I wrote it all down—all the suspects. But I don't think any of them would take it."

I bent over to read the column of words that had been printed in surprisingly good penmanship: "mom, dad, aunt, cousin, grandma, grandpa."

"My cousin is too small to get it out," Kylan said. "She's only one, and she's afraid of going under the bed."

"What about friends?"

He shook his head. "They spend all their money on candy, and they'd want to spend mine, so I don't tell them anything. I think it must be a robber."

"Is anything else in the house missing?"

"I don't think so. But it's a lot of money, so maybe that's all they wanted."

His innocence was endearing. "Maybe. Why don't I give it a try?" I removed the ring Shannon had given me a month ago to mark our engagement. It was set with small stones of two alternating colors, our birthstones, and so far the only imprints on it were positive ones from Shannon. I didn't usually imprint on most items, but removing the ring would prevent any chance of that happening.

As I reached for the sides of the chest, I could feel the tingling that indicated a strong imprint. Not at all surprising. Imprints are almost always left on objects people treasure or commonly use. I let my hands touch the wood, exactly where I imagined someone might grab and pull it out from under the bed. As always, the boy's most recent imprint came first. Emotion took over, filling me as if I had lived the moment with Kylan. As if I *were* Kylan.

I clenched my teeth with determination. I was going to find who took my money. The lady at the old-things store would help. She had to.

When reading imprints, I always envisioned an imaginary calendar that highlighted the day and time of the event. If the imprint was older than a couple months, exact times were harder to pinpoint, but an approximate date was usually enough. This imprint had been left on the chest earlier today.

A second imprint followed the first, coming from only two days ago, an imprint that made me feel as if my heart had been ripped from my body.

Tears wet my face. I couldn't breathe except in tiny gasps. It was all gone! Who had taken it? Who was so mean? I wanted to scream and yell and kick the door. I could never earn that much again. Not in time.

"Now I can't get Mom something nice," I whispered between sobs. It was all gone.

The part of me that remembered I was Autumn Rain sympathized with the child. I remembered too well the days that seventy-six dollars might have stood between me and foreclosure on my shop.

Then came the imprint I'd been hoping for, left on the chest just under two weeks ago.

I peered into the chest. As expected, the bills were there, all neatly stacked inside a rubber band, except for the last few scattered on top. I'd borrow the money for a few weeks like the last time. I'd get paid the Saturday before his mother's birthday—that was plenty of time in case he decided to buy her something. The kid probably wouldn't notice. The bills on top had to mean that the last time he'd slipped money inside, he hadn't even taken the chest from under the bed. No one would ever know I borrowed it or what I bought.

The imprint vanished as whoever was holding the chest set it down to take the small stack of bills that must have seemed like a fortune to this little boy standing in front of my counter. Kylan was right; someone had stolen his money. Someone who knew him.

Next came a more faded emotion. *Satisfaction as one chubby hand opened the rounded chest top and placed a wrinkled bill on top of the others.*

There were more similar faded imprints, but when the first imprint began to repeat, I knew I'd seen all there was.

"Good news," I said, removing my hands. "I can't tell you who took your money because I didn't see them or even their hands, but I can tell you it was someone you know. They borrowed your money and planned to return it before your mother's birthday."

It was a mean thing to do, but adults didn't always treat children with the same respect they afforded others.

Kylan's eyes widened. "Really? That's great!" A line appeared between his brow. "I mean, they shouldn't take it without asking, but I'm glad they're going to put it back." He sounded hopeful now.

I hesitated before saying, "You might consider getting a lock for your chest." If the person had taken his money before, it was likely he or she would do it again.

"That's a good idea. But I should wait until they put it back."

I grinned. "I think that's best."

Setting his notebook and pencil on the counter near my cash register, he shut the chest and stowed it in his backpack. Then he grabbed his notebook and turned in the direction of the connecting doors to the Herb Shoppe.

"It wasn't your mother," I called after him as I slid my ring back onto my finger.

He stopped and turned around. "I knew that," he said with the first smile I'd seen. "My mom would never do that. She knows how hard it is to earn money because she works and goes to school. She's so tired at night that sometimes she falls asleep before she can read her half of our story. That's why I want to get her something special."

"What are you going to get her?" After all that, I was curious.

He glanced toward my section of jewelry boxes. "It's over there. Do you want to see? I'm not sure how I'll get her to bring me back here, but maybe dad will, or my grandma."

I joined the boy from behind the counter, and together we walked over to the music boxes. These were on shelves instead of in cases. Currently, I had twenty jewelry boxes, eleven of which played music. Three of those had little ballerinas.

To my surprise, he continued past the jewelry boxes to the handheld mirrors in the case beyond that. He pointed at an ornate, silver-plated Victorian mirror. The piece was lovely, but at eighty-five dollars, it was the most expensive of all my handheld mirrors.

"I'm sure I can earn nine more dollars before my mother's birthday," he said. "Do you think it will still be here?"

"What if I save it for you? If you decide to get her something else, go ahead and get it, though. I can always sell it later to someone else."

"Oh, I want it," he assured me. "She says it reminds her of the mirror in *Beauty and the Beast*."

I laughed. "That's what I thought when I found it." The piece had beckoned to me at an estate sale of a woman who had passed away after a very long and apparently satisfying life. She'd looked in the mirror each day, but instead of being upset at the passing years, she'd taken joy in her memories.

I put on my gloves, opened the case with my keys, and removed the mirror. "It's a deal," I said. "I'll keep it in the back for you."

He started walking away but hadn't gone far when he stopped to say, "Thank you."

"You're welcome."

I didn't think Kylan would be back, but if he did return any time in the next two weeks, the mirror would be waiting for him. And for that show of politeness, I'd even give him a discount.

It bothered me that someone, probably a member of his family, would steal his money when the child would have most likely been willing to lend it to them. Why take it without permission? Or why not borrow the funds from an adult instead? Maybe whoever had stolen the money had something more to hide than simply taking the cash. Had I missed something important?

Well, the situation was out of my hands now. A glance at the clock told me it was almost lunchtime. My fiancé, Detective Shannon Martin, would be here soon to take me out for a late lunch. Our relationship was new and a little nerve-racking, but as long as we could figure out a way to let each other be who we really were, I was hopeful it would work out.

Both my fiancé, Shannon, and my friend Jake were charter members in the Autumn Needs to be More Careful Club, but at a time when I'd decided to quit reading imprints altogether, it had been Shannon who made me see that I wouldn't be happy if I didn't use my gift to help others—even if that put me in danger. Maybe he understood because his job as a homicide detective was also dangerous at times, but being a detective was who he was.

Jake, on the other hand, had gone from supportive to actively wishing I wouldn't try to solve anything more serious than a misplaced set of keys. He would applaud using my gift for Kylan.

I had barely stowed the mirror and locked my day's receipts into the safe under my counter when the electronic bells above my outer door rang, a deeper sound than the real jingle bells Jake kept above his door in the Herb Shoppe. Shannon was coming through my single outer door, and behind him I caught a glimpse of Kylan and his mother out on the sidewalk, probably heading home after leaving Jake's with the licorice.

"Hey," Shannon. He was thirty-six, only a few inches taller than I was, and broad-shouldered, his compact movements undeniably graceful. His hair was that color between brown and blond, streaked with lighter blond from his time in the sun at work and on the acre of land he owned on the outskirts of Portland. His hair was slightly curling at the ends as it always did when it grew longer than police bureau regulations. As a detective, he usually wore a suit to work, sans tie, but he must have left his jacket in the car, and probably his under-the-arm holster and gun as well.

"I'm just about ready." I let him come to me at the counter as I put away a few items, removed my gloves, and retrieved my purse. I'd worn a floor-length sleeveless summer dress today so my going barefoot wouldn't be too noticeable wherever Shannon would end up taking me. He was man enough to endure my eccentricities, but I didn't feel the need to flaunt them.

Shannon's arms came around me, and I turned into him,

breathing in the faint aroma of aftershave and coffee. His eyes captured mine. There was something in the green-blue color and the heavy frame of light brown lashes that made them compelling and the most beautiful I'd ever seen. I especially liked the way his skin prematurely crinkled at the edges. He kissed me for a long, satisfying moment before drawing away with a little sigh. His face was clean-shaven today, and while I preferred the rougher look of a few days' beard growth, kissing him freshly shaven was a lot kinder on my skin.

"I'm thinking pasta," he said, releasing me.

"You're always thinking pasta."

He leaned over and nibbled my ear. "Not always."

I laughed. "We can have pasta, but they'd better have something on the organic side." I leaned over to dig through an organizer I kept on one of the under-counter shelves, looking for a pen. "Let me just write a note to Jazzy and Thera. I need to see if they can work more hours next week. My sister is a nervous wreck with her parents coming from Kansas, and I'll have to be on hand occasionally to run interference."

Shannon groaned. "Does this mean I'll have to endure dinners and endless polite conversation?"

"Only if you still want to be my fiancé," I said with a laugh. "Tawnia's my sister, and that means her adoptive parents are going to be in the picture for most of our lives, even at a distance." I'd met the couple once before at their own home soon after learning I had a sister, and they'd been kind and welcoming. I wasn't sure why Tawnia was so nervous. "Now, where did my pen go?" Apparently, it was time to order new ones.

"Will this do?" Shannon said, holding up a pencil with a grin. The pencil was covered with little cars.

"Oh," I said, frowning. "He left it."

"Who?"

"A little boy. He wanted to see if I could find out who took his money. He was using the pencil to write down suspects."

Shannon laughed. "Smart little kid."

"Yeah. I'll keep it for him in case he comes back." Before I could reach for the pencil, my electronic bells jangled again.

Shannon and I both looked toward the outer door as a muscled man pushed into the shop. The first thing I noticed about him was the myriad of colorful tattoos covering the exposed parts of his chest, neck, and huge arms, which were set off perfectly by his sleeveless black biker vest. The second thing that popped out at me was that everything about him—except the vibrant tattoos—looked sad and dragging. His greasy, dishwater-blond hair was cut short, but his mustache drooped to cover his mouth, and his gray-streaked beard sagged limply to his chest. His eyebrows were so long that they looked like caterpillars over his sad, stricken eyes. Ignoring my antiques, he strode directly to the counter, a paper in his hands.

"Hello," I said. "Can I help you?"

He set the paper on my counter, and I saw it was the same Internet article little Kylan had shown me. "Are you Autumn Rain, the psychic lady?"

I stifled a sigh. I didn't like being called a psychic because I couldn't see the future or things that were happening at the moment. I could only read emotions that other people left on certain objects. But people persisted in using the psychic moniker no matter what I said, so I bit back a protest.

"I'm Autumn Rain. How can I help?"

"My wife's gone missing," he said urgently. "I looked for her all night and all morning. Everywhere I can think of. She's nowhere, and it ain't like her." He patted a black leather bag strapped to his upper thigh over his jeans. "I brought some of her stuff. Will you take a look?" A world of despair radiated in his tone, as if at any moment, this tough man might break down into tears.

"Sure." I sent an apologetic glance at Shannon. Maybe this would teach him not to be late for our lunch dates.

"Have you gone to the police?" Shannon asked, setting Kylan's car pencil down next to my cash register.

The biker's gaze flicked over Shannon, taking in his dress pants and shirt. Could he tell Shannon was a cop? "I went this morning. They took my report, and I gave them a list of friends and relatives. But they haven't called me back or come out to the house yet. They told me she'd probably come home on her own and to call all her friends to see if they've heard from her. No one has." The sound of laughter came from Jake's store as if in counterpoint to the biker's despair.

"How long has she been gone?" I put my heel on the metal support ring of my stool and lifted myself onto it.

"Only since last night," he said. "But we're supposed to go on a trip tomorrow for our seventh anniversary. Today's when we were gonna finalize our route. We're heading to California like we did for our honeymoon. It ain't like her to disappear."

Shannon started to speak, but I gave him a hard stare. This was my case, not his. "Tell me when you first realized she was gone," I said.

The biker's expression wilted. "I was late getting off work last night and stopped to have a beer with my work buddies. When I came home, she wasn't there. I wasn't even more than an hour and a half late, maybe two tops."

"Was she okay with you going out with your friends?"

He shrugged. "She don't mind if I go out and have a beer. Long as I don't come home drunk."

Silence fell over us as I considered what to ask next. I was aware of Shannon watching and waiting, not impatiently but intently. Before working homicide, he'd been in missing persons, and we'd discussed his past cases enough that I knew he was thinking the same thing I was—that the woman might have more against the biker's co-workers than he knew. Maybe she'd been angry and had gone somewhere to cool off. If that was the case, it shouldn't take long to discover where she was, as long as he'd brought the right objects.

"Is anything missing?" I asked. "Clothes, suitcases, purse, car?"

"No. That's just it. Nothing is gone except her bike—her Harley—though how that's gone when I have both sets of keys, mine and hers, I don't know. She just disappeared."

"No money missing from your accounts?" I asked next, knowing Shannon was burning to voice the question. He believed money was the root of most marital problems, and maybe he was right.

"No. Uh, I don't know." The biker's brow creased. "I can check. We set up our phones for electronic banking." He pulled out a phone and began to punch numbers with large, clumsy fingers. "Nope. It all looks the same as when I made sure my check was put in."

"There haven't been any charges since yesterday?"

He looked again. "Just gas for my bike."

"Okay, let me see what you brought." I patted the countertop.

"Oh, right." He unzipped the bag on his leg and withdrew

a cell phone, a set of keys, a deck of face cards, and a tube of lip cream. "Sariah never goes anywhere without this stuff."

"She didn't take her phone?" That seemed unusual, to say the least, and for the first time, a twinge of apprehension filled me. Even I always took my phone with me, despite my adoptive father's insistence that the emissions caused cancer.

I pushed back that thought before it could overwhelm me. Winter was gone now, and his death had nothing to do with any kind of emissions.

"No," the biker said. "And she loves playing one game or another at stops while we're on the road, so that makes me more worried. If she went to a friend's house—and none of them admit that she has—she wouldn't have left her phone or her lip stuff." He gave me a completely serious look and added, "Sariah kind of has dry lips, especially on the road, so she don't want to get a cold sore."

That was the moment I knew I had a serious case. Not because of the phone, the keys, or the mysteriously missing motorbike. But because of the lip cream. In an abusive situation, a woman might leave behind her clothes, her phone, and her vehicle, but if she was prone to cold sores, she'd slip that tiny tube of lip cream into her pocket.

Wherever this man's wife was, I didn't believe she'd left willingly.

Chapter 2

"Okay, let's see what we've got." I removed my engagement ring once again and held my hands over the objects on the counter. They tingled with imprints, but only the keys radiated strongly.

I set a finger on the lipstick. Nothing except the impression of hurry, so I moved on. The phone had various imprints, but only one frustrating conversation two months ago with a dentist's office was very clear. Besides this, there were only vague emotions—happiness, frustration, anger. All of it quite normal and nothing that pointed to her whereabouts now. If she'd made any emotionally significant calls, they hadn't been on this phone. The cards held only a few glimpses of past games in various hotel rooms.

Time for the keys. I set my fingers on them, ready to jerk away if the imprint was horrible—not that I'd be able to succeed. Sometimes it was easy to get so caught up, I couldn't pull away, but I was getting better at figuring my way out from under those kinds of imprints.

The most recent imprints on the keys were nonconsequential. Faded, hazy things that didn't detail anything. Maybe because she usually wore riding gloves when she used this set of keys. The first major imprint was from nine months ago, but it sucked me in immediately.

I stared down at my hand, gripping the keys hard as I walked to the bike. A thousand dollars is nothing, I thought. I'll pay him that and more. I need to know. I can't live without knowing.

Out in front of the house, a woman waited for me, a huge grin on her face.

"Hey, Brynn," I said.

"Ready to find that new jacket?" she asked. "You need a really awesome one to go with that awesome bike. They have cool riding gloves too. I like the fingerless ones best."

I was more than ready, not so much for the jacket, but to finally know.

So, there was some kind of secret there, but I'd have to wait to learn what because another imprint was already coming to me.

He grinned as he handed me the keys and pointed out the window. "What?" I asked. "You know I have to—" Then I saw the bike, and a thrill rushed through me. "Manny! You didn't! You spent your bonus on that?"

The part of me that was still Autumn registered that the biker at my counter was named Manny, but this was the only outside thought I could manage before the imprint swept me on.

Manny nodded. "Oh, yeah, baby. I did."

I ran out the front door to the bike. It was beautiful. I let my fingers glide over the pristine leather of the dual seat and across the glistening paint. It was finally mine. This beautiful bike was all mine!

Sticking the key into the ignition, I threw my leg over the seat. The glorious sound of the powerful engine roaring to life made my pulse race. Putting the bike into gear, I sped away. The wind streamed through my hair as I heard Manny yelling at me to put my helmet on.

Not yet. Not for this first ride. Be patient, my sweet, wonderful husband. Just a turn around the block. I'll be right back.

I couldn't help smiling at the imprint. This event had taken place a year ago, which would have put it at the couple's sixth anniversary. Had the motorcycle been an anniversary present? Whatever it was, it had been a good day for Sariah, and probably for Manny too.

"What?" Manny asked. "You see something?"

"Sariah really loved her new bike."

Manny stared at me for a moment, and then his brown eyes turned soft. "We saved a long time to buy it. Before that, we always rode double. I miss having her behind me, but she has more fun on her own bike."

"She was surprised that you'd spent your bonus."

He shrugged. "It took us over the top is all. We both work, and all our money goes into the same pot. I'd do it again, and more."

"There was also something about a thousand dollars nine months ago," I said. "I think it was money Sariah was going to pay someone. It feels like she was trying to find out something she felt very strongly about." I didn't add that it was information Sariah felt she couldn't live without. Emotions like those were exaggerated all the time, even in imprints. "Did she ever pay someone a thousand dollars for something?"

Manny's forehead creased as he shook his head. "That doesn't sound like Sariah."

"You'd know if a thousand dollars was missing from your accounts?" Shannon asked.

Manny nodded. "Yeah, of course. We ain't got a lot to spare, and what we have, we save for retirement, or for excursions. We want to have good memories to talk about when we're old." He paused before adding, "You sure about the money?"

"Yes. But it was nine months ago, so it might not be related to why she's gone missing. It was on a day she went shopping with a woman named Brynn for a new riding jacket."

Manny's eyes opened wide. "If you know that, then it's real. What you do, I mean. Anyone could have guessed about the bike, but you couldn't have known about Brynn and the shopping."

I'd have thought people would believe in my ability before walking through my door, but most people were skeptical until I told them something I couldn't possibly know. Even Shannon had indulged in a hate-love affair with both my gift and his feelings for me for the better part of a year, before not-so-gracefully succumbing to my charms.

"Yes," I said. "It's real. Tell me about that day."

He shrugged. "She found a jacket, a really nice one. Gloves too. Cost over two hundred bucks together. But she must not have liked the jacket because she ended up exchanging it a couple weeks later for a different one about the same price. I thought the first one was a little better, but whatever makes her happy is good for me. As for the thousand bucks, I can go back through my bank statements, but I don't see how I could have missed something that big." Manny's big hand clenched on the countertop. "But didn't you see anything about where she went?"

"I'm sorry," I said, shaking my head. "Imprints are usually left on objects if the emotion surrounding them is significant. That's why I could see the new bike so well. But if she didn't touch these things as she was thinking about leaving, or when something important happened—like someone kidnapping her—there wouldn't be a significant imprint that could tell us anything."

His eyes reddened, and his jaw worked as he stared at me. "Then you need more things to check," he said finally, surprising me with his astuteness.

"Yes. It's no guarantee, but I'm willing to try. The more I read, the more likely we'll find something that will tell us what happened."

"Like what kind of things?" He began shoving the other items back into his bag.

"Nothing cloth, unless it was really special to her and you don't wash it much. Cloth tends to lose bits of itself with each washing, so it doesn't hold imprints well. Leather would be fine, however. And anything else solid or special. Also, things she might use every day." The more often something was used, the more opportunities to imprint on it.

He thought a moment. "I have her riding jacket. And her leather pants, though she mostly wears jeans these days. She didn't take none of it."

"Those would work."

He thumbed over his shoulder. "I'll come back with more. How long will you be open?"

"Look, it would be better if I could go to your house," I said. "I just don't know what might have the imprint. I mean, the door at your house might be what will give me a clue. Or the floor." Floors didn't usually have many imprints since most people wore shoes, but it did happen.

His face brightened for the first time. "You'd do that? When? I called work already and told them I wasn't coming in until I find her. So I can do it anytime." His eyes begged me to come now.

I cast an apologetic glance toward Shannon, who sighed. "I guess this means a raincheck?"

"Sorry," I told him. Turning to the biker, I extended my hand. "I learned from Sariah's imprints that she calls you Manny, but if we're going to be working together, I should have your full name—and your wife's." That should make the background check Shannon would insist on much easier. More importantly, I wanted to check out the fingerless riding gloves Manny was wearing over his large hands. If he'd done something to his wife, I'd rather know now than before I followed him to his house. "You already know I'm Autumn Rain, and this is my fiancé, Shannon Martin."

Manny held out his hand without hesitation. "I'm Manny Barnes," he said as he took my hand, which meant that whatever he thought might be imprinted on his gloves, it didn't have anything to do with his wife's disappearance. My palm touched his leather glove, and instantly, I was somewhere else. I was *someone* else.

I raced through the streets, my eyes searching frantically. My heart pounded as if threatening to leave my chest. No sign of her.

Screaming to a stop, I jumped off and ran up the walk. I banged on a door, trying to push back panic. A woman answered. "Have you seen Sariah?" I begged. "Please tell me she's here."

I barely registered a negative reply before stumbling back to my bike and driving to another house. Now my breath came only with difficulty, my mind numb to everything but helplessness and fear.

The terrible, life-consuming fear.

Dear God, she can't be gone, I thought. She can't have left me. She wouldn't. She knew I'd walk over hot coals for her, that

I'd even give up riding for her if it would make her happy. Where could she have gone? She has to be somewhere. Please, God, bring her home to me.

With effort, I pulled away from Manny. I didn't need to see more—I didn't *want* to see more. If the glove was any indication, he was barely holding things together enough to stand in front of my counter. No wonder he'd been desperate enough to come to a "psychic."

"I'm sorry," I told him gently. "I'll do my best to find Sariah."

"Her full name is Sariah Killigan Barnes," he said. "Killigan is her maiden name."

"Is her family local? Do they know she's missing?"

"Yeah, they know. But there's only Sariah's mom and an aunt who lives in Vegas. And two cousins." Bitterness tinged his voice, and I guessed there was no love lost between him and his in-laws. That might bear looking into.

Shannon inserted his face between us. "Would you excuse us for a minute?" he asked Manny.

"Sure." Manny nodded vigorously, as if willing to do anything as long as I agreed to help him.

Gripping my arm, Shannon led me to the back room that ran the width of the shop behind my counter. "You need to take your gun," he said in a low voice. I'd expected something more along the lines of "No way are you going there alone," so this was a nice surprise.

"I will. Don't worry." I didn't remind him that I was testing for my second-degree black belt in three weeks. He had far more trust in guns than in taekwondo.

"I won't because I'm going with you."

I rolled my eyes. "It'll probably take longer than a lunch break."

"Probably, but by then I'll have his name run through my computer and the plates on his bike or whatever he's driving as well. And I'll let him know I'm a detective."

"No," I whispered back. "Not one word about you being a cop. You can come and play the concerned fiancé, but once you check it out, you'll go back to work so I can do mine."

We glared at each other for a long moment, and it was he who backed down first. "Okay, but if you need anything, let me know. I'd rather you solve this before it becomes my problem."

In other words, a homicide. We both knew that it might already be his problem, but neither of us would say it aloud.

"You can follow me."

"Okay, let's go."

Out in the shop, Manny Barnes paced before the counter. He stopped when we appeared, his face anxious as if expecting me to change my mind. I grabbed my purse from the counter where I'd left it and squatted down in front of my safe.

At least we know he isn't a purse snatcher, I thought wryly as I opened the safe and put on the ankle holster that held my new Glock 26. He also hadn't touched my engagement ring, which I now put into the safe.

I locked my outer door on our way out. Customers knew they could come into my store through the Herb Shoppe and pay Jake for anything they might want to buy while I was out. The same was true when he had to close early. The setup worked well for both of us, and even through the ups and downs of our relationship, we'd held that part of our association sacrosanct.

I drove my own rusty red Toyota hatchback, following Manny's motorcycle, with Shannon's white Mustang in my rearview mirror. I was glad not to have to find the address alone, because whatever ability I had didn't extend to directions, even with the help of my phone's GPS, which always seemed to show the map facing the wrong direction. My sister was likewise directionally impaired, so I liked to think it was an inherited thing.

Manny lived on the east side of Portland on Taggart Street, in lower-cost housing that was a step up from the apartments where I lived. The houses might be near the freeway and crammed close together, but they had a bit of land. Most of them also had garages, and a few even had nice porches. Manny stopped in front of a one-story house with tan siding. Everything about it was nice, from the narrow patch of grass in the front to the vibrant flowers in the carefully designed flowerbeds. Rows of colorful potted plants hung above the pristine white railing on the porch. Instead of a sidewalk up to the door, interlaid stones wound across the grass. Several small trees shaded the house. Everything about the property screamed a love of order and growing things.

The white garage door opened. It was made for two cars, but currently there was only one. Manny drove his bike inside and parked while I climbed out of my car. Shannon joined me on the sidewalk.

"A quick check hasn't revealed anything on this guy except a speeding ticket," he said, "but that doesn't mean there isn't something in his past. If his wife really does turn out to be a missing person, we'll have to dig deeper."

Right. Because missing people usually go missing because of someone they know.

We headed up the drive where Manny waited for us inside the garage. "Is Sariah's bike usually in here too?" I asked Manny.

Manny nodded. "Yes. It'd move without the keys, but it wouldn't start. So it just doesn't make sense that it's gone." He hesitated. "If the bike and the keys were gone, I might not be so worried. I mean, she could have gone for a ride."

"All night?" Shannon asked, arching a brow.

Manny sighed. "I guess not. None of this makes sense."

"May I?" I asked, holding up my hands.

"That's why you're here. You'll find out we ain't perfect, but I love my wife more than anything else in the world."

I began touching things in the garage. First inside the car, then his bike, the shelves, and the tools. Whatever Manny did for a living, it was clear he did his own automotive repairs, and the imprints on the tools were all his, except for a glimpse or two of a woman laughing as she hung paintings or sanded a homemade puzzle.

There was nothing on the garage floor except grease, but most of it was old and didn't cling to my bare feet. When he took me inside, it was immediately apparent that Sariah loved figurines. There were three curio cabinets crammed into the small kitchen alone.

"We get one figure from every place we ride," Manny explained. "Usually from garage or estate sales."

Most of the figurines were modern, inexpensive things and held no notable imprints, except from the day of purchase. The rest of the kitchen also didn't yield much. Sariah liked to cook, and it soothed her, so not many strong imprints there. In the sitting room was another, smaller curio cabinet filled with more knickknacks, and I did a doubletake as I recognized what looked like six Lladro figurines from the mid-eighties that I would have been happy to sell in my shop. Reverently, I touched each of the figurines. The imprints they held were nostalgic and faded, but it was clear they'd been well-loved. I checked the bottoms to make sure they were genuine Lladro.

"Do you realize that some of these figurines may be worth thousands of dollars?" I said, closing the case. "Maybe tens of thousands?" Exactly how much, I'd have to research, but the value was there.

Manny looked surprised. "Really? Sariah will be happy to hear—" He broke off, shaking his head morosely. "Most of these are from Sariah's grandmother from her father's side, and it's sort of what got us started collecting. Sariah got them when she died—Sariah's father had already passed by then, and she's the only grandchild. But Sariah's mother nearly threw them away. She isn't into collecting anything but stamps on her passport."

The figurines would have been a sizeable investment, even back when purchased, but time had made them far more valuable. "Sariah's mother likes traveling?" I closed the cabinet.

"As long as it doesn't have anything to do with a motorcycle. Maren—that's her name, Maren Killigan—works for an airline and gets discounted travel, so she's always jetting around. I tried to make her see that Sariah is just like her in that—we both love to see new things and visit new places, except we do it on our bikes, but she thinks I've corrupted Sariah."

"I see." I moved to the furniture in the room, but Shannon's hand fell on my shoulder long before I was finished.

He drew me out to the porch, his voice lowering. "I have to go back to work now. You let me know if you need anything."

"I'll be fine," I said. Because if the imprints had told me one thing thus far, it was that Manny wasn't violent. He'd never lifted a hand to Sariah. Not ever. Not even when he'd had a beer too many. Drinking only made him morose and weepy.

After Shannon left, Manny loosened up. "He's kind of scary," he said, looking out the window as Shannon sped off in his unmarked Mustang.

I laughed. "Not really. He's just protective."

"You can say that again. What now?"

I sighed. "There's still a long way to go. If you don't mind, I'd like to have one of those bananas in your kitchen. I'm missing lunch." I was starting to flag, and the banana would give me a little strength. "Then I'll need that list of friends and family you gave to the police. Yours and hers too. I want to talk to all of them."

Manny frowned. "They're a nice bunch, but they may not open up to you."

"We'll figure it out. And I want the names of other people you know who might not necessarily be friends or related. Make sure you include phone numbers, addresses, and how you know them. Include everyone, even if it's someone you don't socialize with but come into contact with regularly—delivery people, colleagues from work, neighbors, and the like. And if you think anyone might be important, note that as well."

Manny went to retrieve the banana while I continued working in the sitting room. On the coffee table sat a garish ceramic bowl full of clear marbles that invited people to plunge their hands into the bowl and play. The marbles didn't radiate imprints, but vivid tingling signaled a strong one on the bowl, so I squatted by the table and placed a forefinger on its gaudy surface.

Disgusting creature. I had no idea what my son saw in the little tramp. He didn't see Sariah for what she was, how she was always making eyes at other men behind his back. I had to get rid of her somehow, if it was the last thing I did.

The imprint was so malevolent that I rolled back on my heels, which took my finger from the red spot on the bowl. That meant I had to touch it again and relive the imprint before I could check if there was more. There wasn't. But at least six months ago, Manny's mother wanted to get rid of Sariah.

I was still squatting there, recovering, when Manny returned to the room with a banana. "Are you okay?" he asked. His gaze wandered past me to the bowl.

I nodded, coming awkwardly to my feet. "Your mother doesn't like Sariah, does she?"

He shook his head. "About as much as hers likes me."

"You should get rid of this bowl." No one should have something in their house that reeked of hatred that strongly.

His dark eyes were curious, but he didn't press for more. "We never liked it anyway. It was a gift from my mother, though, and Sariah didn't want to hurt her feelings. We put the marbles in to make it better."

"The marbles are great. Just use another bowl to hold them."

I ate the banana while Manny began adding to the list of names he'd given the police, not a list on a piece of paper but on his phone. His big fingers tapped away with the same awkwardness he'd shown earlier at my antiques shop. After examining everything in the room, I left him behind and continued into the hallway. I touched paintings, walls, doors, vents, and every piece of furniture. I opened cupboards, drawers, and closets, and explored everything in the bathroom. I touched coats, shoes, jewelry, and Sariah's leather clothing. I inspected the back patio and the surprisingly large back yard that I learned was the envy of the neighbors.

Gradually, an image of Manny and Sariah's life together came into focus. They had married seven years ago, after a whirlwind romance of barely a month. Manny had fallen head-over-heels with Sariah from the first day they'd met, and she had felt the same for him. Manny worked at a garage fixing cars, while Sariah was a secretary at a local school. They worked hard, enjoyed playing cards, watched game shows on television, and drank the occasional beer. They loved pizza and ice cream and Doritos. Manny used to smoke, but he'd quit long before his marriage to Sariah, when his beloved father died of lung cancer. They enjoyed having friends over, but mostly they loved planning trips and riding their Harley-Davidsons. They helped serve breakfast at the homeless shelter every Saturday, and Manny had fixed up and donated eleven old cars to charity over the past five years. They had no children, not from preference, but because in the five years they'd been trying, it had never happened. They'd been happy for most of their seven-year marriage. Their sometimes loud and passionate fights never lasted long and always ended in equally passionate love-making. Sariah was eagerly awaiting their anniversary trip. In short, they were like any other couple who were in love and on equal footing in their relationship. They were good people.

What I didn't find was any hint that Sariah planned to leave, or that someone planned to take her.

Frustrated, I went to the front porch to touch the vibrant hanging baskets of flowers I'd noticed when I arrived. Again, there was nothing. The railing and floor were equally devoid of information. Soon, only a small watering can sat untouched in the corner of the porch, inconsequential and almost unnoticed. I picked it up, and emotion fell over me.

I focused on the water pouring over the plants as a motorcycle roared to life. I hate him, I thought. Why doesn't he leave me alone? It's enough to make me stop riding altogether. I have to tell Manny, but what would I tell him? That I have a "feeling" when I'm around him?

Ah-hah. This was something recent, from Tuesday of last week at four-twenty. For the first time, I might have a lead. Sariah didn't like one of their riding friends, and maybe she had good reason. I touched it again to make sure I hadn't missed anything.

Imprints never change, but they are fallible because what I experience always comes through the eyes of whoever imprinted on the object. Their emotions, perceptions, and biases were all a part of what they saw. For instance, I'd experienced imprints of serial killers who felt no remorse or shame in what they did, as if killing was as okay as buying groceries. I always tried to ban these horrific imprints to a corner of my mind, but inevitably, they became a part of my experience and a little more of my personal innocence died.

Was it worth it? I didn't really know, but it was a risk I was willing to take.

As a last resort, I walked out to the mailbox and touched that too. An unexpected imprint fell over me like a net, holding me in place with excitement and worry. *I'm finally going to see her today.*

Just that one imprinted thought, but it was so powerful that it repeated three times before I could take my finger away. No clue as to who "she" was, but the calendar in my mind narrowed the date to early January, six months earlier.

Manny came out on the porch. "I think I'm finished," he called, holding up his phone.

So was I. Except for one more thing. I met him at the bottom of his porch stairs. "Can I see what you have so far?"

"Want me to text it to you?"

"Yes, but let me see the list first."

What I really wanted was to touch his phone. I believed in him after touching his gloves and everything in the rest of his house, but I had to be thorough. His wife or whoever had taken her could have imprinted on his phone as well.

He passed me the phone, and in the next second, I regretted my request as more panic and fear filled me, from the deep recesses of my heart to the tips of my toes and fingers. Manny had used this phone to call everyone he knew, often sobbing by the end of the conversations.

I endured it all, going back several months before handing back his phone. I was lucky the frantic images of his panic were preceded by normal, fainter ones, or I might have collapsed altogether, clutching the phone in a grip I wouldn't be able to release until I passed out. If I'd had any lingering doubts about this man, they were utterly decimated.

He gazed at me a little warily. "What was that all about?" When I didn't answer, he said, "Oh. The, uh, imprints are that bad, huh?"

"Sometimes. And you've been very worried about Sariah." Reluctantly, I added, "I need to see your keys and wallet too. I have to rule everything out."

He emptied his pockets of keys, wallet, and a cigarette lighter.

"I thought you quit," I said.

"I did. But we sometimes make fires on the road with it." He sighed. "Although I could really use a cigarette right now."

"Then you'll have to quit all over again when we find her."

He gave me a watery smile. "And if we don't?" His eyes begged me to tell him everything would be okay. "I don't know who I am anymore without her."

"We won't give up," I said, trying to comfort him without giving him promises I didn't know if I'd be able to keep. Sometimes people died, and people also disappeared and never came home. My job was to find Sariah before she became one of those statistics.

"I'll never give up . . . unless—" He didn't finish the sentence, and I couldn't fault him for it.

To my immense relief, the imprints on the keys (worry) and lighter (guilt) were not strong and not important.

"Let me give you my card," I said, my voice strained. Digging in my purse, I gave him one. "Email me the suspect list and text it to me as well. I'll want to print a copy back at my store. I'll check everyone out for imprints. We'll find something."

"Okay." He gripped the card so tightly, it bent in his big fingers.

"I did find something that might be a lead." I pointed at the watering can in the corner of the porch. "Did Sariah have issues with any of your friends? Your riding friends? Did any of them visit a week ago on Tuesday afternoon?"

Manny thought a moment. "I had to work late, and there wasn't anyone here except Sariah when I got home. As for anyone Sariah might have issues with, there's my ex, but they've been getting along great for years."

"You still hang out with your ex-wife?"

He shrugged. "We're part of the same biker group, the Road Rollers. But it's Sariah who hangs out with Brynn, not me."

Understanding dawned. "Her friend Brynn is your ex?"

"Yeah. We were young when we got married. It was stupid. We're both happier with someone else."

"You're sure Brynn feels the same way?"

"Of course."

"What about any men? Has Sariah ever told you someone made her uncomfortable?"

"Someone who rides with us?" He thought a moment. "Not that I can think of."

"What about anyone else who rides a motorcycle?"

"Well, my mother's new husband has a bike, but he doesn't use it much. Sariah doesn't like him, but maybe that's because I don't. He's a self-righteous prick." He colored. "Excuse the French."

I'd heard a lot worse. "I'll have to talk with all of them. I know you already have, but someone must have information that will lead us to a clue."

Manny shook his head. "Our friends are a good bunch. A lot of them have families like me and Sariah—parents who don't approve or care about seeing them. We've become each other's family. We stick together. I don't think . . . they don't open up with outsiders much."

I thought about that a moment. "They don't have to open up. I just need to get close enough to touch some of their things."

He grinned at me, though the amusement didn't reach his eyes. "That's even harder."

If the police became involved, my pull with Shannon might force them to capitulate, but a court order would take time.

"What if I was also a biker?" I asked. "Your cousin or something."

He snorted. "Not my cousin. They all know my real cousin and my parents. Some of these guys I go back to high school with and some of them work at my shop. They know my family."

"What about Sariah's family?"

"Yeah, that might work. Sariah's mom won't be caught dead anywhere near us, so our friends know nothing about her family. Or practically."

"Maybe I'm a cousin who came to help you find Sariah."

He scratched his beard, studying me doubtfully, from my short brown hair that was dyed a bright auburn on top to the tips of my bare toes peeking out from under my dress. "Excuse me, but you don't look much like a biker chick. We usually ride in leather jackets—for protection, you know." He looked down at himself as if realizing he wore only his vest. "Well, it's more a statement for most of us. I just took off with what I was wearing when I realized she wasn't home. Sariah ain't big, but she's tall, and her jacket would be too long on you. And to be authentic, you'd need a bike."

That, I could manage. "Is a leather jacket with an embossed skull on the back okay?" I asked.

"Of course. The skull means brotherhood, you know. We also all use a Road Roller logo—that's our riding club—either on the back or sleeve, but seeing as you're visiting and not a member, you wouldn't need that."

"All right then. When can I meet them? The sooner the better."

He thought for a moment. "The Road Rollers are meeting here at five to participate in a search through the city. One gal's printing off a bunch of flyers, and she invited another riding group to help us get the word out. Will that work?"

"Perfect. I'll be here a little early. I'd like to go through your family album again to memorize a few names so I can carry off the cousin connection."

"Okay." He gave me a miserable smile that didn't reach his eyes. Pity rose in my chest. I wished I could assure him it would be okay.

Back in my car, I considered what I knew so far. Nine months ago, Sariah planned to give someone a thousand dollars, perhaps to uncover a truth she couldn't go on living without knowing. Six months ago, Sariah was excited or worried about seeing someone referred to as "her." A week ago on Tuesday afternoon, Sariah had a visit from a bike-riding man she strongly disliked.

It was precious little but more than the police had bothered to uncover.

I texted Shannon. *Please get a missing person's detective over to Manny Barnes's house. His wife didn't plan to go anywhere, and their marriage appears solid. Something is wrong.*

Having done what I could on the police front, I drove home faster than I should have. There wasn't much time to become biker Autumn Rain.

Chapter 3

Three months ago at an estate sale, I'd made an impulse purchase of a set of vintage leather female biker gear that included pants, jacket, and gloves. The jacket was a thing of beauty, with a black, textured skull on the back and silver flourishes on the sleeves and bottom edges. The pieces were soft cowhide and fit me like the proverbial glove.

I already had a helmet from when I'd been dating Jake, and I'd learned how to ride, thinking I might buy a bike myself someday. The appeal of the leathers had soon worn off, though. Maybe being engaged had something to do with it. Shannon had endured a lot of my craziness already, and now that he'd finally worked up the nerve to ask me to marry him, I didn't want to make it harder for him.

So I'd tagged the vintage biker pieces and thrown them into a display case. That the price was slightly higher than I might normally ask for them was only because I'd had them professionally cleaned. At least that's what I told myself.

Now, I admitted that it might not be true since I was eager to try them on again.

I texted Jake from my car the minute I pulled up at the store:

Really need to use your bike tonight. Is that okay? He'd entrusted his bike to me before, and he had a truck to use, so I was hoping it wasn't an issue.

About then, my stomach protested, and I remembered I'd missed lunch. I darted across traffic to Smokey's, pulling on my dollar gloves. It didn't matter that they made me look eccentric, because not wearing shoes already did that, but after the tumult at Manny's, I needed a rest from imprints. Smokey's was a mostly organic, airy place with spotless tables and a long snack bar along the wall opposite the kitchen area. The place always smelled heavenly, especially to someone who was as voracious as I was. Within minutes, I was back at my store with a potpie and a strawberry smoothie.

No one was inside when I unlocked the front door to my shop, but as I looked around, familiar objects seemed to be missing, which hopefully meant Jake had done business for me after all. Then I heard music coming from the back of the shop, something upbeat and guttural. It had to be fifteen-year-old Jazzy Storm, or Jessica Sandstrom as she had been born, my second part-time employee.

What was she doing here on her day off? I never scheduled her to work alone.

I tried not to worry as I hurried to the back room. My morning proceeds had been locked up in the safe, and I hadn't really been worried about her stealing for months now. Maybe Jake had been so busy, he'd called her in to help.

Sure enough, Jazzy was seated at my long workbench, eagerly typing on the laptop that her guardian, local attorney Claire Philpot, had purchased to help her catch up in school.

"Hey, Autumn," Jazzy called as I entered, her voice light and her eyes barely leaving the screen. Today her blue hair was secured in a braid down her back, and her very short shorts and halter top probably hadn't been approved by her guardian, who had also nixed her nose ring until she was eighteen. "Glad you're here. I gotta show you something, but wait a minute, okay? I'm almost done with this."

"Okay," I threw down my purse and studied the child. The former runaway had filled in a little since Shannon and I had rescued her from a child trafficking ring six months earlier, though she was still thin. Then, she'd been rebellious, angry, and hard to handle, but through a connection with Shannon's partner, Claire had become involved in the girl's life, and things had begun to change for her. When Jazzy found herself with online classes and too much time on her hands, Claire had asked me to let her help in the store—with Claire secretly paying her wage. Jake and I both agreed to put her to work, but it wasn't until this last month or two that she had started to become useful. Two weeks ago, I'd finally stopped taking payments from Claire. About that time, I'd also given in to Jazzy's pleas to put some of my products online.

Stabbing a plastic fork into my potpie, I bent down to look over Jazzy's shoulder. She was uploading numerous digital pictures of a music box to an eBay listing. The music box in question sat close to her elbow next to a handful of toy cars. A few figurines, three vintage Chinese bowls, and my Fisher-Price Little People schoolhouse were also strewn out on the table.

"It's going to be a bid situation for the music box," she explained, "so we can't keep it out on the floor. Same with these others. But the stuff in our online store we can keep for sale in the shop as long as we make sure to delete the listings before we actually sell the pieces. I'm putting a blue sticker on the bottom of each one I've listed, and if you'll show me how, I'll put a note on your inventory list as well, so it'll pop up and send me a message when we sell it."

Jazzy finished and clicked save. "There. I've listed twenty more products, and I need more."

"I thought you weren't working today." I pulled myself onto the table, folding my legs under me, and concentrated on my potpie.

"I wasn't supposed to," she said, grinning up at me, her blue eyes alive. "But after that whole mess with me not figuring in the shipping, we barely broke even on the items you took to the post office yesterday. But I think I've figured it out now, so I want to make up for it." She jumped up from the table. "And you know what? I think I've found what I want to do in life. I *love* selling online. I love researching prices, taking pictures, creating posts. But I need more stuff."

I swallowed the food in my mouth. "Anything in particular?"

"I'm not sure. But you've already priced everything in the store, so as long as I get that price plus shipping, I should be good to sell any of it, right? Once we see what sells, you can look for more of that."

"You need to figure in eBay fees," I reminded her. "Because they charge a fee to sell the items."

"Oh, right. And you need to show me how to pack stuff so it won't break. We'll need insurance on the expensive things, just in case. I'm learning how to do that on this reselling group I joined on Facebook. Did you know there are places that have online auctions for abandoned storage units? You can buy the whole thing and dig through it all after."

"Yes, I've bought a few," I said. "And admittedly, some of the contents might be a lot better for reselling online rather than in our store." The small abandoned storage units I bought had held a respectable number of vintage items, which had netted a nice profit, but the rest I'd ended up donating to Goodwill or tossing in the garbage. "I don't have space to store items I can't sell here, but if you keep up an interest in online sales, maybe Shannon wouldn't mind us parking a trailer on his property."

"That's what I was thinking," Jazzy said, typing something into her search bar. "Meanwhile, I need more stuff to list."

I laughed. "You can start with those new baseball cards I found last week. We'll need to get at least sixty from each to cover all our costs and make something."

"I'll research what they're going for, just to be sure. Because they might be going for more online." She disappeared into the shop to retrieve the cards.

Her excitement reminded me of how I felt each time I found an estate sale with decent pricing. Garage sales were actually better for my bottom line, but those weren't as reliable.

I continued eating my potpie and drinking my smoothie while watching Jazzy take pictures of the three cards and post them online. She did it all a lot faster than I could. "I'll help when I can," I said. "Right now, I have to go somewhere."

Jazzy looked up from her computer with a knowing grin. "Hot date with Shannon?"

"Actually, my date is with a group of bikers." When I saw her eager expression, I added hastily, "I'm on a case. A man's wife is missing. I already went to his house, but I didn't find any imprints that point to her disappearance. Which is why I'm going back tonight."

She wanted more details, of course, but I didn't have any, so I gulped the last of my food and left her busily typing away. Back in the main room, I went to the front case to get my biker gear. The jacket radiated the slightest tingle of pleasant imprints that made me feel invigorated.

Jazzy looked up as I reentered the back room. "Nice," she said, eyeing the jacket. "I bet I can get a lot more than you're asking for online."

I laughed. "You can't post this. At least not yet. I need it for my case." I dug a simple collarless peach blouse from a storage cabinet to complete my ensemble and hurried into the bathroom, aware of her curious gaze following me.

Sitting on the toilet, I washed my feet with a sprayer in the floor basin I'd had installed in the space between the toilet and the pedestal of my sink. People were often appalled that I didn't wear shoes, but everything could be washed off, and for the most part, there were more germs on a doorknob than on the floor.

I donned the biker outfit. It fit a little snugger than I remembered, but maybe it was okay. The pants were wide enough at the leg so I could wear my Glock, though the maker probably had boots in mind. Using some water and some gel, I spiked my hair more than normal. My brown roots were showing, but that shouldn't matter. Different colored roots seemed to be all the rage these days.

I slipped out of the bathroom, intent on digging out a pair of moccasins from a cupboard. Moccasins sans the decorative fringes, of course. I hated anything on my feet, but unlike regular shoes, these didn't make my back ache, and they'd protect my feet from the spiky foot pedals on Jake's bike. If you didn't look too closely, they might even pass as boots.

"Woah," Jazzy said, gaping. "You weren't kidding about the biker thing, were you?"

"Nope. I have to look the part."

Jazzy shook her head. "Then you need more makeup."

"That's just a stereotype." I'd actually curbed my makeup tendencies the past few years since meeting my sister, in favor of a more natural look that was easier to upkeep.

She rolled her eyes in the way all kids master before their eleventh year. "And the tight leather clothing isn't?"

"That's more of a symbol of brotherhood. Especially this." I turned and showed her the skull.

"Awesome." Jazzy jumped up. "Come on, you have to. I'll help."

We returned to the bathroom for more eyeshadow. I already used a lot of mascara, but I drew the line at base. I wasn't clogging up my pores for this case or any other. When Jazzy was finished, I had to admit that I did look like a biker chick, or at least my perception of one.

"That'll get anyone to answer your questions." Jazzy squinted at me. "But it sure makes the different colors of your eyes stand out."

"That's okay. Look, I'd better get going. I'll lock up, so go out through Jake's when you're finished, okay?"

Speaking of which, Jake hadn't texted me back yet. I was halfway to our connecting doors to look for him when my sister, Tawnia, called on my phone.

"Where are you?" she demanded. "I stopped by the store a while ago, but Jake said you went out for lunch with Shannon and never came back."

I checked the time on my wall of antique clocks, surprised to see that one was missing. It was four now, and I wanted to be back at Manny's well before five, so I could prepare to meet his gang as they arrived. "I'm here now, but only for another thirty minutes."

"Okay, I'll be there in ten." She hung up before I could ask if she was bringing Destiny, my niece, who was ten months old and my favorite person in the world, including Shannon, though I didn't tell him that. Unlike my fiancée, Destiny Emma Winn never contradicted anything I said, and she didn't have a fetish for pasta.

I looked away from the clocks just in time to run into Jake. "Oh, sorry," I said, shoving my phone into a pocket of my leather jacket.

"No problem." Jake's gaze ran down my body appreciatively, making me flush. He was a muscular, good-looking man, with creamy chocolate skin and black hair arranged in finger-sized locs, or dreadlocks as my sister insisted on calling them. He had a charming, dazzlingly white smile that made women want to buy things just so he'd focus that smile on them. Despite his tough-looking exterior, he was gentle in the extreme and had a patience that might rival Job's from the Bible stories my adoptive father had read to me as a child.

"Hey," he added, "wasn't that jacket on display a little while ago when I had to get down one of your clocks for a customer? You and Shannon must have a hot date. Is that why you want my bike?"

"No date. Unless you count an entire biker gang." I laughed at his shocked expression. "Actually, I have a case. A biker's wife has gone missing, and I'm trying to blend in. And thanks for selling the clock."

"Well, you'll more than blend in. They'll be eating out of your hand. Would you like some backup?"

"No, just your bike. Shannon's already done a check on the guy, and I've got my Glock."

Jake started to say something, then shook his head. "Okay, but please don't—"

"Do anything dangerous," I finished. "I won't. They probably had a fight, and I'll find her at a hotel in town."

"Yeah, probably." He brightened at that. For my part, I didn't want him anywhere near the bikers. Jake had already gotten mixed up in my cases in the past and had almost been killed.

He handed me his keys, and I gave him mine in exchange. He was familiar enough with my old Toyota that he'd be able to get her to behave. I knew from experience that his keys held imprints about me from the time we dated, and though we'd both moved on, I didn't need a reminder of that now, so I was grateful for the biker gloves. He'd only recently introduced me to his new girlfriend, Melinda Jones, after a month of dating her, which made me a little jealous, even though I was happy he'd found someone. Emotions are crazy that way. Whatever happened, I didn't want to get on her bad side because I loved Jake too much to lose him. One more reason to keep him at arm's length for a while.

I was grateful when the invisible thread of connection I always felt to my sister thickened like rope, which indicated my twin was close. I also knew she had her baby with her. For as long as I could remember, I'd felt that connection with family, first with my adoptive parents and then with Tawnia when she'd come to the city, even before I'd met her and understood how we'd been separated as newborns. More recently, it happened with Destiny, and later with our biological father after I'd learned the truth of my past and resolved some of my negative feelings toward him. It was a comforting sensation that I didn't really discuss with anyone, though I was sure Tawnia felt something similar with me as well—or would if she let herself. She often discounted things that she felt might be too weird, especially in relation to her own unique ability.

"Tawnia's here," I said to Jake, pocketing his keys and removing my gloves, tucking them under my arm. "Thanks so much for letting me use the bike. I'll text you when I'm finished."

"No problem." With a wave of his hand, Jake retreated to his shop.

I met my sister at the door, taking Destiny from her arms and showering her with kisses. Destiny's eyes, two big blue eyes that held no sign of our inherited heterochromia, immediately fastened on the embossed silver swirls embedded in my leather jacket. She began trying to pluck them off.

Tawnia took one look at me and shook her head. "No and no and no! You can't start dressing like that," she said in an aggrieved tone. "You know my parents will be here on Sunday. I came to see if you'd consider nixing the red in your hair for once, not to give them something more to worry about."

I laughed. "Don't worry. It's for a new case. I promise on Sunday I'll look normal. My normal, that is. And, no, I'm not changing my hair color for your parents. I don't care what they think of me."

Tawnia gripped my arm. "But I care what they think of you. You're my other half."

I snorted. "I thought Brett was your other half."

She shrugged. "My other fourth then, along with him and Destiny."

"You're worrying too much." I cocked my head to study her anxious face. My sister had my same mismatched eyes, set slightly too far apart for real beauty, and looking at her face wasn't like looking at a mirror image, which was backward, but at a picture of myself. Her hair was our natural glossy brown, longer than mine, past her shoulders. She tended to wear dress pants and nice shirts, while I gravitated to broomstick dresses, flowy pants, and old jeans. She always wore shoes, except inside her house. She was a junk-food addict who was a lousy cook, and who used a microwave more than anyone ever should, while I loved cooking health foods from scratch. She also had an unusual gift, though it was much different from the one I shared with our biological father.

Tawnia was what I'd deem a real psychic. She worked part-time as a graphic designer at an advertising firm where she'd once been the creative director and was an incredibly talented artist in her own right, but sometimes there was more in her drawings. She'd draw emotion-driven scenes, only to later see the actual people those events happened to in the newspaper or on the news. Her glimpses were always of people who lived in or around Portland, so range was an issue. Occasionally, her "special" drawings were related to my cases, but not consistently.

She'd inherited her gift from our paternal grandmother, who'd died in a sanitorium long before we were born, before we were given to two different families to raise. I'd gone to the flower child couple who'd housed our mother during her pregnancy, and Tawnia had ended up with the planned adoptive family in Kansas who'd paid the adoption company. The difference between Tawnia and our paternal grandmother was that she didn't only see scary, negative events, but also positive ones that lifted and strengthened her. She seemed to have a limit too, as if she turned off after seeing as much as she could handle. Our grandmother might have lived if she'd had that internal limit.

For all our differences, Tawnia and I were identical twins, and the moment she'd entered my life, I'd finally understood the urge that had taken me all over the country. I'd been searching for her. Yes, for my other half.

Tawnia met my stare. "I'm doing it again, aren't I? Giving my parents too much power."

I nodded. "Look, you're an adult. I know they were strict and hard on you growing up, but you believe they did that to give you a leg up in the world, right? You are who you are because of them, and you love them. I thought your relationship with them was going well now that you've finally stopped moving from state to state."

"Things are going well—as long as they're in Kansas. And this is the first time they're staying with me at the house for their visit. It's nerve-racking. Do you know I even paid my neighbor to clean my house—and it was already clean!"

That didn't surprise me, but I had a more immediate problem to deal with. Destiny had finished her futile attempts with the silver swirls, and when I didn't let her lick them, she motioned toward my counter where she knew I kept a glass jar full of soft, honey-sweetened candies from Jake's store.

"I know, baby," I murmured, moving toward the counter.

"Destiny is feeling the pressure," Tawnia continued as she shadowed me.

My mouth fought a smile at her use of Destiny's name. For months after the baby's birth, Tawnia had insisted on using Destiny's middle name, Emma, probably to impress her parents, and I'd been the only one to call her Destiny. I didn't see the point in giving the child a first name and not using it. Brett, Tawnia's husband, had switched the name up so much, he'd finally started calling her Sweetie, and now it seemed even Tawnia had given up. Destiny was Destiny now, for everyone.

I dropped my biker gloves on the counter, opened a candy, and tore it in half for the grinning baby. "Destiny will be fine."

"I hope so. Anyway, I wanted to change the menu for Sunday dinner. That's why I'm here. Remember that brined pork tenderloin you made with the roasted carrots and brussels sprouts? Could you make that instead?"

"Sure. It's easy enough."

She looked relieved. "Okay, but nix the cauliflower rice. Let's just have plain white."

"How about multigrain?"

She made a face. "The kind that looks like it has bugs in it?"

"They'll love it."

She raised her hands. "Okay. I'll trust you. I can get the ingredients on my way home."

"Really?" I asked. "You'll get exactly what I want?" Because if it was going to taste good, it couldn't be just any piece of pork, and trying to explain that to my very educated sister would take as long as explaining why one vintage music box could sell for thousands while another was only fifty bucks. "Maybe you should concentrate on everything else and leave the food to me."

"There's not much else to do." She began listing her completed tasks, numbering them on her fingers. "I have a new bed set up in the guest room, new towels, fresh shampoos and soap, and a daily reminder to take out the meals you made from the freezer to serve on the days we don't eat out." She sighed. "Why am I so nervous?"

"It's going to be fine." What wasn't going to be fine was my vintage leather jacket if I didn't stop Destiny from smearing it with her candy.

As if reading my mind, Tawnia dug in her large purse for

wipes and reached to take Destiny from my arms. "But I really will get the ingredients. I'll even go to that store you like, even if it does cost three times as much as where I shop. Just write down exactly what to get. I promise not to ask why or to make substitutions."

Maybe she could do it. I had no idea where my case would take me in the next few days. And Tawnia was smart, even if she didn't have the patience to understand cooking. "All right."

I bent over to search for a pen, and it was only then that I remembered the note I'd been planning to write to Jazzy and Thera about additional hours while Tawnia's parents were in town. I'd been interrupted before I could write the note, and I apparently still didn't have a pen, though now that I thought about it, I'd seen a couple on the desk in the back room.

My eyes riveted on Kylan's pencil. Hopefully he wouldn't mind. Yet as my hand neared it, I could feel the buzzing of the imprints. Strong imprints. Which meant I needed to see what they were right now, if only to assure myself that I hadn't missed something.

Tawnia was talking to Destiny as she cleaned her hands, but she fell silent as she watched my fingers hovering over the pencil. "What is it?" she asked.

"Just a little boy trying to catch a thief who borrowed his money without permission. He left his pencil. There's a strong imprint on it."

"Then maybe you should sit before—" she began, but the pull was such that there was no way I could have stopped my hand from dropping. My fingers closed around the pencil.

I held the phone to my ear with my shoulder, my neck straining at the pressure. "What's that again?" I asked, keeping my voice low, almost a raspy whisper.

Wait. Was that someone in the corner? I turned rapidly, but nothing was there.

"Eight Oh One, Southwest Tenth Avenue," the voice on the other end repeated as I scribbled the address down on a piece of paper ripped from a tiny notebook. I didn't look at the paper as I wrote. Instead, I watched the corner where the shadows danced and the door with the batman poster hanging on it. I couldn't let anyone catch me in here.

"I'll be there in an hour," I said. "How will I recognize you?"

"Same as before." The caller hung up, and so did I.

It was that simple. I'd pick up the stuff, start dosing their food, and then it would be over.

"They'll be gone, gone, gone," I thought, "and I won't have to deal with them anymore. No one will ever know."

I wanted to laugh and do something to celebrate, but the hidden voices pressed in on me like always. Scary, threatening, and teasing voices. This time, they told me to be quick. I needed to get Kylan's money before anyone came home and found me here. If they found out what I planned, they'd try to stop me. The voices wouldn't allow that.

The imprint wasn't evil, but whoever had left it was obviously unstable. Without a breath, it started to repeat. I relived the event again, unable to release the pencil, but as it started a third time, hands closed around mine, and the pencil was wrested from my tight grip.

"Autumn?" came Tawnia's worried voice.

"I need to call Shannon," I said, experiencing the oddest sensation to check the corners of my shop to make sure whoever owned the voices weren't hiding there. This was one imprint I didn't want to read again. Ever. "I think someone at that little boy's house is planning a murder."

Chapter 4

awnia took the pencil and slipped it inside an envelope, still juggling Destiny on her hip. "Who exactly is this boy?"

"That's just it. I don't know. His name is Kylan, but I didn't catch his last name, or his mother's, and I've never seen them here before. The boy found me from an Internet article."

"Just how young is he?"

"Maybe nine or ten. I don't really know." The only child I had experience with was Destiny.

I was already calling Shannon's mobile phone. When he didn't answer, I called his partner, Paige Duncan. She picked up instantly.

"Hey, Autumn, how are you doing?"

"I need to talk to Shannon right away."

She hesitated briefly, as if the detective in her was kicking in. "He's doing interviews," she said. "Some kids and their dog found a human femur along the Willamette, and since then we've found the rest of that body and another one, mostly bones. They've still got the cadaver dogs out and are canvassing the area in case we have a dumpsite."

My stomach clenched. "You're talking serial killer."

"Right. Shannon's interviewing the neighbors. And I say that very loosely because it's in a manufacturing area that hasn't been in use recently. Service isn't much good there because of interference from some power lines. Kind of like some voodoo black hole, so I'm not surprised he didn't pick up. I'm working with the coroner's office right now to identify our corpse, but these victims have already waited this long. If you need something, I can help. Is it about the missing biker case?"

"No, it's about another imprint left thirteen days ago on a pencil a little boy brought to my store this morning. It's bad." Like the rest of the officers at the station, Paige knew about my gift. Even when Shannon was fighting not to use my talent or to put himself within my clutches, Paige had eagerly brought me items from their cases to read.

"How bad?" There was a little too much eagerness in her voice, but that was Paige. She came from a family of cops, and she loved nothing as much as getting the jump on the bad guys.

"Really bad. Of course, everything I see is filtered through the person's thoughts and experiences, and this person might have mental instability, so—"

"Yeah, yeah, but if you say something's wrong, I know it is." Paige sometimes had more faith in me than I did.

"Whoever it was made arrangements to pick up something they planned to sneak into someone's food. The imprinter seemed certain it would make multiple people be 'gone, gone, gone' in a way that no one would figure out."

"Poison then. Was it a man or a woman?"

"Unknown. Whoever it was watched the door as they wrote down the address, not their own hand. And the voice was low—I think so he or she wouldn't be overheard. Definitely not a booming voice or a prissy one either." It was surprising how alike men and women were with only glimpses to go on.

"Do you have anything else?" Paige asked. "I need to know where to start looking."

"I have the address where the buy was going to take place around ten-thirty in the morning." I rattled off the address that seemed seared into my brain. "Unfortunately, they've met before, and I don't know how they recognized each other the first time."

"Well, I know that address," Paige said. "It's the Central Library."

"Do they have surveillance?"

"Some, but without a way to recognize the perps, we may only see them walking in or out with dozens of other people. What else do you have?"

"The boy's name is Kylan. Blond hair, brown eyes. He's about nine or ten." I paused before adding, "Or eight or eleven. I can't say for sure. His mother and her husband are both in college. She has a job, but I don't know what it is. It's not much to go on, but it's all I have besides the imprint. The pencil might have prints on it, but they're probably not in any database."

"Save it for me. Meanwhile, I'll do what I can," Paige said. "We may be able to track the boy through the schools, even though it's summer. He's definitely in elementary school?"

That I could tell her. "Yes."

"It'll take time. I'll let Shannon know if I see him before you do. But call me if the kid comes back."

"Okay. Thanks." I hung up and turned to meet my sister's eyes, gripping the countertop with my bare hands.

"It's not your fault," Tawnia said.

But it was. I should have read the pencil before he left.

I should have touched his notebook, backpack, and whatever else he'd had with him. At the very least, if I'd noticed and read the pencil sooner, I could have stopped him and his mother before they left the Herb Shoppe. I could have saved them from walking into danger.

Of course, they might not be the targets. Who could possibly want to hurt the child and his mother? But I knew the answer to that only too well. Bad and crazy people hurt others for profit, for revenge, or for no reason at all. Maybe Kylan's mother's paleness wasn't because of going to school full time and working too hard, but because someone had been poisoning her. If so, I'd utterly failed them both.

Tawnia hugged me then, and Destiny's chubby fist patted my face. The actions calmed me.

"Find me a pen in that purse of yours," I told Tawnia. "I'll write down the ingredients. But if you want the food to taste great, get the right stuff."

Tawnia removed diapers, wipes, extra clothes, and a sketchbook before she found not a pen, but another pencil. That didn't surprise me because she always sketched her drawings first before adding color.

I jotted down the ingredients for the brined pork tenderloin. As I wrote, I said casually, "You could try to draw the boy. Or the missing biker."

"You know that's not the way it works," she said. "It just comes—usually when I'm working on something else, and only when there's strong emotion involved. From what you're saying, the boy doesn't know he's in danger, and your biker might be happy she's left."

I sighed. I knew that, but sometimes, for both of us, it was frustrating to have a gift and only see glimpses. Maybe if Tawnia weren't so intent on pushing hers away, she might be able to control it better. Then again, if her gift were stronger, she'd probably end up in a crazy bin like our paternal grandmother.

"Well, let me know for the next few days if anything strange pops up in your sketches, okay?"

My sister gave me a sad smile. "I think I'm too worried about my parents for anything important to come through, but I do have a project I should be working on, and I'll try. Meanwhile, I can make a few calls and post online to see if anyone knows a child named Kylan. It's a long shot, but you never know. There are also a few teachers I can email."

It was all I could ask. Short of dragging her to come to Manny's with me, which I absolutely would not do. Not after what happened during the theater case when she and Destiny had almost been killed.

I grabbed my personal helmet from under the counter, and Tawnia walked me outside. She waited until I locked the outer door to my shop before giving me another hug.

"Be safe," she said.

I kissed Destiny's soft cheek. It was crazy how much I loved that little kid. After her mom, she also loved me best, maybe even before her dad. Perhaps that was because her mother and I were so alike in looks and mannerisms, if not in much else, but it also could be the hours we spent together at my shop every time her mother had an important meeting.

"If you find out anything about the boy, text me," I said, "I'll have my phone on."

"And the location too, right?"

"Yes." I'd promised her to leave it on whenever I worked a case, which went against all my hippy, no-government-interference upbringing.

Jake's bike was waiting for me along the road. Parking was sometimes terrible in the Hawthorne District, where our shops were located, but Jake arrived so early that his bike was always in the same spot—in a corner stall in a small public parking lot right down the street. I fastened my helmet, saying goodbye to my perfectly spiked hair, and rode off. Without someone to follow to my destination, my directional impairedness soon got the best of me, and I had to stop and give Google a chance, fastening the phone to a holder on the bike Jake had installed for just this purpose. Following the phone was almost worse than figuring it out myself, but after only two wrong turns, I pulled up at Manny Barnes's house with ten minutes to spare.

Manny opened the door, greeting me with a sad smile. "Someone from the police department called. They're gonna send a detective over. Since they didn't show much interest when I went this morning, I guess I have you to thank for that."

I sent a silent thank-you to Shannon, who had likely set a fire under the missing persons detectives. "Consulting with the police does have some perks," I said. "Now, why don't we go through that album again?"

We sat at the kitchen table, flipping through pictures of Sariah and Manny together or with only one of them posing with their respective mothers. There were no pictures of both families together, not even at their wedding, which it appeared only friends had attended. In all the pictures where they were together, from recent or previous years, Sariah and Manny were smiling and hugging or holding hands. Somehow, despite Sariah's taller height, sleek jet-black hair, and numerous freckles that contrasted with Manny's much broader girth, beard, and tattoos, the couple seemed to belong together.

I could identify many of the people in the images from

imprints on the pages, but a few of the friends' names weren't in the imprints, and I had to ask as I matched them to names on the list Manny had given me earlier. I paid special attention to see if any anger was imprinted on pages of the photo album, and I found none except on the pages with Sariah's sturdy, unsmiling mother-in-law, Lucy Barnes Newman.

Mrs. Newman was a diminutive older woman with a large chest, perfectly coifed brown hair, massive eyelashes, and a prim expression. She resembled her tough-looking son more than she'd probably want to know. The anger Sariah had left on the pages was mixed with sadness about the relationship and liberal glimpses of her continuing love for Manny.

In stark contrast, the imprints connected to the pages of Maren Killigan, Sariah's mother, weren't angry or resentful but vague and resigned, so whatever Sariah felt for her mother had been tempered through the years. Mrs. Killigan resembled her daughter in height and slender build, though her hair was a yellow blond that was probably a realistic dye job to cover encroaching gray. Her smile seemed easy enough, but happiness didn't reach her eyes.

Since I was pretending to be a cousin from Sariah's side of the family, I was glad to find a photograph of a trip Sariah and her mother had apparently made to Las Vegas three years ago to visit her aunt, Maren's sister, Sadie Frey. Sariah's two cousins, a man and a woman in their mid-thirties, were also in the picture, which had been taken around a table in what I assumed was the aunt's house. I studied the picture, fixing details of the family in my mind. The more I learned about them, the more likely I'd be able to pull off my pretense with Manny and Sariah's friends.

"Is Sariah's aunt married?" I asked Manny.

"Yeah." He shrugged. "But I don't remember her uncle's name. I've only met him once, and the rest of the family maybe two or three times. Like I said, Sariah's mom doesn't like me, so we don't spend time with her family. Sariah's cousins, Lizzie and Angus, seemed nice, but we never had enough in common to pursue a relationship." He paused before adding, "None of our friends ever met them, and if their names ever came up, I doubt they'll remember Lizzie's name or think it strange if Lizzie changed it. A lot of people in our group go by nicknames."

That was something I was used to, having grown up with parents who had always been flower children at heart. "Good," I said. "It'll be easier to use my own name. Now, are there any pictures in here of your ex-wife?" She was probably someone Sariah might have discussed with her cousin, had they been close, and that meant I should know at least a little more of how Sariah felt about her. So far, I hadn't seen a picture of the woman. Of course, I wouldn't want photos of my husband's ex-wife in my album, so maybe there weren't any here, even if they had become friends. "Is she even here?"

"Of course." Manny flipped through to the back pages before coming to rest on a photograph of Sariah and a brown-haired woman standing next to a large Harley, their arms linking and their cheeks touching. Behind them, on the other side of the bike, a man leaned forward, a hand on each of their shoulders, his face on the other side of the woman standing with Sariah. I immediately recognized the woman from the imprint on Sariah's keys.

"That's Brynn," Manny said. "And the man's her husband, Travis. Travis Shepherd. They have two kids—both little boys. They're four and seven now. I think."

I peered closely at the photo, surprised that only a vague, contented imprint marked the page. From the happy smiles, it seemed clear Sariah liked Brynn—and that the feeling was mutual. The two were as different as Sariah and her husband. Brynn was shorter and had at least thirty pounds on Sariah, and she had curves in all the right places. Her skin was smooth and without freckles, so if she spent much time in the sun, that wasn't apparent in this picture. Her long, gently curling, brown hair reached halfway down her arm, and there was so much of it, even I felt a little envious, and I never gave much thought to my hair. Brynn looked a little older than Sariah's thirty-one, and her laugh lines gave character to her otherwise smooth face. She seemed like someone I would like to know.

The only thing similar about the women were the leather biker jackets, jeans, and the large, thin hoop earrings they both wore, visible only on the sides opposite from where their cheeks pressed together.

Brynn's husband, Travis, had short, dark brown hair, a cropped beard, and a tattoo of some kind of bird on his muscular forearm. He was taller than Sariah, but not by much. Like the women, his smile also seemed real. Was there something sinister behind those happy smiles? If so, the contented imprints gave no hint of them.

I shut the book. "Okay. I think I'm ready."

Manny nodded. "Thank you. I know we're no closer to finding her, but somehow it feels like we are."

"Can I do anything to help you get ready?" I checked the time on my phone. "It's five now."

He gave me a strained smile. "It's called biker standard time. They'll be here soon. I usually put out a couple cases of beer, but I didn't get anything today."

"That's probably for the best since they'll be passing out flyers." I didn't know how many would show up, but a bunch of drunk bikers wouldn't help Manny or Sariah.

"You look good, by the way," Manny added, flushing slightly. "I mean, like you'll fit in. I-I'm not hitting on you."

I smiled. "I knew what you meant. I hope it works."

The doorbell rang then, and Manny hurried out of the kitchen. I trailed along, wondering if it would be one of his friends or the police. When Manny opened the door, his ex-wife, Brynn, stood on the porch, carrying a huge, plastic-covered platter of rolled sandwich meats and cheese. A heavy-looking cloth bag dangled from one black-jacketed arm. Her wonderful hair curled gently over her shoulders and down her back, just like it had in the picture, and while her face was expertly made up, the hoop earrings were nowhere to be seen. Her husband, his dark hair bushier and longer than in the picture, his beard still as trim, trailed behind with four plastic grocery sacks hanging from his hands.

"Still no word?" Brynn asked, her eyes staring into Manny's almost pleadingly.

He shook his head. "No." The word sounded strangled.

Brynn shifted the platter to the arm with the bag and put her other arm around his neck, pulling him in to rest her forehead against his cheek. "I'm so sorry," she said. "We'll find her." Without waiting for a response, she let him go and pushed past him, stopping short when she saw me.

"This is Sariah's cousin from Vegas," Manny said. "She came to help."

"I'm Autumn," I said. "And you're Brynn Shepard. I recognize you from Sariah's pictures."

"Hi," Brynn responded, looking me over. "Sariah's mentioned

your family a few times, and I'm glad to finally meet you. I didn't know you were a biker."

I shrugged. "Sariah's been a big influence." I leaned in closer and said in a confiding tone, "But with how things are between Manny and my aunt, well, I keep a low profile."

Brynn smiled a little tearfully. "That I can understand. Your aunt is . . . well, never mind. I don't want to send out those kinds of vibes to the universe when we're trying to find Sariah. I can't believe this is even happening."

"Me either. Here, let me help you." I reached for the platter, which she relinquished.

"We need the table set up," Brynn said to Manny. "We brought an extra if we need it, but yours is newer. I want it in the front, though, not the back. We don't want people to get comfortable and linger. We want them working. We'll go through the garage and find it, if you don't mind." Without waiting for agreement, she continued into the house.

Her husband, pausing only to murmur something to Manny that I couldn't hear, followed close behind us as we went into the kitchen and through the garage, where she opened the automatic door. She had their gang's Road Roller patch sewn into the left sleeve of her leather jacket, but Travis's was etched directly onto the back of his jacket and covered the entire expanse. I recognized it as the same logo Manny had on his vest.

Travis deposited his sacks on a workbench and helped Manny set out a folding table in the driveway close to the street. Once it was up, looking solitary and forlorn, Brynn placed her cloth bag on one half and began helping her husband unpack his sacks of paper goods and rolls on the other.

"I think we'll need the other table," Brynn told her husband,

"We'll use this nicer one for refreshments and ours for the flyers."

Travis nodded and headed for a battered green truck parked in front of the house behind a motorcycle I assumed also belonged to them, as neither vehicle had been there when I arrived.

Other bikers began pulling up at the house, and for a time, I heard nothing but the roar of engines as riders climbed off motorcycles and came forward with plastic food sacks and somber expressions. Each of the bikers, most of them familiar from the photographs, hugged Manny or pounded him on the back. One wide, square-faced man, who I only vaguely recognized, hugged Manny longer than the rest, talking to him with their heads close together. He was a startlingly handsome man despite the pockmarked cheeks and beer belly that hung six inches over his tight pants. His brown hair was a shade or two darker than Manny's dishwater blond, and he wore an open black jacket with the Road Roller logo on the back.

"Who's that guy with Manny?" I asked Brynn, who was directing the others to set out folding chairs that were leaning against a wall of the garage.

She glanced at Manny, and then back at me, with a puzzled line between her eyes. "That's Drum—or Owen Drummond, rather. I'm surprised you don't know him. He's Manny's best friend."

Five minutes into it, and I'd already messed up. I remembered the name from Manny's list, though. "Oh, the guy who works at the RV place." Like Manny, Drum had started out as a mechanic, but now he managed a dealership that both sold and repaired RVs.

"That's right."

"Because of my aunt's feelings about Manny," I added, "I haven't met many of his friends. I may have seen pictures of Drum on Sariah's phone, but there aren't nearly as many as there are of you." I hesitated before adding, "Which I still think is kind of weird since you used to be married to Manny."

Brynn's smile was back. "Yeah, it is weird, but Sariah knows Manny and I are just friends and that she has nothing to fear from me." She bent to pull out a huge stack of flyers from the cloth bag she'd laid on the second table. "I have more in the truck."

"What's the plan for distributing them?"

"I thought we'd canvass all the streets around here in sections. I have a color-coded map to give everyone that shows each area. We'll knock on doors and talk to everyone we see. And we'll also plaster them to every pole or fence or storefront we can find."

"Good idea."

"Honey," Brynn called to her husband, who was talking to one of the bikers. "Can you get the other flyer bags?" He nodded and hurried to the truck.

Usually cloth didn't hold good imprints, but this bag wasn't something Brynn would be washing regularly, and if she was as close to Sariah as she indicated, she should have felt something strong while first ordering and then carrying the flyers. So while Brynn spread out her maps, I touched the canvas bag that had held the flyers.

Poor Manny, I/Brynn thought, holding the bag tightly as the clerk rang up my order. He was going out of his mind. It wasn't fair, not when he was such a good guy. He'd gone through enough in his life with that mother of his. The old bat was probably gloating now. Manny deserved more. A lot more.

That told me Manny's ex-wife hadn't gotten along with his mother any better than Sariah had, which probably meant there was some reason for both women's feelings.

Another imprint came seconds later. *I won't be treated this way. If Travis had told me his love was conditional, I never would have married him. He promised to stand by me and love me no matter what happened. Even if it was this big. I feel so dead in this relationship. Manny would never have treated me this way.*

There was nothing more, and I pulled back my hand, studying Brynn more closely. Obviously, she was having some kind of marital difficulty, and she regretted the past, or at least she was comparing her current husband unfavorably with her first one. Probably not all that unusual, given that the two were still apparently good friends.

But what did the "this big" refer to? Was it something to do with Sariah, or was Brynn dealing with something else entirely?

Brynn was staring at me a little oddly, and I wondered if she'd asked a question I'd missed. "Will Manny's family be joining us tonight?" I asked.

She snorted. "No way. Manny's mother is probably ecstatic. I bet she hasn't celebrated this hard since Manny and I divorced."

"Right, Manny's mom didn't like you either. I think I remember hearing that from Sariah."

Brynn laughed, placing her hands on her curvy hips. "Are you kidding? Lucy *hated* me. I was never good enough for Manny. She thought I was a floozy out to seduce first Manny's dad, and then that lecher she began dating after Manny's dad died."

"He died of lung cancer," I remembered aloud. "Poor guy."

Brynn snorted. "Poor guy is right. But not for the cancer. That was God's way of setting that man free. He was trapped in that witch's clutches for forty years as it was. Lucy was right about one thing—I loved Manny's father. My own old man was a drunk who abandoned me, but Manny's father was the best dad either of us could have. He took us camping and fishing, played baseball and soccer with us, and helped us with homework. He didn't have much education, but he read a lot. He taught us about the stars and how volcanos worked and how to rebuild an engine. Manny worshipped him, and so did I. I'm sure he would have left Lucy, if not for Manny, but by the time Manny grew up, he was diagnosed, and I think he needed all his strength to fight the cancer. I'm telling you, he's the reason I married Manny in the first place. I wanted to be a part of their family." Her face twisted in a sneer that seemed to cover an urge to weep. "That was before I knew how Manny's mom would poison everything. There was no winning her over, no matter what I did. It was heartbreaking that Manny's dad had to depend on Lucy near the end when she treated him so coldly. Once he was gone, I just couldn't find enough reasons to stay. I've said it before, and I'll say it again: the best thing God ever did for Manny's dad was to take him from that witch."

Okay then, I thought. "Sariah didn't tell me all that."

"She never knew Manny's dad. Sariah married Manny for the right reasons—because she loved him." Brynn gave me a sad smile. "I loved Manny more like a brother."

Or so she said. While she seemed sincere enough, maybe there was something she was hiding behind all her helpfulness. Were her continuing feelings for Manny what was coming between her and Travis?

"I'm not saying there wasn't romance," Brynn added, flicking a brief gaze in Manny's direction. "And it might have developed into something more eventually, but we never had the chance, not with Lucy's fireworks every other day. Maybe if we'd had more between us to begin with, Lucy wouldn't have mattered so much. But after we met other people, we understood why it didn't work. The sparks were there but not the fire, if you get my drift." She smiled, but her eyes slid past me to where her husband was coming up the drive with two more cloth bags of flyers. As he set them on the table and nodded at her, a stillness came over Brynn's expressive face, as if she was fighting not to show anything at all.

"This is all so crazy," I said to them. "I really appreciate everything you both are doing. Manny does too." I touched the cloth bags Travis had set down. No imprints on those except a vague sadness.

"We'll find her," Brynn said, blinking back tears. "We have to."

"The sooner, the better," I agreed.

Travis's gaze met Brynn's and bounced away quickly. Something was definitely off between these two. If it was related to Sariah's disappearance, it didn't make sense that they'd be spearheading this search. Unless it was to avoid suspicion.

Whatever they were hiding, I would find out. I just needed the right object to touch.

Chapter 5

More and more bikers were arriving, conversing in hushed voices and darting glances at Manny, who was still talking to his friend Drum. A small woman with short black hair and tight jeans now clung to Drum's arm. Most of the bikers, men and women alike, wore jeans and leather jackets, most of which had the words Road Rollers stamped across the back, though there were at least a few plain T-shirts and leather pants in the mix. A few bikers looked at me curiously, but my presence seemed to be accepted as word of my identity spread through the growing crowd.

I knew Brynn would start handing out assignments soon, so I'd better finish my questions. "You didn't notice anything different about Sariah this week, did you?" I asked her. "Did she mention being afraid of anyone?"

Brynn shook her head. "I've been wracking my brain all day about what could have happened, but I didn't notice anything out of the ordinary. Not recently." The way she said it seemed to imply that something had happened, but long enough ago that she didn't connect it to Sariah's disappearance.

"Did something happen that wasn't recent?" I pressed.

Brynn sighed. "There was something a week ago. At her new school—Ainsworth Elementary. But speaking of that, now that I think about it, her changing jobs halfway through the year was strange, especially the change from being the main receptionist to only an assistant. Ainsworth might be a higher ranked school, but it's a good twenty minutes further away. That didn't seem like Sariah. Plus, the principal is a big jerk, and she knew that going in. Manny and I both thought it didn't make sense to leave her position at Richmond Elementary, but Sariah was happy about it, and it's her life, right?"

"How many months ago was this?" I asked. "That she changed jobs, I mean."

"About six."

That would coincide with the excitement on the mailbox about finally seeing the unnamed "her." Maybe Sariah had been thinking about the principal. "The principal is a woman?" I asked.

"No. A male. And a real chauvinist."

So maybe the imprint wasn't connected unless Sariah had been hired by a female administrator further up the line and not the principal? Or maybe "her" was a child at the school. It bore looking into.

"So what happened last week?" I pressed.

"She had a run-in with the principal at her new school. Sariah was helping a student who needs catching up this summer, and he told her she was too involved."

That meant there was a child, but had Sariah known her before or only after switching jobs? "He told her to stay away?"

"Right. But she wasn't going to listen. This girl's mother died of cancer near the beginning of the year, and right after Sariah started there in January, she began helping her with homework and making sure she had lunches and rides home. The girl lives with her grandmother and her father, apparently."

"Would you say it was unusual for her to get involved?"

"Not at all. Sariah is a favorite with all the kids. They love her, and she loves them right back. But this child needed more than she's getting at home, and Sariah recognized that right from the beginning. She's trying to help her catch up to her grade this summer, so she isn't held back." Brynn rolled her eyes. "The gall of the principal, telling her to stay away from the poor child. As if a little more love would hurt her any more than her mother's death."

"So did the complaint come from her family or just the principal?"

Brynn snorted. "I don't know, but I suspect the principal probably wanted to make sure nothing would happen. There was no official complaint or reprimand, but Sariah was upset. I believe she went to see the grandmother."

It seemed like a visit to the school was in order. Even during the summer someone must be at the school part-time. But it was the weekend, and that meant any leads there would be cold by Monday. I'd have to figure something else out.

"There was nothing else unusual?" I asked. "You two must be pretty close. She told me how you went jacket shopping together." Which was true, in a roundabout way. "Did she ever mention owing a large amount of money to anyone?"

I expected Brynn to shake her head, but instead she scrunched her nose and nodded. "Well, there was this guy awhile back. In fact, now that I think about it, it was the day we went shopping for the jackets."

"Guy?" I asked.

"Right, this was back in September, just after my boys started school." Brynn thought a moment.

"So about nine months ago."

"Yeah, I guess. Anyway, we were at the Lloyd Center at this leather shop I know, and I came out of the dressing room to find her gone. When I looked for her, I found her outside of the shop talking to some guy. She took money from her wallet and gave it to him, and he gave her a paper in exchange."

"You're sure it was cash?"

"I was close enough to see the bills. I have no idea how much she gave him, though."

"What did the man look like?"

"Big guy. Overweight with glasses and a short beard like my husband's. Clothes that were popular a decade ago. You know, like the smart tech guys in the movies who don't have time to keep up on style."

"Brown hair?"

She nodded.

"How big?"

Brynn pointed to Drum, Manny's best friend. "Like that, only taller. And his hair was about the same brown. Hard to tell what his face looked like with the facial hair and glasses, though."

"What happened next? After you saw her with the guy?"

"I went back inside the shop, and she came back a bit later. I never asked her about it, and she never said anything. But when she bought her jacket, she paid for the whole thing with a card, which I thought was weird, because she'd talked about charging only a little to the card and paying the rest with her mad money."

"Mad money?"

Brynn smiled. "Whenever we went to the store, Sariah would get a little bit of cash back to add to a rainy-day fund. Sometimes she'd use it to buy presents for Manny that she didn't want him getting wind of. Or to buy little luxuries that weren't in the normal budget. I started doing it too. Basically, mad money is cash you don't have to feel guilty about using for something you really want because it's already counted as spent. I thought she'd use it to get a nicer jacket, but she put all the charges on her card."

"How much?"

"Over two hundred." Brynn's chin went up. "You probably know that's a lot for her, but I don't think it's a lot at all for something you'll use for a lifetime. She did end up exchanging it, though, so maybe she used some mad money the second time. I'm pretty sure both jackets cost about the same."

"You think Sariah gave the man her mad money instead of using it on the first jacket?"

She nodded. "I can't prove it, and when I commented on her not using the mad, she just laughed it off."

"Besides that, did she act strange?"

"No. Just excited." Brynn's tense expression relaxed into a smile. "We both had a good day. That's when we first became better friends. Before then, it was more forced."

The memory of the shopping excursion seemed to be a good one for her, though the glimpse from Sariah told me it had been something altogether different for her. One thing was certain—I needed to find that man.

"Well," Brynn said, straightening a stack of flyers that didn't need straightening. "Let's get this show on the road. I think enough people are here to start assigning areas and handing out flyers."

At least fifty people had gathered, and more were still coming. The newest arrivals, however, didn't wear the Road Roller logo on their jackets, which indicated they were from the other group Manny had mentioned.

"About that," I said. "I'd like to take the area around the house, if you don't mind. I can do it with Manny. I think the neighbors will respond better to family members." It was also more likely that a neighbor might have noticed something important. Someone knew what happened to Sariah; I just had to find that person.

"That's a good idea," Brynn said.

Standing up on a chair, she shouted for everyone's attention. "Thank you all for coming. We'll be going out in sets of two," she said. "When you finish with your flyers and the area, please come back for another assignment. If you hear anything at all that might be useful, call me immediately or come back here. Please help yourself at any time to the refreshments. And thanks to those who brought food to share. This is going to be a long night, but I believe that together we can help find Sariah."

As Brynn handed out assignments, I introduced myself around, especially to the Road Rollers, shaking hands whenever I could and testing imprints. I wouldn't be able to clear all these people today, but seeing me here would pave the way for later visits if they became necessary. As the bikers were sent out, two by two, Brynn recorded their names and their assigned areas.

Brynn smiled at me when I returned to the table after the crowd had left. She handed me a small stack of flyers and pushed her thick hair back. Sweat sheened her forehead. "Manny says he needs to wait for the police, but Drum volunteered to go with you."

From Brynn's side, Drum smiled at me, his white, even teeth matching his good-looking face. No smoke or coffee stains there. "Nice to finally meet Sariah's cousin," he said, extending a bare, ringless hand.

"Autumn," I said, shaking his hand. His grip was limp, and his hand surprisingly small. I wondered what had happened to the tiny woman he'd been with before, but then I spotted her, climbing onto a bike behind another woman, her eyes staring at me with more than a little ill will. Someone was not happy at all about letting her man run off with me.

Holding a stack of flyers, Drum made his way to an oversized Harley that made Jake's bike look woman-sized, which it wasn't. "Guess we won't need our bikes. I'm going to leave my jacket here." He shrugged out of it. "At least while we're walking this street."

Feeling warm myself, I unzipped my own jacket to let in any stray breezes. "Hey, you have a nice ride." I hoped I didn't sound too green. For all I knew, words like those were only used on television. I tried to touch one of the handles of his bike, but he shoved his flyers at me.

"Thanks." He opened a locked compartment on the bike and put in his jacket and a pair of gloves that were dangling from his back pocket. Taking back his flyers, his stare slid down my body approvingly. "And may I say, that's a really nice outfit you have there."

"They're vintage."

He laughed. "It figures. They don't make them like they used to, that's for sure. Sariah bought a jacket last year that was so cheaply made, I couldn't believe they could even sell such garbage."

"It wasn't real leather?"

"No, it was definitely fake. Cost less than fifty bucks is my guess."

That was odd. Because both Manny and Brynn seemed to think the cost of the second jacket was equal to the one she'd exchanged. I had seen the jacket earlier, but I'd been paying attention to imprints, not labels or quality at the time. Nothing had jumped out at me, which meant Sariah hadn't worn it enough or maybe hadn't cared about it much.

"There were two jackets," I said to Drum. "You sure that wasn't the first she bought?"

"I don't know about any first jacket. I'm talking about the new one she's been wearing around. I never saw any other besides her really old one that she gave away. Because it was too small, I think."

If Sariah had returned an expensive jacket for a less expensive one, had she kept the difference? The only reason for that would be to raise money she didn't want Manny to know about. Had she needed more cash for the mystery man?

"If her bike is missing, why do you suppose her jacket is still in the house?" I asked Drum.

"I don't know. Maybe she didn't feel like wearing it. Maybe she finally realized it was junk." He started in the direction of the house, and I paused to run my fingers across his handlebars. Nothing notable, except a brief impression of anger, followed by a sensation of thrill. I'd expected more emotion from him regarding his bike, but maybe he always wore the riding gloves.

"You know she didn't take her keys, right?" I said, hurrying after him.

He shrugged. "She probably had another set. I keep a few for my truck and my bike. There's a place up by the mall that does them fairly cheap. Come to think of it, I remember telling her about the place a few months ago. She probably had them made then."

"You think she left on her own?"

He looked like he wanted to say something, but we were already nearing the neighbor's porch. Having him around would make it more difficult to manage the conversations if I felt I needed to test objects for imprints, but that couldn't be helped. I needed to visit all the neighbors myself, or I would have suggested splitting up to get rid of him.

We went up the three stairs to the porch, and I'd raised a hand to knock when the door opened to reveal an older lady. Her hunched back and rounded chest were covered in a black shirt splotched with hand-sized purple flowers, and her comparatively tiny legs were clad in black leggings. Her nose was elongated and her eyes bulged in that way that affected some older people.

"May I help you?" she asked, her lips forming a tentative smile.

"Hi," I said, not waiting for Drum to speak. "I'm Sariah's cousin, and we're helping Manny search for her."

The woman's smile faltered as she came outside and let the door shut behind her. "I already told him I didn't see or hear anything," she said, leaning forward and twisting her head to peer over at Manny's, where he and Brynn were alone now by the table. The old woman's steel-gray hair fell forward with the motion, waving halfway down her chest. "I was watching TV all evening. I had the windows open, though, so if there'd been a loud noise, I might have heard it."

"You didn't hear her bike?" I shifted my position, pretending to lose my balance so I could check the door for imprints.

"Well, I hear motorbikes over there all the time," she said. "So I'm not sure I would have noticed that. And my show might have been a turned up a bit high. I don't hear as well as I used to." She cast another glance toward Manny's house. "It's a shame, really. They're a nice couple. She's always bringing me food, and he fixes my fence or my sink when I have a leak. You don't think anything bad's happened to her, do you?"

"She's probably just gone away for a few days," Drum said.

I frowned. Where was he coming up with that idea? I handed the woman a flyer and absently reached out to the porch railing. An imprint assailed me—of someone, presumably this woman, watching with tears dripping onto a gnarled hand that clung to the wood as the ambulance took away a sheet-covered Gurney.

Five years ago, I thought, feeling sorrow for the woman at her loss. I suspected it had been her husband, and bringing it up now wouldn't give her comfort.

Drum was already down the stairs, but I lingered. "You didn't see anyone strange here in the past few weeks, did you? Or any strange vehicles?"

"No. Nothing like that." She pointed across the street. "But you should ask Fran and Joseph over there. They always see everything that's going on, even if you don't want them to—if you get my drift."

I laughed. "I do. What about money issues? Did Sariah ever mention needing money?"

"No. They both work, you know."

"Okay. Well, thank you." I was all the way down the steps when the woman spoke again.

"Sariah and I did have a garage sale together last August. She said she was trying to raise money for a new jacket. She rigged a wire between my trees to hang clothes, and even baked a bunch of cookies to sell."

August would have put the garage sale before the thousand-dollar payment to the mystery man. "How did it go?"

"Like gangbusters. Her husband put out all kinds of signs, and we listed it on Facebook and online newspapers. We sold most of the clothes and furniture and tons of other stuff. We both made about five hundred bucks."

Along with Sariah's mad money and the possible difference between the two jackets, that might explain the thousand dollars Manny hadn't noticed going missing.

"Sounds like a lot of fun," I said.

"Sariah's a good lady," the old woman said. "And friend. I'm praying that you find her."

"Thank you. We all are."

The muscles in Drum's face worked as I joined him on the sidewalk. I waited until we were out of earshot of the woman before asking, "Is something wrong?"

"I'm not sure you should be asking about money."

"Why not? Brynn said she saw Sariah giving a man money. That may be important."

Drum stopped walking and faced me. "She did?"

"Yes. What about you? Did you ever see a man hanging around?"

"Of course not." He thought a moment, his brow wrinkling. "Wait, was he a tall man with a beard and glasses, big stomach?"

"You saw him too?"

He nodded. "Last October."

"Where?"

"Here at the house. Manny has the biggest backyard of

us—well, besides Brynn's cabin in Scappoose, which is farther away—so we bring our chairs and have a bonfire for Halloween in his firepit. He invites the neighbors, so no one complains about the noise. It's an annual gathering. We were all here."

"The man you saw is a biker?"

"No." His upper lip curled. "Of course not. He didn't belong, and he didn't come into the house. The only reason I saw him was because I left my case of beer on my bike, and I had to come out and grab it. Sariah was talking to him on the sidewalk."

"Did she give him money?"

"Not that I saw. But he gave her an envelope. They talked awhile, and then he kind of folded himself into a little blue car and drove away."

"Did you ask her about it?"

"Yeah. She said he was asking for directions. I knew she was lying, but what could I do?"

I paused at the next neighbor's walkway. "You never saw him again?"

"No." His face darkened. "But that doesn't mean she didn't meet him elsewhere. After he left, I saw her hold that envelope to her breast like it was important. Maybe a love letter. She might have been having an affair."

I doubted that. More likely, Sariah had hired the man for some reason, and the resulting information had been in the envelope, but I didn't want to say as much to Drum. Like everyone else, he was still a suspect.

"Anyway," Drum continued, "the last thing Manny needs is all his neighbors thinking they were in financial trouble. So maybe tone it down on the money angle."

"Manny doesn't care about that now. All he wants is Sariah back."

"Maybe he won't always feel that way. I mean, if she left purposefully."

I stared at him. "Are you saying that's what she did? Do you know something you haven't told Manny?"

"No, of course not. It's just . . ." He hesitated. "Look, Manny's been my best friend since high school, but Sariah is out of his league."

"What do you mean?"

"Well, Sariah would have been a teacher if she'd finished her credentials. She loves books and learning. Manny's grammar is terrible, and he can barely read. His hands are always stained with grease from the shop, and he only wears jeans. Sariah doesn't need to dress up to turn heads, but when she does, everyone notices her. She's always had that something special, you know? Manny lucked out the day they met." Clear admiration shone in Drum's blue eyes.

"You sound like you wish you'd have met her first."

"Oh, no," he backtracked quickly. "We're friends, that's all. I'm just saying Sariah is a lady, and she put up with a lot from Manny. He doesn't know how to treat a woman like her the way she deserves to be treated, so I understand if she left. But my loyalty is always with Manny. I have to protect him."

His observations about Manny's treatment of Sariah went against the imprints I'd read at the house, but I didn't immediately discount the information. Imprints were screened through the creator's perception, so it was possible Manny didn't treat Sariah well, but she didn't realize it. But wouldn't at least some imprints show that abuse? I believed so. Which meant that maybe there was another way of looking at this altogether. Maybe Drum was completely wrong. Maybe, best friend or not, he had a thing for Manny's wife. In my book, that put him firmly on my list of primary suspects.

"Sariah never said anything to me about that," I felt compelled to say. "She loves Manny, and she's happy with him."

Drum bristled. "Then what's she doing sneaking around with that guy?"

"Unless you saw something more than what you're telling me, it's probably not what you think. I trust Sariah, and you should too."

Because I did trust Sariah. She'd had a reason for paying that man, for meeting with him. I didn't think it had anything to do with Manny.

Remembering Brynn's something big and her issues with her husband, I asked, "Are you thinking Manny is cheating on Sariah? Is that what you mean when you say he's not treating her right?"

"No," Drum said shortly. "Manny wouldn't do that." He thrust his hands into his pockets and started up to the next house, leaving me to hurry after him.

The other visits on that side of the street and back to Manny's were almost identical to the first visit, minus the garage sale. Manny and Sariah seemed to be friends with all their neighbors, and several mentioned Manny's Halloween bonfire and an annual neighborhood park barbeque that Sariah spearheaded every summer in July. By the time we crossed the street and were nearly back at Manny's, I despaired of finding anything, but I was interested in interviewing Fran and Joseph, the nosy couple the first neighbor had mentioned. If anyone had seen something, they might have.

As we walked to their house, a police car and an unmarked vehicle similar to Shannon's police Mustang arrived. A tall, very dark black man in plainclothes climbed out of the Mustang and started up the driveway to Manny's place. I could only see one officer in the police car as well, and that seemed like too few officers when I knew for sure Sariah hadn't left voluntarily.

Not a good sign. That meant I needed to question the rest of the neighbors quickly, so I could get back to help Manny convince the police that Sariah really needed help.

Chapter 6

Both Fran and Joseph were home. She was a thin woman with short brown hair, while he was a decidedly rounded, balding man.

"Did you notice anything strange last night?" I asked after introducing myself and Drum. "Any cars or delivery people that didn't belong?"

"No," Fran said, but something in her tone was off.

"Are you sure?" I asked. "Because any little thing could be important."

"There's always a lot of movement over there." Fran glanced across the street at Manny's. "What with all the motorcycles coming and going." Her stare traveled pointedly down my leather-clad body. The vintage outfit might have won me points with the bikers, but not with this nosy neighbor. "Anyway, I didn't see Sariah yesterday," Fran said with a frown. "Only her husband when he knocked on our door late last night looking for her. He looked terrible, by the way. Frantic. I really felt for him."

Her husband, Joseph, nodded emphatically. "Terrible."

"You didn't see or hear anything, either?" I asked Joseph.

"No," he confirmed. "Our granddaughter turned two

yesterday. We were at our daughter's for the party from about four to six, but besides that, we were home."

"Thank you for your time," Drum said before I could ask about money.

But I wasn't leaving, not until I knew what was behind Fran's odd tone. "Do you mind giving me a drink of cold water?" I asked. "We've gone to all the houses on both sides of the street that way"—I threw an arm out to my right—"but we still have the rest to go." There were drinks on the refreshment table across the street, but Fran might not know if there was water.

"Sure, dear. Be glad to get you a glass with some ice." Fran looked at Drum. "Would you like one too?"

"No, thank you," he said, his voice impatient.

Fran disappeared inside the house, and we spent an awkward moment on the porch with Joseph as we waited. Joseph smiled and nodded, and I smiled and nodded, and then he started the whole process over again. Drum, his hands shoved in his pockets, didn't say anything, but he scowled at me. I was surprised he didn't continue to the next house without me. Maybe it was some biker code of ethics not to abandon your partner.

When Fran appeared in the doorway, I hurried to ask, "Are you absolutely sure you saw nothing unusual? Even on another day? Anything you tell us might help."

Fran's gaze went from me to Drum and then back again. "No. I'm sorry." She handed me the water.

The moist glass nearly slipped from my hand as an imprint took me. *Should I tell her I've seen this man before? Going over there when I know Manny isn't home. Something fishy is going on between them if you ask me.*

That was all, just a stream of imprinted thoughts and a glimpse of Fran's view of us as we stood on the porch. I gulped down the water and handed the glass back before it could repeat too many times.

But what did it mean? Maybe nothing. Drum was Manny's best friend, so his being there without the other bikers wasn't unusual. He didn't work with Manny and wouldn't know all the times his friend might have to stay late. Stopping here on his way home from work might be a habit. Still, given Drum's apparent attraction to Sariah, maybe the visits weren't only because of Manny.

Or maybe he knew far more than he was telling.

"Thanks for the drink," I said to Fran, taking a business card from my pocket. "Please let me know if you remember anything more."

I'd told the other neighbors to contact Manny's numbers on the flyer if they had additional information, but I wanted Fran to have my personal contact in case she felt she could talk to me without Drum present.

To my relief, she didn't read my card or the antiques shop's information aloud. That might ruin my cover with Drum, and I didn't want that to happen until I'd cleared him.

With Fran and Joseph still watching us from their porch, we talked to the other neighbors, going to the end of the street, before crossing to the other side, and canvassing on the way back to Manny's. No one had seen anything. They had either been at work, coming home from work, making dinner, or watching television. It had been warm enough that not even kids had been playing in the street.

Almost as if the time had been planned for the least atten-tion, I thought. That would have to mean someone close to the family. Brynn, Travis, and Drum all bore further looking into, as did the principal at Sariah's school, the brown-haired man with glasses, and maybe the family of the little girl Sariah had helped. Also suspicious was the absence here tonight of both Manny's mother and his mother-in-law.

It was discouraging that I'd learned so little from the neighbors, but that was the way investigations went. Knowledge sometimes came from the least expected person, which was why I had to keep going and talk to everyone. Most of the clues I had so far had come from Brynn and Drum and Sariah herself, but it wasn't yet a clear picture. Since it was only seven-thirty, once I checked in with Manny and the police officers inside the house, I'd go see Manny's mother.

After letting Brynn know I wouldn't be delivering more flyers, I waved at the still-watching Fran and Joseph and started inside the house. Drum remained behind, preparing to canvass another area with a newly arrived biker. I was glad to be rid of the man for the meantime, though he'd seemed nice enough, even engaging, when he wasn't talking about the way Sariah was being treated by Manny.

Inside the house, Manny was sitting at the kitchen table being grilled by the black detective I'd seen earlier. Sitting next to Manny, as if trying to offer support, was a uniformed police officer I knew well. He was Peirce Elvey, a short, red-haired man, who gave me a grin that wrinkled the many freckles on his nose. From the beginning of my consulting with the police bureau, he'd stood out from the others. Not only for his flaming red hair, but because of the way he'd diverted his colleagues' attention from the odd psychic girl in the worn jeans, who told them things they didn't want to hear. On his off days, I knew Peirce drove his two kids and wife around in a minivan, though I'd never met them. Working this late meant he was on the swing shift, or maybe filling in for the detective's regular partner. That might explain the two vehicles.

The detective was definitely in charge and had to be from missing persons. He hadn't sat with the others but towered over the table like a dark avenging angel.

"Hey, Autumn," Peirce greeted me. "Nice to see you. Do you know Detective Cole Howard from missing persons?"

"No, we've never met."

Howard barely looked up from a tablet in his hands to nod his close-cropped head in my direction before continuing his questioning. "Have you ever suspected your wife of having an affair?" he asked Manny.

"No, I already told you. We ain't having affairs. Neither of us," Manny said with a touch of despair. His long beard was bedraggled, and crumbs had settled into the greasy strands. "It's our seventh anniversary tomorrow, and we planned to go on a trip."

"And you never lost your temper with her?"

"What?" Manny stared. "Of course, I've lost my temper. Like everyone does. But I love my wife, and I didn't do anything to her. Why ain't you out looking for her instead of asking all these stupid questions?"

"We have an APB out on her bike," Peirce said. "And someone is checking local hospitals for motorcycle injuries."

"She ain't on her bike," Manny insisted. "Whoever took her also took the bike. Our keys are both here."

"You sure she didn't have another set?" Howard asked.

"I never seen one." Manny's gaze met mine in frustration, his eyes begging me for help. "They think I did something to her. Or that she left me."

Despite what Drum had said, I didn't believe Sariah was having an affair. "Can I talk to you for a moment?" I asked Detective Howard.

His brow rose in surprise, but he nodded. "Sure."

I led the way into the sitting room, which wasn't exactly private, but it was good enough. "You know who I am?" I asked.

He nodded. "And what you do." The statement didn't say whether or not he believed in what I did, just that he knew. I was used to that, but I'd proven myself enough in the past year that most officers were willing to suspend their disbelief. For those who couldn't, Shannon's reputation and high case closing rate kept their mouths shut.

"There isn't a single imprint in this house or on Manny that hints of any wrongdoing on his part or that Sariah was planning to leave."

"If you'll excuse me for saying," Howard added, "it's always the husband. Or almost always."

"Not this time."

Howard's jaw set. "You may be right. Quite frankly, with the bike being gone, the likelihood is that she left because she wanted to leave."

"No. There's more." Lowering my voice, I told him about the brown-haired guy with glasses, the thousand dollars, the issue with the principal, Brynn's secret, and Drum's attraction. "Drum and Brynn are both outside," I added. "If you hurry, you should be able to catch Drum before he leaves to pass out more flyers."

"You found out all that today?" Howard asked, his expression still unreadable.

I glanced behind me at the kitchen doorway. "I also learned that Sariah was afraid of someone who came here a week ago late Tuesday afternoon. This person owns a motorcycle, and whether you take my word for that or not is up to you. But you know as well as I do that the longer she's gone, the worse it'll be for her."

"That's if she's really missing."

So he was back to that. "Look," I said, "you need to check her phone records to find out if there was anything unusual and find out why she moved to another job at a school halfway through the year. It could be related."

"And what are you going to do?" The words were a direct challenge.

I didn't answer to him, but I responded anyway. "I'm going to see Manny's mother and give her my condolences. Though from all accounts, she'd rather see Sariah in a grave than married to her son. So there's another suspect for you. Her and her husband both."

"This is my case," he growled.

I met his gaze steadily. "It's also mine. And for the record, I was here first. But I'm working undercover as Sariah's cousin, so please don't talk about what I do."

His jaw worked, but when he spoke it was only to say, "Guess that explains your clothes." He pulled a card from his pocket, which I took as a good sign despite the terse words. "Let me know if you find anything." No doubt he was torn between closing his case quickly and making sure he didn't come out of it looking like an idiot.

I took the card and returned to the kitchen. Detective Howard didn't follow me, so maybe he was considering my advice. Manny jumped up from the kitchen table where he'd sat and gazed at me expectantly. His eyes were red from crying.

"I have a few leads," I said to his unasked question, "and I've told Detective Howard about them."

"He's talking about searching the crawlspace under the house," Manny said. "I barely knew there was a way to get under there. It's obvious he thinks I hurt her." He gagged on the words and added hoarsely, "I'd never do that."

"I know you wouldn't. Don't let his questions get you down. Everyone has to be cleared. When they don't find anything, they'll move on." I wanted to ask him if he knew about Drum's feelings for Sariah, but I wouldn't do that with Peirce Elvey here.

"I'm going to talk to your mother now," I added. "And then Sariah's mother, either tonight or in the morning. I'll be in touch. Please let me know if you hear anything." Though it was unlikely Sariah had been taken for ransom, it was always possible.

"My mother?" He sounded pained. "She can't have anything to do with this, can she?"

"Everyone has to be cleared," I repeated. Until I'd met his mother and stepfather, I couldn't begin to know if they were connected to his wife's disappearance.

I turned to leave, but Peirce bounced to his feet and moved closer. "For the record," he said in a low voice, "I believe Manny too."

I nodded, glancing over his shoulder at Manny, who was now staring miserably into the air. "Look, I'm undercover here. So don't mention imprints, okay?"

"I wondered," he said. "Bikers are a tightknit bunch."

"So I'm finding out." Raising my voice a little, I asked, "What are you doing with Howard anyway?"

Peirce shrugged. "His partner is out of town on another case, so I volunteered. I'm thinking about going into missing persons. This might pave the way."

"Good thought. I'm glad you're on the case. Sorry to run now, but I'm sure I'll be annoying Howard again before long."

He grinned. "You always do."

"Always do what?" Drum asked, appearing in the kitchen doorway with Detective Howard.

Peirce turned his grin on Drum, ignoring his impassive partner. "I was telling her that we always appreciate help on a case. Police officers do, I mean. The flyers were a good idea."

Drum nodded. "We're glad to do it. We all love Sariah."

Some of us more than we should, I thought.

"Drum," Manny said with relief, seeming to come out of his reverie. "I'm so glad you're here. Do you think you can stick around while these officers finish up? I need you, buddy."

"Of course." Drum hurried over to where Manny sat and pounded him comfortingly on the back.

"As I said," Howard said to Drum, "I need to ask you a few questions anyway."

"Sure, sure." Drum waved his free hand. "Ask away. Anything I can do to help."

I took the opportunity to leave. I wasn't too worried about the officers blowing my cover. I'd made myself clear, and they knew I was connected to Shannon and would have to answer to him for any mistreatment. Usually his protectiveness drove me batty, but since our engagement, I found it useful at times.

Outside, I waved goodbye to Brynn and threw my leg over Jake's bike. After searching my phone for the address, I attached the device to the holder before pulling on my gloves and fishing for Jake's key.

Why had Lucy Barnes Newman not come to support her son after his wife's disappearance? There was a story there, and I would find out what.

Chapter 7

*L*uckily for me, Manny's mother and her second husband lived nearby. The street was nearly identical to her son's, and the houses were a similar size. I pulled up in front of the house behind a gray Ford sedan. The Newmans' single-story house had blue siding and three wide, railing-lined cement stairs leading to the door, which had been painted a darker blue than the house to match the faux shutters on either side of the windows.

The house was close enough to Manny's that had Lucy Newman been friends with her daughter-in-law, the two might have spent a lot of time at each other's homes, and for all purposes, it looked as if they had. Like Sariah's house, Lucy's was well cared for, from the carefully weeded plants in the flower beds to the decorative flower vases that lined the walkway to the porch. These women obviously cared about many of the same things, including planting flowers and Manny, but those similarities evidently weren't enough to bridge their differences.

Attaching my helmet on the seat hook, I went up the walk, planning what I'd say. My cover as Sariah's cousin wasn't going to pull weight here, and membership in Manny's biker gang might not hold much sway either. On second thought, I returned to Jake's bike and removed my vintage jacket, folding it carefully into his storage compartment, which at the moment held only his gloves. I added mine to the mix. The pants still screamed biker, but the peach blouse with its cap sleeves was nice, and it beat going home to change.

I knocked twice before someone finally came to the door—a man in his late sixties with thinning gray hair, wide lips, and watery brown eyes. Both his eyes and nose seemed to disappear into the puffy, sagging cheeks. Those eyes went past me to Jake's bike and then ran lingeringly over my outfit. Though he seemed heavier in person compared with the pictures I'd seen, I was guessing this was Hutch Newman, Lucy's second husband, who Brynn had said Lucy thought she'd been out to steal. More likely, she'd had to fend off the man's lecherous advances. Even this man's gaze made me feel slimy.

"Hello," I said. "I'm a friend of Manny's. I'm here to see Lucy and Hutch Newman."

"I'm Hutch," he said.

Taking his cue, I left off my last name. "I'm Autumn. Nice to meet you. I need to ask you and your wife a few questions."

Turning his head, he yelled into the house with a dull, expressionless voice, "Luce, someone's here to see you." He turned back to me and motioned me inside. I trailed my fingers along the doorknob, but there were no notable imprints.

As the door closed behind me, I wondered if this was a good idea, my coming inside the house without backup. After all, Sariah was missing, and by Brynn's account, Lucy's second husband was a lecher. What if his wife really wasn't home, and he'd had something to do with Sariah's disappearance?

Hutch looked at me, and I looked at him. The man didn't look strong, so I could probably take him easily, even without my gun. The silence hung pregnant between us as we waited in what was apparently a front room and not an entry. The walls were crammed with pictures and wall hangings, none of it matching or in very good taste. And that was saying a lot coming from me, whose apartment bulged at the seams with mismatched antiques. The unappealing array was a stark contrast to their tasteful yard. It definitely explained the garish bowl Lucy had given to her son.

Finally, after what seemed like five minutes but was probably closer to two, the sound of approaching feet came in our direction, and Lucy Newman appeared, looking exactly like her pictures—short but large-chested, with her brown hair pulled tightly back in a knot. The resemblance to her son was even more notable in person, except for Manny's facial hair and Lucy's heavy frown line. Her brown eyes were outlined with heavy brown eye shadow, and her lashes were so long and thick that they looked like she'd robbed an eyelash technician of her entire stock.

She came to stand next to her husband, the two of them effectively blocking my way from the rest of the house. "Can I help you?" she said in a suspicious tone that told me she most certainly didn't want to help me with anything.

"I'm a friend of Manny's," I repeated, which now that I thought about it wasn't exactly true. It only felt that way because I'd come to know him so well through the imprints at his house.

"Oh, really?" Lucy started to smile, but my next words ended that.

"I'm looking into Sariah's disappearance."

The woman huffed, her nostrils flaring. "Oh, that. I'm sure Sariah has gone off on her own," she said dismissively. "Her bike is gone, after all. Her *brand-new* bike that Manny spent who knows how much on last year. It's probably the most expensive thing they own after the house."

"Now, Luce," Hutch began.

Her eyes narrowed as her face swung toward him. "It's true, and you know it. Sariah only married him until she found something more to her liking—and I'm guessing that's exactly what happened."

"Actually," I said. "I've verified that Sariah had no plans to go anywhere except on her anniversary trip tomorrow, and the police are now on the case. I'm sure they will be here to interview you before long. But I'm here now because your son asked me to look into her disappearance. I was just with him, and he knows I'm here."

"What are you, some kind of private investigator?" This came from Hutch.

"Along those lines," I agreed. "Currently, I'm looking into this as a favor to Manny, rather than on an official basis, but I am a paid consultant for the local police bureau, and I may be called in officially once the detective on the case gets further into his investigation. Could we sit down for a few moments? I have a few questions, and you might as well be comfortable." I certainly couldn't check for imprints stuck here at the door.

"Okay," Lucy said ungraciously, gesturing toward an out-of-date floral couch behind her.

I sat on the far end of the couch near an end table, which contained a lamp, a small framed picture, a book, and a pair of reading glasses. I peered at the picture of a much younger Lucy and a little boy. "Is that Manny?" I asked.

Before Lucy could respond, I leaned over and brushed my finger along the side of the frame.

Deep sadness, tempered by love. My boy was all I had left now.

The imprint had been left fourteen years ago, which meant Manny would have been twenty-four at the time. So either Manny had a son I didn't know about, or this was a picture that dated much earlier, perhaps chosen for display now precisely because Manny's father wasn't in the picture.

Lucy came over and picked up the photograph. "Yes, he was only twelve then. His father was out of town, and we were on a picnic."

I could hardly imagine this woman on a picnic with a child, but the memory had softened her expression. Could she at some basic, faraway level also feel the bittersweet memory of how she'd mourned her husband's death?

She stared down at the picture for a moment and then passed it to me. "He was a handsome boy, even then. Of course, you've probably never seen him without that beard."

I hadn't, but I was too busy reliving her emotion to respond. I handed back the photograph, murmuring appropriate words of agreement. Sitting on the couch, I set my hand on the armrest. Nothing there but faint satisfaction. The gray carpet looked so soft that I wished I could remove my moccasins, but both the Newmans wore shoes and hadn't asked me to remove mine. At least the house was well air-conditioned, so I was no longer sweating.

"Sariah disappeared last night," I began after the Newmans sat on the two rose chairs opposite me. "What were you doing? Did you hear from her at all?"

"I'd be the last person to hear from Sariah," Lucy said, her mouth puckering. "We don't get along."

"Really?" I said, feigning innocence. "With how you both love flowers and growing things, I thought you'd have a lot in common."

Lucy's nostrils widened again in what I took to be offense. She had the most mobile nostrils I'd ever noted in anyone, and it was fascinating to see. "No," she said, her tone clipped, "we most certainly don't."

"We didn't hear from her," Hutch said, smiling at me with apparent unconcern for his wife's anger. "We were here all night watching TV."

I looked at Lucy, who met her husband's gaze for a brief second before nodding. "That's right. We were watching TV."

If that was true, they could give each other an alibi, but that didn't mean they didn't do something to Sariah together. Not that I thought they had Sariah in a crawlspace somewhere, but they might have done something else to their daughter-in-law. It was possible, and the way Hutch kept looking at me set off my creep alert.

"What about today?" I asked. "Your son is frantic. Have you helped search for Sariah?"

Lucy blew out an exasperated breath. "My son didn't ask me for help."

"I just came from his house where all his friends are gathered to help look for her. We've been plastering the city with flyers."

"It's Sariah's fault I'm not there," Lucy shot, her face flushing. "I barely see my son since he met that . . . that tramp." Hurt laced the venom in her voice.

"Tramp?" I asked, not feigning shock at the word. Given Lucy's statements so far, the sentiment wasn't a surprise, but it was crass, to say the least, especially in front of a stranger.

Crass even if Manny hadn't come to her for help, though why he'd have to ask, I didn't know. Staying away didn't make sense, no matter the bad blood between Manny's mother and her daughter-in-law.

"Now, Lucy," Hutch chided.

Lucy looked ready to explode, but I spoke first, feeling defensive on Sariah's behalf. "There is zero indication that Sariah has ever been unfaithful to Manny. What would make you think such a thing?" When Lucy didn't immediately reply, I added, "Please. It might have something to do with why she's missing."

Lucy's nostrils again signaled her disapproval, but when she spoke, it was to her husband. "Will you get us something to drink? I need some coffee. Decaf, though. I don't want to be up all night." She gave me a mechanical smile. "What would you like?"

"Herbal tea, if you have it," I said. "Any kind." A hot drink didn't sound good at the moment, but I wanted Hutch gone long enough to allow Lucy to talk plainly, if that was what she intended. "Or ice water, if you don't have it."

"Sure, sweetheart." With another leer at me, Hutch came heavily to his feet and lumbered from the room.

The instant he was gone, Lucy arose and came to sit next to me on the couch. "Hutch is my second husband, you know. I married him two years after my first husband died. That was twelve years ago. He's not perfect, but he's mine, and we're happy." Her mouth pursed as if tasting bile. "Sariah is a flirt. Every time I've seen her, she practically throws herself at Hutch. I trust him, but with temptation like that under a man's nose, it's nerve-racking." She sucked in a breath and plunged on before I could say a word. "And it's not just Hutch. It's a lot of other men too. They're always staring and flirting with Sariah, and she flirts right back."

Many women had been called flirts when they were only being nice, and the same thing might be happening here. After all, Brynn had told me that Lucy thought she was after both her husbands. Yes, Sariah might be a flirt, but it was clear there was something weird in the way Hutch looked at me. A little kindness might be enough to make him think a woman was after him. On the other hand, Drum obviously had a thing for Sariah, enough to diss his supposed best friend, so maybe on some level she did have an issue with flirting.

"What about Manny?" I asked. "How are they together?"

Lucy snorted. "Like newlyweds. Always holding hands, or hugging and kissing." Her tone was accusing, as if needing physical affection was something they should have gotten over by now, at least in public.

"That's sweet," I said, risking her wrath. "Does he get upset when she talks with other men?"

"Not in the least." Once more, the telling nostril flare. "I've told him again and again and again that he needs to watch her, but he just laughs me off. He's so utterly blind when it comes to Sariah that I refuse to even mention her now. I don't know what he thought he was doing marrying someone he barely knew."

"They've been married seven years now, right?" It seemed more than enough time to prove that the relationship was real.

Lucy thought about that for a moment. "Yes, I guess. But look what's happened now. She probably cleaned out his accounts before she left."

"There's been no activity on their accounts," I countered. She would know that if she were there supporting her son.

Lucy shrugged. "So far, maybe. But there's something else." She leaned forward confidentially. "One time when we were at a lake, shortly after they married, her shirt came up in the water, and I swear I saw stretch marks on her stomach. I asked Manny about them, and he said they were just growth marks, and that she had some on the middle of her back too because she'd grown so tall as a kid." Her lips pursed. "I don't believe it, because when she saw me looking, she turned downright pale."

"She is really tall, so the stretchmark thing could happen." I'd read about it before, though I couldn't remember when. "Maybe she was embarrassed."

"With everyone else her age there wearing bikinis, stretch marks and all? I doubt it. I think she's hiding something shady in her past from Manny." Slowly, Lucy came to her feet. "I'll go see what's taking Hutch so long."

The stretchmark thing was interesting enough that I'd follow up on it. Was it possible that Sariah had a child before her marriage to Manny? He hadn't mentioned such a thing, though, and it should have been important enough for them to talk about. Or maybe it was exactly what he said. I had once known a man with stretch marks that resembled tiger claws on his back.

For now, Lucy was giving me exactly what I wanted—to be left alone. It wasn't the entire house, but I only needed a few minutes for this room. I ran my fingers over the book, the glasses, the lamp. Nothing of interest. I held my hands above the knickknacks on the coffee table but barely a tingle registered. Stronger imprints registered from the case of pocket watches on the bottom level of the coffee table. I touched the tip of my finger to the wood . . . and was immediately engulfed in a hurt so deep that tears sprang to my eyes.

I'd never expected this. When we married, I'd thought it was us against the world. How could he have betrayed me? Betrayed us? This was definitely not what I signed up for. Should I stay or go? And what about Manny? They were so close—would I be able to take him from his father?

The agony in the thoughts was profound, and I was grateful that no more followed. Brynn had spoken glowingly about Manny's father, and this revelation was completely unexpected. Knowing about it, I couldn't dislike Lucy as much as I had seconds earlier. Manny's father may have stayed with Lucy for his son, but he hadn't been innocent in what had happened to his relationship with his wife. Whether he'd acted because of how he was treated or whether Lucy had become a harpy after his betrayal, it didn't matter. But maybe this explained why Lucy had been suspicious of Brynn and now Sariah. She could be afraid of a repeat. Manny's father might have continued to betray Lucy after that first time. If it had been the first time.

There were no more imprints on the watch case, and I removed my hand after the imprint played a second time. I moved to the chairs, the pictures on the wall, and the light switch—again coming up with nothing other than a vague upset that had been left two months ago. Whatever the Newmans had felt about their daughter-in-law, they hadn't felt it strongly enough in here to leave any telling imprints.

When footsteps alerted me to the Newmans' return, I sat back on the couch, bending over to pretend to study the pocket watches. I straightened as Hutch entered in the lead carrying a tray and three steaming cups. Also on the tray was a plate full of cookies, which impressed me, though as an organic health food nut, as my sister called me, the treats weren't ones I normally ate.

"It's chamomile," Hutch told me with a smile that seemed sincere. "I didn't know how you take it. I have sugar here, if you'd like some."

Chamomile was a nice, unoffensive tea, and suddenly I was thirsty. "No sugar, thanks. Plain is great."

I was about to take a sip of the tea when I realized that maybe drinking with this couple wasn't a good idea. If they were responsible for Sariah's disappearance, there could be a drug or something mixed in with the chamomile. Then again, I'd told them Manny knew I was here and that I worked with the police regularly. Surely they wouldn't drug me.

The tea only smelled like chamomile, so I took a tiny sip. Surprisingly good, though I suspected that was more from accident than design.

Lucy was gulping her coffee as if she needed to recoup from my questioning. The coffee must have worked, because in the next minute, as I took another ginger sip, Lucy said confidentially, "You can probably tell that there was no love lost between Sariah and us. In fact, I wish Manny had never broken up with his first wife. You know he was married before, don't you? Her name was Brynn. Such a sweet woman."

I choked on the tea, spluttering a little as I jerked with surprise, sending more of the hot liquid onto my face and shirt. Could Lucy's memory be so terrible? Or had Brynn lied about her former mother-in-law? Someone was lying, that was for sure. My bet was on Lucy.

"Oh, here's a napkin." Lucy set down her coffee cup and sprang to her feet, snatching a napkin from the tray and handing it to me.

I wiped my face and then dabbed at my blouse. It wasn't a fancy affair, and the material wouldn't be damaged, but I knew an opportunity when I saw one. "Thanks. Could I use your bathroom? Just to make sure it won't stain."

Lucy gave a swift glance at her husband before replying. "Of course. I'll show you where it is."

I followed her out the doorway and down a short hallway to the right. She paused about halfway and opened a door. "Feel free to use the hand towel to get out the stain," she said. "I'll replace it later." She left me as I shut the door.

I wet the towel and dabbed quickly at the stain, mostly to have a larger wet spot to show them later. That accomplished, I opened the drawers in the vanity. Imprints jumped out at me as my fingers glided over the contents, but most of them were old. Only two were still potent enough to bring clear images, both reflecting minor arguments between Hutch and Lucy, but nothing recent and nothing about Sariah. I checked the wall hangings, shower curtain, bathtub faucet, and showerhead in the bathtub with similar results.

Giving it up, I replaced the towel on the rack and opened the door. Lucy was nowhere to be seen, so I began retracing my steps to their sitting room. In the hallway, I noticed a half-circle decorative nook set into the wall like a shelf, where a cell phone sat next to a vase of lilies and roses.

Score! I thought and reached for the device. Most people left a few imprints on their phones. Maybe now I'd find some answers. Before I'd even touched the phone, a tingling in my hand told me there was an imprint. A significant one. I let my finger drop to the shiny surface.

I stood clutching the phone to my ear as Manny talked about Sariah being missing. I wanted to tell him that I'd been right about her after all, but the lump in my throat was too big. If he ever found out we'd gone to the house, he'd never forgive me.

The imprinted memory was neither male nor female, but the imprinted memories had to come from Lucy because I doubted Hutch felt that strongly about the stepson who had already been an adult before he'd entered Lucy's life.

The imprint vanished, and a new one began.

"No," I said, my voice clipped. "I don't need any geranium starts."

"Okay," a woman spoke in my ear. "If you change your mind, they'll be at the bottom of my front steps until morning. I thought they'd look good in your front flowerbed, but I'm sure my neighbor will want them."

Probably they were rejects from Sariah's flowerbeds. I stifled a surge of jealousy as I thought about my daughter-in-law's yard. Her geraniums had a brightness mine didn't, and I still couldn't figure out how she got her hibiscus to grow so well.

"I don't need them." I hung up without another word. As if I'd want any flowers from her. The girl probably wanted a chance to throw herself at Hutch.

Both imprints had occurred the day before, only hours apart, and sometime between them Sariah had gone missing. The imprints that followed these were older and barely noticeable. Lucy's mobile phone didn't have much importance in her life.

I lifted my finger from the phone to stop the old imprints, then touched it again to replay the most recent memories. While in Lucy's memories, my anger at Sariah felt justified, but afterward my real anger was only for Lucy. Manny's mother obviously knew something, even if she might not be directly responsible for Sariah's disappearance, but she hadn't been forthright with her son.

My phone buzzed then, and I fished it out to read a text from my sister.

Still no boy in my drawings, but this man keeps popping up. Is he important? Looks like it's at that mall food court we sometimes go to.

I studied the accompanying drawing of a heavy-set, bearded man wearing glasses. He sat at a square table staring at a piece of paper. In the background were several restaurants, and I recognized it as the Lloyd Center where Sariah and Brynn had gone shopping for riding gear.

Yes, I texted back, excitement rushing through me. *I think he's related to my missing biker case. I think she paid him money. I'll check it out. Thanks!*

If my sister had drawn him, maybe she was getting vibes from me, and he was even more important than I'd suspected. Maybe if I hurried over to the Lloyd Center, I might spot the man. But first, I had a few more questions for the Newmans.

I found Lucy and Hutch waiting for me in the sitting room, still drinking coffee. My own tea remained nearly untouched on the coffee table except for the tiny bit I'd either sipped or spilled. I was glad I hadn't drunk more because they were looking more and more guilty to me. I hadn't caught any inkling of premeditation, but at the very least they were hiding a phone call from Sariah and a visit to Manny and Sariah's house.

They looked up as I entered. "I hope it doesn't stain," Lucy said, studying my blouse.

Hutch's interest in the wet part of my shirt was even more apparent, but he was in for a disappointment if he was trying to see anything underneath.

I pulled on my best game face. I couldn't lie well, but I could tell them a truth that might make them start talking. "You should know that the police will be looking at Sariah's phone records, and I've personally questioned all her neighbors about visitors to the house yesterday."

"What does that have to do with us?" Lucy said. The side glance she sent her husband told me better than words that I was on the right track.

"I believe she called you about four o'clock. What was that about?"

This time Lucy didn't look at her husband. Her shoulders sank, and her whole body seemed to curl in on itself. "She called about some flowers."

"And you went over there," I said. It wasn't a question, and the resulting gleam of fear in Lucy's eyes made it apparent she thought a neighbor had seen her.

"Just to pick up some geraniums."

That was interesting. From the imprints I'd read, Lucy hadn't planned on picking up the flowers. If she was telling the truth, what had changed her mind? If the couple had lied about going there, it could mean they had something to do with Sariah's disappearance.

"You talked to Sariah at the house?" I pressed.

"No."

"So you drove over, picked up the flowers, and didn't see Sariah?" I let doubt enter my voice. Something didn't ring true here.

Lucy sniffed. "We don't get along, so it's better we don't meet."

Better for Lucy, maybe. "And you didn't knock on the door or see anything out of place?"

"No," Lucy said quickly. Too quickly. "The geraniums were at the bottom of the stairs."

I eyed Hutch to observe his reaction, but he was staring down at his coffee cup. "Did you see anything?" I asked him.

"We didn't see anything." His set jaw and the determined glance he shot at Lucy told me he was sticking to the story. Sweat broke out on my back, though I could feel cool air coming from the vent near the couch. Neither of them looked threatening, but what if there had been an accident and they'd hidden Sariah's body?

I made a mental note to ask Detective Howard to search their house and crawlspace as well, if they had one. Maybe he'd even let me come along so I could read more imprints.

"What time did you go over?" I asked Lucy.

She shrugged. "Six or seven, I guess."

"And when did Manny call you about Sariah going missing?"

"Maybe nine or ten. I don't know." Lucy's eyes watered. "Does Manny have to know?"

"That you took the flowers without trying to see Sariah?"

She blanched. "Yes."

"Probably." I planned to tell him myself. "I'm sure the detective on the case will want to question you further about this, so if there's any more you're not telling me, now's the time."

I waited, but neither one of them spoke.

"Thank you for your time," I said, pulling out one of my own cards. "You can reach me anytime at the number or come to my store."

Lucy stood and accepted the card without glancing at it. Her hand trembled. "Okay."

She remained in place while Hutch went to open the door

for me. Like his wife, he wasn't wearing a ring on his right hand, so I didn't offer to shake it. Truthfully, I didn't want him touching me.

As I stepped onto their narrow porch, his gaze went past me to Jake's bike. That reminded me of one very important question I'd neglected. "Do you own a motorcycle?"

He pulled his gaze back to mine, a genuine smile on his face. "Yes. Want to see it?"

I weighed the opportunity of touching his bike against the chance of finding the brown-haired man still at the mall. I opted for the sure thing. "Yeah, I'd love to."

He passed me on the stairs, his bulky arms brushing against mine. I followed him to the two-car garage, which he opened with a code in a side panel. Lucy appeared on the porch, glaring at us suspiciously.

That he kept his bike under a cover even inside the garage told me it was his baby. He reverently pulled off the cover to reveal a big Harley-Davison with black leather seats and gleaming chrome.

"Nice," I said, reaching out my hand. He didn't object as I read the imprints on the seat (faded satisfaction) and the handles (strong pride). Only from the mirror did I receive a visual imprint.

I reached out to adjust the angle of the mirror. Just a few centimeters to the left. There. She was one sexy woman, that Sariah. I could stare at her all day. Long as Luce didn't catch me at it, though she might not mind if she knew.

Nothing after that. The imprint was shocking since it referred to his stepdaughter-in-law, though it was surprisingly lacking in emotion or other physical response. Hutch might have admired Sariah, but he didn't appear to be driven to her very powerfully. I wasn't sure what to make of that or of what Lucy "might not mind if she knew."

"You have the bike long?" I asked, stepping back and purposefully running into the white sedan, also parked in the garage. I put my hand behind my back and touched the door handle.

"Five years."

For most of which the bike had probably been in the garage and undriven, by the new looks of the bike.

I started to reply, but imprints were coming through the handle of the car behind me.

Ooh, that man is an idiot.

That was kind of Betty. I'll have to return the favor.

What does he see in her?

If he ever cheats on me, I'll kill him.

What a fabulous sale. I saved at least a hundred bucks.

She never lets me see my son.

On they went, spaced by weeks and sometimes months, going back for years.

"Are you okay?"

Vaguely, I became aware of Hutch staring at me. The thoughts imprinted on the car door weren't strong for the most part, but brief and jarring. None of them told me anything I didn't know except that maybe someone—most likely Lucy— wasn't about to take another cheater lying down.

I pushed away from the car. "Yes, I'm fine. But I have another appointment. Thanks for showing me your ride."

Hutch looked disappointed, as if maybe he'd hoped I'd ask him to take me for a spin on the bike. *Not a chance, you old goat,* I thought.

Back at Jake's bike, I gingerly fished his keys from my pocket, laid them on the seat before his imprints could play too far, and pulled on my gloves. For now, I'd leave the jacket off. The Newmans didn't shut their door until I drove off, an expression of disapproval on Lucy's face.

Lucy's imprint on the car indicated that she'd kill her husband if he cheated on her. Was that an idle threat, or did it hint that her first husband's death might not have come from cancer as Manny believed? Lucy might have helped him along, and if she had, maybe she was involved with Sariah's disappearance.

Chapter 8

The wind blew me and my blouse dry, and by the time I reached the Lloyd Center, I was feeling a little chilly. I donned my biker jacket again and hurried through the parking garage into the mall, becoming self-conscious as heads swung my way. I was either smoking hot in the leather outfit or I looked ridiculous and out of place. Either way, a lifetime of not wearing shoes and living with a hippy father had inured me to stares, and I quickly forgot them.

Within seconds of entering the top-floor food court, helmet under my arm, I could see that the table where the brown-haired man with glasses had once been sitting was empty. I drew out my phone and compared the image with the reality, marveling as I always did at my sister's ability to capture details so correctly.

Sinking down at the table, I ran my hands over it and then over the backs of the chairs. The mishmash of imprints revealed nothing usable. My next step was to ask the employees at all the restaurants if they recognized him.

Most of the workers in the various restaurants that made up the eateries were teenagers or older people. No one recognized the man in the drawing until, finally, an older Hispanic woman at Subway nodded. Her nametag said her name was Luna.

"Yes, I know him. He comes in a couple of times a week." Her eyes went past me to scan the seated diners. "He was here tonight, but I don't see him now."

"Do you know anything about him?"

She shook her head. "He usually has a computer in a backpack. Sometimes he talks on the phone."

"Does he come in alone or with someone?"

"He always comes to the counter alone, but sometimes people sit with him."

Excitedly, I scrolled to the picture of Sariah that Manny had texted me. "Ever see him with this woman?"

Luna's eyes squinted as she pulled back from the screen. "Uh, yes. I think so. But that was a long time ago. Before Christmas last year. I remember her because that day he bought two sandwiches, and she ate with him. And because she was almost as tall as he was. Very beautiful woman, better than in that photograph."

"You are sure it was her?"

"Yes. She came up to the counter to ask for mustard, walking like a model, and all the men were staring at her." Luna shrugged. "I thought maybe it was a new girlfriend, but she never came again."

That was interesting. Whoever the brown-haired man was, he'd been seen with Sariah at least three times that I knew about.

"Do you have any idea when he might be back?"

"No. He ate here tonight, so probably in a few days."

"He ever mention where he lives?"

"No. But probably close since he's here so often."

I extracted a card. "The woman I showed you is Sariah Barnes, and she's missing. Her husband is looking for her, and the police have been called in. Can you call me if you see him again?"

"Are you a cop?"

"No. But I consult with them, and I'm afraid Sariah's hurt. She had a trip planned with her husband tomorrow. For their seventh anniversary."

The woman's face darkened. "It's always the husband. I watch the crime shows."

"Not this time."

"How do you know?"

I stifled a sigh. I could touch her wedding band and prove my ability to her, but the idea of reading even one more imprint tonight made me nauseated. "Because I've tracked killers before, and he's not one."

"You think this guy did it?" She gestured to my phone.

"For now, he's just someone who might know where she is. Thank you for your time."

I left her then, not looking back. She'd either call me or she wouldn't. Meanwhile, I'd have to contact Detective Howard and see if he could lay hands on the mall's video feed. Maybe that would tell us something more.

My steps dragged through the parking garage to the motor-cycle as the many imprints I'd read that day took their toll. I needed rest and food. Before climbing on the bike, I slipped a drawing from my pocket—one Tawnia had drawn for me from a photo we'd taken together during one of our very first meet-ings. Love rushed through me as I relived my sister's feelings for me and her gratitude that we'd found each other.

Maybe I'd been wrong to listen to Dr. Godfrey and keep

wearing gloves around even the good imprints. Except for
the time when I'd temporarily overloaded my senses, and any
imprints had made me dizzy, the good ones had always made
me feel stronger. I missed touching happiness and having it fill
me to the brim. Maybe good imprints were like healthy exercise that strengthened a damaged bone.

I still needed food, and a lot of it. And I was feeling oddly
guilty for not touching the Hispanic woman's ring. What if she
had problems at her house, and I could run interference?

No, I thought. *I already have a case.* Spreading myself too
thin wouldn't help Sariah.

The sun had already set, though the sky was still light
enough that headlights were extraneous. When I pulled up at
my apartment building, I texted Jake. *Too tired to return your
bike, but it's in my parking place if you need it before morning.
I'll probably need to use it again, though. I have more bikers to
question.*

Jake's text came back quicker than expected. *Keep it till
Monday. Or longer if you need to. I can use my truck tomorrow,
and I'll be driving up to Washington with Melinda on Sunday. We
already dropped off your car at your place, in case you'd rather use
that.*

I remembered vaguely that his new girlfriend had been
born in Washington. Did that mean she was taking him home
to meet her parents? I hoped her very white family didn't have
anything against Jake and his black skin and locs. Or maybe
I did.

Thanks, I told him.

*Will you be at work in the morning, or should we call Jazzy to
come in? Both Thera and Randa will be there, but you know how
Saturdays are.*

One person could handle the traffic in my store on Saturday mornings, but business tended to be brisk in the early afternoons, and I'd need two people then.

Jazzy's already coming in, I told Jake. Mostly because I'd originally been planning on going to an estate sale.

Good. Because when you're on a case, you tend to disappear.

He was right about that, at least. I'd probably end up missing the estate sale altogether.

Sometime later, I stumbled into my apartment, located on the left side of the apartment building's main floor. I briefly debated if I was going to pass out on my bed or eat all the leftovers in my kitchen. I opted for shedding the leather jacket and collapsing on my reupholstered Victorian couch, whose back faced the door and was the main focus of my living room.

Closing my eyes, I gave myself up to the quiet imprints buzzing gently from all the antiques I hadn't been able to part with. This was the heart of my apartment and being here revitalized me. The two bedrooms, one bath, and my kitchen all opened up to this room.

My mind still raced as I went over what I'd learned. So far, I had more suspects than any leads. First, there were Brynn and Travis Shepherd, whose helpful smiles held a secret. Next were Lucy and Hutch Newman, who were lying about something connected with their visit to Sariah's. In my opinion, Hutch was creepy enough to have stashed Sariah in a crawlspace or hidden room, but the Newman's house was small, and I hadn't picked up any of Sariah's imprints there. Maybe a peek at their financials would help to see if they had other properties, but for that I'd need police help. Drum was another suspect high on my list because of his weird fascination with his best friend's wife. I'd need to see if he had an alibi and check out his house. There was also the brown-haired man with glasses, and, finally, the principal at Sariah's job, or perhaps someone else related to the little girl she was helping. The principal wasn't a suspect exactly, but I needed to follow up with him as quickly as possible.

That left me with six solid suspects and not enough information. And for all I knew, the postman or Sariah's extended relatives could be involved.

I was going through it all again when the click of my lock told me someone was entering my apartment. My eyes flew open, going past the overhead antique chandelier toward the direction of the door. I couldn't see past the back of the couch, though, so I sat up, my hand instinctively sliding to my ankle holster. Once, that wouldn't have been my first thought, but searching for missing people and consulting on Shannon's cases had changed me.

Any number of neighbors and friends had keys to my apartment, so it was anyone's guess who might walk through the door. I was hoping for Jake since Shannon was working a homicide, but when Shannon appeared in the doorway, my exhaustion vanished. Jumping up, I propelled myself across the room and into his arms. This was so much better.

"Hey, you," he said, giving me a kiss that burned a path of heat through my body.

"Hey," I answered. "I'm glad you're here. How'd you even know I'd be back?"

It was a casual question, to which I thought he'd say, "Lucky guess," or something as inane, but his face was instantly wary. "Uh, I checked your phone's location, and saw you were heading here."

"You did what?" I stepped away and glared. He knew how I felt about that location feature.

He kept his arm around me. "Hey, I had to take a break to eat, so I picked up food and came here. It might be the only time we'll see each other this weekend. Desperate times call for desperate measures."

That's when I noticed the arm that wasn't around me carried take-out bags. If he wanted forgiveness, food really was the best way to get it. I checked the mini grandfather clock on my fireplace mantel. "Does that mean you're going back to work? It's nearly ten."

His face turned grim. "The cadaver dogs found another body at the dumpsite. This time the death was far more recent. We're waiting on the medical examiner to show up and give us some ideas as to how long. We're positive they're all connected. Each of the victims were wrapped in black plastic and then stuffed inside a large, water-resistant polypropylene bag anyone can buy for twenty bucks. We're working on matching dental records, and I'm pushing to fast track the autopsy on the last victim."

That meant there was enough preserved to do an autopsy.

I stepped closer and stroked the curling ends of his hair. "Definitely a serial killer then," I mused. "All the victims are women?"

He nodded. "Near as we can figure from the clothes and remains. The oldest of the bags had been ripped open by animals and much of the contents scattered, which is why the kids stumbled on it, or we may have never found any of them. We have some queries out to the manufacturer now, to see if they can help date the bag styles that are slightly different."

"The other bags were buried?" I took the food bags from him and led him to my couch. With three homicides on his docket, he wouldn't be getting a lot of time to eat or sleep.

He sat close to me with a faint sigh. "Only partially. Like a lot of the areas in the manufacturing sections, there are piles of refuse lying around, and the bags were under those. The county has been pushing for a clean-up, but it's difficult forcing owners to be responsible. The cadaver dogs didn't have much problem finding the first two bodies, including the rest of the first one the kids found. The newest one we found was harder because it was under a load of grass clippings and tree trimmings."

"Any leads on who might be responsible?" I peered into the food bag, unsurprised to see the pasta we'd missed for lunch, but since Shannon had bought it from a restaurant known for healthy ingredients, I was happy with his choice. It beat leftovers by a long shot.

"The second body was wearing a men's high school ring that hadn't fallen off, despite the decay. I traced that to a local high school. We're researching the jewelry too, but I was hoping . . ."

"That I'd read it." Despite knowing it was a murder, and that I might get caught in a loop, I wanted to help him. I wanted to help find the person who'd ended the lives of three women.

"Tomorrow, though. The ring has to be processed first, along with the rest of the evidence."

"Let me know then." I shoved a container at him. "Come on. Let's eat."

As usual, I was faster eating than he was, so while he finished, I caught him up with my suspects. "I may need you to run a drawing through the database," I said when I was finished, "though he may not have a record—he doesn't look the type, but he's definitely connected to my case. And do you think Detective Howard will get mall surveillance recordings for me if I ask?"

"Cole Howard?" Shannon sighed. "That guy has promotion on the brain. He wants to solve as many cases as possible as fast as he can, so it depends on if you're trying to prove his theory or disprove it." He brightened. "But Peirce will help you out with anything you need."

"It was a nice surprise seeing him on the case."

"Yeah, he's smarter than Howard deserves."

Shannon took a final bite, set down his food container, and leaned back on my couch. "You know, in these cases, it's usually the—"

"Husband. I know. But it's not this time."

"What's your gut say?"

I frowned. I wasn't sure. "I like the ex-wife," I said. "I hope it's not her. The best friend . . . he's a little odd, but he seems devoted and Manny trusts him. So if I had to guess right now, I'd say it was related to the guy with glasses. Or maybe something to do with the school. I haven't been able to check that out yet."

"The husband and the other two have been friends since high school?"

I immediately bristled, sensing something under the comment, something directed at Manny. "A lot of people have been friends since high school. Doesn't mean they're covering for each other. I checked Manny's Franklin yearbooks at the house, and nothing traumatic was imprinted on them. I tell you, it's not him."

"Did you say Franklin?" Shannon sat up straighter.

"Yes. He hasn't gone far."

"The ring we found on the second body was from Franklin High."

I stared at him. "You think it might be linked?"

"Anytime a woman goes missing, and others are found dead, there might be a connection. Did Sariah go to Franklin?"

"I don't know. Her yearbooks weren't at their house, but I'm going to see her mother tomorrow. I'll ask."

"Okay, let me know." Shannon stood up to go. "I'll call when I can. Oh, and don't go easy on Howard on my behalf. The guy's definitely a pain in everyone's neck."

I'd already surmised that, and since half my courtship with Shannon had been knocking heads, I was up to the task.

I walked him to the door, where he paused, his eyes scanning my body. "By the way, what's with those pants? Should I be concerned?"

I laughed. "Only if you don't like leather."

He pulled me close and faked heavy breathing in my ear. "Oh, I like it a lot. Which reminds me, have you given any more thought to a date?"

For the wedding, he meant. "Um. Next summer, maybe?" The weather had to be at least somewhat warm so we could exchange vows in the same meadow my parents had been married in.

He groaned. "I know where your mind is, and it's not on our wedding. We'll talk about it after you find Sariah."

If I find her, I corrected silently. I reached past him to the doorknob and let him out with a distracted kiss.

Okay, maybe I was using the case as an excuse, but marriage was a huge commitment, and we'd spent the better part of a year at each other's throats before admitting our feelings. A few more months of settling into each other's lives shouldn't make a difference.

Leaving the remains of our meal where they were, I went to the little alcove in the living room where I kept my laptop. The

Franklin high school ring from Shannon's case had made me curious about Manny and his friends, and I was sure I could find pictures from that time on the internet.

Five minutes later, I hit pay dirt. Franklin didn't appear to keep a database of old yearbooks, but they were available through Classmates.com. I scrolled through seniors until I found Manny Barnes. Except for the beard and thirty pounds, he hadn't changed much in nineteen years. He was better looking without the facial hair, and his eyes met the camera confidently. He'd played football, but there weren't many pictures of him with the "in crowd," and in most of the few team pictures, he was near the back looking bored.

Brynn Shepherd, then Brynn Tucker, looked like the typical "bad girl," who might have dated her way through half the football team. She wore skin-tight jeans and too much makeup, but her thick hair was perfect even back then. She was an eye-catching handful. In one of the group pictures, she was seated close to Manny on the bleachers, and they were holding hands.

Owen Drummond, aka Drum, was the surprise. A definite nerd, he'd been an overweight kid with a severe acne problem who had probably endured more than his share of teasing. The square line of his ravaged face was familiar, as was the shape of his eyes, but he'd worn glasses, and his greasy hair lay over his face like a curtain he was trying to hide behind. It didn't work. The weight and red acne beard were impossible to mask, and they overshadowed everything. He was one of the few people on earth who had improved dramatically with age. Good for him.

I wondered if Drum had ever married or had a serious girlfriend. I did a little social media stalking and found numerous public pictures of him with various women on Facebook. None of the women were around long except for Sariah, who was pictured both alone and with Manny, and less often with Brynn. Most shots of Sariah were casual, and she seemed unaware that someone was taking her picture. She was surprisingly photogenic. In one image, her freckled face was framed by the sun as she looked off into the distance, laughing with apparent enjoyment. The photograph looked as if it had come from *Vogue* or some other high fashion magazine, which made me wonder if Sariah might have missed her true calling in life.

But three months ago, things shifted, and all the pictures of the various women ceased. Either that, or he'd stopped posting publicly, and since we weren't friends, I couldn't see additional posts. There were only a few public photos of the small, dark-haired woman I had seen him with at Manny's today, whose name turned out to be Tina. She was pictured with Drum, with Sariah, and in a group picture of the Road Rollers. Apparently, Drum had found someone to love.

I could see that Drum was friends with both Manny and Sariah on Facebook, but their posts were private except their profile pictures. The last one for Sariah's account had been uploaded over a year ago. I didn't know if that meant she hadn't logged in at all, or if she'd simply been too busy to post. Brynn was friends with all of them as well, her feed private except for scattered pictures of the Road Rollers. Had something happened between Manny, Drum, and Brynn back in high school? I couldn't rule it out, though I believed Manny wasn't involved with his wife's disappearance.

Another thought occurred to me. Even if Sariah hadn't posted on Facebook, that didn't mean she hadn't used Messenger for private messaging that might contain clues. I shot off a text to Manny, relatively certain he wouldn't be sleeping.

He wasn't. *I don't have her password,* he answered. *Or for her email either. Our computer at home used to be logged in, but it's not now. Police said they maybe can get in.*

I wondered if the password issue was important. Was Sariah hiding something from Manny after all?

Thanks, I wrote. *Now get some sleep.*

His reply was heartbreaking. *I don't think I'll ever sleep again.*

Try, I responded. *You need to be at your best for her.*

Saying that felt a little like a lie. With each day that passed, it was less and less likely that we'd find her alive. Unless she really had run away, which I didn't believe for a moment.

Giving up for the night, I scrubbed a toothbrush across my teeth, peeled off everything except my underwear, and slipped under the covers of my unmade bed. The last thing I thought as my exhaustion overtook me was that if a serial killer was loose in Portland, had he somehow caught up with Sariah?

Chapter 9

At six the next morning, I awoke alert and refreshed and ready for my usual two eggs and herbal tea. It was too early to visit Sariah's mother, so I drove my own car to my normal black belt class that now met at six-thirty each Saturday for two grueling hours. That usually left me time to get to the shop at nine to open or to attend an estate sale.

I went barefoot inside the gym, where I changed from wide-legged, white pants and a sleeveless fuchsia blouse into a dobok and rubber-lined socks. Unlike most other places, there were always stray imprints on the mat, and I didn't want to read them. The strenuous workout allowed me to work off a bit of frustrated energy, but after an hour and a half, I made excuses and cut out early.

I wasn't fooling my teacher, Steve, who could tell I was preoccupied. "Another case, huh? Well, keep your fists up." He brought his own into position in front of his face.

"I will. Thanks." I appreciated his efforts to keep me alive.

After a quick shower, I headed to see Sariah's mother. She lived in my neck of the woods, north of the Willamette, in an apartment instead of a house. I passed her street once before looping around and finding an open parking place shortly before eight-thirty.

A text had come in from Shannon's partner as I navigated, but I waited until I was parked to read it.

No luck finding the boy from your shop, Paige wrote. *I've talked with five of the seven school districts. The biggest one, Portland Public, hasn't responded. My bet is he's from there.*

I'd managed to shelve my worry about Kylan, but now it came back full swing. We'd find him, but would it be too late? Was he even now ingesting poison? My stomach churned at the thought.

Paige's foray into the school districts reminded me of Sariah's job change. *I need to talk with George Shank,* I told her, *the principal of Ainsworth Elementary where Sariah works. Can you get me his contact info?* The principal's home number hadn't been on the list Manny had given me, though his name had been. I didn't want to wait until Monday.

I'll get back to you on that.

Sariah's mother answered the door on my second knock. She was taller than I expected, and much younger, but easily recognizable from her pictures. "Maren Killigan?" I asked unnecessarily. "I'm looking into the disappearance of your daughter. Do you have a moment to talk?" I handed her a card.

She gazed at the card, but her reddened eyes didn't seem to take in the words. "Please come in," she murmured, moving backward with an unmistakable grace.

I followed her into an apartment that was sparsely but tastefully furnished with paintings of picturesque European villages, elegant vases, and a Madonna statue that stood guard near her fireplace. She motioned me to sit on a beige leather loveseat and then settled her willowy figure on the matching chair. Maren Killigan was an attractive woman, and I caught glimpses of Sariah in her looks, despite the mother's blond hair that was so different from her daughter's ebony locks.

"Mrs. Killigan," I began.

"Please call me Maren," she said with a gentle smile. "I've been a widow for fifteen years—since I was forty, actually. To me, Mrs. Killigan is still my mother-in-law."

"Maren, then. When was the last time you saw your daughter?"

"Last week." Maren pursed her lips. "We don't see each other much since her marriage to Manny." Her tongue clicked in disapproval.

"You don't like him?" I already knew that, but it didn't hurt to probe.

"He's just . . ." She paused. "Not educated, or something. I don't know what Sariah sees in him. And I don't like the whole biker scene."

I guessed that was the biggest rub for her, but instead of pointing it out, I said, "They seem to share a love of traveling and new places. Manny tells me you like to travel too."

"On a plane or a boat," Maren said. "It's hardly the same thing. Motorcycles are low class." She looked around her small apartment as if painfully aware of the size, despite the nice furnishings.

"Well, I guess it's hard to resist someone who is completely in love with you."

She blinked at me. "Well, yes. I suppose. He is smitten with her." A frown creased her forehead. "But that's not new. Everyone loves Sariah."

A mother's pride? First Drum's crush, Hutch's fascination, and Lucy's jealousy—was there something more to Sariah than

I'd first thought? What kind of woman was she? From her imprints, I thought she was someone I'd like, but there had to be things I hadn't touched. Maybe secret things she'd hidden from everyone.

"I want to believe she finally woke up and left Manny," Maren continued, her blue eyes meeting mine, then flitting away guiltily. "It wouldn't surprise me. Except she wouldn't leave me worrying like this. I've been waiting here ever since Manny called, but she hasn't come by, and she hasn't called like the last time."

"The last time?" I asked, sitting up straighter.

Maren swallowed before giving a faint sigh. "Some years ago, before she met Manny, Sariah was in college and dating a teacher. A nice man with family money, or so we'd thought. Good looking. A definite charmer."

Someone Maren would approved of, I thought. At least at first.

"I was already thinking of a wedding, even though she was only twenty-two. Then she found out he was already married, and it broke her heart." Maren frowned, shaking her head at the memory. "Sariah went into her room and practically didn't come out for two months. She quit her job at the college, dropped out of school, and let her phone service lapse. She only ate when I brought her food. It was awful." She sniffed hard and dabbed with manicured fingers at the tears in her eyes. "Then one day, I came home from work, and she was gone. Her note said she'd taken a job in Washington because she needed to get away."

"How long was she gone?"

"About six months. But she called me every couple of

weeks from a payphone, or she sent me a card. Wouldn't tell me where she was."

"And then what?"

Maren shrugged. "She just came home one day. Right around her birthday."

"How was she?"

"She looked better. Like she'd been eating well. Not so thin."

"She never told you where she'd been?"

"No. Just that she'd needed to get him out of her system. She wasn't the only girl he'd bamboozled, you know. His wife eventually left him, taking their two boys. It might be terrible to say, but I was downright glad when I heard he'd gotten prostate cancer and died last fall."

Fall had been when Sariah met with the brown-haired man. I filed that away for further consideration.

"Did you tell Sariah about his death?" I asked.

"Yes."

"And?"

Maren shrugged. "She didn't say anything, but she acted relieved. Anyway, it was only a year after she came back that she met Manny. They got married so fast. I know it was because she was still upset."

"But she's been happy these past seven years, right?"

Maren bit her lip, as though reluctant to admit it. Then she nodded. "Yes. But it was never the same between us."

"After she married, or after she went away?"

"I don't know. But do you think he's done something to her?"

"No, absolutely not," I said. "Look, did you ever see Sariah with this man?" I held out my phone opened to Tawnia's drawing of the brown-haired man.

Her head swung back and forth. "Never seen him before. But as I said, I don't see my daughter much anymore." Pain laced the words. "I just wish I'd . . ." Whatever it was, she didn't say, and I didn't ask. We both already knew.

Silence fell for long seconds, and then Maren shook herself. "Excuse my manners, but can I offer you something to drink?"

"I'm fine, thanks. But tell me, does Sariah have an old room here? Did she ever live here with you? It might help if I can see her room."

"No, that was another apartment. And she got rid of practically everything when she moved in with Manny. I got the feeling she wanted to start completely over."

"Can you think of anyone who would want to hurt Sariah?"

Maren snorted. "Besides Manny's crazy mother and that womanizing father-in-law? It could be any of those scruffy bikers. They're all a bunch of crazies."

I didn't protest because it wouldn't change her prejudices. "Anyone in particular?"

She shook her head. With that, she put her face in her hands and burst into tears. I stood and patted her back awkwardly. When she recovered, I asked about the Madonna statue and her paintings. That distraction seemed to work, and she threw herself into the task of showing me her few treasures. I touched what I dared, but there were no imprints from Sariah or any interesting imprints at all. Maren's tasteful collection was relatively new and not remotely as valuable as the figurines her daughter had inherited from her grandmother.

Finally, I excused myself, seeing that an hour had passed.

I needed to call my shop and make sure things were running smoothly. At the door, Maren looked around for my shoes. When she didn't find mine among the few pairs stowed carefully on a shelf near the door, she looked puzzled.

"One more question," I said, not explaining. "What high school did your daughter attend?"

"Jefferson. Why?"

"Just part of the investigation." But I was relieved that Sariah hadn't gone to Franklin.

Back at my car, I paused for a moment to let my feet soak up the warmth of the sidewalk, losing myself to the connection I always felt with the city. Only barefooted did I feel rooted, though that was probably due more to my flower child upbringing than reality.

After texting Jazzy and learning that she and Thera had everything under control at the store, I reluctantly called Detective Howard.

"It's Autumn Rain," I said when he answered. "Manny's parents were at his house on Thursday night. I think they're worth checking into. Do they own any properties we might want to search?"

"We?" His sarcasm was clear. "For the record, my partner and I are just leaving the Newmans now, and they told us about the visit."

"Of course they did. They knew I'd tell you."

"They don't like their daughter-in-law, but that doesn't make them kidnappers."

"Maybe not. But Hutch is as slimy as they come."

Howard snorted. "I think he's a nice guy. Awkward but nice."

I blinked at that. Okay, so Hutch's gaze hadn't made Howard's skin crawl, but he had to know the man's type. "Anyway," I added, "I do have a lead on the man Sariah met with and paid a thousand dollars to."

"And that would be?" he said when I didn't continue.

"Can we meet?" I said. Yes, I could text him Tawnia's drawing, but then I couldn't appeal to his partner to search the police database and the mall's surveillance records, and if Howard knew it was something from Tawnia's head, it might never see the light of day.

"We have an appointment right now," he said. "But we can carve out some time later. I'll call you and let you know."

"Fine." Gritting my teeth, I said a polite goodbye and hung up.

What now? I still needed to visit Brynn and her husband, and also Drum, but the identity of the man in glasses was eating at me. Why had Sariah paid him money? I'd thought maybe it was for information, but it was possible she was being blackmailed. If so, about what?

One thing was clear, I wouldn't find the answers standing outside Maren Killigan's apartment building. I decided to return to my shop and use the computer for a little research. Maybe I could find the principal's number myself and convince him to talk to me.

A short time later as I arrived on the street where my shop was located, I began to feel the connection between me and my sister thickening. What was she doing here? Thera and Jazzy should have been able to handle the Saturday morning opening alone.

Inside, I found Tawnia ringing up a 1925 Underwood typewriter that I'd bought for forty bucks at an estate sale.

Even at a hundred-dollar mark-up, it was a good deal for my customer, and it put me one step closer to paying my next mortgage payment. Standing near Tawnia behind the counter, Jazzy happily bounced Destiny on her hip.

"Aren't you supposed to be at home worrying about your parents?" I asked my sister when she'd finished with the customer.

Tawnia made a face. "If I go into that guest room and straighten their pillows one more time, I'll go crazy."

"Okay. I get that. How did buying the food go?" Slipping around the counter, I plucked Destiny from Jazzy's arms and buried my nose in her sweet-smelling hair. "No substitutions?"

"I got everything." Tawnia scowled. "Though there was another slab of regular pork that was a third of the price."

"You didn't," I said threateningly.

She raised both hands to ward me off. "No, but I wanted to."

Tawnia was normally an assertive person, so that surprised me. She must really be anxious if she hadn't deviated at all from my list.

"Good," I said.

"I still keep imagining them coming here and hating all of it. Then they'll insist on me moving to a larger house with a bigger yard, and Brett and I'll get so far in debt that we'll never be able to retire until we have great-grandchildren and are too old to walk to the mailbox, much less do any traveling to foreign countries, and they'll spoil Destiny so much that she'll become an entitled brat, who will steal my credit cards and run up large bills buying name-brand clothing for herself and all her college roommates."

"Stop," I said, holding up a warning hand. Tawnia shared our biological father's tendency to run off at the mouth with wild stories when she was stressed. Usually, it was endearing, but I had my own stresses today.

"Right." Tawnia let out a long sigh. "With you as an aunt, Destiny will never care about name-brand clothes."

That's all she could come up with? "And Brett would never agree to a mortgage you two can't afford."

"Plus, he's hot for an old guy," Jazzy added. When we stared at her, she added, "I only meant that he'll charm your parents so much they won't notice anything else."

"Good point," Tawnia said. "They do like him."

"So stop worrying." I bounced Destiny to make her smile. There was nothing I wouldn't do for this child.

The thought made something tap at my subconscious, hinting of something important. But what it might mean eluded me completely as Jazzy made a little squeal.

"Look! It's the couple who bought the desk I posted on Facebook marketplace," she said, looking at the couple who were coming inside the shop. "I recognize them from their picture. They prepaid and everything."

For the first time, I noticed the *SOLD* sign on the desk that sat in the corner beyond the connecting door to Jake's. "That's great. I've been trying to sell that for over a year now."

"I know, right? And I'm going to show them some more." With a happy grin, Jazzy tucked strands of blue hair behind her right ear and hurried to meet the couple.

"Ever since I showed up, she's been online checking sales," Tawnia said. "She's really excited about it. You might want to think about paying her on commission instead of hourly. I'm betting you'd both make more in the long run."

"You're probably right." Still holding Destiny, who was playing with my earrings, I pulled the stool closer to my computer and sat on it. "Can you help me find a number? I need to talk to the principal of Ainsworth Elementary."

"Is that where the boy from yesterday goes to school?"

A lump as slimy as processed cheese formed in my stomach. "No. It's where my missing biker works. No word on the kid yet." I didn't have to add that it worried me; I could see my concern reflected in her mismatched eyes. I was glad when she didn't comment on it.

Fifteen minutes later, we still had no luck finding Principal George Shank's number. Unless we wanted to pay fifty bucks for a number that might possibly be the right one.

"Well, what about that guy in the drawing I sent you?" Tawnia reached for her drawing pad and opened it to the original sketch. "He's been popping up all over my work since yesterday—and believe me, he doesn't have the physique to please my creative director. They want a gorgeous hunk of man for our client's ad campaign, not an overweight computer nerd." She made a face. "Not that he is a computer nerd. Man, I can't believe I just stereotyped an entire career."

I laughed. "I found where he was eating, but he was gone by the time I got there. I'm hoping the police will request the surveillance footage."

"Well, at least you have an in with the police." Tawnia waggled her brows.

"Unfortunately, it's not Shannon's case."

"Still." She turned the page and shoved the pad in my direction. There were two more drawings of the man, one talking on a phone and the other going into a house. Not helpful.

"Any of Sariah?" I asked.

Tawnia shook her head. "No. Sorry."

"Not your fault you're getting vibes from an entire city."

She shrugged and turned to help a customer approaching the counter with one of my boxed dolls.

I was debating on paying for the principal's home number when my phone rang. Balancing Destiny on one hip, I dug it out of my bag, seeing Paige's face on the call screen.

"Hello?" I answered, maybe a little too eagerly.

"Autumn, glad I caught you in time. You didn't hear it from me, but Cole Howard is on his way to Ainsworth Elementary as we speak. The principal and some of his staff are meeting there to answer questions and to let him search Sariah's workplace. Peirce is going with him and says if you hurry, you might be able to get in on it. He couldn't text you with Cole breathing down his neck."

"Thank you. I'll be there as soon as possible."

Three more customers had walked into the store, but Tawnia took Destiny and waved me away. "I got this," she said. Lowering her voice, she added, "Some of them don't even know I'm not you."

That made me smile. All my regulars knew who my sister was, but the casual visitor would have no idea my twin wasn't me wearing more tasteful clothes. And anyone who cared that I wasn't around to talk about the antiques was quickly won over by Destiny's near-toothless smile.

"Thanks, I owe you."

"Just show up tomorrow—and pretend to help me cook."

"Don't worry. We'll impress them." I figured her parents had to know she was hopeless in the kitchen by now, but she was my sister and that meant I would back her all the way.

"One more thing," I called over my shoulder. "I still need to find that little boy."

Tawnia nodded. "I'll go in the back and do some sketching when Jazzy doesn't need me."

With Paige's attention being co-opted by a serial murderer, it was all either of us could do.

Chapter 10

Fifteen minutes later, I parked on the street near the elementary school behind the unmarked police car. Hurrying over the sidewalk and down some stairs, I cut through a courtyard to a pair of locked doors. A woman was walking in the entry hallway, and I banged on the glass, waving my arms for attention. With a frown, she came toward me and pushed open a door.

"May I help you?" She was a thin woman about my age, wearing a tight blue skirt that hit five inches above her knees, a white blouse that was see-through enough to show the hint of a lacy white bra, and dangerously high heels. Her long hair was blond and cascaded down either side of her face to partially hide the bra, making the shirt almost modest. Her thin lips were tinted a deep ruby red, and thick gray shadow enhanced her blue eyes. Despite a narrow, pointed, too-pale face, she was an attractive woman, though maybe she worked at it a bit too hard. I thought she'd be a lot prettier with twenty extra pounds.

"I'm here to talk with George Shank about Sariah," I said with a confidence I didn't feel.

She blinked, her gaze roaming down my white pants to the

tips of my bare toes. "He's with the police right now," she said rather importantly.

"I know. Someone from the department called me. That's why I'm here. I consult with the police on a regular basis."

"You do?" The words were doubtful.

"Please take me to Mr. Shank. I've been working closely with Sariah's husband, and I believe he has important information."

Her forehead wrinkled in indecision, but I was already moving toward her, crowding her. She'd have to move back or let me barrel into her. She made a decision at the last moment, stepping back to let me pass. I was well into the school before I stopped to wait for her to precede me through the hallway.

Strange how the floors in the silent halls were cold, even though it was summer. I remembered vividly another elementary school and a principal who had required me to wear shoes. It had felt like a prison then, and this school didn't feel much different now.

The woman took me into an outer office where a long counter divided the reception area, perfect for standing customers—or parents, rather—to sign papers or rest their hands while talking to the receptionists. The other side, where the employees sat, was desk level, the top of two computer monitors showing only partially above the counter. An electronic sign-in tablet and two nameplates sat on the counter facing the public, one plate reading Sariah Barnes, while the other was stamped Hadley Mellow. The setup effectively blocked most of what was on the reception desk, which was where I needed to be, but the woman turned down a short hallway and paused in front of another door. I'd have to come back to the desk later.

"What's your name?" she asked.

"Autumn Rain."

"Really?" Her brown eyes narrowed.

"Yes. Don't worry. The officers know me."

She tapped on the door hesitantly, and I steeled myself for Howard's irritation. When a male voice called for her to come in, she opened the door wide enough to let us both be seen. "There's a woman here who knows these officers. She's trying to find Sariah and needs to ask you some questions."

Again, I pushed my way in, while the secretary hovered uncertainly. "Hello, Detective Howard," I said cheerily, nodding at him. Then I smiled at Peirce. "Officer Elvey."

Howard's dark face scowled, but Peirce jumped up and offered me his chair.

"I brought the drawing I need to show you," I added to Howard as I sat. "I thought it would kill two birds with one stone if I met you here instead of at the police station when I go in later to look at the evidence from Detective Martin's homicide case." There, that would make it hard for him to tell me where to go.

"Homicide?" Principal George Shank asked before Howard could speak. He was a round man with a bad comb-over and small eyes. His florid face told of too many sweets and not enough exercise. Whatever neglect he gave his body, however, didn't extend to his abnormally clean desk.

"Yes," Peirce said. "I heard they'd brought in evidence." To the principal, he added, "Miss Rain has helped solve a bunch of our cases."

I silently thanked him. "Sariah's husband gave me your name, Mr. Shank," I went on. "When I realized the police would be here, I thought it would be easier to meet here now than to make you come out again." The chair, though padded, was hard and uncomfortable—or maybe it was the evil eye Howard was leveling in my direction.

"Right, right." Shank looked nervously from me to Howard, as if expecting the detective to object. To my surprise, he didn't. "As I was just telling the officers," Shank continued, "all we know is that Sariah didn't show up for work yesterday. She's supposed to come in part-time to help us get ready for the coming school year. She has a month off beginning Monday, though, and we figured"—he waved a hand to indicate the still hovering woman—"there was some misunderstanding and that she started vacation early. We knew she was going on a trip."

"We'll need to see her desk," I said. "And I'm sure the detective here will want to review her communications."

Howard glared at me. "First, tell us about the reprimand you gave to Mrs. Barnes," he said.

"Reprimand?" Shank's eyes opened wide. "I don't know what you're talking about. Sariah never received a reprimand that I am aware of."

Howard's eyes flashed my way and then back to Shank. "A friend of Sariah's told us there was an incident with one of the students here."

"Right, that." Shank shrugged dismissively. "Sariah has been helping a student whose mother died of cancer this past January—with the father's knowledge, of course. This summer, she's been continuing to work with the child, since the girl fell behind these past years while her mother was sick. Everything seemed to be going along fine, but recently, there was an incident in the parking lot where Sariah had some kind of altercation with the girl's father. I was worried he'd press charges, so I told her to stay away."

"Press charges? Why?" I asked at the same time Howard said, "When was this?"

"It was last week on Wednesday. I don't know the whole of it, but he followed her inside, raging. When Hadley"—Shank indicated the woman—"called me about the incident, I came right in. Mr. Rodgers shut up when he saw me, and when I asked him what was wrong, he said 'nothing' and stomped out." Shank paused and then added, "He had a red mark on his face."

"Because she slapped him!" Hadley interjected, her pale face flushing. "I'm sure whatever happened he was under a lot of strain. It's not easy taking care of a child alone." Her glare told me she felt the blame rested solely on Sariah. She opened her mouth to say more, but after a glance at her boss's stern face, she apparently changed her mind.

Shank continued as if she hadn't spoken. "When I asked Sariah about what happened, she wasn't forthcoming about the reason for the altercation, except to say that it wouldn't happen again." His little grimace told me he hadn't been pleased about Sariah's secrets. "Under the circumstances, I felt it wise for her to discontinue her extracurricular activities with the child. Sariah persuaded me otherwise. After all, educating children is our mission here. End of story."

The whole event interested me. Had Sariah and the girl's father argued about the child's needs, or had their relationship been more intimate?

"This is the only thing that stands out to you about Sariah?" Howard asked.

Shank nodded. "She has her own way of doing things, but she's a good worker. She's friendly with the staff, and the children like her."

It was clear that Shank knew nothing about Sariah's disappearance, and I was betting what Hadley had to say would be of far more interest. Besides, I wanted to get my hands on Sariah's desk.

"We'll need the name of the child," Detective Howard said.

"Well, uh . . ."

"Your supervisor already promised us full disclosure," Howard added.

"Sure." Shank glanced at Hadley. "Print up the information for them."

Before the woman could turn, I bounced up from my seat. "I'll go with you. I need a drink of water anyway."

Hadley's jaw dropped a little, but she didn't protest. I could feel Detective Howard's eyes digging into me as we left, and I wondered if he'd hurry his other questions to catch up to me.

In the hallway, I asked, "Does Sariah have an office, or does she only use the front desk?"

"The front desk. We have our separate stations, though, and drawers we use exclusively for our stuff."

"Are they locked?"

"Some of them. But I have keys, of course. I'm in charge of the office." No mistaking the pride in her voice. I bet she never hesitated to remind Sariah of her superiority whenever the opportunity presented itself.

"I'll need to see everything."

Hadley glanced back the way we'd come, rallying her courage. "I'll have to clear it with Mr. Shank."

"Of course. I'm sure the detective will want to see everything as well."

"The water fountain is out there to your left." Hadley indicated the main doors inside the office.

"That's okay. I'll get a drink on my way out. Look, you seem to know more about the event with the girl's father than the principal. What weren't you saying in there?"

Hadley's thin face showed conflict. On the one hand, she was dying to speak, but on the other, maybe she didn't want to get involved.

"I won't tell anyone," I promised. "I'm just trying to find Sariah. I know for sure she didn't leave of her own will, and that man may have something to do with it."

"It's not him," Hadley burst, her need to speak, trumping her reticence. "Weston—that's his name—took Sariah's interest in his daughter as flirting. He's lonely, that's all. And now he might be ruined because he misunderstood." Hadley's chin jutted out. "Just because she can't have kids doesn't mean she can string Weston along so she can spend time with his daughter. He's lonely and vulnerable now after losing his wife."

"I take it you like him."

Hadley flushed, her expression becoming more alive. "I talk with him is all. I mean, his wife just died. Maybe someday when he's healed, there could be something more between us, but not now. Anyway, Sariah's a flirt."

"What happened?"

"He tried to kiss her in the parking lot."

"She told you that?"

Hadley nodded. "I think maybe it was something more, but that's all she said. And later he swore to me he didn't know she was married."

I wasn't sure I believed that. How could he miss the ring I knew Sariah always wore?

"Thanks for telling me," I said. "Can you print two of those sheets about the student? I'll need to talk to Weston Rodgers directly."

"You still think he's a suspect?" Hadley looked horrified.

"We just want to make sure he's not involved or has any information. I'll make sure to tell him you vouched for him."

Hadley nodded, somewhat appeased. She went to the nearest chair, sat in front of the computer, and started typing, while I went to the second chair and the computer where I'd seen Sariah's name. This side of the desk looked far different from the other side. Here, numerous photos lined the short wall behind the computer monitor, some framed, some stuck into the carpeted wall with tacks. Most of Sariah's photographs were of her and Manny, but there was one of the Road Roller gang and another of her with her mother and cousins. The picture that caught my attention, though, was one of Sariah crouched next to a little girl with sad eyes, who was neverthe- less smiling in the picture, her arm wrapped around Sariah's neck. Sariah's expression as she stared over at the child showed an expression I recognized but found hard to identify: Want, need, passion. Naked yearning. These were only a few of the words that came to mind.

Was this the little girl Sariah was helping? Because, for good or ill, there was something much deeper here than anyone realized. I reached for the simple snapshot pinned next to the computer monitor where Sariah would have stared at it every day.

But would she have touched it?

I was vaguely aware of the men coming into the reception area. I should have known Howard wouldn't leave me alone to do my thing.

I pulled out the pushpin and took the picture.

Love surrounded me. So much love. Love that somehow managed to compete with the heartache that would have otherwise crushed me. I could hardly believe how perfect she was. This little girl, whose heart was broken and who had no idea who I was.

"I'm so sorry, Grace," I whispered, clutching the photograph. "I would never have let you go if I'd known what would happen to you. If I'd known I'd meet Manny."

What had I done? Was it too late to fix her life? Or would she hate me forever if she knew it was all my fault? No matter what, I wouldn't let her go. I would die before I hurt her again.

Would Manny ever forgive me?

I barely had time for a breath before the imprint repeated. The love would have made it a positive imprint, but the intertwined guilt and heartache made it a negative one that drained and captured me. I was vaguely aware of my knees buckling and my body collapsing into the chair. My fingers wouldn't release the picture, and that meant I was imprisoned until I passed out.

So much love. So much heartache. I'd experienced imprints from child molesters, serial killers, and other violent crimes. For the most part, I'd learned to disconnect, to not get caught in the loop, but this was something different. Something stronger than all of that.

I knew Sariah's secret now.

It began again. *Love surrounded me. So much love . . .*

The photo was yanked from my fingers. I took a gasping breath and stared up into the face of Detective Howard. Before I had any time for gratitude, he said, "You shouldn't be touching things. We may need to dust for fingerprints."

Since it wasn't a crime scene, I knew that was a cover, though he could use his authority to prevent me from touching anything else, if he wanted. I swallowed hard, my bare arms going to the armrest of the office chair.

There she is, I thought. Finally.

My hands gripped the chair, the only thing keeping me erect, giving me strength for this long-anticipated moment.

Dear God, I prayed, my gaze wandering over her little face, she's more perfect in person. But such sad eyes.

I needed to be calm. Whatever I did, I couldn't frighten her.

I lifted my arms before I could see more of the imprint. Feeling eyes on me, I met Peirce's gaze. He gave me a smile that was both questioning and encouraging.

"Here are the keys," Hadley was saying, dangling them on a finger.

Howard took them and waved me away. Staying in the chair but careful to keep my hands in my lap, I rolled back to allow him room. He opened the two bottom drawers under the computer. In the first was a tablet, charging cords, and snack items. The final one held changes of clothing, both for an adult woman and for a little girl. Some of the small ones still had purchase tags on them.

"Nothing odd here," Howard said.

I stood and reached inside before he could stop me, placing my knuckle gingerly on the objects one at a time. Even the clothes, yet unwashed, held imprints.

This top is more like what other kids are wearing. She'll love the purple.

I hope she likes these snacks.

This game will help her with math.

These imprints were interspersed with instances of pure emotion: joy and yearning, anticipation and need, love and guilt. They intermingled until I couldn't tell them apart.

I moved to the objects on the desk and in the first unlocked drawer. Sariah's alternate life continued to unfold before me.

That stupid man. What's wrong with Mr. Rodgers? He doesn't seem to care about Grace. At least his mother loves her.

What a horrid mess. How can I ever fix this? I have no one to blame but myself.

He'll never let me near her after this.

At the house she'd shared with Manny, Sariah had kept her mind on her husband and their life together, but here at the school, all the imprints were about the little girl and Sariah's longing to be with her.

I pointed to the picture on the desk without picking it up. "That's Grace Rodgers, right?"

"Who is Grace . . ." Howard began, looking up from the computer where he was reading Sariah's work emails.

"Yes," Hadley said, passing both of us a sheet. "And here's her family information."

"Thank you." I glanced at the paper, grateful it didn't hold imprints, before folding it into my pants pocket. I'd seen enough here, unless Howard found something unusual in her emails, which he hadn't indicated.

Howard's phone vibrated loudly enough to attract everyone's attention. He stood and motioned Peirce into the chair. "We'll need copies of all this. Can you transfer it?"

Peirce pulled out a thumb drive and moved forward as Detective Howard answered his phone.

"Yeah, what's up?" He listened for a while, furrows of concern on his face. "We're finishing up, but we'll be right there. Don't let him leave." He hung up. Peirce glanced back at him, but Howard didn't explain.

My time was running out. I turned to Hadley Mellow. "Do you have a student named Kylan?"

She thought a moment. "Yeah, a kindergartener."

That wasn't the boy I was looking for. "Thanks."

"What does he have to do with this?" Howard demanded.

"Another case," I said.

His jaw worked, and I sensed it was only the presence of the school personnel that prevented him from digging into me. "What about that evidence you have for me?" he asked.

"Right." I pulled up Tawnia's drawing on my phone as Peirce finished his task and rose from the chair. "This is the man three different people saw Sariah with last year. Brynn Shepherd saw her giving him money." I held out the phone for all of them to see. "He ever come in here?" This last, I directed to Hadley.

"I've never seen him," she said. Shank also shook his head.

Detective Howard's lips pressed tight, but Peirce nodded. "Yeah, we know him. He's Eli Stone, a local PI. Nice guy. Smart with computers too. Incredibly smart."

Howard looked away, his irritation clear. "He doesn't have anything to do with this."

I knew Eli Stone had vital evidence, but I couldn't fault Detective Howard because he couldn't possibly realize how much more information I'd discovered in this office. While I was almost certain I knew Sariah's secret, until I had verified the imprints, I wasn't going to enlighten him.

"Thanks," I told Peirce.

"He's got a great website on the internet," Peirce added. "Just search for Eli Stone private investigator in Portland."

"Okay."

We said goodbye to Principal Shank and Hadley Mellow and left the office, Peirce dropping back to walk with me.

"What was on the picture?" he asked. "Or any of it. Was it important?"

"I think so," I said. "But I have a few things to check out before I should talk about it."

"Right." He nodded. "I understand."

Howard glanced back at me, telling me he'd heard the whole exchange, but he waited until we were outside before turning to confront me. "How did you know we were here?"

I gave him a flat stare. No way was I going to rat out either Peirce or Shannon's partner. "I'm psychic, remember?"

He snorted. "Martin better not be mucking around in my investigation."

"He's not," I assured him. "But I believe Mr. Rodgers is a person of interest."

"We'll get around to talking to him. In the meantime, we have another lead."

"What lead?"

"Sorry." He smirked at me. "We have a few things to check out before we can talk about it."

My words thrown back at me. As Howard stalked away, Peirce glance back, shrugging. That's right, he had no clue what the lead was either, but I was sure he'd brief me when he could. Or have Paige do it.

I followed them out and watched them ride away. Something in the mocking smile Howard gave me made me feel uneasy. Where were they going?

I texted Manny. *How are you? I've got a good lead. I'll stop by later and update you.* I actually wasn't looking forward to that, because if I was correct about what I'd learned, Sariah had lied to him—and lied big.

I wondered if that lie had turned deadly.

No response came to my phone. Maybe he was finally sleeping.

Where to next? It was either to question Weston Rodgers or Eli Stone. After a moment's consideration, I chose the private investigator. If I was right, he held the evidence I'd need to confront Mr. Rodgers.

I brought up my browser and searched for Eli Stone, private eye. His listing was the first to come up. The photo on the front page was obviously the same man in Tawnia's drawing, though he was wearing a black blazer and no glasses. He looked smart and able. His phone number was on the contact page.

I dialed the number. *Let's see what you have to say, Eli Stone.*

Chapter 11

By mutual agreement, I met Eli Stone at the nearly deserted food court in the Lloyd Center. Despite Peirce's wholehearted endorsement of the man, I was wary. When I arrived, he was nowhere in sight, so I nodded at the Hispanic woman, Luna, who was once again behind the Subway counter, before slipping into a seat at the table Tawnia had drawn him at yesterday.

Eli Stone's profession as a PI explained the money Sariah had paid him, but I needed to verify my suspicions and probe for details. The mall had been closer to him than to me, so I didn't understand his tardiness, but it was ten minutes after eleven by the time he finally rolled in. Traffic in the food court was picking up as it neared lunchtime.

"You must be Mr. Stone." I stood and offered my hand, noting that he didn't wear a ring, which in this case was unfortunate because I would have liked to learn more about him. He was just as Tawnia had drawn him—tall, thirty pounds overweight, glasses, and a short beard. What her drawing hadn't shown me was the green color of his eyes and how intelligent and kind they looked. His beard was short and well-groomed, and I knew that like Jake's locs, he probably spent more time keeping it that way than if he'd shaved. He wore jeans that had seen better days and a short-sleeve, plaid button-up shirt with a green tee underneath. Besides the kind eyes and well-kept beard, he was a walking stereotype of an intelligent computer nerd.

His hand was cool, and his handshake firm. "Nice to meet you. I'm sorry it's under these circumstances. I heard about Sariah only last night when someone gave me a flyer with her picture on it. I was right here, in fact. It was quite a shock."

"I'm sure it was," I said, wondering if that was when Tawnia had first sensed him. We both sat. "Have you heard from her recently?"

"No. Not since late October when our business was finished."

"You mean since you found her daughter."

He started at that. "She told you?"

"I've never met her, but yes, in a way."

"Her imprints then."

I wasn't sure what to make of that. "You've done your research."

He gave me a boyish smile. "That's why I was late. But there is only the one article about you. For the rest, you might be mentioned a lot, but you've done a good job of keeping your gift out of the limelight. Probably a good idea, or you'd have masses of people knocking at your door."

"Right. I still get people. Mostly by word of mouth."

"Requests to know if he's cheating or if she really loves him, I'll bet."

"Something like that." With a little bit of organized crime and serial murder thrown into the mix. "Tell me about Sariah," I said.

"I can't. I know she's missing, but she hired me. If I told a client's business, then I wouldn't have clients for very long now, would I?" He shrugged off a backpack that clunked onto the table, but he didn't remove anything from it.

"Then let me tell you what I think I know. First, you should understand that I've checked her home and workplace, and I can't find any evidence that Sariah planned to go anywhere except on her anniversary trip today. She wasn't cheating on her husband, but she was afraid of someone who may be in their biker group. I also found no evidence that her husband wished her ill. I believe someone took her and that she may even be dead."

He gasped. "Dead?"

"Yes. And the longer she's missing, the more likely that is. It might be related to what you did for her."

"Miss Rain," he began.

"Call me Autumn," I said.

"Autumn, then, and you can call me Elliot."

That surprised me. "Elliot?"

He groaned. "I meant Eli, but yes, Elliot's my birth name. It just doesn't seem like the name of a private investigator. Thanks to a certain fictional dragon."

I laughed. "I like it. But then, I'm named after a season."

"You could have been Summer or Spring or Winter. That would have been worse."

"Summer and Winter would be my parents."

"Touché."

I gave him a smile, liking him despite his awkwardness—or maybe because of it. "I also know that eight and a half years ago, after breaking up with a man she thought she loved, Sariah disappeared for about six months. Supposedly, she was in

Washington. When she came back, she'd gained a little weight and seemed over the breakup, but according to her mother, she was never the same. A year later, she met and married Manny. Eventually, they tried to have a baby, but those attempts failed." I stopped and waited for him to catch up, though he seemed to be following me. "I think she had a baby during those months away, a baby girl, and placed her for adoption. I think she paid you at least a thousand dollars, and probably more, to find her daughter, and when you did, Sariah changed schools to be near her." I cocked my head and studied him. "The girl's name is Grace Rodgers. How'd I do?"

"Pretty good," he admitted. "But since Sariah's missing and can't defend herself, I think it's only fair to tell you that she had no intention of entering Grace's life. At least not now. She planned to wait until the girl was of age and they gave her the letter she'd written. Sariah only hired me to confirm that her child was happy and that her parents were treating her well. That's all. A lot of mothers who place their children want proof of well-being, and I'm glad to provide that assurance. Like with my other cases, I made sure Sariah was okay with pictures and DNA verification rather than a location. I'm not in the business of upsetting children's lives."

"But you found out about the cancer."

He nodded. "And I've broken a half-dozen privacy laws by telling you that much."

"If it helps find Sariah, who cares?" I cracked a smile. "So you told her the location and that's when she changed schools, to be near Grace in order to help her through her adoptive mother's death."

He gave the slightest of nods. "It didn't help that the adoptive father was a jerk. I wanted the girl to have someone."

He may not have intended it, but that comment said a lot about him. "Why do you say the father's a jerk?"

"Because Weston Rodgers was cheating on his wife while she was in for treatments. He's a commercial refrigeration mechanic, so he travels a lot. In fact, they moved from northern Washington to Portland because of his job. It's more central to his maintenance route."

"What kind of man is he?"

"Strong. Impulsive." He shrugged. "Wouldn't want to meet him in a dark alley."

"You think he'd be capable of hurting Sariah?"

"Definitely," Elliot said without hesitation.

Not good news. I wasn't sure what refrigeration mechanics did, but Weston Rodgers could have access to old machines that might hide a body for months, if not years.

I sat back, tapping my fingers on the table, thinking. "Who takes care of Grace?"

"The grandmother. She's good people. Even if she's old."

That confirmed Sariah's imprints at the school and made me somewhat happier to think the little girl had someone steady, especially now that Sariah was missing and might be missing forever.

I watched the food lines growing in the food court for long seconds, my mind going over what I'd learned. "When you were working for Sariah, did you see anything suspicious? Did she ever confide in you?"

"No, ours was strictly a business relationship. The only thing I knew about her personally, aside from the baby, was that she was currently married and that I had to contact her through her work number to set up meetings. She never even gave me her cell phone number."

"You always met here?"

He brought a hand up to rub his beard. "Usually it was here at this mall. But when I finally got the DNA results, I went to her house to give them to her instead of meeting at a neutral location, which is my normal requirement. Her biker group was having a Halloween party, and when she came out of the house, she was flushed. I could tell she was upset about something, but when I gave her the information about Grace, all of that disappeared. Even with the cancer diagnosis for the adoptive mother, we'd at least found the right child. She paid me the rest of the money, and I left. I didn't hear from her again."

"Any guess at who upset her?"

"I thought it was her husband, and that was why he wasn't at any of our meetings and why she didn't want to use her cell phone to contact me."

"Did he know about the baby?"

"No idea."

"How'd you find Grace?"

"Trade secret." The words were softened with a smile.

"I'm assuming you knew her date of birth and where the adoption took place."

"Right. I used a computer algorithm that narrowed it down, and my contacts in Washington did the rest. Plus, once I laid eyes on the child, there was no doubt in my mind. She looks like Sariah when she was young."

"How'd you get the DNA?"

He grinned. "From the trash."

"What about the birth father? Did Sariah ever contact him? Or ask you to?"

"She didn't want him involved. I did a little research on my own, though, after I learned about the cancer. He's also dead."

"So, not a suspect."

"Right." Elliot reached into his backpack and removed a small manila envelope. "I have something of Sariah's. She gave them to me at the initial visit. I forgot to bring them that last day, and they've been sitting in my folder ever since. I'd forgotten about them until you called. She told me she'd already digitized them, so she probably forgot about them too." He dumped out a handful of pictures and began separating them. "These six are of Sariah at different ages, but these two are of Grace. One was taken at the hospital, and one was taken a year later and sent to Sariah in accordance with the adoption agreement." He pushed two pictures toward me, one of a newborn baby and another of a slightly older child, sitting with a huge grin on her face.

My hands were on the table, still inches away, but the imprints tingled strongly, beckoning to me. Elliot was still talking, but I didn't hear the words. I placed the tip of a finger on the photograph of the baby. It looked like a photo from an instant camera.

Hard to breathe. Pain. Loss. Grief so deep I knew it would never, ever end. Was life even worth living?

My breath whooshed from me as I lifted my finger, fighting panic. My heart pounded furiously, and I had to remind myself that these were Sariah's imprints. Sariah's life, not mine.

I touched the same photo once more. Again, I experienced the terrible loss that made me want to curl up in a ball and die, but I was ready for it now. There were no other imprints on the image.

I tried the next photo, allowing only a sliver of my fingertip to touch the edge.

Cute kid. Who can she be? Why has Sariah hidden this picture between the pages of her Bible? Unless . . .

Sounds came from the other room, and I shut the book.

The imprint cut off abruptly, but another soon followed.

My chest felt too tight, like a band choking the life from my body. But she looked so happy. Maybe we could both be okay now. Maybe it was time to forgive myself.

The first imprint had been three years ago this past April. The other seven years ago when Grace Rodgers had turned one.

"When did Sariah first contact you?" I asked Elliot.

"In May last year." His eyes searched mine. "Was there something on the photos?"

I nodded. "I'm just not sure what it means. Can I keep these for a while? And the others too?" I needed to learn if Manny had left the imprint three years ago, or if someone else had discovered Sariah's secret.

"If you think it will help. But if—when you find her . . ."

"I'll give them back." I took out my thin gloves from my pocket and used them to put all the photographs back into the envelope and then into my bag. "Thank you."

I'd started to push back my chair when Elliot leaned forward suddenly, his hands under the table, his big shoulders angling toward me. "I can help. Do you have suspects?"

"The police think her husband is responsible."

"Do they have any proof?"

"Not yet. But Manny didn't do it." I considered a moment. "There are some things I need, but I can't pay you. I'm not doing this for a paycheck."

"I don't need payment for this one. Just tell me what you need."

His willingness was refreshing, unless . . . Maybe he wasn't all that he presented himself to be. If he was involved in Sariah's disappearance, inserting himself into the investigation might be a way of making sure he wasn't discovered.

"If you want to help, let me touch your computer," I said.

His jaw gaped. Seconds ticked by, then he nodded slowly. "Okay. I guess that makes sense." He pulled out a laptop and set it in front of me.

I opened it—and found nothing. Or rather, I read a lot of imprints, some that would make him blush if he realized they were there, but nothing about Sariah except worry and a deep remorse that had been imprinted only today. Worry, remorse, and something more.

"You have a thing for her," I said tentatively.

He sighed. "Not by choice. But you're right. I do admit to a bit of a schoolboy crush where Sariah is concerned. From the first time we met, I realized she had a certain something that compels you to want to be with her. It's hard to explain, at least intellectually. I mean, she wasn't pretty or gorgeous in the sense that some women are, but she's just . . . attractive and really kind." He smiled ruefully. "So, yes, I had a silly crush, but I got over it. Still, at the time I probably worked twice as hard on her case as I did any of my other cases, and I definitely charged her half as much."

"And that was?"

"Three thousand dollars." He sighed. "I still can't believe she's missing."

Elliot's confession was interesting, but maybe that explained why Tawnia had drawn him here last night. He was not only connected with my case but still felt strongly about Sariah, even after all these months.

"I'll text you some names," I said. "I need background, properties owned, that sort of thing. I believe Sariah was taken by someone she knows, and if she's alive, they're hiding her." With Shannon and Paige working the serial murder case, they didn't have time to help me—and the clock was ticking for Sariah. I could use Elliot's help.

"One more thing," I said as I stood to go. "Do you have any contacts in the Portland Public School District?"

"Some. Why?"

"There's a boy I need to find. His name's Kylan. Blond hair, brown eyes. He's somewhere between eight and eleven, but I'm leaning toward the older side of that. His parents are college students, and his mother works. I don't know about the father."

Elliot stared up at me thoughtfully from his seat. "How's he related to Sariah?"

"He's not. So I'll pay you for this one." And I would, even if it took me months to find the cash. "I have contacts in the police department who are working on it, but it's a weekend, and they have other high-profile cases."

"Why do you need to find him?" When I didn't respond right away, he added, "I won't do something unless I understand the reason. Especially where a child is involved."

It was something I might have said. "Okay. Fine. Yesterday I read an imprint that leads me to believe someone is trying to poison his family. I need to send the police there. That's all."

He didn't show surprise, but my words ended his questions. "Autumn Rain," he said. "You lead a very interesting life."

If he knew about the debt I still owed to a certain New Jersey crime boss named Nicholas Russo, he might choose a different adjective.

"You have no idea," I said.

He slipped on his backpack and came to his feet. "I'll be in touch."

We shook hands and parted ways.

On the way back to the car, my phone vibrated with a message from Tawnia. All was in hand at the shop, but she had a drawing for me to see. Eagerly, I downloaded it, holding my breath. But instead of Sariah or Kylan, the drawing showed Manny, hands held to his head, his expression one of despair.

After thanking Tawnia, I checked to see if Manny had replied to my text. He hadn't. This time I called him, but no one picked up. I was tempted to drive to his house, but what he needed most was Sariah back, not more sympathy. Or at the very least he needed information that would explain what had happened to her and why. That meant I had to go see Weston Rodgers, who, according to Elliot, was hotheaded and capable of violence.

My hand went to my ankle holster, appreciating the hard feel of the grip under the slick material of my pants. I was ready.

Chapter 12

The existence of Grace Rodgers changed everything. Because people did crazy things when love was involved, perhaps more so for the love of a child. The fact that Tawnia and I had been separated was clear evidence of that. Love was a motivation I understood far better than greed or revenge. Now what I'd been feeling earlier today when I was holding Destiny made perfect sense. There was nothing I wouldn't do for Tawnia's daughter, and Sariah's connection with her baby, especially now that she knew her child was motherless, must be even stronger. But did it somehow figure into why she was missing?

The Rodgers lived a block northeast of Ainsworth Elementary, near the corner of Vista Avenue and Laurel Street, so that meant retracing my path. The neighborhood was far more upscale than where either Manny or his mother lived, but the Rodgers' two-story house was an oddly shaped affair, narrow in the front but extending deep onto the property. The shingles were in obvious need of replacement, and the white and red railing needed a new coat of paint. The older trees, sprawling bushes, and decorative rock on the property were in keeping with the neighborhood, if more overgrown than the rest of the street. On the right side of the house, the yard was a good five feet higher than the street, necessitating seven stairs before coming even with the desperately thirsty lawn. There, a short landing led to the two stairs going up to the covered porch and the door.

I'd reached the landing when rushed sounds from the right side of the house made me turn around—only to have a figure slam into me. As my body bounced toward a bush, I kicked out, catching solid flesh. In the next minute, I was entangled in the brush with a man who had at least a foot and forty pounds on me. He lashed out with a fist, but he was slow. I easily blocked him, then rammed an uppercut to his chin. His head snapped back.

I rolled away and jumped to my feet. "I just want to talk," I said, tossing my bag to the side and holding my fists ready.

This had to be Weston Rodgers, but why he'd come out swinging was anyone's guess—unless he knew something about Sariah. That meant I couldn't let him go.

Recovering quickly, he launched himself at me, landing a lucky blow to my ribs, which sent me flying back into more bushes. Branches raked my arms. My feet skittered against a rusted trowel on the ground next to a water hose. He sneered, face twisted, his shaved head flushed and his eyes wild. Was he going to attack? I felt for my gun, just in case, but he was already turning away—and taking with him any information he might have about Sariah. I pushed off the bushes and grabbed the pack he was carrying, yanking him back, pulling him past me and tripping him. A roundhouse kick sent him to his knees in the bushes.

"I said I want to talk. What did you do to Sariah Barnes? Where is she?"

With a guttural growl, he leapt to his feet and came up swinging. I got my hands up late—my taekwondo instructor would have been disappointed, but the first hit only grazed my jaw. By the time the second came my way, I dodged to his other side and kicked him again. My move made him furious, but my confidence was growing. He was bigger and knew how to punch, but he was slow and knew nothing about martial arts.

He reached for his pocket. I heard the pop of a switchblade before I saw the glint of metal. All my focus was on that hand now. "Look, I just want to talk," I said. There wasn't enough room to run away. He'd be on me before I moved two steps. I wouldn't be fast enough to pull the gun either. I needed to control his knife.

He jabbed at me. I sidestepped, grabbing at his wrist with one hand and his upper arm with the other. I twisted, going down to the ground on one knee, pulling him with me, pinning his arm between my chest and my other leg. He cried out as I twisted, but the knife came free from his fingers and fell to the dirt.

He jerked, bashing his head into mine. Something popped in his arm, but it didn't stop him from squashing me flat. I felt something on the ground dig painfully into my side. Not the knife, but something else. A rock, maybe? I released him and rolled, jumping up, my hands ready.

He also rolled, but the other way, down through the dirt and bushes to street level, where he bounced to his feet and ran, heading for the corner, holding his arm awkwardly to his chest.

For an instant, I thought about following, but the pain in

my side and a drip of liquid there convinced me otherwise. Seconds later, an engine roared to life, and a gray Toyota truck screamed around the corner, disappearing before I could see the license plate number.

The police should have him on record, I thought. They'd have to pick him up if I pressed charges. Well, if they could find him.

Lifting my shirt to expose part of my side, I found a long cut. *Not a rock,* I thought, my eyes landing on the old trowel that lay where I'd been pushed. It had cut me good, but not deep enough for stitches. A little herb poultice and I'd be as good as new in a few days, even with the rust. For now, I retrieved my bag and fished inside for a shawl I kept there, tying it around my waist and over the wound. I pulled my blouse down to cover all but the ends of the shawl. There was only a little bit of blood on the blouse and my pants, but I could fix that with a little water later. It hurt, though.

Sighing, I squatted down and touched the discarded knife with a fingertip.

My hot hands closed over the cool metal. I'll cut her good. I'm not going to jail for that frikin' tramp.

That was from only moments ago as he'd drawn the weapon. But it was followed by another imprint from twenty minutes earlier.

I gripped the knife, staring down into the bag. I had money, a change of clothes, my important papers. It was all I'd need. I should be grateful that pretty little number from the school had given me a heads up about the police visit. She said it had been nearly an hour though since they'd left. Why hadn't she called me earlier?

"What about Grace?"

I turned to see my mother. "What about her?" I shot back.

"She just lost her mother. You can't travel for work now. She needs you."

"I don't have a choice."

My mother would never understand. The kid wasn't mine. Not really.

My eyes dropped to see the kid watching me from behind my mother. Watching me with those large blue eyes that always reminded me I was a failure at the one thing that should have come so easily. Animals could reproduce. So could every loser on the street. But not me. And the kid knew. She'd always known who I was. I'd tried for Patricia, but now that she was gone, there was no more pretense. Not for either of us. I hated even looking at her scrawny face.

Guilt infused me then. Remorse. It wasn't the kid's fault. It was Pat's for dying. Everything that happened this past week was her fault. She was why I now had to run.

The next imprint was from months earlier at a bar, when Weston had fingered the knife in his pocket while deciding how to approach an attractive blonde. There was nothing about Sariah.

I withdrew my finger, thinking to leave the knife where it lay on the dirt, but remembering that a child lived here, I used a tissue from my bag to pick it up and slip it into my pocket. I'd figure out what to do about it later. Standing, I brushed the dirt off my pants, which still looked remarkably good despite my run-in with Mr. Rodgers.

Weston had blamed his wife for dying and for the events of the past week. Was that a reference to his run-in with Sariah at the school, or did it mean he'd done something worse? I'd need to go inside the house to touch more things to know for sure. First, I texted Peirce about my run-in.

Tried to talk to Weston Rodgers. He attacked me with a knife. I want to press charges. Can you find him? There, that ought to light a fire under even his temporary partner.

"You have to ignore him," came a soft voice in the direction of the porch. "He misses my mom."

There was so much longing in the words that my breath caught for a moment in my throat. I turned to see a child in cut-off jeans and a faded yellow shirt standing on the porch. Her likeness to Sariah's childhood photographs was noticeable. Her very blue eyes and freckled face was topped by dark hair a shade lighter than her birth mother's was as an adult, though it would probably darken with age. Like me, she was barefoot.

"Hi, Grace," I said. How long she'd been there and how much she'd seen, I could only guess. She seemed tall for her eight years, as tall as the boy, Kylan, at my shop—or maybe I'd misjudged his age.

She blinked. "You know my name?"

I nodded. "I'm a friend of Sariah Barnes. I came to talk to your father and grandmother about her."

"I was supposed to have lessons with Mrs. Barnes on Friday, but she wasn't at the school. And now my grandma says she's missing."

"That's right. I'm trying to find her." I walked to the bottom of the porch stairs.

"I hope she's okay. She's super nice. The nicest of all the teachers. I mean, the grownups cuz she's not really a teacher. Except she's my teacher right now until I catch up." She gave a little shrug. "Maybe I'm always going to be behind." The thin face was too somber for a child her age, as if everything that had happened to her had stolen her belief in anything good.

"You won't," I said, sitting down on the top stair. "But it

doesn't really matter when. Everyone catches up in the end, even if you're like me and learn differently than others. I missed a ton of school growing up, especially after my mother died."

Grace took a step closer, staring down at me intently. "Your mother died?"

"Yes, of breast cancer."

"So did my mom."

"I know. I'm sorry." I hadn't known what kind of cancer exactly, but it didn't really matter in the end.

"Thanks. I'm sorry for you too."

"She was my adoptive mom," I said, because it was something else I had in common with the girl, and I wanted her to know.

Grace's brow drew tight. "One of my friends said I shouldn't care so much since she wasn't my *real* mom."

"Well, that's just silly. Of course she was real. And so was mine."

Grace nodded. "That's what Sariah—Mrs. Barnes—says."

"You call her Sariah?"

"Only when we're alone. I'm supposed to call her Mrs. Barnes at school." Grace's hands went to her little hips. "Anyway, that girl isn't my friend anymore. I told her she was the meanest, rudest girl ever, and I didn't want to talk to her ever again."

I wanted to cheer her courage, but she might need a friend, even one who didn't understand. "She might be sorry now."

"I guess I could try playing with her again. Maybe." She looked toward the street where her dad had disappeared. "She's kind of right, in a way. My dad isn't real. He doesn't even like me."

For a vivid instant, I fought fury at Weston Rodgers for

not being the father she needed. My own father had somehow managed to look past his grief to become everything to the ten-year-old child I had been. Grace deserved much better.

I rose, standing on the dirt landing where our eyes were level. "Well, *I* like you, and so does Sariah Barnes. I think your dad has problems that don't have anything to do with you."

She smiled shyly. "It was cool how you knocked him to the ground."

Okay, so she'd seen at least that much. "He sort of surprised me."

"He thought you were with the cops. Did he do something wrong?"

"I'm not sure yet. But I hear your grandmother takes care of you. Is she home?"

The child's face relaxed. "Grandma's always home. She's in her room right now. She and Daddy had a fight."

"About him leaving?"

Grace nodded. "I'm glad he's gone. He's always mad."

"Is it okay if I talk to your grandmother?"

She nodded. "Maybe." She started for the door, her movements like those of a dancer. No awkwardness there, despite her height.

I went up the stairs and paced on the porch for nearly five minutes until the door opened again and a tiny woman with a ramrod-straight back opened the door. She was dressed in stretch pants and a loose, flowery dress that reached mid-thigh, and she wore tastefully applied makeup on her wrinkled face. Her short white hair was combed and curled slightly under. If she resembled her son, I couldn't see it.

"May I help you?" she asked, her accent ever-so-slightly flavored with a southern drawl.

I nodded. "My name is Autumn Rain. I am helping Manny Barnes with the disappearance of his wife, Sariah Barnes. May I ask you a few questions?"

Her already pale face blanched further. She looked around, her eyes landing on Grace peeking out from behind her, almost as tall as she was. "Sweetheart, I need you to go upstairs to your room for a while. Okay? After, I'll take you to the swimming pool."

Grace gave her a smile. "Really? Thank you, Grandma!" The little girl rose up on her toes to press a kiss on her grandmother's cheek. "I love you."

The old lady caught her in a brief hug. "Love you too, sweetheart." Mrs. Rodgers watched Grace until she disappeared up the stairs to the second level of the house. Only then did she invite me in.

I touched the doorknob and the door itself on the way inside, finding nothing of value. She led the way to the small sitting room that was in the very front of the narrow house. An old loveseat with carved wooden legs was the focal point there, next to a real-wood fireplace whose brick floor was stained with soot but swept clean. The room smelled like dust, though the coffee table and the pictures on the wall were clean. The thin throw carpet that covered most of the wood floor was worn through in places, and I could see glimpses of varnished wood underneath.

She sat stiffly on one end of the loveseat, barely taking up half the cushion. She patted the other cushion, and I sat next to her. "This is about my son, isn't it?" she said.

I nodded. "I tried to talk to him before he left. Why was he in such a hurry?"

Tears welled in her eyes, making her irises look like brown

stones under water. But her back remained perfectly straight. "Because of what happened with Mrs. Barnes last week. When we heard she was missing, he said the police would be coming for him. I told him that was ridiculous. He should never have assumed she was going to fall into his arms like those hussies at the bars he goes to. She isn't that kind of person."

"He told you what happened?"

She lifted her hand as if to push the idea aside. "No. He was picking up Grace, and she saw it all." She shook her head. "Imagine causing a problem with the only person she's opened up to since her mother's death—and right in front of her. It made me so mad when I heard."

"Did you confront him about it?"

"Only yesterday when we heard Mrs. Barnes was missing. I told him I knew and asked him if he'd done something to her. He denied it, but today when that receptionist from the school called, he got all frantic and packed a bag and left. He didn't even say goodbye to Grace."

"Do you think he's capable of hurting Sariah Barnes?"

Her voice quavered as she said, "I don't know."

"Where was he Thursday night?"

The old woman's calm evaporated. Her shoulders slumped, and she clasped her hands to her face and began weeping. "I don't know that either. The good Lord help me, I just don't know."

She looked frail and so desperately sad that I reached out and laid a hand on her shoulder. There was a faint streak of blood on my pointer finger, blood from my wound, hopefully dry enough that it shouldn't stain her blouse. I searched for something to say, but in the end, like with Sariah's mother, there was nothing I could say that would help her.

When the flow of tears subsided, I pulled back my hand. "How did Grace become involved with Mrs. Barnes?"

The old lady blinked as if she'd been expecting more questions about her son, and I did have more, but they could wait. "She, uh, she called me in January after she started working there. Right before Patricia died. She said she would be willing to work with Grace, and I was grateful. I don't know all that new stuff they teach kids these days."

"And Grace likes her?"

"Grace *loves* her." There was a catch in her voice. "Without Mrs. Barnes, I think Grace would have taken her mother's death much harder."

"How often do they meet?"

"It was most days after school during the year, and every day now during Mrs. Barnes's lunch break. It's very kind of her, spending all that time. Grace is almost a year behind. Patricia didn't make her go to school much that last year. She wanted time with her. To record videos and make memories."

"They lived here?"

"Yeah. When she was diagnosed two years ago, I bought this house. I thought my son would spend more time with his family if he didn't have so far to travel." Her tone hinted that it didn't quite work out that way.

"It was a good idea."

She nodded. "I've been able to give Grace stability. I'm seventy-eight, and my health isn't great, but I plan to hang on for as long as possible. I only wish . . ." She stopped talking, and a fat tear rolled down her withered cheek.

"How did they come to adopt Grace?"

Her watery eyes lifted, scanning the room as if making sure they were alone. "When Weston and Patricia learned he couldn't father a child, Patricia wanted to have a sperm donor. Weston wouldn't agree. He didn't want some other man's child growing inside his wife." Her southern accent was slightly stronger now. "I tried to explain that it wouldn't be that way, but he wouldn't listen. After four years, he did agree to adoption, though. Guess he thought they'd be even that way. They weren't. Patricia loved Grace from the moment they put that baby in her arms, and she was a good, good mother. The best. But Weston, he never bonded with her. It was like she was a daily reminder of his infertility."

I knew what she wasn't saying—that her son hadn't liked being a father.

"How did your son feel about Grace working with Mrs. Barnes?"

Mrs. Rodgers sniffed. "Oh, he didn't care. He kept saying it was close enough that Grace could walk, and that pleased him, but Mrs. Barnes wouldn't hear of it. She made sure Grace always had a ride to and from school, and even during the summer. I agreed. She's only just finished second grade. When he wasn't traveling, Weston would sometimes take her during his lunch hour when I was feeling too poorly to walk with her." She rubbed her hands on her stretch pants, her eyes clouded with memories, and sighed. "I don't know why that boy had to go and mess things up. Mrs. Barnes is the best thing that happened to Grace since Patricia." That started a new wave of tears.

"I guess you and Patricia were close?"

"Oh, yes. Patricia's mother lived in England, and she died shortly after they adopted Grace. Patricia was always the daughter I never had."

I pondered what to say next. Mrs. Rodgers might not have the information I needed, but I had to try. Even if it meant spilling Sariah's secret. "Did you ever wonder why Mrs. Barnes took such an interest in Grace?"

"I believe it was because of Patricia's cancer. She's helped so much. Making sure Grace has her hair combed and the right clothes. She never even asks me for money to pay for anything she buys. Which is good. I'm in debt up to my ears for this house."

That didn't tell me if Weston had known Sariah's identity or not. "What about your son. Did he talk to Mrs. Barnes about Grace?"

"He said she couldn't have kids and that she was living her dream of being a mother through Grace and the other kids at the school. It didn't bother him, but he tried to use that against her. She's just too pretty for her own good."

"Then you've met her personally?"

"Of course!" Mrs. Rodgers met my gaze. "As if I'd let Grace spend so much time with just anyone. All the teachers and employees at the school also have background checks, you know."

"Look," I said, reaching for my bag to retrieve the photos. "Did Mrs. Barnes ever talk to you about Grace's birth mother?"

"No." She peered over at the photographs. "Why do you have pictures of my granddaughter?"

I handed them over. I'd grown up knowing I was adopted, that my adoptive parents had been planning to help my mother keep me instead, but she'd died. I believed the truth could now help lead me to Sariah.

Mrs. Rodgers began thumbing through the photographs, shaking her head. "These are Grace, unless—"

"The two baby pictures are Grace. The others are Sariah Barnes."

A little burst of air came from the old woman's chest, sounding like a mixture of relief and resignation. "Of course."

"You knew?"

She shook her head. "But when I saw them together that first day after the Christmas break, they looked so much alike, that my heart kind of . . . you know, jumped. I brushed it off at the time. Patricia had gone into the hospital by then, and I knew we had only days before she'd be gone. Both Grace and I needed Mrs. Barnes—or someone like her—so badly. Then after Patricia died . . ." She trailed off, one finger touching the photograph of a young Sariah. "She looks just like Grace, down to the exact shade of hair."

"She does," I said, wondering if I had made things worse.

Mrs. Rodgers put a hand to her pale cheek with a little slap, as though checking to make sure she was awake. "How did she find us? Aren't there laws against this? She has no rights here."

"No, of course not. And I don't think that was her point. When Sariah finally realized she couldn't have more biological children, she started thinking about the past and wanted to know what happened. She wanted to make sure the baby she gave up was happy and well cared for. So she hired someone to make sure. I talked to the private investigator today, and that was supposed to be the end of it." I waited for a heartbeat before adding, "But then she learned about the cancer."

"Right." Mrs. Rodgers's mouth pursed. "I do understand her motivation. But after all these months—why hasn't she said anything?"

"I don't know. Like you said, she has no rights here. But if she approached your son and said something . . . could he have been willing to make sure she didn't try to get Grace back?"

Mrs. Rodgers considered that a moment. "I'd like to say

no, but he can be vindictive at times. If she threatened to press charges about the groping last week unless he gave her more time with Grace, he might have . . ." She heaved a sigh. "He might have done something."

So it hadn't been just an attempted kiss. No wonder Sariah had slapped him. "Okay," I said. "The police will have to ask him questions. In the meantime, can I look around to see if I can find anything connected to Sariah?"

The old woman didn't reply for a moment, but then her shoulders straightened, and she resumed her original stiff posture. She handed me the photographs. "Not without a warrant. He may be a lousy father, but he's all Grace's got. He's all I've got."

"What if Sariah Barnes is still alive?" I asked. "What if something here can lead me to her?"

She shook her head. "I'm his mother. I have to protect him."

"You have to protect Grace too." I slipped my hands into my pocket and pulled out the knife, still wrapped in tissue. "I told you I tried to talk to your son. This was his response." I placed it in her hands.

She stared at it, her face flushing. "No," she whispered. "No. Please go now, or I'll be the one calling the police."

I came to my feet, pulling out a card. "Okay, then. Please let me know if you change your mind, and I'll be sure to let the detectives know they'll need a warrant." I let irritation show in my voice at this because Weston Rodgers was exactly the kind of man who might have decided to teach Sariah a lesson, and the delay in getting a warrant might be fatal.

Mrs. Rodgers didn't reply but hustled me through the house and out the door, shutting it in my face. I was going down the steps to my car, trying to decide what I should do next when a flurry of texts came in. All three were from Peirce, and I paused to read them.

Are you okay? I'll get someone looking for him, said the first one.

The second was more urgent. *You better get to Manny's now. We found her bike. That's all I have time to say. Hurry.*

And the third. *You are okay, right? Please let me know.*

I texted back. *I'm okay. On my way there now.*

My phone was still in my hand when soft footsteps came to my ears. I whirled, keeping one hand up and the other ready to reach for my gun in case Weston Rodgers had come back. Instead, it was Grace.

"Wait," she called. "Will this help?" She rushed down the stairs. On her outstretched hand, she held a mobile phone. "It's his. He was hurrying too much to get it from the charger."

"Why are you giving it to me?"

"Because I snuck down the stairs and heard what you said to my grandma just before she made you leave. Maybe he made calls to Mrs. Barnes."

"Thank you." I reached for a tissue and wrapped the phone before placing it in my bag. Besides reading the imprints, which I would do as soon as I arrived at Manny's, I personally couldn't do anything with it, but maybe I knew someone who could.

Grace's blue eyes welled with tears. "Please find her. She's my best friend." Her gaze dropped to the sidewalk. "I mean, since my mom . . ." She didn't finish the sentence. She didn't need to.

Chapter 13

Even from two blocks away I could smell the smoke. When I arrived at Manny's, the road in front of the house was lined with two fire trucks and two police cars. Definitely not good. No wonder Manny hadn't answered my call, and this must have been why Detective Howard had rushed away from the school.

I'd have a thing or two to say to him about that.

As I parked, one of the fire trucks pulled away. I could see people inside the house through the open door, so though the house was still smoking, the damage obviously wasn't extensive. Neighbors from up and down the street were milling about in the street, talking excitedly.

Pushing through them, I hurried up the walkway. A police officer I knew only vaguely started to stop me at the door but let me through as he recognized me. I found Peirce, Detective Howard, Manny, and Drum in the kitchen, standing near the sliding glass door that was open to the back yard.

"What happened?" I asked.

For a moment, no one answered. Manny gazed at me with

a broken look, Howard with irritation, and Drum with an angry glare.

"There was a fire in the Barnes's crawlspace under the house," Peirce said, his red hair looking more than ever like fire in the quiet room. "They were able to put it out before it did any damage to the main house, except for one of the bedrooms, but they've found Mrs. Barnes's bike inside the crawlspace."

"Pieces of it, you mean," Manny shot. "Her perfect bike." He stumbled to a chair and sank into it. "She loved it so much."

"They think he did it." Drum growled. "And used the fire to cover it up." He glared at Howard. "No freakin' way. You got this all wrong. Manny would never, ever hurt Sariah."

Ignoring the outburst, Howard said, "That's not the only evidence they found."

"What else?" I demanded.

Howard met my gaze. "Some clothes and personal items that may have belonged to Sariah Barnes. We believe the fire was set to eliminate evidence—and it may have succeeded."

He was probably right. I hadn't found anything that obliterated imprints on objects, though they faded with time. Burning by fire might do the job.

"It wasn't me," Manny said, popping up from his chair with a sudden burst of energy. "Why would I hide her bike?"

Detective Howard rounded on him. "To make us think she left you. What did you do with her?"

His sureness ignited my fury, but it was to Manny I spoke. "I know you didn't do this, and I will find out who did with or without Detective Howard's help. In the meantime, don't say another word." To Howard, I added, "Are you going to arrest him? Because if not, he'll be leaving with me now."

"Oh, I'm going to arrest him." Howard tossed a pair of handcuffs to Peirce. "Especially if he's done talking."

"He's done talking," Drum said. "We'll get you an attorney. Don't worry, buddy."

Manny turned to him, eyes leaking. "Life's not worth living without Sariah. I can't do this."

"You can and you will," Drum insisted. "You have to be strong for her."

It might have seemed cliché, but Manny nodded and straightened his shoulders. "For her." He held out his hands, and Peirce clamped on the cuffs, his freckled face pale and maybe a tad resentful.

"I'll wait outside in the car with him," Peirce told Howard. "Let me know if you need me."

"I'll call the others," Drum said, following them from the kitchen. "Don't worry. We've got your back."

I waited until they left the house before facing Howard. "You've got the wrong man. Sariah Barnes is the birth mother of Weston Rodgers' adopted daughter. He was given a heads up by that receptionist we talked to today and was prepared to run when I showed up. He attacked me with a knife when I tried to stop him."

"Birth mother?" Howard said. "Then maybe that fight they had in the parking lot wasn't about romance."

"It definitely wasn't romance, at least not on her part. And the child was a witness. And for the record, I'm filing charges, so you have to find him."

Howard's full lips pursed. "I'll put someone on it. But finding this bike pretty much wraps it up as far as I'm concerned. I knew it was strange none of the neighbor heard Mr. Barnes leave on her Harley."

"Bikes come and go here all the time," I said. "I doubt the neighbors would have registered the sound as unusual even if she had left. You could at least see if there's any evidence on Weston Rodgers's phone."

Howard nearly gaped. "You took his phone?"

"No. His daughter gave it to me and asked me to look inside it. I was going to pass it along to the private detective Sariah used, but you might as well do the legwork."

I reached into my bag, purposely allowing a finger to touch the phone. No way was I allowing it out of my possession without reading it.

My heart beat heavily in my chest. The police were at the school. They must know about the phone calls. I had to get out now.

That was from today and was similar to one of the imprints he'd left on the knife, but what followed was far more interesting.

Pick up. Pick up. Why won't that woman answer? I have to see her again. I have to convince her to give me another chance. I need her cell phone number. This calling the school isn't working.

A click and she was on the phone. "Stop calling me," she said, her voice low and angry, "or I will press charges for sexual assault. I mean it. And if you don't allow your daughter to continue her lessons, I'll still file. Don't ever call here again. I'll arrange with your mother to get Grace a ride to school. You don't need to bother." She hung up.

I gripped the phone, cursing and raging. I felt as impotent as I had each month Patricia couldn't get pregnant.

That had been from Wednesday a week earlier, after the incident at the school.

But it wasn't the only call. Rodgers had called the school three or four times a day for weeks before that, sometimes talking to Sariah on one excuse or another, and other times hanging up when the other receptionist had answered.

He'd been stalking her.

A firm hand on my arm tugged my finger from the phone. Howard was glaring at me again. "The phone?" he asked.

I carefully pulled it out, using the tissue to prevent the imprints from replaying. "He called the school repeatedly," I said. "He was stalking Sariah."

"If we do find anything, it'll probably be inadmissible since you got it from his kid without a warrant."

I lifted my chin to gaze directly into the tall man's eyes. "See, detective, that's the difference between us. As long as it helps us find Sariah, I don't care."

"Okay, then. I'll have it looked at and bring him in for questioning."

Silence fell between us until I asked, "How do you know Manny put the bike in the crawlspace? Or that he's trying to destroy evidence?"

Howard lifted his hands, palms up. "He's a mechanic. If he didn't dismantle that bike and put it in there, who else could have?"

"Someone trying to frame him," I retorted. "Everything you have is circumstantial evidence, especially without a body."

"I will find her body," Howard said.

"Can I at least touch the bike parts? I only need a tiny spot."

He gave a flourishing wave. "Be my guest. It was in the worst of the fire. No way we'll lift any prints. But you'll have to wait for the CSI team to clear it."

"I promised Sariah's daughter I'd find who did this, and I intend to do just that." I'd taken a step toward the glass doors where I'd glimpsed pieces of blackened motorcycle on the back lawn when his voice stopped me.

"For what it's worth, I want to believe him. But I have to follow the evidence."

"I *am* evidence," I shot before turning my back on him.

Outside, two suited but helmetless firemen were surveying the objects they'd rescued from the crawlspace, their faces streaked with ashes.

"I think it's safe for us to turn it over to the police as soon as the arson investigator signs off on it," one of them was saying. "No doubt about it being arson, though."

"That's my take."

"Any sign of a break-in?" I asked. If someone had pried the entrance to the crawlspace open with a crowbar or left the side gate open, maybe I could push Howard toward thinking someone else besides Manny might be responsible.

The men turned to me, surprise in their eyes. "Yes," said the first man. "Apparently, the police put a lock on the crawlspace entrance yesterday. I guess so no one would tamper with anything that might be inside before they had time to search it today. But the lock is missing now. Whoever did this probably cut it and took it with them."

"Neighborhood hoodlums," the other grumbled.

From their conversation, they either didn't buy into Detective Howard's pet theory of Manny being responsible, or Howard hadn't enlightened them.

I passed the burned clothing, the strap of a purse, and a pair of shoes, all so destroyed they were barely recognizable. I bent for a closer look.

"You can't touch anything," one of the firemen said. "We only hauled this stuff out because the detective thinks it might be related to his missing person's case."

Howard had followed me outside and now loomed above us all, his black skin glistening under the hot sun. Ignoring him, I held my hand over the objects and wasn't surprised when not even a tingle registered on my senses. The clothing might still contain DNA evidence, but if there had ever been any imprints on them, they were ashes now. Next to the clothing lay scorched boards and pieces of vinyl fencing that had apparently been stored beneath the house. Nothing strong emitted from them.

The bike pieces, still radiating heat, came next.

"Those got way too hot to have fingerprints," the second firefighter said. "Maybe even still too hot to touch."

Aware of Howard's intent gaze, I ran my hands close to them without touching. Nothing jumped out at me, so maybe the surface that held the imprints, just like fingerprints, had been burned off. Except imprints were generally more durable than fingerprints, and not even strong cleansers could remove them. Maybe I just needed another part.

"Are there handlebars?" I asked. That would be the most likely to have strong imprints.

"Over there, between the engine and the tank," said the second firefighter. "Twisted mess. There was gas in the tank, and that's what blew the hole into the room above."

I hurried past the other bits and pieces. The handlebars were still recognizable as belonging to a motorcycle, but only just. The rubber was completely missing from the blackened and twisted metal. No imprints, not even faint ones, radiated out at me when I held my hand near. The gas tank gave off such an intense heat that I wouldn't have been able to touch it, but there was no tingling there either.

How hot would something have to be to remove imprints? I wondered. Depending upon how hot it had to be, it might work for objects with negative imprints that I could clean up to sell in my store. If so, that meant no more passing up good profit. And if extreme heat eliminated imprints, maybe it was the clothes dryer and not so much the washing and losing lint that faded imprints on clothing.

Straightening, I studied the objects again. Something felt off about the whole situation. I believed Manny was innocent, but hiding the bike had been a good way to deflect the police investigation. Officers would naturally assume she was on the bike somewhere, that maybe she'd run away. Torching the crawlspace, however, had only brought down more notice on Manny, even if the flames had destroyed important evidence.

"You need anything else?" The first fireman asked me.

I shook my head. "There much damage to the house?"

"Only the master bedroom in the back. The rest of the crawl-space should probably be inspected and maybe a few supports replaced, but for the most part, it's just that one section." He waved a hand in the direction of Manny and Sariah's bedroom. "Poor guy. First his wife takes off, and now this."

I had to agree.

Could Weston Rodgers be responsible for the fire? Could he have been that angry at Sariah for her threats? If he'd set the blaze, it would be one more reason for him to duck questioning.

"Thank you," I told the men and began picking my way carefully through the debris, this time avoiding Detective Howard by walking around the side of the house near the damaged bedroom.

Out in the front, Drum was on the phone, pacing by the unmarked police car where Manny was seated, the door open.

Peirce was standing nearby talking to a neighbor. Eyes turned in my direction.

"We're going to stage a protest at the police station," Drum told me, his good-looking face flushed. For an instant, I saw the pimple-faced teenager he'd been. "I've alerted everyone," he continued. "We know Manny had nothing to do with it. Are you with us?"

"Yes, of course." To Peirce, I called, "Can I talk to Manny for a moment?"

"Go ahead," he said.

"Thanks." I gave a pointed glance at Drum, and Peirce understood immediately.

"Hey, Mr. Drummond," Peirce said to him. "Can you please go over this timeline with me? You say you were here until ten last night, right? Then you came back this morning. Why?"

"Manny texted me after he called the fire department," Drum said. "I was at my dealership and came right over."

Whatever else they said was lost to me, as I squatted down next to the police cruiser in front of where Manny sat facing the door, his feet half out of the car. "I'm not going to lie to you," I said. "This looks really bad."

He sighed. Sweat beaded on his forehead and dripped down the sides of his hairline. "It's like a nightmare that won't let me wake up."

Unfortunately, it was about to get worse. I had to tell him about Grace because now that I'd given that weapon to Detective Howard, I didn't trust him not to use it to hurt Manny further. Besides, I was here under Manny's request, and I believed in him, which meant I worked for and reported to him.

"What do you know about Sariah's past?" I asked. "I mean before you met."

He shrugged. "I know her dad died when she was young and that she lived in Washington for a while. I know she earned a college degree, unlike me." He grimaced. "I'm just a grease monkey compared to her." He struggled to maintain control. "But I always tried to make her happy."

"I think you did a good job. But I found out today that she was hiding something."

He swallowed noisily, his eyes begging me to go on.

I pulled on my thin gloves and rifled in my bag for the two photos of Grace as a newborn and extended them to his cuffed hands. "That time she was in Washington? She had a baby and placed her for adoption."

He glanced at the photos but didn't take them. "I seen them before, or at least one of them. Right after we moved here three years ago. They were in a box of things. Mementos. Inside the pages of a Bible that I assumed belonged to her family. I don't know what happened to it."

"You didn't ask about the photo?"

His eyes dropped to his lap. "No. But she has stretchmarks on her stomach, and I asked her about them once. She got all weepy and didn't want to talk about it. So I didn't bring it up again."

"Not ever?"

His chin lifted, and his reddened eyes met mine. "She never tortured me about my past, and I don't want to be that kind of guy. She was either with me or not. I think she chose me."

"I think so too."

"Then what does it matter? I love Sariah with my whole heart. I'll do anything to make her happy. I don't care about her past. Whatever happened, she did what she had to. That's all anyone can do."

"It matters because last year she hired a private investigator to find her daughter. That's what the money I asked about was for. She ended up paying him three thousand in all."

Manny's brow creased. "Must have been after we decided to stop trying to have a baby. But we've been talking about adoption." He let a few seconds of silence pass and then, "Did she find her?"

"Yes. Her name is Grace. And it probably would have ended there if things had been okay." Quickly, I outlined the rest of what I knew, and Manny listened with growing fury. But it wasn't directed at his wife.

"You think this Rodgers guy set the fire?" He motioned to the house. "You think he did something to Sariah?"

"I don't know that yet. Everyone seems to think he's capable of violence, but I don't know if he knew Sariah is Grace's birth mother, and even if he did, he doesn't seem to care enough about Grace to do anything that would risk his own future."

Manny's fists clenched. "Why didn't Sariah tell me? She think I was going to leave her for wanting to know that her daughter was okay? I'd never do that. That poor kid."

"Maybe she'd been hiding for so long that she didn't know how to start talking."

Manny twisted toward the front of the car and leaned back in the seat, his face pointing toward the ceiling. "Sariah has an independent streak, that's for sure." His Adam's apple moved as he swallowed several times. "I should have kept asking."

"Look, I asked you once before if there was anyone in your biker group she wasn't comfortable with. Did she ever complain about anyone?"

"I don't remember her saying anything." He frowned. "But maybe I wasn't listening. The only thing I remember is how lately, she sometimes wouldn't want to go out with Brynn and Travis because they always talk about their children. It made her sad."

Angry voices pulled me from the conversation, which I didn't really resent because my hurt side was furious at the squatting position.

"He's under arrest," Detective Howard growled. "Of course you don't let him talk to her or anyone alone."

"Never mind," I said, holding up my hands in mock defeat as I came to my feet and backed up. "I'm finished."

"His attorney will spring him soon enough." Drum hurried over, coming around the open door. "You hear that, buddy? Don't tell these idiots anything. Not a single word."

Manny nodded gratefully and squared his shoulders. "Thanks, Drum."

Detective Howard slammed the door between the men, while Peirce hurried around to the passenger-side door. Howard remained near the car, talking to new arrivals from the crime scene investigations team.

Drum approached the section of grass by the sidewalk where I stood, his eyes dropping to the tips of my toes that were just visible in the grass. "Kind of hard to ride without shoes," he said with a smile.

"A little," I agreed. "But it's as freeing as going without a helmet, you know."

His grin widened. "I do, but it's a sure way to end up dead."

"You have a point."

"Well, I'd better get to the station to meet the others. I'd offer you a ride, but I'm picking up someone."

"Thanks anyway." It would have been nice to touch his jacket if he opted to put it on over his T-shirt before taking off on his bike, but I was just as glad not to have to go with him. "I'll see you there."

I waited until he was gone to approach a knot of neighbors, who had retreated to the lawn in front of the house across the street. I recognized the nosy Fran among them, the woman who'd imprinted on the glass of water I'd requested. It was time I talked to her about the imprint.

"What's going on?" Fran asked as I approached her. "Are they arresting Manny? Or is he in protective custody?"

"Did someone try to burn down his house?" someone else asked.

"I don't have any answers right now," I said. "Sariah is still missing, and that's my priority." A little lower, I said to Fran, "Could I talk to you alone for a few minutes?"

She nodded, and we walked off a short way from the others. "Last night when I was here," I said, "I had the feeling you weren't saying everything. Was it because of the guy I was with?"

"Well," she began reluctantly.

"I don't know him at all," I hurried to add, "We were paired up to deliver flyers."

"In that case, yes, it was because of him. Or partly." Her face turned up and down the street as if searching for Drum.

"He left," I told her.

"Well, what I wanted to say was sometimes he'd come over before Manny was home from work. Now, I love Sariah. She is a very sweet woman, but in my opinion, she shouldn't allow another man, not even a good friend, into the house when her husband isn't home. It's not seemly." Fran sniffed. "But she's a grown woman and doesn't ask my advice." Her tone hinted that things might have gone better for Sariah if she had listened more to Fran.

"How often are these visits?"

Fran shrugged. "Maybe once a week or so. The past two times I saw them, though, they stayed out on the porch. It's still weird."

Being engaged and having a best friend who was dating someone else, I didn't really agree, but Fran was right that it could be opening the door to something more, depending on the intentions of the people involved.

"What about when Manny was home?"

"Oh, he's over there then too. They go riding together. Sometimes the whole group."

"Is he the only one you've seen over there when Manny isn't home?"

"That's what else I was going to say. I also saw that guy who was here last night at the table handing out flyers, you know, the one with the woman who has all that hair."

She could only be talking about Travis Shepherd, Brynn's husband. I took out my phone and scrolled to Brynn's Facebook page. "This guy?"

She squinted at the page. "That's him."

"When was this?"

"Let's see . . ." Fran scrunched her nose and pursed her lips. "It was a week ago on Tuesday. I had gone out for mail at about three-thirty or so, and then I watered my roses. That's when he came. I water them every Tuesday, Thursday, and Saturday, you see. It takes me twenty minutes to soak them all, and I weed a bit while I wait. Anyway, he hung out in front of the house until Sariah got home. From work, I guess. They went inside, and after a while, he came out and got on his bike and left. When I looked out the window a while later, she was sitting on her porch with her hands in her lap, staring straight forward at nothing. I never saw her like that before."

A week ago on Tuesday at four-fifteen had been when Sariah had left the upset imprint on the watering can. That meant Sariah had been afraid of Travis. Unless he hadn't been her only visitor that day. "So you went inside after he left?"

"Yes. One of my shows was on."

"Could she have had another visitor?"

Again the pursing of her lips. "I suppose, but it'd have to be quick. I wasn't watching TV all that long."

"When you looked out the window, did she seem afraid?"

"No, just sad." Fran sighed. "I wish I'd been a better neighbor. I should have gone over there. It's obvious to me now that something wasn't right. I wish I'd at least told Sariah how lovely her flowers were."

I hoped she'd get her chance.

If I was going to the biker rally at the police station, it was time to head home and change clothes. I might see Shannon there, and he wouldn't miss the bit of blood on my pants and blouse, even if Peirce and Howard hadn't seemed to notice. I was also starving.

At my apartment, I stripped and cleaned my wound. It was deeper than I'd thought, stretching as long as my pointer finger, and blood had completely drenched the inner part of the scarf. Drying off the wound as best I could, I squirted Super Glue into the gap and held it tightly. When it was good and sealed, I rubbed a comfrey salve around the wound and took a handful of herbal supplements to attack the problem from the inside. I finished with a large bandage.

Determined to question Drum and the other bikers again, I pulled on my leather pants and a fresh green T-shirt. I was contemplating the jacket when my phone rang. It was Shannon.

"Hey," I said. "What's up?"

"We've cleared the ring for you to touch. There were no prints or DNA on it. Can you come down?"

"I was heading there anyway. The bikers are going to protest Manny's arrest."

"I heard about that. Sorry. Howard says he's following the evidence."

I rolled my eyes. I'd heard that already from the man himself. "Then he should follow the guy who attacked me with a knife today," I retorted.

"Knife?" Shannon's voice had become tense, but I didn't feel like talking about it. I'm sure he didn't tell me every time someone pulled a knife on him.

"Later," I said. "I'm fine. Did you find out whose ring it was?"

"The owner of the jewelry store said that generally there are fewer than half a dozen rings the same size with the same birthstone, but they updated to a new program fifteen years ago and didn't input that information. They do still have the hard copy information, and they're willing to turn over everything from that year, but there's a good chance it may not be a comprehensive list, especially if anyone paid cash and bought from the stock on hand. They typically have one or two rings on hand from each of the popular sizes, and they change out the stone as needed. Paige is bringing over the files now, but anything you can do to narrow the field will help. The faster we find this guy, the better. Before he takes someone else."

"I'll be there as soon as I eat something." It was barely after one, but I felt ravenous. Dodging a knife apparently made my habitual hunger even worse.

"I can order in, if you're interested."

"Lunch on the police bureau? Hey, I'm there. Just don't take it out of my consultant fee." A good meal would eat half the minimum fee they paid me.

His laugh was tighter than normal, which told me he was still upset about the knife comment. Either that, or he'd learned something about the deaths that made him worry about what might be imprinted on the ring. "I never do."

"One more thing before I hang up," I said. "Does Paige have any news on the boy?" It was eating at me, how I'd let him walk out of the store without checking the pencil.

Shannon was silent a moment. "I'm sorry about this kid, I really am, but we've been up to our necks with these murders. The moment I can, I'll carve out time to find him. Right now my priority has to be to stop this guy."

"I know," I said. "I'll see you in fifteen minutes."

Chapter 14

I was hurrying out to Jake's bike, dressed once more in my vintage leathers, when my phone rang again. This time it was Elliot Stone.

"Talk to me," I said.

"I researched the people you gave me. I emailed you the details, but here's the summary. It's a big negative for the Newmans. Lucy and Hutch are barely making payments on their current house. They don't have any other properties. Ditto for Sariah's mother. The other couple, Brynn and Travis Shepherd, have a cabin northeast of Portland in Scappoose. It's a shared five-acre property with his family. Fairly isolated area."

I made a note to see if Peirce and Detective Howard had searched the place already as Elliot continued.

"Manny Barnes is a co-owner of his auto shop, but there isn't much land. Just enough for the building and parking area. They have good reviews, and it always seems busy."

"What about Drum—uh, Owen Drummond?"

"He owns a lot where he sells new and used RVs. Also great reviews and a lot of happy customers. Started out fixing them, and still does some repairs, mostly cosmetic, not engine related. That he contracts out."

"Probably to his good friend Manny."

"Probably," Elliot said. "I did a drive-by. It's a fairly large lot, but RVs take up all of the space. I can't find any other address for him, so my bet is that he lives onsite in one of the RVs."

"What about the others?"

"Nothing notable on Manny's co-workers, and I'm still working on the rest of the list of bikers from your not-likely list. I anticipate that most don't have extra properties lying around, except the one guy who seems to have family with land, but he was so far down on your list that I didn't start there."

"Right." I vaguely remembered talking to a Road Roller who'd been a little more well-dressed than the others and his English more cultured, but he'd also been wearing rings that had told me he knew nothing of Sariah's disappearance. That's why I'd included him in the not-likely list.

"Thanks for the information," I said. "Meanwhile, I've learned there's a good chance Travis Shepherd might have been the man Sariah was afraid of, so maybe dig deeper on him, if you can. And I have another name for you to check out right away: Weston Rodgers."

"Really? Why him?"

"When I went to see him after our meeting, he was adamant enough about not speaking to me that he felt it necessary to pull a knife. I want to know if he has access to a place he could have hidden Sariah."

"You think he's good for it?"

"He called her repeatedly at the school. Maybe he also went to see her at her house. Things might have gotten rough."

"Dead rough?"

"Or hurt bad." I wanted to believe she was still alive. "That's why I need to know if he has property or access to anything at his work."

"You'll need warrants—unless you have good break-in skills."

I sighed. "Maybe I'll just call and ask the people he works for to check their discarded refrigeration units and the like. They won't want to be party to a homicide."

"Right. I'm on it. And I'll dig deeper into Shepherd's family."

I had reached the bike and was anxious to be on my way. "Thanks. I appreciate your help."

"Wait, there's one more thing. I checked with my contact in the school district. She was able to pull a few favors with other districts, so I have a list of Kylans for you from the area, including charter schools. Some you can eliminate for age, I'm guessing. I was surprised at how many kindergarteners and first graders there are with that name. I've emailed you the list. I'm working on pictures. That requires more strings."

"Pictures might save a lot of time," I said. "And this boy is definitely not in kindergarten or first grade. My guess is fourth through sixth."

"There are still private schools," he said. "Getting those records will be tough, if not impossible."

"The family doesn't seem to have much money, so I'm guessing that's out."

"Okay. I'll check in later. Bye." A click sounded in my ear.

The drive to the station was enjoyable. I wasn't hot with the wind ripping at me, and it was nice to clear my head. Of course, I had to cross the Willamette to get to the precinct, and

I could never do that without thinking of Winter and how he'd died. Nearly two years, and sometimes I missed him like it had happened yesterday. He'd be proud of me, I knew, using my gift to help others. Knowing that helped somehow.

Blocks away from the station, I began to see motorcycles parked along the street. A stray biker or two walked with purpose in the same direction I was heading. I left the bike at the first vacant parking space, tucking my helmet into a backpack. My phone buzzed with an unknown number, and I answered it as I walked.

"Hello?"

"Is this Autumn Rain?" came a woman's familiar voice.

"Yes. Who's this?"

"It's Lucy Newman."

Ah, Manny's mother. "Hello, Mrs. Newman. What can I do for you?"

"They've arrested my boy," she blurted. "They're saying he hid Sariah's bike under the house so investigators would think she took off. But he didn't do it! I know he didn't!"

I stopped walking. Was this the break I'd been waiting for? Maybe Lucy had been an involuntary witness to something her husband had done.

"Do you have information for me?" I asked.

"There's something I didn't tell you about when I went over to get the geraniums Sariah gave me."

"The ones you picked up at six or seven without talking to her," I prompted.

"Right. There was something strange about the geranium starts. The pot they were in was knocked over. At the time, I thought it was because she hates me, and she knew I'd come for them even though I said I wouldn't. Now, I'm thinking maybe it was because there was a struggle. But Manny was at work at the time, so it doesn't have anything to do with him."

"And your husband was with you the whole time?" I still didn't trust the man.

"Yes, yes, of course. Oh! If I'd knocked on the door, maybe I could have reported her missing sooner, and Manny wouldn't be arrested."

She'd been there at least two hours before Manny, so she was right, and I couldn't offer her solace. "You should have knocked on the door," I agreed. "And you should definitely tell the police about the flowers." Howard probably wouldn't believe what he'd see as a mother's desperate attempt to save her son, but that wasn't my problem.

"I'll do that right now." She hesitated a moment before adding, "I know you think my husband is involved, but he isn't. He loves me."

"I only know that for whatever reason you weren't nice to Sariah," I said quietly. "I hope you have a chance to make that up to her."

A sniff came from the other end of the line, and I imagined her nostrils flaring. The line went dead.

I hurried the last block to the station, where bikers lined the front of the building, some with signs. Newspaper reporters were speaking into microphones, and I bet the interviews would be appearing on the six o'clock news. I saw Brynn, Drum, and his black-haired girlfriend near the entrance and angled toward them. Brynn's sign was glued to a two-by-two board and read, *Do your job. Find Sariah Barnes. Manny Barnes is innocent!*

"They won't let us see him because we aren't family," Brynn said, her face tight. Today her hair hung in a thick braid down her back. Her face looked puffier with the hair back, and her makeup did little to mask her exhaustion. Was that the cost of a guilty conscience? If the police didn't check out her cabin, I'd go myself. And where was her husband, Travis? He had a lot of explaining to do about his visit to Sariah.

"They did let the lawyer in," Drum said. His pockmarks looked pale under the afternoon sun, not in the least detracting from his good looks. If anything, they added to his ruggedness. Sometime between Manny's arrest and now, he'd put on his Road Roller jacket that masked the inches of belly hanging over his belt.

"Hi," said the woman next to him, thrusting out a hand in my direction. Red stained her high cheekbones. "We haven't had a chance to meet yet. I'm Tina, Drum's girlfriend." Clearly, this tiny woman was marking her territory.

I pulled off my gloves and shook her hand, noting the heavy eyeliner and the small black rings that created flesh tunnels in her stretched earlobes. "Nice to meet you," I said. "Though I wish it were under happier circumstances."

"Yes. Me too." Tina gave me a fake smile as she took a possessive hold on Drum's arm.

"Right now, we're organizing a silent auction to raise money for Manny," Brynn told me. "Because no way can he pay for an attorney."

"Good idea. I can definitely donate items." I paused a minute before asking something that had been on my mind since Manny's house. "How fast do you figure a bike like Sariah's could be disassembled? I mean, enough to get into the crawlspace."

Brynn and Drum exchanged a look. "You'd only have to remove the outer fairing, the handlebars, and maybe the tank to get it in," Brynn said.

"And the two side touring boxes?" I asked. I'd seen them both in the picture and as melted remains in Manny's back yard.

"On her bike, those are easy," Brynn said. She shut her eyes and added more softly, "Were easy, I guess we have to say now since they're ruined."

"How long would that take?"

Brynn looked at Drum, who shrugged. "Depends on how careful you were. And how experienced. I've seen Manny strip a bike in a few hours."

"But Manny wouldn't do that," Brynn protested. "There's no reason."

I nodded. "I know. But someone did."

"Even I could do it," Tina said, obviously not wanting to be left out of the conversation.

"Sure you could, Tiny," Drum said, leaning over to kiss her nose.

At first, I thought I'd heard the name wrong, but Tina punched him. "Don't call me that."

Brynn sighed. "The police think Manny hid it so everyone would think she left him and wouldn't search for her. And then torched it to hide evidence when he knew they were going to look in the crawlspace."

"Right," I agreed. "But it makes more sense to me that whoever really took Sariah hid the bike to make Manny think she'd left. Then they worried about the evidence they might have left."

"Do we even know the bike's hers?" Tina said. "Maybe it was some old one the previous owner junked."

"It was hers." Drum took his arm from her grasp and laid it across her neck. "Manny and I both identified it."

"Such a waste of a beautiful ride," Tina murmured. The others nodded morosely.

I stared out over the sea of bikers. They had confirmed that just about anyone here was capable of disassembling a bike. But as a commercial refrigeration mechanic, Weston Rodgers would know his way around tools too. So he could also be responsible.

Did he have access to a motorcycle? It would be a good question to ask.

Brynn caught sight of someone and waved. "Excuse me a minute. There's Manny's mom. I'd better go talk to her. I don't like the woman, but I'm glad she's here." A sob cracked her voice. "At least he'll have someone."

Drum lifted his free hand and squeezed her shoulder. "Go," he said. "I'll fill Autumn in about the silent auction."

"When is it?" I asked.

"Tomorrow night."

"That's soon."

"Yeah. I thought so, but we need money right away for a retainer's fee. And we'll need more money along the way, so there will be more for those who can't make it to this one."

"Where's the auction tomorrow, and what time?"

He smiled. "That's still up in the air. Brynn's cabin is kind of far, but there's an amphitheater nearby and plenty of room for people to camp. My RV lot is closer, and it has a small indoor showroom. I can move the RVs out. But there's no seating or camping room for those outside of Portland who have to drive for hours to get here. We also might be able to use a local church."

"I'm voting for Brynn's cabin," Tina said, snuggling up to Drum. "We could stay a lot later."

"And it would be easier to sell food and drinks," he agreed.

By drink, I was sure he meant beer, but I only smiled. I'd already kept Shannon waiting too long.

"Brynn will decide soon, so we can send out the address," Drum said. "She's already assigning people to collect auction items. She's good at planning."

"I'll give her a call. I'm going inside now to see if I can learn anything about Manny."

Drum nodded. "That's right, you're family, of a sort."

Of a sort, of a sort. The phrase reverberated through my head as I extracted myself and went into the station. Did that have a second meaning, or did he only doubt that my cousin status would get me very far?

Shannon had an officer waiting for me inside the station, a big, smiling recruit who couldn't take his eyes off my biker jacket. "Detective Martin said you'd be undercover," he said in a low voice that didn't mask his obvious thrill that the biker demonstration was taking place during his shift. "You know, we're going to arrest them soon if they don't leave peaceably. They're scaring regular people from coming inside."

Regular people, of which I knew I wasn't one, given my eccentricities, but he was young and eager, so I didn't bring that up. "I'm sure they are. But it's a peaceful demonstration."

"Without a permit on government property."

"Right." I'd leave it to him to sort out.

"I'll have to check your gun, though. You knew that, right? But I can wait until we're out of sight of these people." He glanced behind him as he motioned me into a room to the right of the metal detectors. "In here."

That taken care of, we entered the recesses of the station. Heads turned as we passed officers in the hallways, especially those who knew me by sight. Some nodded, others simply stared, and I wondered how many sarcastic comments Shannon would have to endure on my behalf. I didn't feel too sorry for him, though. He could hold his own.

The recruit led me to an examination room, where Shannon met us at the door. The young officer gave me another of his happy grins and Shannon a nod before moving back down the hallway.

Inside the room, I set my backpack with my helmet down by the leg of the table before removing my leather jacket and the gloves. Throwing my jacket over the back of a chair, I slid into it, noting that the food had already arrived, which meant Shannon had likely ordered it even before he called me. He knew me too well. It was a good thing, but it felt different from the uneasy truces we'd had in the old fighting days.

"So, what have you learned?" I asked Shannon, more to settle the worry in my stomach than for the information. Reading the items of a murder victim was never pleasant, and I was fully expecting the worst.

"We've identified the first two victims through dental records." Shannon pulled another chair to my side of the table. "The first is Liberty Kingston. Remains show signs of possible strangulation. She's been missing nine years. The last time anyone saw her was at her ten-year high school reunion at Franklin High School."

Franklin, which meant another connection to the ring he'd found on the second body. "You found out all that from bones?"

"Not me, but yeah. The weird thing is that the bag we found her in wasn't sold until nearly two years later."

"You think he kept her alive that long?"

He shrugged. "Or maybe he didn't bury her before then."

"If he moved her later," I said slowly, "her bones might contain an imprint." My breath stopped, and for a terrible moment, I saw only blackness. Then my reflexes kicked in, and I was breathing again as if nothing had happened.

"Yeah." Shannon sounded wary. "But if it were me, I'd have worn gloves."

"Right. I'll do whatever you need me to do. But let's hurry. I still need to find Sariah." And Kylan. I reached for the bag of food, though my appetite had abandoned me, a thing that almost never happened, and removed a gourmet turkey and rye sandwich. There was an organic label which normally would have made me smile. Now I felt nauseated.

Shannon nodded at an unfamiliar officer standing by the door, who disappeared.

The blackness still seemed to hover near me like a cloud waiting to pounce. I unwrapped the sandwich.

"I'm sorry about this," Shannon said in a low voice.

I met his gaze. "It's my job."

"I know."

He kissed me then, long and deep, and the black cloud receded. That was some magic trick. Even my hunger returned.

When he released me, I bit into the softest rye bread this side of the Willamette, and maybe in all of Portland. I might have groaned a little. My stomach certainly did. From his perch against the edge of the table, Shannon smiled.

I finished the first half before slowing down. "What about the second victim?"

"Rose Caldera. She's been missing five years this month. We haven't been able to determine the cause of death from the remains. But she was pregnant when she died."

A brief image of Destiny flashed over my eyes. I swallowed a mouthful of sandwich and put the rest back inside the bag. "Next time remind me to eat before I ask you questions. How far along was she?"

"The medical examiner estimates about six months, but both suffered from malnutrition, so it's hard to be sure."

"Was she pregnant when she went missing?"

"The family has since moved to California, and when local officers asked, they said no way, and certainly she couldn't have been six or seven months along. The family is devout Catholic, and even the suggestion made them extremely upset. At the time, Rose didn't have a boyfriend and had been accepted to a private religious college. She went missing right after her family took a three-week summer vacation together. The mother says Rose had her cycle during that time. So no pregnancy, unless the mother is lying, which we have no reason to believe."

I gnawed on my lower lip, thinking that through. "Then Rose was alive for months after she disappeared. She could have run off with someone, I suppose, but if she was abducted and held prisoner, it would go along with the idea that the first woman didn't die right away."

Shannon nodded grimly. "Agreed. My current theory is that the murderer kept her somewhere and killed her when he found out about the baby. The only good news is that when we do get a suspect, we should be able to match his DNA. We're also looking for connections between the first two victims, but so far, we've come up empty."

"And the third?"

"We don't know."

"Why not?" I would have thought the most recently deceased would be the easiest to identify.

"There's no match to the missing person's database, which might mean she's a runaway who was never reported missing. Her wrists were cut, but definitely not a suicide. She didn't wrap herself in that bag. The medical examiner says she was in her mid-twenties."

"That means they ranged from eighteen to twenty-eight when they first went missing. No connection there."

"None career-wise either. Liberty was an attorney, while the pregnant Rose was planning to become a biologist."

"And the third was a runaway."

"Maybe. We've sent an image mockup of her to all the news outlets. With the other two bodies found, we might get enough press to identify her. We need to find a connection."

"Maybe the connection is that there is no connection."

"Could be, but it's doubtful. He had to choose them somehow, and people are creatures of habit."

My stomach growled, protesting its interrupted meal, but it would have to wait. The officer Shannon had sent away reappeared with a long, narrow box containing four pieces of what looked like arm and leg bones and a ring inside a plastic zip bag. Shannon took the food away without me asking. While he was gone, I withdrew Tawnia's drawing of us from my pocket and removed it from its protective plastic sheath. Love waved through me in a revitalizing rush.

Shannon returned to the room and perched on the edge of the chair next to mine, angled toward me. One elbow lay on the table, the other arm rested on his leg, ready in case I needed him. I held out my hands over the bones.

The Bones—I saw the words in capitals. How sad it was that someone had taken the rest of this woman's life from her, reducing her to bones far before her time. I thought about her parents and loved ones and what they must be going through. Probably something similar to what Manny had endured these past few days.

I became aware of the other officer fiddling with the camera set up in the room. They always recorded the sessions, which was kind of ridiculous as I doubted they'd be admitted as evidence in any courtroom in the US. When he finished, Shannon nodded at him, and he left us alone.

"What was her name again?" I asked.

The set of Shannon's face was grim. "Liberty Kingston."

I felt a wild compulsion to go wherever Liberty's belongings were stored and learn about her before I touched her remains. To touch them without knowing her seemed too personal. Pushing the thoughts aside, I held my hands over the box, anticipating a violent tingling.

There were none. I let my fingers touch the smooth bones themselves.

"I'm sorry," I said, letting out a sigh. "There's nothing." It was more of a letdown than I'd expected.

"He wore gloves."

I nodded. "Probably." Or he hadn't felt anything about disposing of the body. Was that possible?

Shannon swept up the bag with the ring and carefully pushed the box toward the edge of the table where I couldn't see inside anymore. I wasn't queasy at the sight but glad enough to have The Bones away from me.

The door clicked, and Shannon's partner, Paige Duncan, came in, looking as crisp and professional as always with her perfectly ironed, shoulder-length, blond hair and navy suit. She nodded at me before bending to set a huge box of jumbled files by the door.

"Any news on Kylan?" I asked, knowing that Paige was resourceful and perfectly capable of working on her phone in the car as she pursued her other case.

She gave a slight shake of her head, the strands of hair barely moving. "Not in the Portland Public school district, I'm afraid. And the library surveillance shows no strange packages being exchanged, either."

"Thanks for trying."

"There's still a chance to find him in the schools," she said. "Or he could come back to your store for his mother's present."

I nodded, my throat too tight to respond. The poison had been purchased two weeks ago. Was it slow acting? Or had it already been fatal?

Opening the little bag, Shannon poured out the ring on the table in front of me, the ring he'd taken from the clenched fingers of pregnant Rose Caldera, victim number two. It bounced once before settling on its side. It was a typical class ring, big and unwieldy, and more money than they were worth because no one really cared about high school after leaving it.

My fingers weren't close before I felt the tingle of strong imprints. I splayed one hand next to the ring for balance, just in case, then let the tip of my finger fall onto the edge of the silver.

I placed the ring onto my pointer finger, loving the heavy feel of it. So many hopes it had once held for me. Hopes that hadn't come true.

I'll have to give the ring back now, I thought, especially if he asks for it.

Too bad. I still loved what it represented.

Nothing identifying on the thirteen-year-old imprint, but it was achingly sad. The hands I saw belonged to a woman with beautifully rounded fingernails. I waited for more.

Manny finally gave me his ring! That meant he was really mine, and I would finally belong. We'd have a family and do it right. So what if Manny didn't care about college? He was strong and hard-working like his dad, and he could fix any car.

I couldn't wait to tell Shasha and Liberty. And everyone else.

I'm so happy, I thought. This is the best graduation present ever.

Shock rolled over me as the meaning of the imprint hit me, an imprint that had occurred more than nineteen years earlier. The imprint had to be Brynn's, and it made the first imprint, the more recent one, make complete sense.

Another scene followed. *The ring felt big in my hand—and heavy. Tears pricked my eyes.*

"I'm proud of you, son," my father said to me. "You've done a good job so far. Just one more year. You're on the home stretch. I know it won't be easy, but it makes your mother happy, and when you're finished, you can be your own man. It'll be your choice what you do next. I wanted you to have a talisman to help you get through the rest of this last year." His hacking cough nearly blotted out the final words.

"Thanks, Dad. It's really great." I'd wanted one of the rings, mostly because the other players had them, but I'd decided against buying one when I'd seen the price tag.

Dad slapped me on the shoulder. "Now go see if Brynn wants to come fishing with us. We'll make her a fish lover yet."

No doubt about it, this was Manny's ring. That meant not only was he a suspect in his wife's disappearance, but he'd soon be a prime suspect in Shannon's serial murder case. The imprints started to repeat, and I let them play out because something bugged me about the imprints. But what? When they were over, I'd learned nothing more. I lifted my finger.

"What did you see?" Shannon asked.

"There are no imprints from Rose Caldera," I said. "The most recent imprint on it was thirteen years ago when Manny Barnes's ex-wife, Brynn Shepherd, was thinking about giving it back to him after their separation. It's Manny Barnes's ring."

The words took away Manny's last chance of getting out of jail tonight. Or possibly ever.

Chapter 15

Shannon stood and moved to the camera, turning it off. "You know what this means, don't you?"

I nodded. "It means the cases are somehow connected. But it also means Sariah might still be alive, if she's being kept like the others."

"It also means Manny is now a person of interest in the homicides," Paige said.

"He might never have seen the ring again after his divorce." It was a lame attempt at controlling the damage, but I had to try. "Brynn might not have given it back."

"So you're saying his ex-wife did this?" Shannon waved his hands at Liberty Kingston's remains.

"We should at least question her." Paige leaned forward from her standing position on the other side of the table, her hands flat on the surface. This close, I could see the slight sideways tilt of her front tooth in the otherwise perfectly straight white teeth.

"There's more," I said. "Brynn Shepherd had a friend named Liberty. What if it's the same Liberty?" I didn't look at or gesture to the bones, but it felt as if I had because Shannon and Paige both glanced at them.

"Are you suggesting Liberty somehow got the ring from Brynn?" Shannon asked.

I shrugged. "It's possible. And it doesn't necessarily mean Brynn was involved with the murders."

"If Liberty took the ring from Brynn," Paige said, "Rose could have found it if they were kept in the same place."

"Right." I frowned.

"That's a huge stretch." Shannon swept up the ring and put it back inside the bag.

"Then maybe the ring was planted later," I suggested.

"Planted. No." Shannon shook his head and folded his arms stubbornly like in the old days. "We found the bag partially buried, so unless the killer risked going back to put in the ring, that's an awful lot of foresight." His tone and stance sparked a challenge in me, but until I had a logical explanation, I'd let it simmer.

No one spoke for a moment, and it was as if I could feel the nails hammering into poor Manny's coffin. "Paige is right. Ask Brynn what she knows."

Shannon walked over to stand next to my chair. "I want every detail of everything you've learned, beginning with that prick who held the knife on you today. Maybe he went to Franklin too. The ring might mean it all started there."

"Okay," I said. "But I want to see Brynn's questioning."

"I suppose she's here for the protest?" Paige turned toward the door. "If she is, I'll need you to ID her."

I gave her a thin smile. "You can't miss her. She's got great hair. Medium brown. It's in a braid right now, but it's seriously as thick as my arm. Or ask anyone out there who she is. She's been organizing things."

Paige nodded and said to Shannon, "Want her in here?"

"No, take her to interrogation three. That way Autumn can watch the interview without breaking her cover."

"Will do."

I pocketed Tawnia's picture, grabbed my backpack, and started toward the door. Shannon's hand stopped me. "I know I don't have to tell you how dangerous this is. If we're right and the cases are connected, I mean. And your guy is looking guiltier by the minute."

"It's not him," I insisted.

He nodded. "I know because I believe in you. And you know what, that only makes it worse, because whoever did this is still out there."

"I'm undercover," I said. "For all anyone knows, I'm Sariah's cousin." But that wasn't strictly true. I hadn't introduced myself that way to Manny's mother and stepfather, or to Sariah's mother.

"Yeah, but Manny knows, and it wouldn't take much research to blow your cover."

"No one has a reason to."

"The murderer does."

"I'll have my gun." I pointed to my ankle before remembering the officer had checked it for me.

"So do ninety percent of the bikers out there."

"I'll be careful."

"I know. I'm just pointing it out." His hand came up, his finger cupping my chin while his thumb slid over my bottom lip. I could feel the roughness of his skin and the desire in his eyes. I swallowed hard, fighting the urge to kiss him again.

With a regretful smile, his hand left my face, the fingers first running down my cheek in a brief caress. For now, it was enough.

"Tell me what you're thinking," he pressed.

"I guess now my bet is on Travis Shepherd, possibly with his wife. Or Weston Rodgers."

"Who is Weston Rodgers?"

"The guy with the knife," I explained quickly, giving an abbreviated rundown of my encounter with the man. "I have someone researching his worksites now," I added. "A private eye. He's the one Sariah paid to find her daughter. Nice guy. Elliot Stone. He's got a thing for her, so he volunteered."

Shannon cracked a smile at that. "Good, forward me the information. Paige and I will check on it."

"What about Detective Howard?"

"It's my case now." His eyes were genuinely amused. "Oh, Cole will fight it, but the chief will see it's connected, and I'll be given access to all his information, whether he likes it or not. Starting with that phone you gave him."

"He still thinks Manny did it."

"Then we'll prove that he didn't."

And find Sariah, I thought.

Ten minutes later, after waiting for Shannon to confer with Detective Howard and Peirce, I was outside an interrogation room, staring through a one-way window. Brynn was seated at the table facing me, a line of worry gathered between her eyes. Her sign, propped against the wall, slid down and hit the floor with a soft *thwack.*

"What is going on here?" she said, glancing between Shannon and Paige, who sat opposite her. "Why did you bring me here? Do I need a lawyer?"

"If you feel you need one," Shannon said. "But I only have a few questions."

"Who are you anyway?" Brynn glared at him.

"My name is Detective Martin," Shannon said with the too-patient voice that told me he was losing patience. He'd already introduced himself twice, so I didn't blame him. He set the school ring in front of her. "Do you recognize this ring?"

Brynn leaned closer. "Sure. That's Manny's school ring. At least it looks like his. Can I touch it?" At Shannon's nod, she picked it up and slid it on her pointer finger. "Yep, seems like the same size."

"When was the last time you saw it?"

She shrugged. "Years. Since before I met Travis, and we've been married ten years. I used to wear it when I was with Manny, but after we divorced, I gave it back." She paused to remove the ring. "At least, I think I gave it back. I don't actually remember doing so. Maybe he just picked it up one day when he was moving his stuff." She shook her head. "I just don't remember."

"You don't remember giving it back," Shannon said.

"I just said I didn't. Ask Manny. He has a better memory for details. Always did." She took off the ring and laid it on the table before saying, "Does this have something to do with Sariah's disappearance?"

"We think so," Shannon said.

"Do you know anyone named Liberty Kingston?" Paige asked.

Brynn's mouth curved in a real smile. "Sure. She was one of my girlfriends in high school. I haven't seen her since our ten-year high school reunion, though. Maybe we'll catch up again on our twentieth." She laughed. "It's coming up quicker than I want to admit."

"For all of us," Paige agreed.

I knew for a fact that Paige's ten-year high school reunion

wasn't for two more years. Most people thought she was older because she was a detective, but she came from a long-time police family and had put in grueling hours to prove herself.

Shannon withdrew a photo from a file he'd retrieved from his desk on the way here. "Actually, this is Liberty Kingston. And no one had seen her since the night of your ten-year high school reunion. Until yesterday."

Brynn gasped. "What? No! It has to be a mistake." She averted her gaze from the photo, color leaching from her face.

"No mistake," Shannon said.

"W-what happened?"

"She was murdered. Strangled, to be exact, though it's hard to tell after so many years."

"Oh, dear Lord," Brynn prayed, crossing herself. "Poor Liberty. She was always the smartest of all of us. Who would ever have done something like this? Wait. Now that I'm thinking about it, I remember someone calling me and asking if I'd seen her. It was a few weeks after the reunion. I gave them all the contact info I had. I never dreamed . . . Oh, Liberty." Her eyes strayed from the photo and away again.

"Is there any way she could have gotten hold of Manny's ring?" Paige asked, her voice gentle.

"What? Why would she? Manny's just—" She stopped talking, her eyes going to the ring. "No way. No freakin' way. Manny didn't do this. He wouldn't! You couldn't have found this ring on Liberty. She couldn't have had it."

Shannon spun another photo onto the table. "It was actually on a second body we found, a young Hispanic girl who disappeared five years ago when she was eighteen. She was pregnant when she died. These bones are all that's left of her and her child."

Brynn held her hands to her face. "No, no, no. Manny is the gentlest person I know." After several deep breaths, she took her hands from her face. "You have to believe me. When I told him I wanted a divorce, he said he wanted whatever made me happy. He helped me move all the furniture we'd bought together. He never hit me or raised his voice. He didn't do this."

Shannon tossed a third photo onto the others. "Have you seen this woman? She's the third victim."

Brynn started to cringe but stopped as she focused on the picture. I strained to see the new image, only to glimpse black hair framing a pale face. Brynn leaned closer. "She does seem familiar, but I can't place her. She's not anyone I know well. You might ask my husband. He has a knack for faces."

"Is your current husband also a gentleman?" Shannon asked. "Could he have any involvement? Because someone cut this girl's wrists."

Brynn stood so fast her chair went flying backward. "Travis has nothing to do with this. And I'm leaving now. Unless you're going to arrest me. Go ahead, put on the cuffs." She held out her hands with an admirable flare.

"You're free to go," Shannon said. "For now. But we'll be talking to both your husband and Manny about the ring. And don't leave town. I'm sure we'll have more questions."

Brynn stalked to the door, pausing to round on Paige, who'd followed her. "Just because Manny knew Liberty Kingston it doesn't mean he killed her. And you know what, maybe she did steal the ring. Because she was always jealous that I ended up with him. She was all over him at the reunion, but he didn't even notice. He wasn't ready for any new commitments back then. That was before he met Sariah."

"When did he meet Sariah?" Shannon came to his own

feet, taking a step toward her. My heart pounded in my chest because I already knew the answer. Manny had married Sariah seven years ago, which would have been right after Liberty's final burial.

Brynn shrugged. "Today is their seventh anniversary, so I guess that would be two years after the reunion. They married really quick. I was happy for him."

With that, she flounced through the door Paige had opened, and both women disappeared from view. Shannon turned to face the one-way glass. I held my breath. Brynn might have been trying to help Manny, but she'd just hammered one more nail into his proverbial coffin.

"So seven years ago when Liberty died," Shannon said, "Manny met and married Sariah. That's quite a coincidence." He paused before asking quietly, "Did anything happen five years ago in Manny's life?"

I'd been thinking the exact same thing, but there wasn't anything for the past five years, Manny and Sariah had been focused on trying to have a baby.

A baby.

Rose Caldera had been pregnant when she died.

It had to be another coincidence. Unrelated, just this once. I pushed the intercom button. "I can ask Manny. If they'll let me see him."

He nodded and was about to say something more when Detective Howard came into the interrogation room, clearing the doorway with his head by only an inch. "I just got through asking Manny Barnes your questions," Howard said to Shannon without preamble. "He says he did spend time with the first victim at the class reunion, but not alone. And he claims he never saw the ring after the divorce. He also doesn't know Rose Caldera or recognize victim number three." He folded his muscular arms across his wide chest. "I don't believe it. I think he's good for all three murders, and his wife's disappearance as well."

"I don't have enough evidence to charge him."

Howard's face showed no reaction to this, but his voice became brusque. "Maybe not in the murders, but I do have enough to charge him in his wife's disappearance. Locking him up is the only way to keep her alive. If she's still alive."

"And if he's not responsible?"

"Whoever did this had access to their house, their crawl-space, and their jewelry. I don't know many friends who have that kind of access."

Shannon's gaze strayed past him momentarily to the mirror, and I knew he was thinking of my apartment and how all my friends and half my neighbors had complete access. "Different people live differently," he said, "and I'm staking my career on the fact that our perp isn't Manny Barnes. But I need help on this, Cole, and that means I need you to think outside the box."

Detective Howard stared at Shannon, apparently stunned into silence. At last, he nodded. "Okay, I'll play your game, and I'll follow all the leads, including the Weston Rodgers angle. But mark my words, something isn't right with Manny Barnes or someone very close to him." Turning on his heel, he stalked out.

Shannon had just levered a truckload of influence against Detective Howard, and all because he trusted in me. A twinge of worry pinged inside my chest. I'd read the imprints, but maybe I'd forgotten that they were all seen through the imprinter's point-of-view. In that context, Manny could be hiding something.

No. I trusted my gift. I remembered all too vividly Manny's

panic—it was part of why I felt so driven to find Sariah. She meant a lot to me now.

Shannon appeared in the doorway of the observation room, looking pleased with himself. "If your PI gets that info about Weston Rodgers, I'll forward it to Howard. I think he's on board."

"He's not very happy about it."

"He doesn't have to be. Not if we're right."

"Do you have the ring?"

He handed it over. The second it touched my hand, a new imprint came to me.

Poor Manny, he doesn't deserve this. And neither do I. I wish I could tell them all where to go.

Nothing that condemned Brynn or Manny. This was a stressful situation, and naturally she would have imprinted on the ring. But now I knew what had been bothering me the first time I'd touched it. People often imprinted on jewelry, and always on jewelry they wore often. If Rose Caldera had been wearing the ring when she died, she would have left fear, terror, hope, and even the memory of her death imprinted on its surface.

"Rose Caldera didn't leave any imprints on the ring," I said, handing it back to Shannon. "That's impossible. Being kept prisoner, assaulted, and finally murdered would have created a lot of emotion. But there is nothing since Brynn's imprint thirteen years ago, and another just now."

Shannon understood at once what I was saying. "So Rose never touched the ring, at least not in life. Or Liberty. Maybe you're right about it being planted sometime after her death. If it was planted a lot later, that could be why there was no DNA residue. But the site didn't look disturbed."

"Maybe it was weeks or a month ago." Thoughts rushed out at me, clicking into place. "Maybe when the third victim was dumped. Things would have settled with the rains."

"We need to learn the identity of the third victim," Shannon said. "And fast."

Paige's voice called our attention, and we turned to see her in the interrogation room with Travis Shepherd. "Please, sit," she said. "My partner, Detective Martin, will be here soon with a photo we want you to identify."

Shannon gave me a rueful smile and hurried from the room.

Travis showed no recognition of the ring, but when Shannon placed the photo of the third victim in front of him, he nodded. "I've seen her before. She was at the Halloween bonfire at Manny's. At first, I thought she was a neighbor, but she was sitting with some of our bikers, so I guess one of them must have brought her."

"Name?" Paige asked.

Travis shook his head. "Not the faintest idea. They probably didn't even say. There was like sixty people there. Maybe if she'd stayed until the end, when things wound down, but she didn't. It was just the diehards by then."

"And who would those be?"

"Brynn and me, Manny and Sariah, Drum, Jason, Gretchen, John and Ange, and Paul." He shrugged. "I think that's all."

"How late?"

"Two, maybe. Most of the others left before midnight."

Paige and Shannon began asking about Liberty Kingston, who Travis remembered faintly from the reunion, but my thoughts raced on. Manny and those closest to him now had a link to the third victim. Could that mean something *had* happened between Manny, Drum, and Brynn back in high school, something that led to these deaths so many years later? They had all known Liberty and had spent time with the third victim, however briefly.

Or maybe it had something to do with Manny's marriage to Brynn. She told a good story about their separation, but maybe it had been Manny who'd broken up with her instead. There was nothing like a woman scorned and all that. Maybe the past was what was wrong between Brynn and Travis. Travis's visit to Sariah might work into it all somehow.

Then again, October had been when Sariah had received the envelope with the news of her daughter. Had Weston Rodgers become aware that a private eye was stalking him and turned the tables, following him to Sariah's?

Now that three murders were connected to Sariah's disappearance, I didn't think Manny's mother and stepfather were involved. They didn't have space at their house or funds to hold victims for years, though it was theoretically possible.

"Autumn?" I looked up to see Shannon watching me from the doorway of the observation room. His handsome face was drawn as his blue eyes searched mine. "That's two for three," he said. "The third victim was at your biker buddy's house. If someone's framing him, they're going out of their way to make it stick. I have no choice but to get a court order for the records at Manny's shop."

"I figured as much." I was still disappointed.

"The big issue right now is Sariah Barnes. With everything that's going on, the killer may decide to cut his losses."

My gut told me he was right. "Brynn's holding a fundraiser tomorrow night. Maybe I'll find something there."

"I thought tomorrow was your sister's dinner." His cheek

twitched as if he wanted to smile but under the circumstances decided against it. "Much as I'm dreading entertaining her parents, you can't let her down."

At least that meant he was still planning on being there. "Dinner's at five. I should be able to get away by six or six-thirty. Especially if I'm there cooking earlier. Even if I miss the beginning of the auction, I'll be there before the end."

"Okay." He looked pained as he added, "You should also know that the Calderas are driving up from California to claim their daughter's remains. If we turn up another link to Manny, I'm going to have to charge him."

I stifled my frustration. "Do what you have to." I started past him, but his arms went around me, pulling me close.

"Hey," he said, his breath hot in my ear. "I believe you. I'm going to do everything I can on this end. We'll find whoever did this."

I pushed away. I trusted him, but I didn't want to be comforted. I wanted to free Manny and find Sariah before she ended up in a bag like the other victims. "I have to go," I said. "I need to interview more bikers."

He shook his head. "They're mostly gone. Chief Sandton was out there reading them the riot act while we were talking to Brynn. The chief's a spitfire when she wants to be."

"It's better to track them down at their homes anyway." I held up my hands. "More imprints."

"Right. I'll walk you out."

By the time we retrieved my gun and reached the lobby, no bikers were in sight. Not a single sign or slip of paper had been left behind to mark their protest. Shannon's gaze was on me, and I turned to meet his eyes, even knowing they would cause my knees to puddle. For a moment, I was sad I had pushed him away, because now, with the eyes of the receptionist and several milling officers, it was far too late.

I took his hand. "Am I going to see you later?"

"I might be working late. I'll call."

The bike was further away than I remembered, or maybe all the running around and imprints were making me tired. I fished my gloves from my pocket. My stomach was grumbling again, but I needed to check in at the store, so I'd go there.

As I reached the bike, I glimpsed a gray truck. *Weston Rodgers?* I wondered, though he should have been long gone and not stalking the police department. Unless he'd heard about the protest and had come to learn more.

Jamming my head into the helmet, I jumped on the bike and darted into an opening in traffic, squealing the tires without intending to. Two teenage boys on the sidewalk stopped and stared. So did two police officers. I let off the gas until I turned the corner where I'd seen the truck disappear.

There it was ahead. Four cars in front of me. I pushed harder on the gas, passing the first car. After another block and too much traffic, I was once again four cars back.

Finally, the opposite lane opened up, and I started to pass. One, two, three cars. But I wouldn't be able to take the last one this time. I braked to get back into the right lane.

Nothing happened. I pushed on the brake again.

The motorcycle didn't slow.

Cars jammed the lane on my right, with no openings, and a blue truck straight in front of me, bearing down fast. If I didn't do something quick, I was going to crash.

Chapter 16

Hitting the truck straight on wasn't an option, and I didn't want to risk getting squished between vehicles in this narrow street if I tried to straddle the road. Desperately. I downshifted. The engine screamed in protest.

It wouldn't be enough.

I pulled to the left and let the truck roar by. But that put me in line to hit a parked car, so I weaved into the left lane again—directly into the path of a yellow Volkswagen Bug.

I swerved left again. A parked black sedan reared up in front of me, and for a moment, I thought I was going over the hood. I yanked the bike into the lane again, my leg brushing against the bumper of the sedan.

My heart raced. The engine screamed. I heard shouts, but I didn't dare look away from the road. I saw only cars as I calculated the space I'd need to weave through them.

I should have hugged Shannon, I thought. *And why had I left him hanging about a stupid date?* If I ended up dead, I'd regret those things the most.

And not finding Sariah.

After dodging another car, I calculated that my speed was low enough. Taking a breath, I darted back into the right lane of traffic, in front of the second car I'd passed. The driver laid on the horn, breaking with a loud screech. Only then did I dare to breathe.

Too soon. The cars ahead of me braked for a traffic light. I jerked to the right, zooming past them next to the parked cars. I swerved to miss a pedestrian. A car nearly hit me as I entered the intersection. More horns and screeching brakes. But by this time, I was slowing. I reached the other side and killed the engine. I rolled to a stop.

Shaking, I stood there, amazed that I was still in one piece. And Jake's bike as well. The light turned, and I looked up in time to see the bed of the gray truck passing me. A few more cars passed, and then a blue car swerved over and parked in front of me. A young man jumped out.

"You okay?" He wore cut-off jeans, a tank top, and was barely out of his teens.

"The brakes went out," I managed.

"Could tell something was wrong. I nearly clipped you when you pulled in front of me back there. I thought you were drunk at first, but that was some fancy driving."

The cop that pulled up next didn't share the same opinion. I was sure I'd end up with a ticket, but the teen hurried to explain. "It wasn't her fault. Her brakes quit. She's lucky she's not a red and black squished mess on the road back there."

"You're a witness?" The officer pulled out a sheet of paper from a folding clipboard and passed it to the teen. "I'll need your information."

"Sheez, really, man? Not cool."

As the teen retreated to fill out the paper, the officer squatted by the motorcycle, running his hand along the brake line. He held up the end. "This has been cut. You'd better file a report."

"Cut?" It took a while for the information to set in. Someone had tried, if not to kill me, then to at least take me out of commission for a while.

The officer stood and met my gaze. He did a doubletake. "Oh, hey, I know you. Didn't recognize you in those clothes and with, uh, shoes. But your eyes . . . You're that psychic lady who helps Detective Martin with his cases. I hear congratulations are in order." He smiled, clearly pleased with himself.

"Thanks. Are there cameras on these roads?"

"Yeah."

"Can you pull the feed? I'm helping with the Sariah Barnes case, and I was following a suspect when this happened. I need to know who did this. Sooner rather than later."

"I can request it. But they'll jump faster if Detective Martin does it."

I gave a silent groan. "Okay, can you write it up?"

"I need to know where the bike was parked. But be warned, there may not be a good angle."

"At least it's a shot. For now, I'd better get out of everyone's way." With a little maneuvering, I moved the bike closer to the curb, right behind the teen's parked car. The boy was giving his paper to the officer.

It was time to call Jake.

Jake brought his truck and a ramp he used when taking the bike across the country, and together we pushed the bike into the bed.

"It'll take me an hour or two to replace it, tops," he said

as he tied it down. Like me, he was a long-time proponent of doing everything he could on his own to save cash.

"I'll pay for the parts, of course," I said. "This was on me."

"Not your fault. But I don't understand how this could happen. I replaced this line a few months back. Wait a minute." He squatted in the bed of the truck and studied the brake line. His locs hid his expression, but I could see the sudden tenseness in his body.

I didn't have to wait long. He let out a soft curse and stood up swiftly. "This was cut, wasn't it?"

"The officer who is pulling the surveillance feed seems to think so."

"I thought you were working a missing person's case."

"Guess I'm getting closer to finding her." No way would I tell him about my wild zigzagging between cars or the homicides that were now connected to Sariah's disappearance. Jake was my best friend, but he was also overprotective.

"I see." His hands clenched and unclenched at his side, and his muscles rippled under his tight T-shirt.

Dropping my gaze before I spilled the whole story and dragged him into it, I studied a stain of brake fluid on the road until he gave a snort, jumped down from the bed, and pulled me into a hug. He smelled of herbs and cologne.

"I don't care about the bike. Well, I do, but it's nothing compared to you being safe."

"I know. You're a good friend."

He let me go, smiling. "This is nothing compared to all the scratches we put on it during that cult case. Remember that?"

Oh, I did. It had been my second big case, and after it we'd begun dating. Shannon had been there too, and he almost hadn't made it in time to save my life. "The fire wasn't my fault."

"I know." He released me and finished securing the line. "We'd better get back to our shops. It's insanely busy this afternoon."

Tawnia hadn't called me for help, but I took Jake at his word. Going to the store made sense. I needed more food and time to decide what to do next.

Jake opened the passenger door for me. "I can probably fix the bike tonight if you still need it."

"You don't have to do that."

"Hey, if it keeps you under the radar with the bikers, I'm happy to." He grinned and added, "But if the line was cut, the undercover thing might not be working. Did you ever think of that?"

I looked back at the intersection. Had I seen Weston Rodgers's truck? Portland was full of gray trucks, so probably not. Also, I hadn't been driving the bike when I'd gone to see him, and with so many motorcycles around the station, how would he know it was my ride? Unless he'd followed me or had been watching earlier when I parked.

I didn't think anyone except maybe Brynn and her husband, who'd been the first to arrive last night at the flyer event, would even recognize my bike.

Where had Travis been when I arrived?

"It might not have been the bikers," I said. "I saw two teens. They might have done it as a prank."

"Some prank," Jake muttered.

I couldn't shake the feeling that it was something more. If one of my suspects had stalked me, Jake was right, and my cover was blown. I'd need to be more careful.

Business was brisk, and Tawnia was ready for a break when I arrived. "Good," she said. "Destiny is fussy. I'm going to feed her and put her down for a nap in the back. You want something?"

"No, I'm good. In a little while, I'll grab a snack."

My sister was the only person I knew whose appetite rivaled mine, but we had vastly different ideas on the definition of food. Her meals were normally frozen and microwaved, while I preferred fresh and organic. I had pressed upon her the need for fresh food while she was nursing Destiny, though, and she normally kept a supply in my small fridge in the back room. We had an array of baby food too, since Destiny had recently started solids, but for the most part, she still only wanted her mother's milk.

It was near four now, and the rush was dying down, so I told Jazzy she could leave at her usual time. For the next hour, I helped customers until it utterly died at five. I went in the back room to find Tawnia asleep, curled up in my ratty easy chair with Destiny cuddled in her lap. Most likely, she hadn't slept at all last night, worrying about her parents' visit.

For a moment, I simply watched them sleeping, the connection between the three of us as thick as Brynn Shepherd's braid. I'd have given up anything in my life to have been raised with my sister, except my relationship with Winter and Summer Rain. Tawnia felt the same about her parents, despite their strictness. We'd been polar opposites growing up, and yet both of us had been driven from place to place to find each other. She'd moved from job to job, state to state, and I'd gone searching for antiques, always visiting the cities Tawnia lived in but never meeting her until finally she'd come to Portland two years ago. The thirty-two years apart still hurt, and yet we couldn't change it—and wouldn't if we could.

Now there was Destiny, who was biologically my child as well since Tawnia and I were identical twins, and Shannon and the possibility of family. Was I afraid?

I knew the answer.

Tawnia cracked an eye and yawned. "Oh, did I conk out? Do you need me?"

"No. You already took care of the brunt of it. No one ever comes after five anyway, unless it's from Jake's store. Sorry about being gone so long this afternoon."

"It wasn't too bad over on our side," she said. "And it kept my mind off stuff." She shifted the baby's weight, glancing at the port-a-crib we'd set up in the corner. "So, what now?"

I'd been debating that very thing. I could start on the list of children Elliot had sent me, which would take a lot of time, or I could visit more bikers and Manny's co-workers. But with the evidence pointing at Brynn, Travis, Drum, or Weston Rodgers, would I be wasting my time vetting the rest of Manny's list?

"Well," I said to Tawnia, "I was wondering if you could draw me a picture of Kylan, the boy who came in yesterday."

Tawnia frowned. "I've tried. I drew a ton of images— people talking, an old lady crying, and even a purse-snatcher, which I did send to Shannon, by the way. But no little boy. I had to stop."

"No, I mean like a police sketch. I think it would help me to have a picture of him."

"Definitely, it would," she agreed. "I posted about him and called around asking, but no one has heard of him. I bet an image would really get the shares going online." She hesitated.

"Maybe if I saw him, I could, you know, *see* him that other way. But I'm not a sketch artist. I don't know how that even works."

I shrugged. "We can try. Right?"

"Okay, then. Let's do it."

She leaned forward, and I helped her out of the chair. Not an easy feat as it seemed intent on keeping her. Once she was on her feet, Tawnia laid Destiny in the crib with a practiced hand, patting her gently until she settled. We both held our breaths, but the baby stayed sleeping. Putting her down without waking her was getting easier these days but was still a miracle this far into her sleep cycle.

Tawnia pulled her sketchbook from her large purse and found a new page. "Okay, then. You said about ten and blond, right? Eyes? Face shape?"

"Brown eyes, round face, though not chubby round. Just young round, and his hair was parted in the middle. I think he had a dimple here." I touched my right cheek. "And his eyes looked big."

"Kids' eyes almost always look big," Tawnia said. "That's because people's eyes are mostly as wide as they will ever be when they're three months old. They do grow front to back until about age eight, and they move further apart as the skull and brain grow, but the front to back isn't noticeable. Anyway, it's natural that his eyes would look large. What about his body shape?"

"He's not thin at all, but not overweight. And he's rather pretty for a boy. Takes after his mom, I guess."

She fell silently to work, and I knew it would be a while before she was finished enough for me to give more input. I busied myself gathering items I could take to Brynn's silent auction. I had some vintage auto signs and license plate holders

I thought bikers would appreciate. Some of the signs even had the Harley-Davidson logo.

When my phone buzzed, I was sure it was Shannon, and I answered without looking at the caller ID. "Hello?"

"Hi," came a small voice. "This is Grace Rodgers. Have you found Mrs. Barnes yet? Is she okay?"

My heart sank. "Does your grandmother know you're calling?"

"No. She's making dinner. I took the card you gave her." The child's voice became even softer. "The police were here. They're looking for my daddy. Did he do something to Mrs. Barnes?"

"I don't know where Mrs. Barnes is yet," I said. "Do you know where your dad is?"

"Grandma told the police he went to Arizona. Some place that starts with an F. I think. He goes there a lot to work. Do you think Mrs. Barnes is with him?"

I sure hoped not. "I don't know, but I promise you I'm doing everything I can." It felt like a lie. I should be out at Drum's RV place, visiting Brynn's house, or knocking on other bikers' doors. Shannon would eventually follow his leads there, but what if he was too late? "When I find her, I'll let you know."

"Please hurry." She hung up, sounding lost and alone, empty.

I understood only too well. She'd lost her mother, and now her birth mother as well, although she didn't know Sariah as such. I had to do more.

"Look at this," Tawnia said when I returned to the back room. "Does it look like him?"

I stared at the drawing. She'd sketched a cute boy, but it wasn't Kylan. "Not really."

"Then tell me what to fix."

"The face shape is right, but the eyes should be rounder." I watched as she fixed one of the eyes. "No, that's too round. Maybe make it not quite so round, but bigger. Plus, his ears stuck out a little, and there was something about his chin. I'm not sure what. And that forehead is too wide, the hair too long."

She fiddled with it as I watched, and slowly, with added input from me, Kylan's face came to life on the page.

I studied it. "That's really close." I hadn't remembered the cleft in his chin until she drew it in. "But make his face a little thinner now. And the hair longer again. Just a tiny bit. And more . . . fluffy, maybe?"

And there he was. At least from what I remembered. "That's him," I said.

Tawnia smiled. "Okay, then. I'm heading home now. I'll post it everywhere and ask people to share."

"Thanks." I took a picture with my phone and forwarded it to Elliot, Shannon, and Paige. "Could you give me a ride to my apartment? Jake's bike had an issue, and I need to pick up my car."

"Sure, but you're coming by later to prep the meat for tomorrow, right?"

I'd forgotten, but it would be better tonight. "Yes. I might come late, though. I have a few people to visit." I couldn't get Grace's soft plea from my head. *Please hurry,* she'd said. I would try.

"Come as late as you want." She rose and gave me a hug.

"What's that for?"

"You look like you lost your best friend."

"I guess I was thinking about our birth mother. And Summer." And Grace losing both her mothers.

"Oh. Well, in that case . . ." She gave me a tighter hug. Exactly what I needed.

We left together, locking the outer door to my shop and putting up the sign directing customers to enter through Jake's. Tawnia dropped me off at my apartment, where I filled the back seat of my car with antiques destined for Brynn's auction.

Afterward, I drove to Brynn's two-story house located in a newer section of houses ten miles north of where Manny lived, but only Travis answered the door.

"Brynn's not here," he said, a touch of annoyance in his voice. He kept the door open only halfway, a clear indication that he didn't plan to invite me in. "She's picking up auction items from Manny's mother. And trying to order food to resell tomorrow night."

"I have some items too. That's why I stopped by." Behind him, somewhere in the background, I could hear young voices squabbling over something I couldn't make out.

He gazed past me to where my car was parked. "It would help if you could bring your stuff directly to the auction tomorrow. A lot of people are coming in, not just Road Rollers, but other various biker clubs from Oregon and Washington, and our cars are already going to be full of supplies."

"Okay, yeah, sure. That's great about the other clubs."

He nodded. "Brynn's been busy."

I hoped the support would hold once news of the serial murders hit the airways. "Has Brynn decided where the auction is going to be?"

"At my family's cabin." He raised his voice to cover the squabbling of his kids. "You need the address?"

"No, I've got it."

"Well, the event is all over Facebook, so you can look

there for the latest info. We made a page called Help Manny Find Sariah." A crash in the background made us both start. He turned and yelled, "You guys better not have broken that chair!" To me, he added, "I gotta go stop the boys from killing each other. Is there anything else?"

"Well . . ." I so didn't want to ask him, but I couldn't let it go. "One of Sariah's neighbors told me you went to see her on Tuesday a week ago. Do you remember that?"

His eyes narrowed. Brown eyes, I noticed for the first time. "No," he said. "I mean, yes, I went over there, but I don't remember the day."

"The neighbor said she seemed sad afterward. Can you tell me what you talked about?"

"It has nothing to do with her going missing."

"Please. I'm just trying to rule everything out."

The muscles in his jaw, noticeable even under his trim beard, flexed as if he was going to refuse. "Okay, then," he said after a long, tense moment. "I asked her if she'd watch the boys next month so I can take Brynn somewhere special for her birthday. Brynn's sister lives too far away, and the last time the boys were with her, my youngest ended up having stitches. Besides, Sariah and Manny are the boys' godparents."

"You didn't text her?"

He snorted. "You don't ask someone to watch two boys for three days in a text." A shout from somewhere inside the house punctuated his words, and Travis glanced behind him. "Boys!" he yelled.

Was he telling the truth? He appeared to be avoiding my gaze. "Did she seem sad?"

He looked at me then, his eyes pinning mine with determination. "Talking about the boys always makes Sariah sad these days. That's another reason I went, to make sure it would really be okay because they are a handful. Now, if you'll excuse me, I'd better go see what my kids broke."

"Okay. Thanks."

He shut the door, and I reached out to touch the knob. Nothing but a faint imprint from an installer thinking about getting home to his new bride. I wished I could touch the other side because I was almost certain Travis was lying.

As I walked back to the car, I eyed the house. It looked similar to my sister's two-story starter home. Not exactly a place they could be carrying out kidnappings and murders, not without alerting their two boys. But if they were having the auction at their cabin, Sariah must not be there either. Of course, I'd found a woman once in a buried root cellar near a house, so maybe it wasn't totally crazy to think something there or in this house might lead me to Sariah.

I pulled out my phone and texted Shannon. *Are you planning to search the Shepherds' house? If so, I want in.* I didn't expect a reply right away, but I wanted to make sure he didn't go without me.

Next, I headed over to Drum's RV lot. When I arrived, his showroom was locked up tight, and the interior lights were out. The sign said they had closed at five. That didn't stop me from wandering the grounds and examining the rows of motorized motorhomes and towable fifth wheel campers. If Drum didn't have living quarters inside his showroom, he had a lot of RVs to choose from. It occurred to me that one of the units would be the perfect place to hold a prisoner, and I began knocking and trying each door, and then listening.

The RVs were all locked, of course, so I touched the doors and exterior handle and switches that people might regularly use. Myriads of images rippled through my mind, imprints left by past owners, and even some from a few people who were searching for a new RV. Nothing out of the ordinary. I experienced frustration, contentment, happiness, peace, anger. There was an imprint of a woman planning to leave her husband, and one of a man thinking about buying a new RV to get away from his in-laws who lived with him. Nothing about Sariah, and nothing that indicated Drum might live in any of the units.

Of course, Sariah wouldn't be here, even if Drum wasn't what he represented. He would no sooner involve his place of work than Brynn would her children. Sighing in frustration, I went to the last unit.

"May I help you?" came a voice I recognized.

I whirled to see Drum behind me. Though I hadn't heard the sound of a bike, he was dressed in riding gloves and a leather jacket, and had a helmet tucked under his arm.

"Oh, there you are. I've been looking for you." I laughed, hoping to sound normal.

His square face was tense. "Well, you've found me. What's up?"

"I have some vintage items I wanted to donate to the auction, but I have a prior commitment, and I'll be late. Could you take the items for me? I've got them priced with their actual value."

His expression relaxed. "Sure. I'm glad to. We may need a lot more money than we initially thought."

"What do you mean?"

He sighed. "You haven't heard? The five o'clock news had a story about three murders. They say they have a person of interest under arrest at the station, and that there might be a fourth victim. They showed Sariah's picture." He frowned. "Don't you see? They think it's Manny."

"He'd never hurt her."

"I know. It's crazy . . . but . . ."

"But what?" I stared at him.

He gazed past his stomach to the boots on his feet. "Well," he said reluctantly, "I talked to Brynn, and we all knew the first victim, Manny, Brynn, and I. Manny even danced with her the night of our reunion. Brynn says they found a ring that might be Manny's on the second victim, and the third woman came to the Halloween bonfire at their house."

I stifled irritation. Brynn had a big mouth, but I guess these two went way back.

Too far back? Maybe what had come between Brynn and Travis had more to do with Drum than her past with Manny.

"He didn't do it," I insisted.

"I know." Drum lifted his eyes to meet mine. "And for sure, Sariah wasn't involved. She didn't even know Liberty."

"Right," I said. "Liberty went missing before Sariah met Manny. I don't think anyone believes she has anything to do with it." Sariah had been pregnant and having a baby at the time Liberty might have been held prisoner. Did Drum know about that?

"I need some clarification on something else," I added. "The other day, you told me Sariah was better than Manny."

Drum's mouth turned down, and he looked miserable. "I didn't mean it like that exactly, but yeah, she is high class, at least more than Manny. He's always been a grease monkey."

"Do you know anything about Sariah before he met her?"

"Just that she finished her degree in Washington and likes children. It's a shame Manny can't give her that."

"He's the problem?"

Drum shrugged. "From what I understand, it's both of them. Her body rejects pregnancies, but they would have a lot better chance of it happening if he didn't have issues too." He hesitated before adding, "That's why I thought at first she left. Maybe for that guy who came to see her at the Halloween bonfire."

"That man was helping Sariah with something, that's all," I told him. For a moment, I debated revealing Elliot's identity, but that was Manny's prerogative. If he wanted Drum to know about Grace, he'd tell him.

Drum stared at me, as though I'd dropped a cup of hot coffee in his lap. "Really? Could it be connected to her disappearance?"

"I think so. But you can't still think she left, not after finding her bike."

"No, right. I meant before."

Something was off about the statement, and I was suddenly very aware that we were alone in the lot. Bad idea when I still didn't know if he was somehow involved. I eased backward to put some space between us.

"I'd better get going," I said.

"What about the auction items?"

"This way." I led him to my car, and we'd started unloading when Brynn pulled up in a white minivan, parking in the empty stall next to me.

"Oh, good, you're here," she said to Drum, slamming her door. "I've got a load of things for you to haul up to my cabin tomorrow."

"The beer?" he asked.

Her smile didn't quite reach her eyes. She looked like she'd been crying. "That's being delivered here in the morning at ten. I hope you can fit it all in your truck."

"It'll fit, and all the other stuff as well."

"You need help?" I asked.

Drum nodded, pulling a pair of work gloves from the pocket of his leather jacket. "Let's just put it all here in front of the doors. I'll bring the truck around later. I have stuff inside I need to unload first. Plus, I'm taking Tina out later tonight."

Brynn forced a smile. "I'm really glad things are working out for you two."

"I think she's the one," he said, grinning. "Maybe."

"Good." Brynn turned and dragged a blue plastic tote from the back of her minivan.

I helped stack more blue totes and cardboard boxes in front of the showroom door, touching the back of Brynn's car and the outside doors to see if there were any important imprints. There weren't. By the time we finished, I was lagging, and Brynn was crying openly.

"What's wrong?" Drum asked. I wanted to know too.

She set down her last box and covered her face with her hands for a few moments, breathing deeply. "I don't even know if any of this is going to help. At the last house, when I was picking up stuff, I saw the Caldera family on the news—that's the family of the murder victim that was found with Manny's ring. They looked familiar, somehow. You know, from the time I was helping Manny with the books at the shop."

"I didn't know you helped him," I said.

"I was pregnant with my second, and I couldn't exactly go out and get a job with a two-year-old tagging along. So I worked for him, doing his books and ordering stuff." She looked at Drum. "Like I did for you, only more in-depth." She paused before rushing on. "Manny never changed the log-in to his server, so I went and checked on my phone. The Calderas went to Manny for repairs before their trip. They were going across the country and needed a new water pump. At least that's what my notes say. That makes a connection to all the murders, even if the ring isn't Manny's."

"No," Drum said, breath whooshing out of him as if the failure was his personally.

"Once the police find out, I think they'll charge him, and there's nothing we can do to help. Nothing."

"You're doing what you can, Brynn," Drum said.

"It won't be enough. Raising money to find Sariah is one thing, but who's going to help him once he's accused of three murders?"

"I'll help." Drum's eyes were red now and beginning to water. "Just tell me what to do. You know Manny's my best friend. I'd do anything for him."

She rounded on him, her face flushing. "Would you really? Because you haven't been there for him these past few years. Cutting out on trips, and all those snide comments about him not being a real man because they can't have a baby. I'll have you know that hurt him."

"He knows I didn't mean anything by it." Drum folded his arms over his stomach.

"I get it. You were just trying to get him back because everyone always liked him. Because you were always second to him. But that was your vision, not his or anyone else's. He's always had your back."

"We're like brothers," Drum said with a huff. "I've always had his back too."

"And you think offering to get Sariah pregnant is what a brother would do?"

"What about your offer to carry their child?"

She flushed. "At least it would be *their* child."

"Would it?" he retorted. "Maybe it would be yours, not hers. I think you don't want to let Manny go."

"Of all the stupid things to say!" Brynn glared at him, hands on her hips.

"Ask Travis if it's stupid."

I was learning more about the two of them right now than I had in the past two days, but this was getting out of hand. "This isn't helping Manny," I broke in. "He didn't do it. Not any of it." I felt like one of the scratched vintage records at my shop, the needle of the conversation always coming back to this point. "Let the police do their investigation. You both have an auction to put on."

And I have to find whoever did it, I thought. *Even if it's one of you.*

Drum's mouth pursed tightly for a moment before he nodded. "She's right. But I think Brynn's also right to be worried. That's a lot of coincidences."

I knew that—and the murders seemed to be coincidences that Weston Rodgers had nothing to do with. Which meant he might not have anything to do with Sariah's disappearance. Unless . . . was it possible that the three murders were still their own case?

Either way, the murders had to have been committed by someone who had it out for Manny or by someone who at least ran in the same circles. I would find out who was responsible, even if I had to touch every belonging of every single person who knew Manny and Sariah. Starting now, before Shannon found out that Manny had interacted with the Caldera family.

I left Drum and Brynn with barely a goodbye and started on Manny's list, not bothering to call ahead. I had visited all of his co-workers and four of the Road Rollers on Manny's list when Shannon called. Normally, I was excited to hear from him, but tonight my stomach sank clear past my knees.

Please let him just be calling to say he can come over to catch a late movie on TV.

"Hey," I said.

"I have bad news, and I want you to be the first to know." He hesitated only a second before plunging on. "We've found a second connection to Rose Caldera, and we're charging Manny with the three murders. Right now, it's all circumstantial evidence, but if we prove the ring is his, and you and I know it is, it might be enough for a trial. Meanwhile, the fire at his house and the Caldera connection is enough for us to hold him on his wife's disappearance as well. Chief Sandton won't let him go, regardless of what I say. The way it looks right now, everyone here believes he's guilty."

Chapter 17

arly the next morning, Shannon texted me to turn on the news. The third victim had been identified as twenty-five-year-old Nora Miller. Her mother, who lived in Indiana, had occasionally heard from her daughter but hadn't seen her since she was seventeen. Nora had been living with friends in the Portland area until October or November of the previous year when she disappeared, taking a suitcase with her. Friends assumed she'd returned home.

No mention of Manny's name, for which I was grateful.

I was about to turn off the television when an older woman with a round, age-spotted face and bleary eyes appeared on the screen. "I got a card at Christmas last year," she said. "Like always. After that, she must have gotten in with the wrong people." The woman dissolved in tears and the camera cut away.

Only a Christmas card? My heart hurt for both Nora and her mother.

But if she'd gone missing in October or November and had presumably been held prisoner by the killer, how could she have sent a card? It was one more thing that didn't fit.

As I ate breakfast, a text came in from Elliot. *Travis Shepherd has additional property in Washington, undeveloped. Sending details now.*

I forwarded it to Shannon, trusting him to deal with it. For now, I had other plans.

I spent the next six hours cruising all over Portland, visiting the rest of the Road Rollers on Manny's list. Jake had delivered his repaired bike to my apartment before his Sunday jaunt to Washington with his girlfriend, and the bike gave me an opening in the conversations. Every single biker invited me to see and touch their own bikes. Then they asked me into their homes for a drink. I learned nothing new, except that a few of the men were secretly attracted to Sariah, and that they all really liked Manny, who was their unspoken leader, though Brynn seemed to be the official planner for the Road Rollers.

In between biker visits, I'd also visited five families on the revised list of children that Elliot had sent me last night. The revised list contained the addresses and pictures of children with blond hair that sort of resembled Tawnia's drawing, but because children changed so much during a school year, I planned to visit all of the original list as well. So far, I'd come up empty.

Disheartened and somewhat exhausted, I pulled up at Tawnia's at three on Jake's bike and let myself into her garage. There, I changed from my biker pants and moccasins to a floor-length summer dress that hid my bare toes. Whipping out a mirror from my backpack, I used a cotton swab to remove some of my makeup and then combed out the gel from the top of my hair. I didn't really look that much different, but I was less noticeable, and that's what I wanted to be at this dinner with Tawnia's adoptive parents.

Stashing my backpack in the garage, I knocked on the back

door before letting myself into the kitchen. Tawnia jumped up from the table where she was drawing.

"There you are. I was beginning to wonder."

"Of course, I'm here."

She gazed at me critically. "Did you even sleep last night?"

I hadn't, so I ignored the question. "I'm fine. Any word on Kylan?"

"No, sorry. Not yet. But I had a hundred shares on Facebook."

It was a start, I supposed. "So where are your parents?"

"Bret took them and Destiny on a walk to the park. They wanted to see our neighborhood and spend a little time with the baby. She hasn't really taken to them yet, so we thought maybe the park would help."

"They need to give her time," I said. "They've only seen her twice."

Tawnia sighed. "Which is apparently my fault."

"They still hinting about you moving to Kansas?"

"Not so far. I think they finally realized we're here to stay." Her hand touched mine, and something deep passed between us. "I'd never leave you."

I nodded. "I know." I felt the same. We also couldn't leave our newly-discovered birth father, Cody Beckett.

That reminded me. "So is Cody coming?" I asked.

"He said no, but I'm sure he'll be here." Tawnia smiled. "I think he's curious to meet them."

"Or he just wants to see Destiny." The old guy brought the baby a toy every time he came and played the silliest games with her, as if trying to make up for the fact that he'd been in jail during our beginning years.

We laughed as we began to pull out ingredients. "Go back

to drawing," I told her when I had everything at hand. "This is relaxing for me, and I know how much you hate cooking. What are you working on? The sleep thing?"

"Yes. We're pitching the company at the end of the week. I think we'll win the bid. We've come up with some impressive advertising strategies. I'm trying to finalize a few drawings before the presentation. Just having a little trouble with one of my female characters looking drugged rather than peacefully asleep."

"That is a problem." It was still a little early to cook the tenderloin, which didn't need more than forty minutes, even at the size she'd bought, so I started the prep for the vegetables. I'd make baby potatoes as well as rice, just because she had the potatoes.

"How's your case going?" she asked after a few moments of silence.

I turned off the water and faced her. "They arrested my client. I need to find something to help him before he ends up in prison."

"You will. Let's talk it through."

"Let's not," I said. "I'm tired of thinking about it." I knew who my suspects were, but until I found imprints implicating them, my hands were tied, and Shannon's hands were tied as well.

"Okay. Sometimes that's the best way to let your brain work—to give it a break." She snapped her drawing pad closed. "That's what I'm going to do with this horrid drawing."

I hoped she was right. "I'll have to leave early tonight to work on the case. You don't mind, do you?"

"Are you kidding? You pull off this meal, and my parents will be so impressed, they won't care that the waffles I give them tomorrow are frozen. Besides, I want you to find that poor woman. Now tell me what to do so I can say I helped."

At five the table was set, all the food was ready, and Tawnia's husband Bret was slicing the tenderloin. His engineering mindset made him the perfect candidate for getting the pieces absolutely perfect. Tawnia joked that his ability to cut meat and bread was one of the reasons her parents liked him so much.

Tawnia's parents, Sherman and Ellen McKnight, were in the small adjoining family room playing with Destiny, along with Cody Beckett, our birth father. The McKnights were well-to-do and looked the part, from Sherman's tailored shirt and dress pants to Ellen's designer dress. Sherman was an economist who worked for a large company, while his wife managed their house and charity events. Sherman was starting to lose his dark hair, and his tall figure had the beginnings of a paunch. He'd had laser treatments to remove all traces of a beard. Ellen's figure was perfectly trim, and every blond hair was in place. She had a standing monthly appointment at the salon and dragged her husband to the gym at least three times a week. They made a striking and impressive couple who looked younger than their sixty-eight years.

Cody was even more well-to-do, but he looked rather like a homeless person and far older than his sixty-seven years. His copious white hair usually poked out at awkward directions from his head. He was as slender as I was, but his bones were larger and protruding, which gave him a slightly emaciated look. Tawnia worried that he wasn't getting enough to eat, which might be true because he often lost himself in his work. His profession was creating sculptures from giant tree trunks and junk, each of which sold for more money than I made in five years. At least today he'd made an effort to wear jeans without holes or stains, and his hair had been slicked down with some kind of grease. From the smell, I suspected olive oil. He was wearing the same kind of thin cotton gloves I'd taken to wearing when I didn't want to read imprints.

While baby Destiny was leery of the McKnights, she adored Cody, which completed some kind of strange circle. He'd gone to prison for a murder he hadn't committed to pay for a sin he had enacted upon our mother. Until I'd appeared on his doorstep, searching for a missing child, he hadn't known Tawnia and I existed. I'd finally forgiven him—and not just because he'd risked his life to save mine six months earlier. Truth was, he was gruff and unmannered and downright surly, but he was all I had left in the parent department.

As I set the salad dressing on the table, Ellen asked Cody, "Why do you wear gloves? If you don't mind my asking, of course."

Cody mumbled something about a skin condition and went right on playing with Destiny, who loved the fist-sized zoo animals he'd carved for her.

Tawnia came up to where I stood in the archway that separated the family room from the kitchen, watching the two of them play. "Great," she whispered, "now she's going to want proof that it's not catching."

I laughed. "Probably. Unless you tell them the truth."

"Not today."

No surprise there. "Okay, it's ready, so let's eat."

"Shannon's not here yet."

"Let's be perfectly honest. With a serial killer loose, he may not make it at all. And you deserve to have this meal be perfect."

She leaned the top of her head against mine. "Okay. I'll call everyone into the dining room."

We were at the table and well into serving the brined pork tenderloin when Shannon finally showed up. I ran to open the door for him before Tawnia could volunteer for the job.

He pulled me into his arms in the entryway and kissed me as if I tasted like his favorite pasta. "Well?" I asked him when we came up for air. "What's new?"

"Several things, actually. Using info on that phone you gave us, Peirce found Weston Rodgers—that's why I'm late. Peirce is flying to Flagstaff as we speak to pick him up. The company Rodgers works for did a complete search of their property and didn't turn up anything, but they have a storage facility in Flagstaff that they'll let us search as well. His record with them isn't very good, though. He's been written up a dozen times for being late on a job. The manager said they'd have fired him already if they had someone else qualified and willing to travel."

"Does Rodgers know Peirce is coming?" I asked, thinking of the gray truck I'd followed outside the police station.

"Since he's in police custody there, I'd say definitely." He glanced past me when a burst of laughter came from the diners. "But we can't find any connections between him and the murder victims, so if he's responsible for Sariah, it's only her. If he'd driven like a maniac to get to Flagstaff, he could have been the one to cut your brake line, but it's a stretch."

"What about the surveillance recordings near the police station?"

Shannon sighed. "It wasn't a good view. I've got a beat officer going door-to-door to see if any of the businesses have their own surveillance cameras that we can review."

"Which means we know exactly nothing more about the cut brakes."

His brow furrowed. "We know someone tried to hurt or at least scare you."

And they succeeded, I thought. "Well, it still could have been those teens. What are you doing next?"

He grinned. "Eating dinner with my beautiful fiancé and her crazy family."

"I meant *after* dinner."

"That's part of what else is new. We found three eyewitnesses that Travis left Manny's Halloween bonfire with Nora, the girl whose name he supposedly doesn't know. It turns out he's from Indiana, where Nora grew up. In fact, his parents still live two blocks away from her old house. And when I called Brynn Shepherd about her husband's property in Washington that your PI uncovered, she knew nothing about it."

I remembered Travis's irritation when I'd been at his house the day before and the feeling that he'd been lying. "Interesting. He didn't mention any of that when you were questioning him yesterday."

"Exactly. The only thing missing is that Travis has no connection to the second victim, Rose Caldera."

"Except that ring," I said. "And they all had access to it, him included."

"Right. With all this, I'm hoping to get a court order to search Brynn and Travis Shepherd's house and cabin, and the Washington property. Paige is tracking down a judge now."

Paige had probably volunteered, but I felt bad that she was likely standing up her doctor boyfriend again. Between both their busy careers, I didn't know when they'd find the time to move to the next step in their relationship.

"What about Owen Drummond?" I asked.

"We don't have enough evidence to request a court order yet. And I can't find a place of residence other than his RV lot."

"I think he lives there."

"Makes sense, even if it's not zoned as residential."

"Would that be enough to get us a court order?"

"Not to search everything—and that's what you'd need. He's not connected to the second victim at all, and no one saw him with the third."

"But he was at that Halloween bonfire."

"Yeah, but it was Travis who left with Nora, so his being there doesn't mean much. On a positive note, any way you look at it, Travis's connection with Nora Miller is good news for Manny."

"Travis works for a department store, right?" I'd contemplated the possibility that Brynn might still be hung up on Manny, but maybe her problem ran in another direction. Maybe she was afraid of her husband.

"He manages a Walgreens."

"Would he have access to drugs?"

Shannon thought about that. "Possibly."

"Drugs would come in handy if you're keeping a woman prisoner."

"Right. I'll put that on my list."

For a moment we stood there, listening to more laughter coming from the other room. Then Shannon asked, "So what's next on *your* agenda tonight?"

A smile tugged at my lips. "To have dinner with my very handsome fiancé."

He kissed me, running his tongue across my lower lip, and making me press against him. "If dinner is anything like this appetizer, he is going to be a very happy man." He pulled back and arched a brow. "And then?"

I grinned. "Okay, okay." Turnabout was fair play. "After dinner I'm still going to Brynn's auction. No court order needed. Now, come on, let's eat." I led him through the kitchen to the minuscule dining room, where Shannon sat between me and Cody.

"I understand you're a homicide detective," Sherman McKnight said after I made the introductions.

"That's right."

"And Tawnia says you're involved with the serial murders that are all over the news," Ellen added. "It must be fascinating."

Shannon chuckled. "It is, but it can also be frustrating, especially when I have a lead I know is real, but I don't have the proof to back it up." His glance at me was pointed, but he knew not to bring up imprints here.

"Well, yes. I can imagine that," Ellen said, delicately slicing off another portion of tenderloin with her knife. "But keeping the city safe . . . it's a brave job."

"We all do our best." Shannon stuffed a forkful of food into his mouth.

The conversation rolled on, with the McKnights full of questions for Shannon and compliments about the dinner. Tawnia gave me credit for the meal, but it was clear Ellen thought her daughter had somehow miraculously learned to cook in the oven instead of a microwave. Between questions that Shannon either answered shortly or deflected, he kept peeking at his phone under the table. I didn't blame him since I was also watching the small wall clock behind Cody.

Cody said nothing during the meal, but he steadily forked

meat into his mouth, eating three times as much as anyone else, including me. Twice, I caught him playing peek-a-boo with Destiny in her highchair across the table.

As Tawnia and Bret served a chocolate truffle cake purchased from Papa Haydn, Ellen said, "Sherman and I are thinking about moving here after he retires."

"You're retiring, Daddy?" Tawnia blinked in surprise.

"Well, I am sixty-eight," he said. "So, I'm thinking about it." That garnered a laugh.

"I'd love having you closer." Tawnia sounded happy at the idea, a complete turnaround from when we first met and she was still wearing contacts to hide her different colored eyes in an effort to fit in with what she thought was her mother's idea of perfection.

"I second the motion," I said, raising my water glass. I was all for Destiny having more people around to love her, even if it meant more trouble to keep our secret.

Ellen started to gather plates, but I stood and reached for them. "You're the guest. Stay and talk. I'll do it."

Ellen smiled at me. "Thanks, dear. The dinner was really good." She sighed. "And I have to tell you that seeing you . . . looking so much like our Tawnia . . . it's like we've gained a daughter instead of losing her to Portland."

That took me by surprise and brought an unexpected lump to my throat. Ellen, with her uptight schedules and to-do lists was so much the opposite of my parents that I hadn't anticipated her wanting a relationship with me too. A dinner or two maybe, and help with antiques, but not anything substantial.

"Thank you," I said, moving toward the door.

Shannon sent me a don't-abandon-me-glare, which I ignored. "You're a big boy," I mouthed. In answer, he peeked at his phone again. Next to him, Cody said something to him I couldn't make out.

In the kitchen, I rinsed off the plates and put them in the dishwasher. I was anxious to get to Brynn's cabin, sure that I'd find the answers there, or at least some of them. Even if I had to confront Brynn, I was going to find out if she was pushing for Manny because of their friendship or if she was hiding something more sinister. It was almost six now.

Tawnia came into the kitchen, carrying more plates. "You're glowing," I said.

She laughed. "It's different having them here. On my turf, and with you here. Yeah, she thought I should get sheets with a higher thread count and that I need a better crib for Destiny, but you know what, I thought of you and your secondhand sheets, and it didn't really matter."

"Not as long as you wash them hot enough to kill any potential bedbugs." Sheets were one thing I always bought new, but I loved seeing her this confident.

She dropped the dishes into the sink and went to the table, flipping open her drawing pad. "Ugh. I thought maybe if I took a break, I'd see it with new eyes, but my character still looks drugged."

"Let me see." The instant my gaze hit the colored sketch, my stomach dropped. The image was so perfect, it might be a photograph, except for the lighter color of the watercolor pencils. "It's her," I said.

"Sariah Barnes?" Tawnia sank to a chair, tucking her brown hair behind her ears and peering closer at the image. "Wait, I've seen her picture on the news and the one on your phone. This isn't anything like her."

"No, it's Kylan's mother. And I don't think she's drugged. I think she's poisoned."

Tawnia paled. "What are we going to do?"

I took a picture of the drawing with my phone. "I'll send it to Paige and my new PI buddy. Maybe he'll have some ideas."

"Doesn't she go to a local college? Someone might be able to trace her that way."

Right. Good idea. I sent an additional text to both Paige and Elliot with that note. To Elliot, I added, *We are running out of time. Don't you know how to hack into stuff? What kind of PI are you anyway?*

It was a low shot, but I was feeling panicky. If this was a current picture of Kylan's mother, she couldn't have much longer. And what shape might Kylan be in?

I'm strictly white hat, came Elliot's return text. *But I have connections at the universities I can tap, and there are a lot of college students online. It should be easier to find the mother than the boy. They're protective of children's information, and he could be homeschooled for all I know.*

Thanks, I wrote back, not wanting to alienate him completely. *Please do what you can.*

Shannon appeared in the doorway. "I have to go. They've found what might be more evidence at Barnes's repair shop, and I want to check it out before we search the Shepherds' residence."

Great, I thought. *Poor Manny is getting kicked again.* Aloud, I said, "I'd better go too."

"Of course," Tawnia murmured, still intent on her drawing.

Shannon stepped closer to me. "I don't like you going to the cabin without backup. Once they hear of the court orders, there might be big trouble."

"I'm undercover, remember?"

"I'll go with her," Cody said from the doorway.

A memory of him nearly dying from a gunshot wound danced before my eyes. "No. It's an auction, with more than a hundred people there. I'll be fine."

Cody looked irritated, his wrinkled face scowling at me. "If it's so safe, you shouldn't mind me coming along."

I looked at Shannon for help. "It's a good idea," he said. "Call me if you find anything. I'll be there as soon as we clear their house."

I was going to murder him later. After I solved his case.

"I'm going to change first," I told Cody. "Then I hope you can keep up in that piece of junk you drive because I don't have an extra helmet."

Chapter 18

Cody's ancient gold Honda somehow did keep up on the fifty-minute drive to Scappoose, which was surprising, given its age. I'd asked him why he didn't buy a new car, but he insisted that he knew this one and was too old to start a new relationship with a car that might not be dependable.

The dirt road up to the cabin was packed with motorcycles, making the area look like a used Hog shop. If even a few had ridden double, I'd way underestimated the number of attendees. There were cars and trucks too, but fewer of them. I considered touching the vehicles as we passed but decided to save my strength for the cabin itself.

"I don't have time to explain what's going on," I said to Cody as we approached the cabin that was lit up and filled with people wearing jeans and leather jackets. "I just need to see if there's anything here that leads to the missing woman."

He waved a hand. "I know all about it. I watch the news, and your sister filled me in."

"Well, Brynn and Travis Shepherd are hiding something, and I can't leave here without knowing what. Brynn was the last person who imprinted on the ring that was found with the second victim, but all of this"—I waved a hand at the display before us—"was planned by Brynn to help my client, so why would she do this if she's involved in the kidnapping or the murders?"

"Got it," he said. "Could be the husband or someone else close to them."

My only comfort was that Weston Rodgers was at least in custody. If Sariah's disappearance wasn't connected to the murders, maybe he'd spill something about it.

"Someone also cut my brake line yesterday," I told Cody. "On Jake's bike. I nearly crashed."

He rubbed a hand over his face, which I knew he'd shaven this morning for the special occasion of meeting his birth daughter's parents but was already growing more white stubble. "We'll check ours before we leave." He patted his waist. "And I got my gun."

"Don't take it out unless you really need it," I warned. "Everyone here probably has one." It was nearly the same thing Shannon had said to me the day before.

The two-story cabin was a misnomer as it wasn't really cabinlike. It was simply a house, painted a bright red. A large deck on huge beams jutted out from the house, which made a carport below for what might normally be used as a parking area. Now it was filled with tables full of food for purchase or auction items. Chairs that looked like they'd come from some church storage room wound around the outside of the tables and gathered in clusters. Lights stood on huge poles and hung from the deck, illuminating the carport area. Stairs led up to the deck itself where additional tables held more items. Lights glowed from the cabin's main window like a beacon.

The drinks were flowing freely and apparently had been for some time if the relaxed atmosphere was any indication. A few kids raced around playing tag, weaving in and out of the adults and shouting gleefully. No one shushed them.

"Let's split up," I said. "Meet back here in an hour."

"Deal." Cody checked his watch while I made sure the location on my phone was turned on. It was, but there was no cell service, at least where I was standing, so at the moment it wasn't doing much good.

While Cody headed into the carport, I started up the deck stairs toward the main entrance of the cabin. As I reached the top, the loud music suddenly cut out, and Brynn began speaking into a microphone. "Okay, people," she called. "Listen up. Table three auction items are going to close, so hurry and see if you can outbid your neighbor. Remember, this is for one of our own. We need to bring Sariah home and free Manny. Thank you."

I slipped by a group of people and headed toward the house. I was almost to the door when raised voices coming from the darker part of the deck that continued the length of the cabin grabbed my attention.

I peered around the cabin and saw a man and a woman. She was completely in shadow, and his back was mostly to me, but they were angled enough that I could see the man's hands were gripping hers.

"No," she said, slapping his hands away. "I'm tired of you flirting with anything that has boobs when you drink. You never introduce me as your girlfriend, and you go off for hours helping with this thing for Manny and don't answer your texts. I don't like feeling this way. Blocked out. Second best."

"I'm sorry. This is all new to me, and opening up isn't easy. But I love you, Tina. You know I do. We're good together."

I recognized the male's voice then: Drum.

"Good enough to meet your family? Good enough to ride together? Good enough to take me somewhere other than a smelly RV and a dollar movie? Good enough to marry?"

"Come on," Drum cajoled, leaning forward to kiss her. "You're being unreasonable. We'll talk about all that later."

"Let me go!" Tina yanked away. "You don't get to tell me how I feel or how I act. You know, people warned me about you, and they were right. No wonder you're still single."

"Come on," he protested. "That's not fair."

She flounced away from him and into the light, glaring at me as she passed. "He's all yours," she muttered.

I was already moving on, but not before I met Drum's eyes. His expression was unreadable; I hoped mine was sympathetic. He passed behind me without comment, moving fast. "Tina, wait. I can explain."

I wondered what he needed to explain, but I wasn't about to stalk them. I'd tackle him after I figured out what Travis and Brynn were hiding.

Inside the cabin itself, there were far fewer people, and most of them wore Road Roller jackets. They nodded to me in welcome. A biker I didn't recognize followed me inside, and one of the Road Rollers moved to intercept him. "Hey, bud, can we help you?"

"Bathrooms?" the man asked.

The Road Roller pointed down the hall. That's when I understood they were keeping an eye on the cabin for Brynn and Travis, in case someone was in the mood to walk off with their personal belongings—a good idea with so many strangers here.

I wasn't a stranger. My efforts the past few days had branded me a Road Roller, even if I wasn't one. I was a member of the inner circle. Cody wasn't, but I didn't worry about him. That old man was tougher than most of these bikers.

I stayed in the kitchen, pretending to clean up and organize, running my hands over everything. A few imprints were worried, but there was nothing guilty in any of them. I needed to search deeper.

When the others were distracted, I slipped into the bathroom. There were imprints here, but mostly from long ago and from people who didn't seem to be Brynn or Travis. Maybe they didn't come to the cabin often, or they used the master bathroom. I went on down the hall to a bedroom, going inside and shutting the door behind me. I was searching through the large duffel bag on the queen bed when the door opened, and someone gasped. I spun to see Brynn Shepherd.

"What are you doing in here?" she demanded. "Is that my purse? Are you trying to steal from me?"

I looked to see that I was holding a black purse from the duffel. "No. Look, I'm . . ." I took a step toward her.

She drew a pistol from a holster inside her pants. "Put. It. Down."

"I can explain."

"Drum warned me about you," she said. "He said something was off. You aren't Sariah's cousin, are you?"

I tried to look past her, but the door was only half open, and we were too far from the main room for anyone to hear us. Unless I yelled. "No, I'm not. But Manny asked me to help find Sariah. He didn't think your group would accept me if I didn't fit in."

"He got that right." She waved the gun slightly. "I said to put that down."

I threw the purse on the bed. "Did you take Sariah?"

Brynn blinked. "What are you talking about? Of course, I didn't take Sariah."

"You and your husband are hiding something. I know that much."

"How could you possibly know that?"

"Because I read emotions and memories imprinted on objects," I said. "That's why Manny asked me to help. You imprinted on the bag of flyers. You were thinking if you'd known Travis's love was conditional that you wouldn't have married him."

She sucked in a breath. "How . . . how . . ." Her voice became hard. "Okay, whatever. But it has nothing to do with Sariah. At least not the way you're thinking."

"What about your husband? He went to see Sariah alone last week, presumably to ask her to watch your kids for your birthday."

"What? No, he never went to see her." The gun dipped a little. Small comfort that it would probably only gut me instead of blowing off my head. "He knows the kids always stay with my sister. They love spending time with their cousins."

"He did go see Sariah. A neighbor saw him, and he told me himself about asking her to babysit."

Brynn's face crumpled. "No wonder she was so sad. Oh, Sariah, I'm sorry."

Before I could ask about that, Travis strode into the room. "Brynn, where are the coolers with the extra—" He took in his wife's face and the gun in her hand. "What are you doing?" He glanced behind him and pushed the door closed. "Put that down." He stepped toward her, but she moved away from him.

"Why did you go see Sariah?" she demanded. The gun

lowered even more, pointing at my knees now, and I took a relieved breath.

His gaze swung to me, but his words were for her. "I wanted to take you somewhere nice for your birth—"

"Don't lie. You told her about the baby, didn't you?"

"Baby?" He stared at her incredulously. "I didn't know about the baby last week."

"Then why did you go?"

"Okay. I went there to tell her I didn't want you to be her surrogate. Our agreement was that you'd go back to work once Darrel was five and in school. You know how much I hate my job. I need to go back to school."

She glared at him. "It would only have been nine months. They're our friends!"

"He's not just a friend. He's your ex-husband." He thrust his hands in his pockets. "And . . . and most days, it seems like you don't remember about the ex part. I don't think you're finished with him."

"That's what this is all about?" Brynn's gaze widened, her body angling slightly toward him. "Honey, I love you. Only you. You have to know that."

He shrugged. "Maybe. But sometimes it doesn't feel that way." The part of his face not covered by his beard reddened. They stared at each other, seeming to have forgotten me altogether.

"I'm sorry. I didn't know I made you feel that way." Brynn's free hand went to her stomach. "But what now? You don't want this baby."

He sighed. "I didn't, but I can get on board. It's the five more years that's killing me, and it may take me time to be happy about it."

"It doesn't have to be five years. We'll figure something out."

Travis nodded, and his shoulders straightened. "Okay."

Brynn turned back to me, the gun still in her hand, now pointed at my feet.

"So, you're pregnant," I said, hoping to keep her distracted from the fact that I'd been pawing through her things.

"It was an accident. I removed my implant when I was thinking about telling Sariah I'd be her surrogate. She asked me last year. I was supposed to tell her after I thought about it. Or never mention it again." She frowned, glancing at Travis. "You know what? Even if you didn't tell her about my pregnancy, what you said might have been enough to send her running away for a few days."

"No," I said, thinking of Grace. "She didn't leave on her own. I can't go into why without violating her privacy."

Brynn stared. "You know this because of your . . . imprints?"

"Because of Sariah's imprints. And it's also why I know Manny didn't do it."

"What are you talking about?" Travis stared between us as if we'd both gone crazy.

"Apparently, she has some kind of psychic thing going on, and that's why Manny hired her. She's not really Sariah's cousin."

"Figures," he muttered.

"So Manny wasn't responsible, but you think we might be," Brynn said.

I cocked my head to study them. "That depends. Are you going to let me touch everything?"

"You can touch whatever you want," Travis growled. He pulled his hands from his pockets and reached for Brynn's gun.

My pulse quickened, but he only lifted his wife's shirt and placed the pistol in her holder.

"Then I'll begin with your keys," I said, holding out my hand.

Gritting his teeth, he fished them from his pocket and tossed them to me. I held the keys with loose fingers, ready to drop them, but all I found was a yearning for his wife and a need to know that she loved him more than her ex. The fact that he really admired and respected Manny didn't help in the least. And he did really hate his job.

"See?" Brynn said as I tossed back the keys a few minutes later.

Travis didn't speak but caught his wife's gaze. "Where are the extra coolers of ice?"

"In Drum's truck. One of the really big ones should still be almost full." Travis nodded and leaned down to kiss her. "We'll talk later." With a glance at me, he hurried from the room.

When Brynn faced me again, she said, "Why did you think it was us?"

"Whoever killed those women might be the same person who took Sariah, and there aren't many people with access to Manny's school ring. You knew Liberty and yours were the last imprints on the ring found on the second victim. And because your husband was seen leaving Manny's Halloween bonfire with the third victim." I searched my memory for her name. "Nora Miller."

She glanced at the door that Travis had left partially open before moving toward the bed and sinking down on it. "So that's why they're searching my house right now. My babysitter called a few minutes ago. I haven't told Travis yet. He's been upset enough at me."

"You didn't bring your kids?"

"Are you kidding? Not when I can't watch them. Too many strangers are here, even if they're good people. I'll be heading home after the auction. Travis will stay and clean up."

"Travis knew Nora, didn't he? From Indiana."

Brynn nodded. "When they asked me at the police station, I wanted to tell the truth, but I knew they'd think it was Travis. He grew up near Nora's family, and they went to the same church. She played with his little sister. He was so much older that he barely recognized her from his visits home, but she recognized him right away. That night at the bonfire, she told him she was crashing with some friends, but one of them was pushing for, you know, side benefits for letting her stay, so Travis took her to a motel and paid a week in advance. He told her to find a job or go home, and she promised she would." Brynn wiped a tear from her left eye. "Now it looks like he was the last person to see her alive. But I swear that he was back within an hour, and he is never anywhere except at work, or with me, or riding. He didn't do this." She bounced to her feet and swept up another duffle that was on the floor. "Go ahead and make sure."

I ran my hands over the objects in Travis's duffle, again coming up empty. There weren't a lot of objects, but the imprints on his beard-trimming kit alone proved that he knew nothing about Sariah's disappearance.

"They'll convict Manny now," Brynn said. "I should have deleted all traces that he fixed the water pump on that RV."

I dropped a belt back into the duffel. "RV? The Calderas drove an RV?"

She nodded. "Yes, they took a family vacation across the US, visiting different sites. At least that's what they said on the news last night. Didn't you see the clip?"

I, of course, had been out visiting bikers and reading imprints. I shook my head. "Does Manny repair a lot of RV engines?"

"I don't know."

"Could you tell if it was a referral and from where?" Because Elliot had said Drum did cosmetic repairs to RVs but contracted out engine work, and if Manny and the Shepherds weren't guilty, and Weston Rodgers had no connection to the murder victims, that left only Drum and Manny's parents, or someone else I wasn't looking at yet.

She considered a moment. "Yes, but I'll have to look it up. Come on." She gestured for me to follow her into the hallway to another room. It appeared to be an office, but the bunk beds against the wall might mean her boys slept here as well.

"I thought there was no service."

"No cell service, but our router is hard-wired to the land-line, so we have Wi-fi in the cabin."

She brought up the page with a few keystrokes and scrolled down. "It was a referral," she said, "but it doesn't say who sent them." She bit her lip. "A lot of people refer jobs to Manny."

"Could it have been Drum?"

"I suppose. But so what if it was? That can't mean anything, right?"

"It could. He's as connected as you and Manny are to the other murder victims."

Her eyes widened. "That's why you asked me to check, isn't it? You think it might be Drum." She shook her head. "But you're wrong. Sure, he had an awful time in high school because of his face, but Manny's always been there for him. He'd never do something like this to hurt him. And he adored Sariah."

I knew exactly how much Drum liked Sariah. "Where is his truck parked?" I asked. "Maybe I can check it out, just to be sure." The imprints at his RV lot had given me nothing, but if he was involved in transporting victims, he'd have used his truck.

Brynn heaved a resigned sigh. "By the time we unloaded it, people had arrived, so he's parked down on the right side heading out. It's a big, metallic blue truck with chrome trim. There are coolers in the back, and a table we didn't end up needing." She paused. "What will you do if you find something?"

"Nothing, except call the police. I'll need your Wi-fi password so I can send an online message once I check it out."

A minute later, I was back in the main room where the Road Rollers were still drinking and having a good time. They nodded at Brynn and me and raised their glasses as we passed.

"I have to make another announcement," Brynn said. "Will you please let me know what you find?"

She seemed anxious, and it came to me that I hadn't finished searching her duffel, and she hadn't handed over her keys. But she wasn't going anywhere, and she hadn't shot me, so maybe that could wait.

Out on the deck, I saw Cody in the middle of a knot of bikers, holding a drink in his hand and now wearing an olive windbreaker that was zipped up tight. He didn't look my way, but I smiled to see him. He was a gruff old coot, but he always landed on his feet.

Down below in the carport area, Travis was dumping more ice into a cooler on a table of beer, while a woman in a Road Roller jacket took money from the customers. Drum and Tina were talking intently in a corner, holding hands again. The din was loud as people shouted over the music. The temperature had dropped since our arrival, and I rubbed my bare arms to ward off the cold. No wonder Cody had retrieved his windbreaker. I'd left my own jacket on the motorbike, along with my gloves, so at some point, I'd have to grab at least the jacket.

With Drum otherwise involved, now would be a good time for me to search his truck. I eased away, keeping an eye on Drum and Tina, who were now kissing and ignoring everyone else in the crowd. All made up, it seemed.

The music died suddenly, and Brynn's voice called everyone to attention. "All right," she announced from the balcony, as the chaos ratcheted down a few notches. "High bidders on table three, you can move over there to pay for and collect your items. And table four will be closing in fifteen minutes, so make sure you have your final bids in there!"

Cody hurried down the stairs and turned in the direction of a table, and I wondered what it was he'd bought. He had a soft heart where charities were concerned, so it could be anything.

When I was on the periphery of the group, far enough away in the dark to go unnoticed, I turned and made my way down the line of cars. Here, the moonlight peeked from beneath the clouds enough that I didn't feel the need to use the flashlight app on my phone. As the music faded, I became aware of how remote the location was and how still and perfect the night.

Before long, a metallic blue truck appeared on my right. I looked around me casually before stepping closer and peeking into the bed of the truck, finding a folding table and four coolers, two huge white ones and two smaller blue ones. Had to be Drum's truck. I slid my fingers around the edge of the bed. No imprints. I touched the driver's door, but besides a clear and distinct satisfaction of ownership imprinted two months earlier, there weren't any imprints except ones from a dealer as he showed it to an interested Drum. He was hoping to sell the truck fast, even if he had to discount.

So the truck was a newer one, but there was no sign of anything related to Sariah, which meant if Drum was involved in Sariah's disappearance, he hadn't used the truck. Surely even a cold and calculating serial killer would leave anxious imprints on a vehicle he used to cart away his latest victim.

I went around to the passenger door, and a recent imprint assailed me, coming from less than four hours earlier.

I glared at him as I climbed down from the truck. It angered me that Drum seemed afraid of telling Brynn no. But I was through with that. I'd break up with him tonight and give him the ultimatum. He was either with me or not, and that bossy Brynn needed to butt out of his life.

But what if he chose her instead?

I shook the thought away. Drum said he loved me, and I loved him. I knew he wanted a family. It was going to work.

Another imprint came on the heels of that one, not filled with emotion like the first, but more practical. It had been imprinted the evening before. *She's the one. I'll ask her to marry me when this is all over. We'll have a couple of kids and move on.*

So that was what was going on with Tina and Drum. She was asserting her territory, and it might or might not be working out for her. It was petty of her to demand anything with Manny in jail, but love's insecurities were often impatient and hard to soothe.

The truck was locked, so I considered a moment before climbing into the bed and trying the back window. Also shut tight. The table held imprints from a woman—probably Brynn—who worried about carrying it when she was pregnant. The two empty blue coolers and equally empty white one also had no notable imprints. Not surprising. People usually didn't feel strongly about coolers. The second large cooler held bags of ice and a strong imprint from earlier this evening, so brief that I couldn't tell who left it.

As large as a coffin. No wonder the boys got a kick out of locking their friends inside.

I kicked the cooler in frustration. I'd missed something in my search, and with every ticking second, Sariah was closer to her final fate, if she hadn't met it already.

Please hurry. Little Grace's plea rang in my ear.

I climbed down from the truck, wondering what to do next.

"Did you find anything interesting?" came a sharp voice.

I lifted my eyes to see Tina staring at me, the glow of a flashlight in her hands.

"I was thinking about using the table to put up some things I brought," I lied. Awkwardly, of course. Tina could probably see the lie a mile away.

"Really? Because Brynn just confronted Drum about referring the Caldera family to Manny. It seems to me you're trying to dig up dirt on my fiancé."

"Congratulations, I hadn't heard you were engaged."

Tina held out a hand, aiming the flashlight down to show the ring. "Just tonight. With everything going on, it's not a great time, but I love Drum, and we don't want to wait."

"Congratulations," I repeated, starting to edge away.

"Why are you trying to drag Drum into this?"

"I'm just trying to find Sariah."

Tina stared at me, one hand on her tiny hip. She looked more like a child than a woman. "Well, wait for me," she said, fishing keys from a pocket. "I need to get something for Drum from the truck. Those clouds are starting to cover the moon, and I don't want to walk back alone if it gets any darker."

More likely she didn't want to leave me near the truck alone.

She beeped the key fob and pulled open the passenger door. I moved forward, determined to find some excuse to check the inside for imprints. But Tina was back at the edge of the seat in seconds, holding something in her hand. "They're having a problem with one of the tables collapsing," she explained. "Drum has a screwdriver on his knife. Hold this while I get down."

She tossed it to me.

It was in a case, but even through it, imprints tingled, calling to me. I opened it and touched the knife.

The girl moaned as I dragged the blade across the ropes holding her. I accidentally cut her wrist, but it wasn't too deep. Not yet.

"Sorry," I said to her, not feeling sorry at all. She didn't matter. Not really. I tucked a long strand of black hair behind her ear. "But you've enjoyed these six months with me, haven't you? No worries about food or where to stay. I know I've enjoyed being with you. But it's time now to go after what I really want. You've always been a stand-in for the real thing. I have to get ready for her now."

She struggled and cried out, but the cloth over her mouth made certain no one would hear. If there was anyone near to hear, which there wasn't. I'd made sure. This would go as I planned, as perfectly as the others. I'd held off for so long, and now it was time to give in to the need. Time to release myself to the craving that filled me.

From somewhere inside me, I knew I was Autumn and

that the horrific, dispassionate imprints weren't mine, but they felt like mine. It felt as if the terror I was inflicting on another person didn't matter, as if it was something that should be done.

And not just to any person, but to Nora Miller, the third victim. I also recognized the hand holding the knife.

Maybe it was the discrepancy of morals that helped me release my grip, or maybe the horror was already sending me into unconsciousness. Whatever the reason, the knife dropped through my fingers. I followed it, hitting the rocky dirt hard with my face.

A scream sounded from above me, followed by a whooshing sound. An explosion reverberated in my head.

Then everything went black.

Chapter 19

*P*ain throbbed in my skull, seeming worse with every heartbeat. For a moment, I didn't know where I was or how I'd come to be there. Someone was sobbing next to me. Who?

"Let me out," a woman's voice begged from very far away. Tina's voice.

Memories came rushing back. I remembered Tina tossing me Drum's knife. The explosion in my head. But most of all the imprints showing the last moments of Nora Miller's life. I hadn't lived through the entire imprint, but the horror and intention remained with me. My horror, because whoever imprinted on that knife hadn't felt any horror or remorse at all.

I knew those small but decidedly masculine hands that had held the knife in the imprint. Drum's hands. I struggled to open my eyes and lift my head from the corner of the window and the seat where it was wedged. The pain in my skull grew worse.

"I told you to give her the knife and leave." The truck lurched over a bump, and it was only then that I realized we were in motion.

"But she fell."

"Exactly. She's a psychic, and I knew the knife would get her."

"What was on it?" Tina screeched. "Poison?"

"Shut up!" He lashed out at her, his fist ramming into her head. She bounced against me, sending a new wave of pain through my skull. I tried to touch my head and found that my hands were tied. Something liquid dripped down my back.

"You ruined everything," Drum gritted, whether at Tina or me, I didn't know.

Tina sobbed louder. "Just let me out. I won't tell anyone."

"Shut up! I have to think."

We bounced along for long minutes more, with only a periodic sob from Tina to break the silence. They didn't seem to know I was awake yet, so I felt for my gun, pulling my leg up to meet my hand. It was missing, along with my ankle holster. Next, I checked for my phone, but it was also gone. If Drum had taken out the battery or thrown it out, not even Shannon would be able to track me once we got back into cell range.

I considered trying to open the door and throwing myself out, but what about Tina?

"Is this about Sariah?" Tina whispered.

"Don't say her name," Drum said coldly. "And no. For you, this isn't about Sariah. For you, this will all be over soon. And for the psychic, once she does something for me."

I didn't like the sound of that. Before I could make a decision about what to do, the truck came to a jolting stop. Drum jammed his foot down on the emergency brake and killed the engine. Jumping out, he ran around to the passenger door and pulled at me, hauling me over his shoulder. I decided to play dead a little longer.

"Wait here!" he yelled at Tina before slamming the truck door. "Don't move."

In long strides, he crossed the moonlit clearing to a motorhome. Not a fifth wheel camper that hitched up to a truck, but one with its own engine. *His house?* I thought. Beyond the motorhome was what looked like a shed built from small logs.

He unlocked the door and staggered inside under my weight. The interior was illuminated by a dim battery lantern sitting on the counter. The place smelled of dust and mildew and alcohol.

He crossed to the end and dumped me on a large bed with a grunt. Then he grabbed the end of the rope around my hands and fastened it to something on the floor. For a moment, I saw only blackness as renewed pain flashed through my head.

When the blackness cleared, I found myself staring at a lifeless figure of a woman on the bed, huddled under a blanket next to the wall as if she'd tried to get as far away from Drum as she could. Her long hair was as black as midnight, her face pale, her eyes stained with ruined mascara. I could also detect the sour stench of vomit. She looked vaguely familiar.

"Sariah?" I whispered, forgetting that I was supposed to be unconscious.

Drum's laugh sounded almost congenial. "She won't wake for at least two hours. I made sure of that."

Instead of dismay, I felt relief at his words. She was still alive then. Unless he was completely insane and didn't realize he was keeping a corpse.

"How did you know about me?" I asked, rolling to face him and trying not to wince at the pain in my head.

Drum shoved his hands in his pocket and stared down at me. "For starters, Sariah set me up with her cousin once right after she married Manny, and it wasn't you. And when I confronted Manny about that Friday night after you left, he confessed." His mouth stretched into a companionable smile. "I have to admit that I was a little concerned about your ability. Even though I'd made sure when we were passing out flyers that none of the neighbors had seen me there on Thursday. I timed that, of course, but I needed to make sure. You were a problem."

"That's why you started the fire," I guessed.

"Little timed device that the fire investigators will never find. Originally, I'd thought if the police found the bike parts, they'd blame Manny, and if no one ever found them, Manny would think she left him. Once the police said they were going into the crawlspace, I couldn't have you doing your hocus pocus and ruining all that. I don't get too emotional for the most part, but taking that bike apart, knowing she was finally mine . . . I might have left an emotion or two around for you to find." Something pure evil glinted from his eyes.

Could I take him out with a well-placed kick? I was still wearing the moccasins as part of my biker disguise, but they shouldn't soften the blow too much. First, I'd have to get into a sitting position. I had to keep him talking.

I shifted my weight, rolling further onto my side. "You killed Nora Miller."

He shrugged. "I was tired of her. I finally realized that it was Sariah I needed."

"But what about Liberty? She was before Sariah ever met Manny." I lifted myself to a seated position, almost surprised that he didn't object.

He shrugged. "Liberty was a snob, and even more so after she became a lawyer. She'd always had it for Manny back in high school. Didn't matter that her best friend was dating him."

"You saw Liberty at the reunion."

He nodded. "She didn't want to dance with me, not even after Manny left. But she learned to love me the two years she was here. In the end, she wanted me, not Manny." His expression darkened as his eyes went to Sariah's inert form. "But then Manny found Sariah, and after that, it wasn't the same. Sariah was . . ." His voice turned bitter. "Manny always got the best. First Brynn and then Sariah. Liberty wasn't good enough."

"Why did you take Rose Caldera?" I swung my legs off the bed.

Drum took a step backward, and then forward again, clearly agitated. "Manny and Sariah were trying to have a baby." He stopped moving and looked at me, almost pleading now. "I didn't want to get in their way. Manny's my best friend." A pause, and when he spoke again, the pleading had been replaced by calculated coldness. "I knew from the moment Rose came in with her father that she would be next. She looked like Sariah, only younger. I thought it would work out, but it wasn't the same."

"You killed her."

He frowned. "Maybe I should have waited. Maybe if I'd given them the baby, Sariah would have liked me more." He shook his head. "Never mind. She's mine now, and once Manny's in prison, we'll be free." His smile sent a chill down my spine.

"You really think you're going to get away with this?"

"I've been careful, for when the bodies were discovered. I made sure Manny had a connection to them all. Like the ring that I found at Brynn's after their divorce. I put it on Rose only last month. I knew they'd trace it to him. And they'll find more. Pictures of him and Liberty at the reunion, her things planted at his shop. I even let Nora send a Christmas card to her mother—as long as she first wrote some other letters I could mail to her friends, letters that talk about her affair with Manny and being scared of him. With her face plastered all over the news, it's only a matter of time until those friends go to the police."

"I thought he was your best friend." I couldn't resist the jab. I scooted to the edge of the bed and let my feet find the floor. So far, he hadn't noticed. If I could get him closer, I might be able to kick him hard enough to take him down.

Drum lifted a hand to scratch at his cheek. "I didn't want this, but he has to go away. I'd thought to keep Sariah like I did the others, but I decided I don't want that. I need to convince her that I saved her from being murdered like the others. She'll love me then. And you'll be my guarantee."

"Guarantee of what?"

Outside, a door slammed. Cursing, Drum turned and raced to the open door. "I told you to stay inside!" he yelled as he hurtled from the motorhome. "Tina! Come back here!" The RV door swung shut and heavy footsteps sounded across the clearing.

I lifted myself off the bed and took a step, struggling to see out the window above the sink, but nothing was visible except the truck. No Tina and no Drum.

"Are you okay?" came a soft voice.

I sat back down, bringing one knee up on the mattress and turning in Sariah's direction. She was sitting up against the wall, dressed in a man's blue flannel nightshirt and little more. Like me, her hands were tied, but with chains instead of rope. I strained to see her clearly in the dimness, past the aching in my head.

"You're okay," I said, releasing a long breath.

She nodded. "Mostly."

"Did he hurt you?"

"Not since the first night." She clasped her chained hands to her chest in a gesture of protection. Protection that didn't exist. "He thinks I don't remember what he did to me. That the drugs made me forget." A heartbeat of a pause. "But . . . why . . . how are you here?"

"Manny asked me to find you."

A heartbeat of a pause. "You're the psychic. Well, you found me." There was irony in her words, and a little jab that I didn't mind.

I had found her. And now I had to get her out.

"Quick," I said. "You need to untie me. If I'm free, I'll have a better chance of getting us out of here."

"I've tried and tried to get out of these chains. Until my fingers are bleeding."

I thrust my hands at her. "These are ropes. You need to try!"

She began fumbling over the knots. "He thinks I don't know," she said. "About those other women. But he talks about them when he believes I'm sleeping. How could he do it?" A sob escaped her lips. "He says it's because I'm so . . . compelling. That no one else can compare with me. But I know it's because he hates Manny. He wants to hurt him, to put him away forever. Oh, why didn't I see him for what he is?"

I grabbed her trembling hands. She was close to panicking. "This isn't your fault. It's Drum's. He's crazy, and that's why we have to get out of here. We have to help Tina. We're all she's got. Now focus on the ropes. Nothing else."

"O-okay."

Her voice was calmer now, but I wanted to be sure. "Why aren't you asleep like he thinks you are?" That took strength, and she needed to focus on that now.

"He gives me pills. I pretend to take them, but there's a place between the bed and the wall, and the first day I was here, I saw pills there. Someone else—" She broke off and then started again. "So every time he gives them to me, I put my finger down my throat and make myself throw them up. And then when he thinks I'm out, I listen to him rant about Manny. Drum thinks he'll convince me that he saved me from Manny. And that you'll be able to tell him if I really believe him and if I love him."

"Then he really is crazy. No way would I ever tell him that."

"And no way would I ever believe a single thing he says— Oh, this isn't working. I can't make my hands work. I haven't eaten since yesterday, and he puts drugs in the food too, so I can't eat a lot. Maybe if I do it with my teeth." She brought the knot up to her mouth. "Tell me about Manny. How is he? Does he think I left him?" She bit down on the rope, tugging, and I noticed her lip was split, and remembered the lip cream Manny had so carefully brought to my shop.

"No. He's never stopped searching. He's never stopped believing that you love him."

She lifted her teeth from the rope. "But he doesn't suspect Drum, does he?"

"No. Drum's been right there supporting him the whole time."

Her lips twisted in a sneer. "I should have told him how Drum made me feel. I should have told him a lot of things." She went back to working the knot.

"He knows about Grace. He doesn't blame you." I was tempted to tell Sariah about my encounter with Weston Rodgers. Now that Rodgers didn't seem to be involved with Sariah's kidnapping, I had no idea why he'd attacked me.

Sariah gasped and let go of my hands. "No! What if Drum finds out about Grace? He says he's going to have a baby with Tina and bring it to me because he knows how much I want a baby. But if he learns about Grace . . . What if he brings her here?"

"He won't. Not if we get free." I shoved my hands at her face. "Concentrate on the knot. Only the knot."

She obeyed as tears streamed from her mascara-streaked eyes.

Outside, we heard a scream and a woman's voice. "Please, no! Please. Just let me go." Tina's desperation clearly came through each word.

"Shut up," Drum growled.

"I think I got it," Sariah whispered, lifting her mouth from the rope. Her hands finished working the loosened knot, and I was free.

I jumped up from the bed, nearly losing my balance with a momentary dizziness. At the window above the kitchen, I could see Drum dragging Tina to the back of the truck by a rope that tied her hands together. He picked her up and threw her into the bed of the truck and jumped up himself. The next minute he was pushing her into one of the big white coolers.

"Please, Drum. No! Please!" She tried to get out, but his hands forced her down.

"Stop struggling, and I'll open the drains so you'll have air," he said. "Either way, you're going in."

With a sob, Tina gave up and collapsed inside the cooler.

Drum snapped the lid shut and struggled for a few moments to tie it shut with a cord. I didn't see him open any drains.

"Do you think it's airtight?" Sariah asked from behind me. She stood next to the bed, straining at her chains, and only her taller height allowed her to see past me.

"I don't know," I whispered. "But get back to the bed and pretend to sleep. He's coming."

I opened the drawer next to the kitchen, searching for something to defend myself. There was nothing. Not even a fork. Too late to ask Sariah for possibilities now. I bent down and grabbed the length of rope where it was tied to a metal ring in a huge cement block, trying to work it free. The knot was tripled and far too tight to get out easily. Giving up, I put the end of the rope around my hands to make it seem as if I were still tied and sat down on the bed.

The door opened. Drum came inside and slammed it behind him, muttering something about getting rid of the evidence. Would he simply wipe off his prints and dump the cooler into some lake and hope no one found it?

"Where's Tina?" I asked.

He stopped muttering. "None of your business. But it's time for you to go nighty night." He walked to the front of the motorhome and removed a bottle from the dash compartment.

"You should let me go," I said. "My fiancé is a homicide detective with the Portland Police Bureau. He will find me."

"You mean the genius who locked Manny up?" he sneered.

"He knows Manny's not guilty. He's researched Brynn and Travis. You're next."

"After the letters and other evidence comes to light, it won't matter. Manny will be convicted. And he won't find you here. Not ever. This land isn't connected to me in any way, but it's private property and totally secure." He opened the bottle and shook out a few pills. "You'll take these, or I'll shove them down your throat."

"Sure," I said. "If you promise not to hurt me."

My response must have been too flippant because he suddenly became wary. I tensed as he approached. He had a good forty pounds on me, anyway I looked at it, and hitting the spare tire around his stomach would likely hurt me more than him. I had to be quick and accurate.

I opened my mouth as he came closer. "Swallow them and then show me under your tongue." His voice held fragments of iron.

I waited until he put the pills on my tongue, slowly pulling the rope off my wrist while he was distracted to avoid becoming entangled. Then I spat the pills at him. In the moment surprise registered on his face, I leapt to my feet, bringing my right fist up under his jaw. His mouth shut with a loud snap, and his head jerked backward.

I followed with a left jab at his eye but overextended, tripping slightly on the cement block. I recovered as his fist angled for my head. Ducking, I slammed into the cupboards on the side and used them to launch myself at him, kicking at his hand as he went for something at his waist. Thankfully, his weapon, if he had one, was under his leather jacket and more difficult to pull than if he'd been in shirtsleeves.

Breath whooshed from him. I kicked out again and sent him to his knees. He scrambled to the door. I raced after him. Too late. He wrenched it open and hurtled outside. I couldn't allow him to go free, to pull his gun and pick me off from the windows of the motorhome. I launched myself onto his back, crashing into him and sending us both to the ground. My head pounded, and I suspected I'd reopened the trowel wound on my side.

I pulled his gun free as he rolled, slamming me into the rocks and dirt. The gun went flying. I didn't mind that because I was worried about a shot going astray and hitting one of the women. Besides, for all his bulk, Drum wasn't trained and didn't seem to know how to take advantage of his size.

I bounced to my feet, sending two punches at his face and ducking away as he tried to retaliate. His strike hit me in the head with enough force that nausea rose in my chest, but it also left him vulnerable. I hit him as hard as I could in the ribs, following with a roundhouse kick that propelled him to the dirt.

I came at him, my hand raised for what I hoped would be a blow that would knock him unconscious, but he twisted, throwing a handful of dirt and tiny rocks in my face. My punched missed. I whirled away to avoid an attack, but he was moving in the opposite direction.

Away from me. To the truck.

"No!" I ran after him, but he jumped inside and roared away without even shutting the door. Rocks and dirt spit out from under the wheels.

The night was suddenly quiet.

He'd be back. I knew it. I had to find his gun because he still had mine and who knew what else in the truck.

I retrieved his gun from a bush next to the motorhome. A Glock. By habit, I checked the magazine and found nine bullets plus one in the chamber. No external safety. One pull away from *ka-boom!* I tucked it into the top of my leather pants, which were tight enough to hold it. For now.

"Hello?" came a faint voice.

I returned to the motorhome to find Sariah sitting on the edge of the bed. "You're okay." Her voice became shaky. "I thought . . . Did you get Tina?"

"No, he took off in the truck."

"The coward," she spat, stronger now.

"I have his gun, but he took mine earlier. We have to be ready. He'll be back."

"Not before he hurts her." She stood from the bed. "You have to go after him."

"How? I doubt he left the keys to this motorhome."

She shook her head. "Even if he did, we couldn't keep up. But I saw the roads on the way up. They're huge switchbacks. He'll have to go down them, but you can cut across them on foot. If you have his gun, maybe you can blow out his tires. Then you and Tina can get away and call for help." She was crying now. "Please. She'll be one more person to die because of me."

I had to try. "Okay. I'll be back. I'd like to free you first, but those chains might take a while."

"Just give me a rock. There's enough space between my hands to hold one. I might be able to get it off the ring." She held up her hands to show wrists chained three or four inches apart.

"Okay."

Outside, I searched for a rock that would be heavy enough, but not too large for her to pick up. I found one with a pointed end from a pile near the back wheel of the motorhome. It was probably too heavy in her weakened state, but it would have to do.

I set the rock down by the cement block and moved the dim lantern there as well. "I'll be back," I promised.

She nodded. "Be careful."

"I'm a good shot." I wasn't sure if I said this to reassure her or myself.

I left the motorhome at a run. Maybe five minutes had passed since Drum had taken off. Was it even possible for me to catch up with him?

If I didn't, Tina would pay the price.

Chapter 20

$\mathcal{I}$ ran through the woods, sloping downward, hoping I was heading in the right direction. I'd been unconscious most of the way here, and I had no idea where I was going. When I crossed the first dirt road, I was relieved. But after skidding and tumbling down to the next one, and still seeing nothing, I began to worry. Maybe I shouldn't have left Sariah. Had he already doubled back?

I pressed on, tripping over small boulders and snagging my beautiful vintage leather pants on the brush as I plunged down the slope. There were no trails, and I believed Drum when he said no one would ever find his motorhome. So why hadn't he left the bodies of the other women here? Had he wanted them to be found? Had something inside him wanted to be stopped? Or had his hatred of Manny been such that he'd planned all along for his best friend to be charged?

Everything began and ended with Manny. They might have been friends, but Drum harbored something far more deadly in his heart. Brynn had been lucky she divorced Manny before Drum had snapped. It might be the only reason she wasn't up there in that motorhome right now.

I tripped and rolled twenty feet to the third loop of road, sprawling on it. My head slammed into the dirt. I bit back a moan.

Was that a light to the right? I sat up to see red taillights. I'd found him.

I scraped myself off the ground and plunged again into the brush. I was more careful now, not wanting him to spot me. Yet.

I reached the next road seconds before he passed and squatted down behind a tree until his taillights faded enough that he wouldn't see me cross the road. At the fifth switchback, I arrived as his headlights appeared to my left. He was coming fast. Too fast. There wasn't much time to act.

I jumped out in front of the truck, pulling his gun from my waistband, aiming at the driver's side. He slowed when he saw me, then gunned the engine.

I fired. One. Two. Three, Four. Five. As I fired, the truck swerved one way and then another.

I jumped back into the brush and up the hill the way I'd come, hoping it was steep enough to prevent the truck from hitting me if that was his intention. I caught a glimpse of shattered glass as he jerked the wheel at the last moment, sending the truck plunging downward into the woods opposite my position. He traveled several yards before crashing into a tree.

I hurried across the road, bending low and ducking behind a tree. "Come out with your hands up!" I shouted.

No response except noises in the brush.

I peered around my tree and saw him scuttling toward the bed of the truck. I stepped out and fired twice more. No way was he going to use Tina as a shield.

He angled away, heading downhill through the brush.

I fired again to keep him moving. I ran forward, maintaining him in sight until I reached the truck. Then he disappeared in the darkness. The truck was at an angle, and the coolers were all shoved in the back corner, as if they'd bounced forward and then back at the impact. I hope Tina was all right.

Keeping my attention on the woods, I crawled inside the bed and tried to release the rope around the white cooler. I heard a moan from inside. I slapped the top. "I'm going to get you out."

I jumped down, still with the gun in my hand, listening. Nothing. No sound. I'd had ten rounds at the beginning and wasn't sure how many I'd fired, but there was at least a couple left. Not many.

Jumping into the open cab, I started feeling around in the dark. My cheek accidentally touched the keys still hanging near the steering wheel, and vivid imprints grabbed at me.

Rage. I would kill her. Kill them all.

I pulled back and reached for the dash compartment that was still miraculously closed. I cringed as I put my hands inside—coming up with another gun inside an ankle holster. My Glock 26. I recognized the imprints Shannon had left on it before he gave it to me. There were no other imprints, not even left by Drum after he'd clonked me.

Cold, I thought.

My phone was there too, still in one piece, though it had been powered down, and also the knife Tina had trapped me with. Taking it all, I scooted outside, listening for steps. Had he circled around? Had he gone back up to the motorhome for Sariah? I had to hurry.

Swinging into the bed of the truck, I used the bottom of my shirt to pull the knife from its cover and cut the rope. Letting the knife clatter to the bed, I opened the cooler.

At first, Tina wasn't moving, and I wondered if I had imagined the moaning. "Tina?" I said, squinting to see in the dark.

A faint moan. "Help me."

I reached in and helped her sit. "Are you okay?"

"Is he gone?" Her voice was panicked and breathless.

"For right now. But we need to get moving."

Her hands were still tied, so I had to awkwardly squat down to pick up the knife again with the hem of my shirt. After freeing her, I helped her stand. The moonlight caught her face for the first time, and I gasped. She looked horrible, as if he'd beaten her with a rock.

What now? Did I try to get the truck working, or did I stash her somewhere and go for help?

"Come on," I said gently, putting my arm around her body and urging her to the edge of the truck.

I jumped down and released the back of the bed. As I reached for Tina, I heard an engine. Dread filled me. If Drum had gone back to the motorhome, maybe he had other keys there. Or maybe he had another vehicle stashed in the shed I'd seen.

"Hurry." I pulled Tina from the bed of the truck and pushed her behind some bushes. "Stay down."

The vehicle was moving closer, slowly though. Ponderously. It was the motorhome. I crouched by the truck until I recognized Sariah behind the wheel. Which meant Drum hadn't gone back, or at least not in time.

I stood up, partially in the headlights so Sariah could see it was me. I heard the window roll down.

"Is she okay?" Sariah asked. "Is he there?"

"No. He's gone. I've got Tina. But she's hurt bad."

I heard an emergency brake go on. "I'll unlock the door. Let's get her inside."

I half-carried, half-pushed Tina to the door of the motor-home. It took both Sariah and me to get her inside on the bed. The chain was still on Sariah's hands, but she was no longer tethered to the ring.

"How'd you get it started?" I asked.

She smiled. "I'm not married to a mechanic for nothing. I've learned a thing or two over the years."

"We have to get her to the hospital."

"Right, but did he leave the keys in the truck when he crashed? It's hard to drive with my hands chained."

I nodded, internally shuddering when I thought about going for the keys. Drum could be lurking around any tree. "I can drive."

"Have you ever driven anything this big? These roads are dangerous."

I hadn't, so I went back outside, listening with all my attention. Back to the truck where I awkwardly used my shirt to yank out the keys. I returned to the motorhome, relieved when I finally locked the door behind me.

"So, it's true. What Drum said about you." Sariah said as I fumbled with the keys, trying to keep a layer of cloth between me and the metal.

"It's true," I said.

"He keeps gloves in the big cupboard."

I jumped up and opened it. There were no imprints on the cupboard or the box of disposable plastic gloves. How that was possible when he'd kept women here for months or years hardly seemed possible. But this was his domain, a place he was in complete control. Nothing special to imprint, at least not on a daily basis.

He had to be completely insane.

I was sure there were imprints elsewhere inside the motor-home, moments that marked changes in his life or times when he'd felt more alive, imprints like the horrific memory he'd left on the knife. I wasn't interested in finding any of them.

It took only a minute to find the right key after donning the gloves. Sariah met my gaze as the chains dropped to the floor. "Thank you," she said.

I waved her back to the driver's seat. "We'd better go. We have no idea where Drum is, and I'm worried Tina is bleeding internally."

"Right."

She hurried to the wheel, and seconds later we were in motion. "Can you look for something to eat?" she asked. "I feel faint."

After a little searching, I found a carton of granola bars and brought them to the front, sinking into the passenger seat and fastening the safety belt. I opened a bar and passed it to her. She munched for a while as I stared in fascination at the tiny road and how it seemed at any moment we might veer off and plunge down the slope like Drum had in his truck.

"I thought it was a scam when Drum first talked about you," she said after starting on a second bar. Her eyes never left the road. "I was sure Manny was paying a charlatan, that he'd lose all our savings."

"He's not paying me," I said, wanting to leave it at that. But I was a saleswoman first and foremost, and at the end of the day, I had to earn a living. "Of course, if you ever want to part with those Lladro figurines you got from your grandmother, I'd be happy to sell them for you."

She blinked. "Figurines?"

"Some of them are worth a lot of money. Thousands. A

couple of them are maybe in the tens of thousands. I'd have to research to be sure, but I can get you top dollar. I have wealthy customers who collect them."

Sariah barked a laugh that held a hint of hysteria. I couldn't blame her. "My mother wanted to throw them away."

That made me smile. "One man's junk is another man's treasure." I pulled my phone from my pocket and powered it up. "How long before we'll have cell service?"

"Probably not until we're mostly down the mountain, I think. I'm not exactly sure where we are yet. Once we hit the main road, we should know more."

My battery looked good, so I left it searching, knowing it would buzz me when we were in range.

We'd gone another five minutes when Sariah gave a slight gasp. "There's a headlight behind me. It's a motorcycle."

"Did Drum have a bike in that shed?"

"I don't know. Maybe."

"We're too big for him to push off the road." I motioned to Drum's gun that I'd placed in the cupholder near her. "Use that if you have to. I have my own." I withdrew my Glock from the holster, which I'd strapped around my ankle over my pants.

The bike approached, the whine of its engine growing. It followed us for a few moments, and then suddenly darted to the right, cutting the corner on the next switchback and speeding in front of us.

"It's Drum," Sariah said as he lengthened the distance between us. She stepped on the gas, and the motorhome swayed back and forth wildly.

For a few seconds, he was in range. I knew that I should roll down the window and shoot him. But I didn't move fast enough, and the moment passed. "He won't get far," I said, lowering my gun to my lap. "I'm sorry."

Sariah glanced at me. "I wouldn't have been able to do it either."

The motorhome was still swaying. "Steady. We don't want to end up in a ditch. We have to get help for Tina."

"Right." Our speed slowly decreased.

"You should probably get checked out too."

"Not before I see Manny."

"Then we need to go to the police station."

When the bike ahead of us vanished completely, I holstered my gun and went to check on Tina. She lay on her back with her hands crossed over her stomach. "Are you okay?" I asked.

"I don't know. He kept kicking and punching me. I hurt all over."

"We're taking you to a hospital."

She swallowed, and the tip of her tongue came out to wet her lips. "I'm sorry about the knife. I didn't know what he planned."

Drum obviously understood himself enough to know that he would have imprinted on the knife when he gave into his lust for death—and that the experience would incapacitate me as surely as any poison. And he'd been right.

"It's okay," I told Tina. "It's all over now. At least for us." But what if Drum disappeared and started killing again elsewhere? I should have at least taken out his tire. Or something.

"Is Brynn okay?" Tina asked.

"Yes, of course. She was never here."

Tina sighed. "Good."

But her question sparked one of my own. "Why would you think she was in danger?"

"Brynn confronted him at the cabin about referring an RV repair to Manny. She said she was going to tell the police. That you were finding proof on his truck that it was him. All the way up here, he talked about how he was going to make her pay."

My gut wrenched at the words. Was Drum crazy enough to follow through with his threat? Or would he do the smart thing and disappear? I thought I knew the answer.

We finally reached a paved road and were following signs to the highway when my cell service kicked in and buzzing notices took over to say I had messages. I called Shannon immediately.

"Autumn?" he barked. "Are you okay?"

"Yes. And I have Sariah. But Drum got away. He's on a motorcycle, and I think he's heading to Brynn's. Not the cabin. Her house." The auction had to be long over by now, and she'd be home with her boys. Alone. Without Travis.

"We're way ahead of you on that," Shannon said. "Your fa—Cody found an imprint on pieces of bottle at the cabin. We've moved her family somewhere safe, and I've got the place staked out. The cabin too. If he shows up, we'll get him."

"Good."

Shannon had caught himself before calling Cody my father. He'd never really be that. But Cody was family all the same, and not for the first time, I was grateful he shared my gift.

"Whatever else was on the bottle made Cody go a little crazy," Shannon continued. "You sure you're okay? I knew you might be out of cell range, but I kept worrying that you'd turned off your location because of the stunt I pulled the other day, tracing you to your apartment."

"It was on. I promised Tawnia. Even if you are a bit of a stalker. Anyway, tell Cody I'm fine, but Drum's girlfriend is hurt. We're heading to the hospital. Then I'm going to the police station with Sariah to see Manny."

"I'll let Cole Howard know you're coming. Text me what hospital, and I'll have them on standby. I'll meet you as soon as I can."

"Just get him."

"I will. I love you."

"I love you too." He was brilliant and sexy and kind, and also more frustrating and annoying than anyone I'd ever known. I wanted to spend the rest of my life with him.

Twenty minutes later, we pulled into the emergency drive of the hospital, and true to his word, Shannon had people waiting. As they stabilized Tina in preparation to remove her from the motorhome, one orderly took a second look at my face. "You should be looked at too. Is that blood on the back of your head?"

Now that he mentioned it, my head did still hurt, but nowhere near as much as it had in the beginning. *Adrenaline,* I thought.

I gave him my best smile. "Could you just give me a few wet wipes? We have to get to the police station."

He could and did, along with an ice pack for my head. Sitting in the passenger seat, I washed my face as my phone called out directions to the police station. Sariah drove like a maniac, muttering under her breath, and this time I didn't stop her.

Cody Beckett was pacing outside the police station when we arrived just before midnight, looking small in his windbreaker. His white hair poked out at all angles, and his hands, once again in gloves, clenched as he paced. He looked up the instant we turned the corner from where we'd left the motor-home and stood motionless, looking me up and down.

"Do I wanna know what the other guy looks like?" His voice grated on my ears. "Because I'm sure it's a lot worse."

I grinned. "Thanks for the confidence." Hopefully, it was true. During my clean-up in the motorhome, I'd learned the glue had actually held on my side, and while I had a golf-ball-sized lump on the back of my head that was beginning to hurt again more than I was willing to admit, there wasn't a cut on my skull. The sticky wetness on my hair and neck had been beer from the bottle. I was bleeding through numerous scrapes after my downward plunge through the forest, but those were all minor. The bruises from Drum's punches would take a lot longer to heal.

"If you need it," Cody said as we reached him, "I've got some glue in the car. It'll work better than stitches. I use it on my hands all the time."

I laughed. Maybe some things were inherited. He stiffened in surprise as I hugged him, which I understood. I'd been a lot less accepting of him than Tawnia had been, even after he'd helped me on two cases. But tonight I had an ulterior motive.

"Can you hold this for me?" I whispered, shoving my gun and ankle holster at him. "It hasn't been fired, but I did fire another gun, and I don't want the police distracted with mine."

"Right. You might never get it back." The gun disappeared into his pocket by the time I drew away. "So what now?" he said louder, including Sariah in the question. "Jake's bike is still out at that cabin, by the way."

I looked at Sariah, whose face was far too anxious for intro-ductions. "I'm going inside with Sariah to make a statement. I don't know how long it will take."

"I'll wait in the lobby then."

"You don't have to."

"I want to."

I nodded. "Any news from Shannon?"

"About the guy who attacked you?" Cody's jaw clenched. "No, but after hitting you with that bottle, I hope they shoot him."

For a bright, world-stopping instant, I remembered when Drum had passed the motorhome, and I could have shot him. If he hurt someone else, it'd be my fault.

Chapter 21

etective Cole Howard appeared seconds after we entered the police station. He did a doubletake at Sariah as if he hadn't quite believed Shannon, and his gaze didn't leave her as he led us to an interrogation room.

We answered questions and more questions.

I learned that Drum had drugged Sariah on the porch, injecting her with a syringe, and the last thing she remembered was him carrying her through the house into the garage. She might have still been in the garage with Drum while he dismantled her bike, probably around the same time Lucy and Hutch had come for the flowers. The next thing she became aware of was waking up in Drum's truck with her hands tied.

Minutes ticked into hours. Detective Howard should have been happy that I'd solved his missing person's case, but instead he seemed annoyed that I hadn't called him from the hospital and that he hadn't been able to interview Tina. He quickly dispatched an officer to the hospital, recovered Drum's gun from the motorhome, and scheduled forensics to examine the vehicle in the morning.

Someone found a pair of sweats to cover Sariah's bare legs,

but she was still wearing the blue flannel shirt that had to be Drum's. Even disheveled, she was the center of stares and small services that had nothing to do with her kidnapping. Elliot hadn't been lying when he'd said she had that certain something. Even Detective Howard was oddly gentle when he addressed her. He'd also found food for both of us when Sariah told him she was hungry. He'd ignored my two previous requests.

"And you really can't identify where the motorhome was parked?" he asked me for the third time.

"Look," I said, finally having reached my limit. I sat back in my chair and folded my arms. "We've gone through this twice already. I was unconscious on the way up and sitting with Tina most of the way down. I have only the faintest idea where we were. Sariah already said she'd be happy to show you. She was awake during her trip with Drum, and she drove here. But you promised to let her see Manny over an hour ago. Does he even know she's been found?"

Howard didn't respond, so I knew the answer was no.

I stood up and leaned forward, my hands splayed on the table. "He didn't do it, not the kidnapping or the murders, and the sooner you free him, the less media backlash you'll have." It was a threat, and we both knew it.

His dark face flushed. Something he should really learn to control if he was angling for management. "Only Shannon can free him now. The homicides are his case."

"Maybe, but you can get him into this room with his wife. Shannon is on his way." This last was a little iffy because I hadn't heard from Shannon since our conversation in the motorhome and wouldn't until this was over. Howard had made me power down my phone during the interview—or interrogation, as I was inclined to see it.

"Please," Sariah said, drawing his attention. "I'm so worried about him."

Howard caved and walked to the door. "Bring me Barnes." He paused and listened as someone else spoke. "I don't care what time it is, or who you have to wake up. Get him in here now."

Fifteen long minutes ticked by until Manny was finally ushered inside. Someone had told him Sariah had been found because there was no surprise in his face when their eyes locked.

"Sariah," he said, his voice a rough whisper. I doubted he noticed any of the rest of us.

"Lose the cuffs," Howard barked.

The officer accompanying Manny obliged, and they ran to each other, hugging and crying. She was a half-head taller than he was, even in her bare feet, and so slender that she looked ethereal. By comparison, his tatts and beard made him look rough and solid and very human. I would never have put them together from a crowd, but the joy they obviously felt at their reunion was blinding. Instinctively, I understood that whatever horrors she'd experienced in that motorhome, Manny would be there for her. He'd also support her with whatever happened with Grace and her family.

"Let's give them some privacy." I pushed my way through the officers.

No one stopped me, so I kept walking right on down the hall, hoping to escape from the station altogether. Powering on my phone, I checked my texts. Nothing from Shannon, but there were three from Elliot. I clicked them open.

Bingo. I found the kid's mother. She's Chrystal Reed. I cross-checked the address with the lists from the schools, and a John Kylan Reed lives there. I never thought it might be a middle name we were looking for. His grandparents, John and Ester Reed, own the house. Here's the address. I know you're probably sleeping since it's after two, but what's next? Guess we have to wait until morning.

I hadn't expected the middle name, either, but it made sense. No wonder the kid had been so hard to find. Elliot's second text had come in twenty minutes later.

Since I'm not sleeping anyway, I think I'll drive out there now. Let you know if I see anything odd. If poison is involved, time could be important.

Then another text that had come in only minutes ago.

The house is dead. No lights or movement. But that might be because it's nearly three. Guess I'll head home.

I pushed dial, and Elliot picked up immediately. "Hey," he said. "Sorry if I woke you with all the texts."

"No sleep here. I've been with Sariah."

He gave a swift intake of breath. "Is she—?"

"She's okay. Are you still at the boy's house?"

"Yes, but there's nothing to see. A while ago, a neighbor came out to confront me, and he said the grandparents are gone on vacation, but that both their adult children live with them. The son has a wife and a little boy, which is your Kylan, and the daughter also has a child—girl, he thinks. He says the house has been quiet, and that he hasn't noticed anything weird. They might all be on vacation, but Chrystal has school tomorrow, so I doubt that."

"Stay there," I said, turning on my heel and heading back down the hallway. "One way or the other, I'm talking to his mother tonight."

"Someone's going to call the police on me," he said.

"That's exactly what I'm going to do. Wait there." I hung up.

Outside the room where Sariah was still with her husband, Detective Howard was talking with two night-beat officers I didn't know.

"I need you to do a welfare check," I said, shoving my phone under his nose. "At this address."

"You're not supposed to have that on in here," he said. "And are you aware of what time it is?"

I gave him a flat stare. "I was right about Manny. I brought Sariah to you. Please, can you do this for me? There isn't time to wait for Shannon."

He studied me for a few seconds, his jaw muscles working. "Why this house?"

"I believe someone is poisoning multiple people there. You know that PI Sariah was working with? Well, he's there now, waiting outside." I hoped bringing up Elliot would add legitimacy to my request. "We need a welfare check."

He sighed, and before he could object, I added, "I could go myself, but someone might call the police if I'm prowling around."

He glanced over his shoulder through a small window in the door. "You stay with them," he told the officers. "Give them whatever they need. I'm going to take a little ride with Ms. Rain."

That was more than I expected. He started down the hallway, apparently leading to some back door. I followed, limping slightly now that stiffness was sinking in.

Howard's police siren got us to the address faster than I imagined. I had to admit he was an excellent driver. Elliot was still at the house, pacing in front of his parked car. Detective Howard nodded at him in greeting.

"Wait here," he told us. He strode up the walk and climbed

the wide stairway to the door under a decorative arch. We waited while he rang the bell. And rang it again. No answer.

He pounded on the door. Still nothing.

"I'm going around the back," I said, starting up the walk.

"Wait." Elliot grabbed me and pointed.

A small, ghostly figure had opened the door. Detective Howard disappeared inside the house. Long seconds later, we heard sirens.

"That's it," I said, fearing the worst. Howard or no, I was going in.

I made it to the doorway just as Howard appeared carrying Kylan in a blanket. Kylan looked small as the detective set him on the porch. "Keep an eye on him."

"Are they . . .?" I couldn't finish the question.

He shook his head. "I'm not sure why we're even here, but they're lucky we are. Morning might have been too late."

Was that a note of admiration? I chose to believe so.

"When the paramedics arrive," he said, "send them in." He turned and went inside, leaving the door open behind him.

"Come over here," I told the boy, drawing him to the side of the stair where we wouldn't be in the way. Kylan sank against me, half asleep. He didn't ask any questions, which bothered me. Had he also ingested the poison?

Elliot joined us near the porch, pacing until two ambulances arrived and half a dozen EMTs hurried past us. Long minutes later, they were out again, carrying a man and a woman on stretchers.

"Wait," I said as the last paramedic reached the bottom. "You need to check this child too. Please."

He peeled away from the others and knelt down by Kylan. He shined a light in his eyes, took his pulse, and then held out his arms. "I think we'd better take you with your parents," he said.

"Are they okay?" came Kylan's soft voice.

"Yes. I'm pretty sure, but we're going to let the doctor fix 'em up even better. And you too. Hold onto my neck now. It's kind of cool inside the ambulance. At least my kids think so. I'll show you around."

Kylan didn't protest as the man picked him up and carried him to one of the two waiting ambulances.

I glanced at Elliot, who stared after them sympathetically. "Poor little guy."

"Yeah," I had to agree.

Two police cars arrived, and Detective Howard came out to meet the officers. "Okay, it's your show," he announced. "I'm not actually on the clock."

One of the others laughed. "You think it's carbon monoxide?"

Howard glanced at me before replying. "No. We believe it's deliberate poisoning. We'll need all the food and medicine in the house tested. Maybe shampoos and the like as well. I'll show you where I found them."

As they disappeared inside, a car skidded up to the curb, coming to a stop with a lurch. A thin woman wearing a short, black halter dress climbed out, reaching into the back for a car seat containing a young child. She hurried up the walk, staggering a little under the weight.

"What's going on?" she demanded, looking from me to Elliot.

"Who are you?" I countered.

"Ivy Reed. I live here."

"With your parents? Your brother and his wife?"

She tucked a clump of blond hair behind her ear and set the car seat with the sleeping child on the cement walk. "Yes. Did something happen?" Her voice was wary now.

"They went to the hospital," I said. "Someone poisoned them. They almost died."

She gasped, her eyes opening impossibly wide. "No!"

"Yes."

"But . . . that wasn't supposed to happen."

A movement at the door behind me made me look around to see Detective Howard watching us. "Please come inside," he said. "We'll take your statement now."

"What? I don't know anything," Ivy protested.

"I think you do." To me, Howard said, "I'll be out to drive you home in a few minutes."

"I can take her," Elliot said. "We have some business anyway."

I jumped to my feet. "Good idea." The less time I spent with Howard, the better. "But take me to the police station."

The drive back to the Portland Police Bureau was more sedate than the trip with Howard but just as quiet. At the station, Elliot walked me to the lobby door.

"About your bill," he began.

"Whatever you want." I raised a hand to fend him off. "Give me a dollar amount. I'll make payments."

"I don't want your money, but I do want something."

I knew what that meant. Here was one more person wanting to use my ability. No wonder he'd stuck around at Kylan's long after I expected him to bail. "Then let's talk about it later," I said.

I'd been stabbed with a trowel, hit with a bottle, tied up, exchanged blows with a madman, and tumbled down the side of a mountain. I was tired and achy, and my head was pounding again. It was a pretty full day, even for me.

"Sure, fine." He thumbed over his shoulder in an endearingly awkward gesture. "Guess I'll take off now. Talk to you later."

I didn't open the station door but turned and called after him, "Elliot?"

He stopped, pushing up his glasses. "Yeah?"

"Thank you. It means a lot to me that you found him."

"I know." He grinned and resumed his journey to the car, his step enviously jaunty for the middle of the night. Whatever favor I owed him, he deserved it, at least on the same terms I'd promised the New Jersey mob boss—that my information couldn't lead to any deaths. For Elliot, I didn't think that would be a problem.

Cody was the only person inside the lobby, and he barely opened an eye as I sat beside him. "You going somewhere?" he asked.

"Just got back. We found the boy."

That made him open both eyes. "He's okay?"

"I think so. And his parents. But have you heard anything from Shannon? He hasn't texted me."

He shook his head.

A million things could have gone wrong, but Shannon was a good officer, and so was Paige. I had to wait and trust him.

Another hour passed, with me alternately trying to doze, furiously pacing, or going outside to look up and down the street. I wasn't good at waiting. The sun was just beginning to hint at lightening when Shannon texted me.

You still at the station?

Yes.

Interview room?

Lobby.

Almost there.

You get him?

No response, but ten minutes later the front door of the station burst open, and Shannon and Paige came inside, dragging a sullen Drum between them. He had numerous cuts on his face, and one of his arms was in a sling. He limped heavily. My knees went weak with relief. I wouldn't be the reason someone else died tonight. I had no doubt that Shannon had come in the front door so I could verify Drum's capture with my own eyes.

"I need a hospital," Drum protested.

"Shut up," Shannon snapped. His gaze met mine, running all over me as if cataloging every scrape on my skin or snag in my clothes.

On Drum's other side, Paige's hair was still iron straight, her clothes unrumpled, but she looked satisfied like Destiny did every time I gave her one of my honey candies. Paige had used her gun was my bet, but she hadn't pulled the trigger or Drum would be dead.

"Ah," Cody said, rising from his chair to stand next to me. "I knew he'd look worse."

Drum stopped moving at the words. Spotting me, his skin between the acne scars grew red, mottling his face. Both his eyes were blackened, and a huge bruise slashed across his neck.

"Where'd you take her?" he demanded of me. He twisted to look back at Shannon. "She has Sariah. You have to believe me. She shot at me. I could have been killed!"

"Too bad you weren't." Shannon shook him, and Drum cringed as if in pain. I hoped that meant a fracture.

"It was her, I tell you," Drum recovered enough to say. "I tried to save Sariah. Manny's a murderer. There are letters! And clothes in the rag box at his office. I can show you."

Shannon motioned to another officer behind him. "Help take him to booking." Paige and the officer dragged Drum away.

"Brynn?" I asked.

"She's fine. We caught him putting accelerant around her house. And he had a timing device that I'm betting we'll find a match to in the remains of Manny's crawlspace, now that we know what to look for."

"I could have shot him," I said, "but I didn't. Because of me, he might have hurt someone else." The explanation was my way of trying to thank Shannon for finishing the job, but I quit talking before I gave in to tears.

Cody's gloved fingers brushed my hand. "You did your job," he said in his gruff voice. "And Shannon did his."

"That's right. Without you, I don't know that we would ever have found Sariah. Or prevent him from eventually hurting Tina." Shannon moved to my side and put his arm around me. "We should get you home."

He hadn't said hospital, so I agreed.

"There's more news," Shannon said as he held the door open for Cody and me. "About Weston Rodgers. Peirce searched the storage unit in Flagstaff. You won't believe what he found."

early two weeks later on a Friday evening, I stopped by Manny's large back yard where he and Sariah were hosting a barbecue to thank the Road Rollers who'd helped look for Sariah and raised money for Manny's defense. Ten thousand dollars had been raised, but after the charges were dropped, the money had gone into a reparation fund for the victims' families.

Grace and her grandmother, Betty Rodgers, were also at the party, which was surprising since Weston Rodgers was in an Arizona jail on drug trafficking charges. Or maybe that was the reason they'd been able to come. Drug trafficking wasn't Rodgers's only crime. Using surveillance feeds from nearby stores, Shannon had tracked down the teen boys I'd seen, and they identified Weston Rodgers as having cut the brake lines on Jake's bike. Before fleeing to Arizona, he'd been following me, trying to ascertain if I knew about his drug dealings, and when I'd shown up at the police station, he'd assumed the worst and tried to get revenge.

The real miracle for me, though, was not Grace's presence but that Manny's parents and Sariah's mother were also at the barbecue. They weren't exactly chummy with their respective in-laws, but they were polite and smiling.

The property showed little sign of the damage that had been inflicted on the Barnes' household. Volunteers had cleaned out the crawlspace and the back yard, and insurance had paid a service to rid the house of the smell of smoke and start the reconstruction of the master bedroom. Sariah's motorcycle had also been covered.

Sariah was the center of attention at the gathering, graciously talking with everyone. She looked healed on the outside, and if she sometimes startled or grasped Manny's hand too tightly, I think he and I were the only ones who noticed.

"Drink?"

I looked up from my lawn chair to see the burly Hutch Newman offering me a glass of soda. "No, thanks. I had juice." I indicated the empty cup on the grass at my feet near the remains of my steak.

Shrugging, he lowered his body into the seat next to mine. He sipped the soda. "Better drink this before Luce sees me. I'm supposed to be off carbonated drinks."

I nodded absently as we both watched Manny and Sariah with Grace. No one had been told of the relationship between them, least of all Grace, but to me the fact that they were mother and daughter was obvious. Most of Sariah's focus was on Grace, the woman's quiet joy making me smile. Manny had shaved for the occasion, and he looked more like the high school football player he'd been. Grace was currently tracing the tattoos on his arm and seemed to be crushing a bit on him, which I thought was good. She needed a safe man in her life.

"Glad she's home," Hutch said. "Thank you for what you did. They're saying that monster would have gotten away with it if it hadn't been for you. It means a lot to Luce."

The comment made me give him my full attention, and I realized he wasn't looking at Sariah but at his wife, Lucy, who stood beyond Sariah by the grill, chatting with Brynn and Travis Shepherd.

"I didn't think she liked Sariah," I said.

He shook his head and sighed. "She's worried I'll have a wandering eye like her first husband, but I wouldn't take that chance, even if it was possible, which it's not. Luce is my girl and always will be, no matter how old we get. I just wish I could be a little more, well, up to my wife's standards. I'm getting older and not necessarily better. Like she is."

It was an incredibly sweet thing to say, and I believed he meant every word. Maybe I'd misjudged him. Maybe this explained the emotions I'd picked up on his bike that his wife "might not mind if she knew." He might admire Sariah, but if Lucy knew how much he loved her, maybe she'd understand that she had nothing to fear. But if I had misjudged him, I wasn't the only one. His wife had too. Repeatedly. Even now, she was coming our way, a determined look on her face and her nostrils flaring suspiciously.

"Maybe things will be okay between Lucy and Sariah now," I said.

"I hope so. Well, I'd better take my turn at the grill. And hide this drink." He deposited his cup on the lawn behind the leg of my chair and went to meet Lucy.

I was glad to have shared this evening with them, especially while Shannon was chasing down the final details of his investigation, but it was time to get back to my own life. I arose and went to Sariah's side. "I need to go. Is it okay if I take those two figurines now?"

"Sure, but you're perfectly welcome to stay and have another steak."

"Thanks," I said. "Another time."

She excused herself, and together we went inside to the sitting room. The curio cabinet now had a lock on it, at my urging, and Sariah opened it with a key in her pocket. She'd also insured the pieces, or I would have been more afraid to move them.

"Just the two?" I asked, pulling off my gloves and withdrawing the first Lladro figurine.

She smiled. "For now. I'll probably want to sell the others when it's time for Grace to go to college, but this should be enough to help us get into a new house. Thank you for getting me such good prices."

"You don't have to thank me. I'm getting a good commission." Twenty-two hundred dollars, to be exact—ten percent of the total.

"I would have never gotten that much on my own." She paused, her dark eyes holding mine. "And you saved us from everything Drum planned. I can never repay that."

"I wanted to help. You don't owe me anything." I snuggled the figurine into the protective nest of packing peanuts I'd brought from the shop. "But maybe you should wait to move. You have good neighbors, and you may feel differently after the remodeling."

Sariah's lips tightened. "The memories here . . . they're just too raw. I keep seeing . . . you know." She straightened and smiled. "I want to start new memories. And I want to be closer to Grace."

"I thought her grandmother didn't want to tell her."

Sariah shrugged. "Not yet, and I agree. Grace had a wonderful mother, and she's still in mourning. She's been through enough for now. She needs to feel safe. Maybe in a year or so we'll all feel differently. Maybe once she knows I'm going to be around forever. Once they both know that." She smiled again. "In the meantime, Betty needs help with Grace, especially now that her son is out of the picture, and she has full custody. She's agreed to let us help. She's even talked about letting Grace stay with us for a week while she visits a friend next month. She's always wanted to travel but hasn't because of the cancer and having to watch Grace."

"That's good," I said, reaching for the second figurine. "It's a start."

"Manny and I are thinking of buying a house with an attached apartment, something that we can maybe offer to Betty and Grace. It would ease Betty's financial burden and give us more time with Grace." She gave a low chuckle. "Funny how Manny and I can't stand our own parents and would hate living that close to either of them, but Betty Rodgers is the kind of cookie-baking grandmother I always wanted for my children."

That set me to thinking about Brynn and her new pregnancy. "Are you thinking about other children then?"

"We're going to save for adoption. Maybe we can do for another child what Grace's mother did for her."

"Adoption is a great idea."

The next day before closing, I finished up my last customer as Jake appeared at my counter, grinning. "The word finally came in. Melinda's family likes me!"

"That took long enough. Does this mean you two are serious?" I was teasing, but not really. He'd been scarce since I'd returned his bike, this time in one piece.

Jake's eyes opened wide, and he breathed out a sigh as if the very idea surprised even himself. "I guess so. Uh, yeah."

"What?" I put my hands on my hips. "Are you serious here? I'm your best friend, and I barely know her. You can't be serious yet." I tried to keep the humor in my voice, but maybe a little hurt showed through. I'd given him space and time because our friendship was important, but I needed to know he wasn't setting himself up for another broken heart.

Jake knew me well enough not to laugh. "Okay, okay. Maybe it is time. What about a double date?"

"Sure. But not tonight. I have plans this weekend." Now that Shannon had wrapped up most of the details of the murder investigation and sent everything to the district attorney, we were finally going to spend the weekend ignoring our phones and everyone else.

The electronic bells above my door sounded, and my smile grew as I recognized Kylan Reed and his mother, Chrystal. She had called earlier in the week to tell me they'd be coming today, but I hadn't been sure they'd actually follow through. This evening Chrystal looked healthy instead of pale and weak as she had when we'd first met, and Kylan was positively jumping, despite the heavy-looking bulge of his backpack.

"We'll talk Monday," Jake said, heading back to his shop.

"I'm here to get the you-know-what," Kylan announced when he arrived at my counter. "You still have it, don't you?

We're having Mom's birthday tonight at our new house. It's like a week and a half late, but we have cake and everything."

"Of course, I have it," I said. "I told you at the hospital that I'd save it for you."

Kylan had been in the hospital for only twenty-four hours, having ingested less of the poisoned food, unlike both his parents, who had remained for three days. I'd also heard from Shannon that Kylan's aunt insisted the poison was only to "encourage" her brother to move out so she and her daughter didn't have to share a room. The woman was in the psychiatric hospital now and would likely serve jail time for poisoning her brother's family.

"Stay right here, and I'll get it. I even wrapped it for you."

When I returned, Kylan had his treasure chest on my counter and was carefully counting out eighty-five dollars. I'd planned to give him a discount, but the pride on his face forbade me from voicing the offer. I was glad I'd also included the tiny pewter jewelry box his mother had admired.

"At least my aunt put the money back," he said. "That was lucky."

I laid the wrapped mirror on the counter. "That is good." I exchanged an uneasy glance with his mother. "A new house?"

She nodded. "My husband quit school and went back to work full time. We've spent the last ten days finding a new place and moving. We love his parents and appreciate their help, but we'd rather take our time finishing school than put our family at risk again. We don't know what will happen, and his sister . . . well, she isn't stable, and her parents have custody of her child and will want to help her when she gets out. So I'm finishing nursing school first, then I'll get a better job and support our family while he goes back to school. He makes a lot more than I do right now, and I'm closer to the end than he is, so it makes sense for me to finish first. We'll both get to spend more time with Kylan."

"I'm glad it's working out." My gaze flicked past her to see Shannon come inside the shop, fifteen minutes early for our date. Apparently, this time he was taking no chances that I'd get involved in another case. Seeing that I was busy, he wandered down one of my aisles.

Kylan shut his treasure chest and started putting it in his backpack.

"Wait," I said. "I have something for you." Bending, I reached into the shelves under my counter and pulled out the antique padlock and key I'd bought for five bucks last week at an estate sale. "This is so you can always protect your treasure."

His eyes grew wide. "Cool! Thank you so much." He turned to his mother. "Can I keep it?"

She grinned. "Yeah, sure." She watched him run down the aisle to the door. "Thank you so much for everything." For a moment, her voice was heavy with all that might have happened.

"Don't look back," I said, coming around the counter to walk with her to the door. "You have a special kid there and a wonderful life ahead." It was what I told myself on the nights that the more horrific imprints haunted me. Going forward was the only way to win.

She nodded vigorously. "Thank you." She hurried outside after her son.

I locked the door and turned over the sign that told people to go in through Jake's. As long as he was open, I could always hope for an extra sale or two.

"I'll get my purse," I called to Shannon, heading for my counter.

He came over. "Looks like the lock went over really well."

I nodded. "And you're early."

"I have a special date tonight." He leaned over the counter to meet me in a kiss. His eyes look more blue than usual and more intense. I closed my eyes and gave myself up to the moment. His mouth moved against mine, causing the world to stop rotating. There was only us. Only this moment.

A clearing throat made us break apart. We looked to see the private eye Elliot Stone standing inside the double doors that connected my store with the Herb Shoppe. I'd been ducking his calls for the past two days, so it wasn't really a surprise to see him. But he had incredibly bad timing.

"Sorry," he said. "I came in through the Herb Shoppe. Your door was locked." He stared down at a paper cup in his hand. "They're giving away free cups of tea." His nose twitched as if he wasn't accustomed to saying the word, much less drinking it.

"I suppose you're here for your favor?" I'd expected him to show up before now, but he just had to pick tonight. I hoped it didn't take long.

Resignation filled Shannon's face. "Well, what is it? Something for her to read?"

Elliot deposited his cup on a shelf and held up empty hands as he approached the counter. His glasses needed cleaning, and a spot of something red stained his blue T-shirt. "It's not what you think."

"And what do I think?"

He shrugged. "I want us to work together. Your talent, my

tech. Your persistence, my tech." A smile tugged at one side of his mouth. "Tech's worth a lot, right? Maybe not as much as your, uh, imprints, but I've got a PI license, and if we're working together, it'll be easier for you to get one too. I could say you work for my firm."

"Why do I need a license? Doesn't that mean more fees to pay the government?"

"Makes it easier sometimes to get information. And you can charge people a fee." He raised both hands to hold back my protest. "I mean for the investigation time, not necessarily for reading the imprints."

Shannon grinned at me. "He's got a point."

"I'll think about it," I said.

Elliot nodded. "Call me then." He gave me a hopeful stare that reminded me a lot of Kylan's when he'd originally asked me to save the mirror. He started back to Jake's, pausing to pick up his cup of tea with an expression of mistrust. "Oh," he called over his shoulder, "and if it helps, we already have a new case. Her name is Luna Medina. She works at Subway in the Lloyd Center. You questioned her at some point in your search for Sariah. She was nervous to call and asked me to talk to you."

"I remember her. What's wrong?"

He grinned. "Does that mean you're in? Because I set up a meeting for Monday morning. If you want to come along, I'll text you all the details. Just let me know." Without waiting for further response, he disappeared into the Herb Shoppe.

"He's like a big teddy bear," I said when he was gone. "A super-smart, persistent, techie teddy bear."

Shannon laughed. "I'm glad you think of him that way. In that case, I think it's a good idea to work with him. Word at the station is that he's reliable and honest, plus, he's good at"—he grinned—"tech stuff. Even better than our guys at times."

"Which could be helpful when you're tied up," I mused.

"Hm, maybe this isn't a good idea after all. But I already know you'll be at that meeting on Monday."

He had that right. I owed the woman at least a meeting for her help.

I laughed and came around the counter, stepping close until our bodies were touching. I took his hands. "Forget all that for a moment. I've decided I want to get married."

"Well, that's the idea." His thumb toyed with the ring I was back to wearing since I had no imprints on my immediate agenda.

"I mean, right away. As soon as possible. I don't want to wait anymore. Let's get married in the same meadow my parents did. I'll wear my mother's dress."

Shannon laughed and pulled me to him, hugging me so tightly he lifted my feet from the ground. "I have time off in three weeks." He set me down and touched a mottled green and black bruise that still showed on my cheekbone and the lower part of my left eye. "If this will be gone by then."

It was way too soon, and Tawnia was going to raise a fuss, but I was moving forward.

I put my hands around his neck, kissing him first on one side of his mouth and then the other until his eyes shut with a moan. "Who cares if it's gone? My sister's an expert at Photoshop. Let's do it."

TEYLA BRANTON grew up avidly reading science fiction and fantasy and watching Star Trek reruns with her large family. They lived on a little farm where she loved to visit the solitary cow and collect (and juggle) the eggs, usually making it back to the house with most of them intact. On that same farm she once owned thirty-three gerbils and eighteen cats, not a good mix, as it turns out. Teyla now has seven kids so life at her house can be very interesting (and loud), but writing keeps her sane. She's been known to wear pajamas all day when working on a deadline and is often distracted enough to burn dinner. (Okay, pretty much 90% of the time.) Under the name Teyla Branton, she writes urban fantasy, paranormal romance, and science fiction. She also writes romance, romantic suspense, and women's fiction under the name Rachel Branton. For more information or to sign up to hear about new releases, please visit www.TeylaBranton.com.